THE
NIGHT BAZAAR
VENICE

THIRTEEN TALES *of* FORBIDDEN
WISHES *and* DANGEROUS DESIRES

EDITED BY
LENORE HART

NORTHAMPTON HOUSE PRESS

Cover design by Naia Poyer. "A Moonlit Night Over Venice" oil painting by Karl Kaufmann (1880); Ribboned half-mask illustration by Naia Poyer. Trattatello font (c) 2005 by James Greishaber.
Interior by Jennifer Toomey.
First edition 2020 by Northampton House Press, Franktown, Virginia USA.

Second Edition
ISBN 978-1-950668-07-6
Library of Congress Control Number: 2020901006.

10 9 8 7 6 5 4 3 2

THE
NIGHT BAZAAR
VENICE

Contents

WELCOME TO A MOST PECULIAR AND UNUSUAL BAZAAR.................... 1

THE CURE *by Aphrodite Anagnost*.. 5

TOWNIES *by Roy Graham* 25

THE EXQUISITE HIDE OF BROTHER EDUARD *by Edison McDaniels*......... 43

MASK MAKER'S BALL *by Carol MacAllister* 69

WELL PLAYED *by Corinne Alice Nulton*.. 93

THE THOUSAND INJURIES OF FORTUNATO *by David Poyer* 111

SIREN SONG *by Rebecca Lane*... 135

IN BRUGES *by Mau VanDuren* 161

POSIONE D'AMORE *by Dana Miller* 189

CINNABAR AND STONE *by Naia Poyer* 219

ISMENE IN VENICE *by Gregory Fletcher* 249

PLENTY OF FISH IN THE SEA *by Lenore Hart* 277

THE BOOK OF AMAL *by Kaylie Jones*...291

AFTER THE BAZAAR 307

CONTRIBUTORS 309

I have wandered in many lands, seeking the lost regions from which my birth into this world exiled me, and the company of creatures such as myself.

—George Bernard Shaw, *Caesar, the Sphinx, and Cleopatra*

Turn and face the strange.

—David Bowie, "Changes"

WELCOME TO A MOST PECULIAR
AND UNUSUAL BAZAAR,

WHICH FIRST APPEARED THAT FATEFUL SEASON
NEARLY 700 YEARS AGO, IN ST. MARK'S SQUARE . . .

Greetings, Gentle Guest. Come and mingle among us, the revelers of the first Night Bazaar in history.

Our marketplace may already be known to you from visits to other cities (possibly in other times). But it first appeared in St. Mark's Square, at midnight, during the week preceding Christmas in 1348. A festival that embraced the strange, the secretive, and the cunning, conceived as an entertainment by the noble wife of a wealthy Venetian merchant, one Signora Vera Fortunato. Intended—or so it was said—to raise alms for poor unfortunates, its wonders briefly graced the famous Square, enticing masked revelers and confounding envious passersby. And inexorably drawing some who came to remonstrate and condemn.

After a mere seven days, it closed. But by then the citizens of *La Serenissima* had more dire concerns. For the Bazaar's appearance, oddly enough, coincided with the arrival of *Yersinia pestis*. The Black Death arrived with such violence that for decades afterward, scribes from around the world wrote of its depredations. But some works, more obscure and controversial, also described the continuation of a supernatural 'night marketplace' which set up shop for one week only, in various places around the world, and then moved on. As happened when the Night Bazaar came to Paris, in 1796 . . . to London, in the 1880s . . . Berlin, in the 1930s . . . San Francisco, in 1906 . . . Manhattan, in 2017 . . . among other venues. Never appearing for more than seven consecutive nights, and never to be seen again in the same city.

Tickets to this mysterious event may not be had for love, political influence, or any amount of money. Or indeed any other means, no matter how under-handed, persistent, lucrative, violent, or fatal the attempt to procure them. Only The Invited, those personally summoned in some way, often by the Bazaar's own Mistress of Ceremonies, can gain admittance. And then, for one night only.

But how is one invited, you ask? Why, in various ways. A tap on the shoulder. An elegantly engraved invitation. A brief text from a stranger, which quickly vanishes from the screen. Or perhaps some cryptic calligraphy on parchment, or a too-pale, slender hand beckoning from an alleyway. We either choose you, or we don't.

The Bazaar opens at midnight and closes just before dawn. Step inside, into an assemblage so large it could not possibly be contained in the modest structure you saw from the outside. Take a deep breath, stroll around, take it all in. The stalls, tents, carts, and booths are filled with an amazing variety of goods new and ancient, all of impeccable quality. Antique oddities of interesting origin; some of great beauty, others of soul-shriveling ugliness. Potions and playthings, poisons and props, peignoirs and paintings. Cast-off white elephants, some as large as their namesake, displayed next to curious objects and devices crafted of ancient oak, rusted steel, the hides of unidentifiable beasts, or cast of finely engraved silver. All meant to perform . . . well, who knows what arcane functions?

But merchandise is not all that's on offer in these thronged aisles. In cur-tained alcoves you'll note various forms of tattooing, piercing, exotic costuming in vintage cloths and fine leathers, certain unusual elective surgeries, odd pottery vessels, *papier-mâché* masks, herbal and alchemical treatments, as well as every sort of body art and alteration, imaginable and not. And of course the expected palm reading, Tarot spreads, tea-leaf scrying, and water-, glass-, and crystal-gazing one might see at any Italian street fair.

The difference being that our purveyors of hidden truths are never mistaken in their prognostications.

But if seeing into a possibly not-so-bright future does not appeal, take heart: other entertainments may be had. The narrow aisles are inhabited by buskers playing contemporary and ancient tunes. Strolling jongleurs, friendly charlatans, retired circus freaks, mountebanks, prostitutes, and dancers move back and forth among the displays. Money-changers and masked vendors offer ready loans to the monetarily embarrassed. These usurers accept various forms of collateral (some tangible, others less so), which may be used to purchase ancient *objets d'art*, mind-boggling curiosities, and vintage musical or medical instruments. Or perhaps you're in the mood to gamble? Our barkers, more discreet and far more exotic than those at an ordinary carnival or casino, tout various arcane and legally-prohibited "Highly Serious Games of Chance and Skill."

The crowded aisles wind and twist back upon themselves for what seems infinity. Only to stop abruptly in some dark and confusing dead end, past the rows of satin-draped booths, billowing silk tents, ebony and mahogany tables. Behind artfully-hung tapestries or clacking beaded curtains, our comely, interesting, or malformed purveyors offer services from the seemingly benign and ordinary to the wildly erotic and life-imperiling.

In short, whatever you desire, no matter how odd, questionable, humiliating, or averse to the light of day, can be found, rented, or purchased here. If, of course, you are willing to pay the price.

But at the end of your week, this movable feast will briskly fold its tents, disassemble its stalls and booths, and steal away into the night, to reappear elsewhere . . . and often else*when*.

But for one night, the Bazaar will be your conduit to gaining the darkest desires of the heart.

We already know what you want. Now, will you be able to set aside our strange invitation? The elegantly engraved card that, once you turn away and then back, has already vanished from your desk?

Of course not. You cannot help yourself.

How do I know so much about this fabled Bazaar? Well, one might say I was there at its inception. The compulsion you feel the moment you glimpse that invitation has much to do with me, its creator and ruler. You may call me Madam Vera: *Lady Truth*. I was once somewhat like you, but that was very long ago. Both before and since that first convening I have lived in many places, under many names, and in various guises: equestrienne, croupier, spy, mistress of ceremonies, dominatrix, purveyor of fortunes. My name still suits me well, for the truth and I are ageless. And both of us terribly hard to hold onto.

So abandon now all fears and expectations. For one night only, you will be permitted to return with me to the long-obscure origins of The Night Bazaar, to immerse yourself in the lost world which spawned it. Or, to discover what became of a rare object, service, or person who once inhabited its ancient tents and booths, now transported to *your* time.

So step in, step closer, and view our marvelous wares!

Ah. You've already spotted something you've always longed to possess. Oh, but wait! Don't head off to fulfill that burning desire quite yet. Instead, hold still as I drape a corner of my silken shawl over your trembling shoulders. There. Isn't that better? Now you may come along with me as guide, and fully savor the experience.

But we needn't rush through. For you have all night. . . .

Though not a single moment more.

This striped silk tent houses one of the Night Bazaar's most sought-after cosmetic vendors. Inside, protected by a leaded-glass display box, three items are arranged: a clay pot of rouge for the lips; a cake of black kohl with its own tiny brush, to outline the eyes; and a wooden box of the finest white face powder, complete with a lamb's wool puff. The vendor supplies these tools of artifice to the fine ladies of the Doge's court, as well as to famous courtesans. And also to more ordinary women of the evening, who must also make their way in a world controlled by powerful men of often corrupt and violent disposition. This purveyor of feminine beauty is known throughout Venice as the most skilled at her trade. The women of the city flock to her stall. So it will be no surprise that the three items in the glass box also will play a part in the story to come: a tale of religion gone wrong, of the sisterhood of the craft, and of hard bargains, secret plots, and cold revenge . . . and also, for some of the more fortunate players, a chance at redemption and escape to a safer and gentler world than this city's narrow and sometimes cruel streets.

THE CURE
by Aphrodite Anagnost

Miriam held the sweaty boy in her lap, rocking him as his breaths came less frequently, and turned even more rasping. The salt and yeast scents of roasting fish and baked bread rose from the busy street below, drifting through the open window, carried on a chill breeze. A holiday festival was riotously in progress over in St. Mark's Square.

Turning carefully on the straw-stuffed mattress, trying not to wake the ailing child, she leaned on the windowsill and stared down. From her tiny attic aerie, through a blurred veil of tears, she could trace the sluggish meander of Rio della Zecca. The torn lace curtain fluttered about her face like tattered wings.

It appeared all of Venice had fled to the Square to celebrate the strangest Christmas Eve Mass in the history of Saint Mark's Basilica. Miriam wondered why this *Bazaare Nocturnalis* had been allowed, as the Doge had cancelled the usual seasonal celebrations on quarantine orders. At least three hundred had died in the City since the last full moon. People always looked to blame some-one, or something, for such misfortunes: miasmas, foreigners, heretics, witches.

This time was no different. She'd heard the gossip and muttering in her own neighborhood. About the rare objects, alchemy, strange and worldly services, the ancient artifacts this bazaar was rumored to offer. Things most would ordinarily condemn as blasphemy, or the tools of witches. Yet even the priests huddled in the cathedral had allowed the celebration, perhaps hoping someone connected with it would miraculously discover an elixir to cure the plague.

Those same priests had more than once declared Miriam herself indecent. A woman alone, with no man to support her, to protect her from the travails of daily life. She had a small business of her own, making and selling perfumes to the ladies of the Doge's Palace. Oils distilled by her own hands from the herbs and flowers of her birthplace, Verona. But women were not supposed to work, save to make lace or sell a few vegetables in the marketplace. Worse yet, her only child had no known father. Or at least none whose name she would reveal. Yet was she not a mother as loving as any other?

She lay down again beside her poor Amadeo, peeling the damp sheets away from his hot, sticky body. The cloth still smelled of goat urine from the physician's useless poultice. She ducked her head to kiss the little boy's smooth, childish belly. His sweat tasted like her own tears.

What if he died now, in her arms?

In terror, her hands gently pressed his shivering shoulders, as if she could hold his soul in place. She slid them down to his chest, counting the breaths which came sometimes too slow, sometimes too fast. His lips, opening now and then to cry out at the shadows painting the moist plaster walls, were rosy petals. He was perfect. Innocent. She had vowed at his birth to let nothing harm him, ever.

The boy coughed. A thin trickle of blood at one corner of his mouth made his skin appear even whiter. Frantically, she held him close again, breathing in his scent, still clean and fruity beneath the faint metallic tang of the sickness. She pressed an ear to his chest. His heart drummed there, faint and rapid as a hummingbird's wings.

A gondolier called from the canal just then, as if summoning Heaven to witness her terror. Miriam cried out, too, to the room's shadows, "*Santo Dio*, send a cure for my Amadeo! An herb, a draught, a prayer, an incantation."

A burst of raucous singing came from below, accompanied by horns and pipes and drums. Drunken laughter interrupted the music: the shrieks and cackling of intoxicated women. The murky salt scent of the sluggish canal was no longer discernible. Instead, the breeze carried to her the odors of coppery blood, hot iron, and invisible airborne globules of fat from herbed joints of wild game roasting on spits. The *macellaio*, the city's butchers, had set up kiosks on the outskirts of the Bazaar to ply their savory trade.

Amadeo whined fretfully, clutching at his blanket.

All the local *medicos* had recommended burning the bedding of the dead as well as their bodies. Instead, more intent on the Day of Judgment and the Resurrection, the priests had ordered all the swollen bodies boxed up and loaded onto carts, then shifted to barges bound for Lazzeretto Vecchio. There, on that small island in the Venetian lagoon, the dead were dumped into mass graves, hastily prayed over, and left behind. Hundreds upon hundreds of men, women, children.

Amadeo was so frail, his soul all but fled. His ailment would surely be fatal. She pressed a gentle kiss against his mouth and her tears spilled over, abandoning her cheeks, dropping onto his chin.

His chest heaved. The next exhalation had a pronounced heaviness, and for a moment she feared the worst.

That was when God spoke in Miriam's ear, whispering what she must do.

Pay attention to each breath. As the exhalation leaves his mouth, look for the sickness. And then, take it from him.

She would do anything, risk anything at all to save her son. And this advice sounded at least as sensible as the foolish nostrums the quack doctors prescribed. Far better than a goat-piss poultice. So she sat very still, holding him, silently waiting for Amadeo's next breath.

When it did not immediately come, she whispered, "Inhale, my love. *Per favore!*"

At last he gave a faint sigh. The narrow, hollow chest rose a little.

She wept in relief. "Again, *mi cuore*. Let it out now. Once more, for *Mamma*."

When his chest moved again he exhaled a tiny puff of air. And Miriam, watching intently, eyes narrowed in concentration, finally saw it: The pestilence. A faint curl of gray smoke escaping his lips along with the breath.

So, as God had instructed, she unhesitatingly inhaled that pale miasma, sucking its poison into her lungs with such force she could feel the plague smoke withdrawing from Amadeo's body and coming into her own. As if the disease itself not only understood her plan, but approved. First, it entered her mouth and settled on her tongue; a bitter taste coating her teeth with an oily film. Next, the smoke trickled down her throat, which opened and permitted it to pass, as a surrendering guard allows the enemy to step inside the castle gates.

All the while, she fought back an urge to cough, to choke, to expel the intruder. It passed on, into her lungs and instantly descended, as if by many roads, down into her belly. Which immediately cramped, offering to vomit it out.

She silently and stoically commanded the protesting organ to yield. To allow the murderous intruder to land and dwell even more deeply inside her.

So the pestilence settled as lead might, even lower, down into the amphora of her uterus. By then she didn't even need to exhale. It was as if her lungs had become capacious caverns. When she sucked down another breath, her toes and fingers stiffened like rods of iron. Her fingernails tingled. Her chest was an iron vault.

In moments her boy stopped shivering and sweating. Little Amadeo had bypassed death. Mumbling in dreams, hair rumpled, tired shadows ringing his eyes. But he slept soundly, skin pinkening with returning health.

Sharp straws from their mattress poked through her thin gown, pricking her back and side as Miriam rolled away. She scooted even farther, to the edge of the mattress. Holding her breath, she imprisoned the plague to keep it away from her son. At the edge of the bed she leapt up, still turned away from Amadeo, and ran across the slats of light falling like a dungeon's bars onto the cold, damp flagstones.

She flung open her door and bolted down the narrow staircase. Beside the first-floor entrance someone had posted on a broadsheet the church's official seal, the Bull of Mark. It was seen everywhere in Venice these days.

By the Grace of Almighty God
We shall find and burn ALL witches
AND STOP THE PLAGUE.

She gripped the large brass door handle, which broke off in her clenched fist. Shoving the heavy iron-banded door open, she stepped out into the court-yard of mossy interlocking stones, tossing the ruined bit of metal into the gutter.

Outside, night was taking over the world. Its dusk lay deepest in the alleys through which Miriam now ran, not breathing, all the way to the canal where gondoliers' lanterns cast warm golden circles on the damp cobblestones at the water's edge. Torches racked at street corners lit a path for her to follow: past

floating houses, striped tents of healers, booths where alchemistral necroman-
cers sold strange brass-banded glass instruments.

On one street a troop of mounted soldiers had donned their best armor in
honor of the festival day. Their black and gray and white horses were rearing
prettily, dancing to music that drifted from the waterside Bazaar. Miriam spared
them only a glance, then lowered her head and bolted past the drumming of
iron-shod hooves on brick and granite.

By some miracle, she kept running even after that. Despite the deadly exhalation beating at her lungs and other organs, she locked the foul contagion within
her body like the Doge's most ruthless gaolers. Cold air pinched at her hands,
face, and bare, bleeding feet. Festival songs vibrated the very cobblestones she
crossed, which led inexorably to the water. Head pounding, Miriam desperately
gritted her teeth and refrained from exhaling, keeping her eyes focused on swinging pinpricks of light out on the canal as she ran toward them. Lanterns at the
bow and stern of a barge—the plague ship which daily carried the dead away, to
dump them into the lazaret, the quarantine islet. Her thigh muscles and tendons
burned, tightening to painful rocks and wires beneath her skin as she ran. Her
air-starved fingers grew numb.

As her bare feet slapped brick and cobble, by sheer will she forced the plague
down even deeper, pounding at it in time to the rhythm of her running. Her bare
toes at last touched the far edge of the farthest city dock and gripped it. The last
plank was petrified solid as rock from years of submersion in sea salt.

And then Miriam, who could not swim, jumped into the canal. Still holding
in the terrible breath which clamored for release.

She stretched her body like a dancer's, toes pointed straight toward the
dark bottom as she broke the surface, and sank deeper, deeper. At last her soles
touched the silty floor. Only then did she open clenched lips and aching jaw,
letting the tainted breath out in a huge rush of bubbles that churned the water
around her.

But as she hung there, suspended by the dark waters, she finally understood. The gray swirl of plague was alive, still burrowed deep within her. For
her vision went red, and she burned from throat to pelvis. And if the disease
was lodged within the vessels and canals of her womb, she was surely doomed.
What else could she do now but surrender and drown? She prayed her uncle in
Verona would take the boy in. He'd raised her after her own parents had died
of the sweating sickness, teaching Miriam first her letters, then Latin, Greek,

and Hebrew. Uncle Massimo had no son and heir, for women could not inherit property. But they had parted on less than amiable terms, though he still made sure she received the regular shipments of blossoms, buds, herbs, and oils she needed to practice her livelihood.

Uncle Massimo was not a cruel man, only a proud one. Surely he would take pity on her orphaned son.

Then she realized her mistake.

I left no note. No directions that her uncle must be contacted, or information about where he lived. So now beautiful, sweet Amadeo would be sent to the orphanage run by the church, raised by the same black crows who had called his mother indecent and whorish.

She would never know if indeed this would've been the case. For just then a pair of hands jerked her up by the neck of her shift. First to the surface, as she coughed and spluttered. Then she was unceremoniously heaved over the gunwales and onto the deck boards of a large gondola.

Lying on the thwarts, Miriam vomited water, then bile, and finally choked on her own sodden breath. Firm hands wrapped her in a blanket. Then someone held her tightly against them to still her shivering. Another figure stood back at the stern, oaring the boat along.

Saved, she thought. But to what good end? Some gondoliers saw me fall and came to my aid. Yet now I may infect these poor devils, too.

But when she looked down, it was not the callused hands of a boatman holding her, but rather smaller, softer, ones. Now they reached underneath the scratchy sheep's wool coverlet to unlace and tug off Miriam's sodden wool kirtle and linen under-smock.

Then those same ministering hands lit a lantern, and finally Miriam saw her saviors.

Both women wore the heavily-painted faces of the street-walking *meretrix*, above fine velvet capes trimmed in tassels. These covered brocaded gowns with gold-worked hems. She'd been rescued by the best-dressed but least decent women in all of *Venezia*.

Now that she was warmer and almost dry, the one who'd taken her wet clothing away dressed Miriam in someone else's smock and pleated kirtle, then drew over her a warm woolen cloak.

The whore moved to sit on the bench across, then took Miriam's hands and chafed them to warm the numb, blue-nailed fingers.

"I'm Rosa," she said, and smiled, face youthful and smooth beneath the paint. The hooded cloak draped loosely around her revealed a few reddish curls and a fine jaw so firm and white it might've been worked from marble by a master sculptor. When she threw back the hood, the moon became an eerie beacon lighting the hair pulled back from her face with silver combs until it glowed the color of freshly-spilled blood. The young woman's green irises were so pale they seemed almost colorless. The lids lined heavily around the lashes in kohl.

"You are one of us now," said the smaller woman who stood ramrod straight in the stern, as she steered the gondola.

"I am indebted to you for my life," Miriam admitted. "And it's true I have no master to answer to. But . . . I do have a child at home."

"Boy or girl?" asked the smaller woman, as Rosa cupped Miriam's chin in one warm hand and began deftly powdering her face with a puff of lambswool.

"A boy," said Miriam.

"As if the world isn't full to the teeth with those," muttered the oarswoman, with a grimace. She looked disgusted and turned away, back to her oaring.

By then Rosa was lining Miriam's eyes with a kohl brush. At last she dipped one finger in a tiny clay pot of reddish grease, painting her lips with a pigment gritty as fine sand.

"May I know your name as well?" Miriam asked the woman standing at the stern.

"You may ask it." She smiled grimly, but said no more.

Rosa opened a basket and took out a small loaf that smelled so fresh it must've just come from the baker's oven. So warm it steamed in the chilly air. Miriam inhaled deeply. And was that . . . yes, dried lavender from Provence, and green rosemary from her own birthplace in the countryside.

Rosa tore off the heel of the loaf. Her fingernails were bleached to a pale perfect ivory, the skin of her hands smooth and moist-looking, smelling sweetly of aromatic oils. "Eat," she ordered. "It will restore you."

Miriam pressed the warm, fragrant bread to her nose and inhaled deeply: flowers, herbs, yeast, honey, virgin olive oil, finely-ground durum wheat. She inhaled again, and the metallic stink of the plague receded from her tongue. Her stomach growled loudly. She could not recall her last meal, for she hadn't wanted to leave Amadeo alone for a second. Now she was ravenous as a winter wolf. Not wishing to appear greedy, though, she took a small bite. The herb-infused bread tasted . . . holy. The crisp brown crust, the soft white steaming center, together created a swirl of sensations intoxicating as a goblet of honeyed wine downed too quickly.

Rosa reached into the basket again and pulled out a hard heel of salami and a small round of snowy goat cheese. She examined each closely as a master jeweler might inspect a diamond before nodding and passing the food over.

Miriam, who accepted it gratefully, nevertheless had begun to feel miserable. Her very presence in the boat was surely endangering these kind souls, however disreputable their trade.

"I must tell you that I . . . I carry plague!" she blurted out. "I dare not stay and accept any more kindnesses, in case—"

Rosa cut her off with a laugh. "*Cara mia*, fear not. That sickness deep within you will not harm us."

Miriam gaped at her. "*Quale?*"

"I saw you running like a pursued hare to the canal. Even saw the plague smoke writhing inside your belly before you jumped in. A woman who swims like an anchor stone! And yet, here you sit, alive. *Che fortuna!* One who will not die—at least not in the canals of *La Serenissima*. And as for *la peste nera* . . . " She paused and shrugged. "*Chi lo sa?* My sister and I are quite immune."

Miriam glanced back at the smaller, darker woman again. The two of them looked nothing like sisters. But then, what matter?

She told them that Amadeo was still at home, recovering. That he must be sent to her uncle as soon as he was well enough to travel. "After I die," she added bleakly.

"You do owe us a debt," Rosa said. "And there is a way you may repay it that is more valuable than a barge full of gold *ducati*."

The bite of cheese Miriam had just swallowed stuck in her throat. She coughed. "What do you mean? Valuable how?"

"Why not use your condition to fight certain corrupt churchmen and politicians in the City? Those who use the pestilence as an excuse to condemn widows and spinsters who live alone, or ply a trade. All in order to seize their lands, goods, and money for themselves. And thus fool their sheep-like subjects into believing they are wise and deserve even more power."

Miriam did not know what to say to that. She felt dizzy. Or perhaps that was just the hunger . . . she greedily ate two more huge bites of bread and cheese, then asked, "But how do I fight? What could I do, alone, against such powerful men?"

The woman at the oar laughed aloud. "Why, infect them of course."

Rosa stood on the bench opposite Miriam, pointing up past the sea wall to a large marble and stone building. "You see this monastery, which lies on the outskirts of the city? There the Hounds of God make wines. Very fine ones, for they continually discover new processes. Such as clarifying cloudy vintages with the whites of hens' eggs, or distilling stronger spirits from fermented matter."

"I see." Miriam nodded, looking up at the gray buildings looming over the canal.

Rosa smiled without mirth. "The monks have become wealthy, for their prized *vini* draw all the thirsty noblemen of Venezia. In the large *taverna* upstairs the self-indulgent princes of the church imbibe rare ports and amontillados with dukes and *baroni*. Many prefer to play a game more exciting than a hand of cards. They keep lists, comparing all the women who have recently drawn their desire and lust. Not those in our ancient trade, mind you. We are quite easily available, if one has the *soldi*. No, they seek to ruin respectable women. To seduce them, if they can. If not, then to force themselves upon these innocents, seizing their most private parts with impunity, and then ravishing them."

Miriam gasped. "But . . . but that is outrageous!"

"Yes, it is. But there's more. To cover up their vile acts, they call in a favor from a friendly magistrate, or else slip a note into the *Bocca de Leoni*, accusing the defiled woman. So that she, arrested for heresy or practice of the Dark Arts, has no recourse—or a powerful man has spoken. The poor wretches receive a sham trail and meals of moldy bread in a damp dungeon. Flames will consume the most unfortunate of them, in the Square."

"But not their feminine wisdom," added the smaller woman. "That lives on forever, in us."

That holy men and nobles behaved as ill, or even worse than, the lowest villain did not shock Miriam as much as it might have. For she recalled the groping, pinching hands of noblemen which she had to dodge whenever she delivered an order from her shop to the Doge's Palace. She did not know if the ladies of the court were treated as badly. But more than once she'd heard a chambermaid or goose girl weeping in the kitchen, after being assaulted by some princeling or baron's son.

Would it be a sin in the eyes of God if she took revenge for these powerless ones? After all, Judith smote her ravisher, the brute Holofernes, and she was a righteous woman.

Still, how did one judge which man truly deserved punishment?

"How will I know which one to choose, though, so I can avoid killing an innocent?" She felt a cramp in her lower belly and paused to press a hand there, where the plague swirled. Was it still growing inside her?

"Few innocents move among those exalted ranks," said Rosa. "But one sinner stands out as more wicked than the rest. Find the priest of their order called Padre Michel. Make love to him. Indeed, the bastard will no doubt approach you first. There are private chambers upstairs for this purpose. But do not be deceived by the smooth lies of this inquisitor, or become infatuated with his fine manners and comely form. He's ordered the deaths of hundreds of innocent women."

Mio Dio, thought Miriam. The sin of fornication was one thing. She was no virgin, of course, and had not been for years. But to seduce a bad man in order to kill him, even to save the women of Venezia? *Perdonami!*

"I will help you," she said at last. "But if I die in the act, or am caught and taken, what of my child? I left him in our room, sleeping. My uncle, Massimo Solari, lives in Verona. I must—"

"Should the worst happen, and your uncle refuses to take him, we will raise the boy," the small woman said. "To be a better man than most."

"We women can only weather the vicissitudes of fortune through our wits, and cooperation. You may trust us on this," said Rosa, "and all else I have related."

These two *cortigianas* speak with compassion, Miriam thought, though their eyes are hard. But then, it was no easy thing to make one's way in the world, with so few choices allowed: only marriage, or whoredom, or slow starvation.

As Miriam swallowed the last bite of bread, she decided to trust the *meretrices*. Amadeo would be saved from the black crows, no matter what happened. So she was to be sent on a mission by indecent women? *Ottimo*. Anything to save her son.

They reached the basin nearest St. Mark's Square. The gondolier tied up between many other boats just like theirs.

"So: tell me the address of your uncle, and where we might find your son, should the worst happen." Rosa leaned forward until her lips brushed Miriam's ear. "You are my Judith, equipped for battle." Her red hair was soft; it smelled of chamomile. Her breath was sweet with mint. "All that is required, once you have the foul serpent wrapped in your arms, is to release your poison, Miriam."

Well before the hour the monks chanted their nightly offices, Miriam rushed home to check on Amadeo. He was still sleeping, no longer feverish. As she tucked the covers in more closely, he briefly opened his eyes and smiled up at her.

She went across the hall to arrange for a neighbor woman to watch over him, promising a ducat. Then slipped downstairs into her tiny perfume shop, and walked all the way to the back, where she stored the flower-infused oils. She reached up onto a high shelf for a small glass bottle banded with silver. There was no label, for she had not yet decided on its name.

To make this new perfume she had blended lemony magnolia blossom, fragrant wisteria, wood sage, precious ambergris, sharp black pepper, and a green hint of juniper in a poppy-infused oil base. The most potent and beguiling scent she'd ever created, and she'd meant to sell it for a good price at the Palace. But then Amadeo had fallen ill. Thus, no one in all of Venice had yet smelled, much less worn this fragrance. She paused and thought for a few moments, a hand to her lower belly. Then took up a parchment label, dipped a quill into the ink pot, and wrote in small, careful script, *L'abbraccio mortale dell' Amore.*

Love's Deadly Embrace.

Miriam slipped the bottle into a small velvet bag, and went back out into the festival-noisy streets. Pressing into the costumed crowd, through the chaos and revelry. In the middle of the Square jugglers were tossing colorful balls. Romani fortune tellers seated inside tents gazed down at crystal scrying globes. Near-naked festival-goers were having colorful scenes drawn on various parts of their bodies. Down the next alley *houris* swayed and gyrated in costumes less modest than their filmy veils, arms stacked with musically-jangling belled bracelets. Farther on, near the water, Musselmen and Orientals tossed stone disks onto carpets, then read the future in the strange runes engraved thereon.

At last she reached the farthest, rankest-smelling block, where cuts of meat from strange animals hung side by side with fly-crusted haunches of beef and pork. The latter were studded with sprigs of rosemary or dried herbs wedged in the creases or stuffed inside cavities to mask the scent of decay. Such things were considered delicacies by some, or so Miriam had heard. She shuddered and waved away a cloud of flies, then pulled her cloak tighter, and hurried on.

At a livery behind the inn called *Lanterna di Marco Polo,* near the Grand Canal Bridge, she hired a covered litter borne by two white horses, one before and one behind. She gave the address to the groom.

The man nodded. A green bycocket hat pulled low on his brow shadowed his face. "*Sì.* I know the place," he said gruffly, glancing at her sideways, as if he also knew why she was going there.

He set off, guiding the litter through narrow cobbled streets until they reached the outskirts of the City. A half-hour later, they turned onto a long lane, a narrow unpaved drive made even darker this night by the towering Aleppo pines that lined either side, so tall they shut out the moon.

Miriam shivered and drew her new cloak around her. At last the gray bulk of the monastery crouched before her, like a huge beast about to spring. They passed under a great stone arch and through tall wrought-iron gates. In the stone courtyard, stunted black oaks creaked as if their ancient warped limbs were slowly breaking.

One thick, knotted root had heaved up the paving stones. But the groom stepped deftly around it, a hand on the bridle so the horses followed, as if he'd trod this road often.

The wind cannot defeat a tree with strong roots, thought Miriam, and she crossed herself twice.

Instead of stopping in front, the groom led the horses past the massive double doors of the facade, and around the left wing of the building, where a walled garden concealed a less-imposing, more discreet side entrance. The litter halted. He took Miriam's hand to help her down, then escorted her to a portico where torches guttered on either side of a narrow, iron-banded door. A yank on a bell-chain announced her arrival.

A few moments later the door swung open. The groom stepped back and bowed. In the torchlight Miriam saw now he was no man at all, but a woman in men's garb: tunic, vest, and breeches. Her dark hair had been carefully tucked up under the long-brimmed felt bycocket that still shadowed her beardless face.

"My lady Rosa sends you greetings, *Signorina* Miriam," the woman said. Then she turned and led horses and litter away.

We women are everywhere, Miriam thought, only one does not always notice. Still bemused, she walked past the servant waiting just inside the doorway.

The Rosso Verona marble tiles in the dark foyer reminded Miriam of her uncle's estate. Would she ever see the old man again? She had not since she'd left Verona, still refusing to reveal the name of Amadeo's father.

They had argued bitterly even before that day.

"The *farabutto* must make it right, and restore your honor," *Zio* Massimo had kept insisting, when she had made her condition known. Normally a gentle soul, he preferred working in the garden to all else, including arguing with his niece. It was to him she owed her love of flowers and herbs.

In the end she'd left a month after Amadeo's birth. And though her *zio* made sure she had enough money to live, and the materials for her work, she'd never journeyed home to the villa again. She understood he'd wanted her to marry so she could inherit the house, not live alone, and be secure after he was gone. But she did not want to wed the man who had made her pregnant. *Duca* Lorenzo's son, the foppish poet whose pretty *terza rima* poems had seduced her—for a time. Until she'd discovered they'd been written by his Neapolitan Greek tutor. *Idiota!*

She was too proud; she could admit that now. But back then she had not wanted to confess those foolish mistakes to Uncle Massimo, and be forced to spend her life yoked to an even bigger fool than herself.

Well, now she would probably not live to return and see her *zio* again. But Amadeo, he could still go to Uncle Massimo, and be his heir.

As she followed the servant up the stairs the disease twisted and turned, a knife unsheathed in her womb, which writhed and cramped and begged to expel it. She'd not known such pain and pressure since laboring to give birth. The disease was distilling within her, growing ever stronger. Her knees felt so weak, they might soon no longer hold her up. She wanted only to go home, to lie down beside her son, and rest. But then what? What if she died, leaving him alone in the world?

No. To protect Amadeo, she must keep her promise.

So she bit her lip and tried to ignore the roiling deep inside her. To focus instead on the carpeted marble steps to the second floor. The horror of the plague had been loosed upon the world. But if Miriam had found a more deserving vessel, perhaps God would allow the transfer of her portion of it to him. And then . . .

Do not think of the future, she scolded herself. Not even the outcome of this night. She prayed that Venice herself would guide her to do her part well. Then pushed damp curls away from moist eyes, and silently prayed for the boy. And for the final destination of her own guilty soul.

Somewhere drunken revelers were singing bawdy folk songs, laughing and jeering as a musician strummed a lute. The silent servant never looked back as he led her down a narrow hallway that ended at another door, this one ornately carved, its lintel topped with a leering gargoyle with a lolling, lascivious tongue.

The singing grew louder as her taciturn guide pulled the door open. She took a deep breath, and stepped inside.

Suddenly she was in the midst of a large, overheated room full of partiers— mostly men—singing, dancing, eating, smoking, laughing, and flirting. Some were already half-undressed. She hesitated at the edges of the revelry, wondering where she might find the murderous sinner called Father Michel.

As Rosa had predicted, though, her quarry found her first.

She was scanning the crowd, searching for a man as bright and comely as Lucifer, when a hand descended on her shoulder. Miriam suppressed a gasp, and turned.

Indeed, the kindly *puttanas* had not exaggerated. At first glance, he was an angel. Over the Alb he wore a long tunic, the dress of his order. His thick, dark hair curled in cherubic ringlets. The Alb itself seemed made of a finer cloth than most clergy wore; a rich black brocade. His fine-boned face had only a short, closely trimmed beard. Above it his cheekbones were finely cut, the skin pale and unblemished, without scar or pockmark or mole or wen, as if it had never been touched by the sun or a human hand. And he smelled of . . .

Miriam closed her eyes and inhaled deeply. A French-lavender water she sometimes distilled herself, for the vainest Palace *bravos*.

"I have never seen you here before, *bella*," he said, and took both her hands in his, leaning in to kiss her chastely on each cheek, as if they were standing outside the cathedral after mass. "I am Padre Michel."

For a moment her belly clenched, and she realized with astonishment it was from a faint prick of desire, rather than pain. Now she understood just how prescient was Rosa's warning, for this priest was indeed as comely as Lucifer, and no doubt every bit as dangerous.

He paused, frowning faintly, and leaned closer to better inhale the fragrance she'd liberally applied to throat and bosom. When he shivered, so did she. Her womb had fallen quiet, finally. The priest had the long, thin fingers of a poet or a musician, and was vain enough to wear a ring on each: blood-red rubies and blue sapphire baguettes set in gold all so warmly gleaming they seemed freshly cracked from the earth.

How young and handsome he is, for a witch hunter hired by the church, she thought. But perhaps youth and beauty were a professional advantage; a way to distract more foolish women, to make them confess more freely to things they may or may not have done.

"Stay and talk to me a while, *per favore*, Signorina. Tell me . . . are you married?" His eyes glittered in the firelight.

"I have never relinquished my sword for a ring," she said. "I speak only of the sword of our Savior, of course," she added, and lowered her gaze modestly.

His eyebrows rose, and he drew in a quick breath. "Indeed? So, *bella* and chaste as well. A rare combination. I feel as if I've been waiting for you all night, *cara mia*," he whispered.

"I feel it too," she lied, making her tone sweet.

The plague awakened again. She took a deep breath as her guts turned, feeling anything but sweetness within her. He was certainly bold. And it had been a long time since she'd lain with a man. The notion of giving in to him might have seemed enticing, had she not known all she did about his evil work, killing women.

Deposit the poison, a distant feminine voice whispered in her ear.

Miriam blinked and glanced around. No one was nearby save a fat laughing nobleman holding a giggling strumpet on one knee, a glass sloshing in his other hand.

"This is not the proper place for you," said Father Michel, taking her elbow. "*Per favore*, let me escort you to a quieter chamber, away from these gross louts. We can pray. I can even hear your confession, if you like."

"*Grazie*, Padre," she said, trying to sound relieved and grateful.

He led her out a different door, down a hallway with damp walls that stank of yeast and bitter grape-skins, then through halls so labyrinthian soon she was no longer certain what part of the monastery this was. The ruse was no doubt deliberate.

It had been hot in the crowded tasting room. She was sweating beneath the fine gown Rosa had given her. She again caught the scent of Love's Deadly Embrace emanating from its tight bodice, and felt lightheaded. It was so intoxicating she struggled to resist its beguiling scent, herself.

He led her to a room which held a chair, a table which held a flagon of red wine and two goblets, and a bed with a blue silk counterpane.

"Please, have a seat." He gestured at the bed, but she sank onto the chair. "I will pour us some holy wine," he added.

"Blessed Mary." She drew back, feigning shock, and crossed herself. "Padre, surely you cannot mean—"

He laughed. "Of course not! My little jest. This is not even a fine bottle from the Brothers' vineyard here, but a Spanish Amontillado. Unblessed as yet, save by the presence of your innocent loveliness."

Such smooth lies. The fine manners. His most comely form. He was surely even more beguiling than the women in the gondola had described.

He carried two brimming goblets over. "Here, refresh yourself," he said and handed her one.

She lifted the cup to her lips, for to be convincing she must take a sip. Only a small amount, to allay any suspicions he might have. The trickle of red spirits flowed like nectar over her tongue, though she was surprised by its bitter after-taste. It struck her belatedly: *he has drugged me.* Before she could voice a protest, he sat down across from her, on the bed.

"Now, *bella donna*, tell me your sins. If indeed you have any to confess?"

Miriam studied his face. His smile seemed far less beguiling now. He watched too avidly, as a cat might stare at a promising mousehole.

The small amount of wine she'd imbibed was making her feel strange. Too warm. Her skin itched, despite the fineness of the cloth. The plague stirred in her womb. If only she might vomit it up . . . she swayed and toppled forward. Someone caught her arms and held on fast, yet still she fell, on and on, into blackness.

It is Death, she thought. Maybe even Hell.

Sometime later her eyelids fluttered open. A silver candelabra glowed on the table where the now-empty flagon lay on its side. She was naked on the feather-stuffed mattress, Father Michel atop her, sweating and thrusting, as a yellow moon peered in through the open shutters like the eye of a cyclops.

The priest was muttering, "Holy *God*, holy *mighty*, holy Immortal, have *mercy* on us. Cleanse me of this *sin,* in your holy *fire* . . ."

Disgust and horror overcame her. She turned her face away from the sight of him, feeling no guilt or remorse now. Only a bitter joy that he would die horribly of the plague she carried.

And what had he just said? *Holy fire.* Fire like the flames licking at a woman tied to a stake, on a pyre . . . so this too was as Rosa had warned. The rogue priest planned to feed Miriam to a dungeon, then to the flames, after he'd taken his fill. A warped offering, for expiation of his own sins.

She forced herself to look up at him again. The lustful grimace, the eyes rolled up now and then as if to regard Heaven. Moonlight illuminated the planes of his cruel face, making the few strands of gray in his hair glisten like silver threads. She hated him and what he did, but in the end he was just a man. And she, just a woman, would be his executioner.

What would happen to her soul after this night?

"We should pray," she said abruptly.

He stopped and looked down as if surprised. "What? Oh yes, we will pray. Many times this evening, if I am not mistaken." He chuckled, but began to recite the prayer of Luke.

"Father, hallowed be thy name. Your kingdom come . . ."

At the words the plague flared up within her, with a sharper pain. "Ah!" she gasped.

"So you like to say your prayers, *bella*," he whispered into her ear, hot breath burning, his bearded cheek grazing hers. She jerked away, but he grabbed her chin and forced her to look again into his eyes. The bitter scent of amontillado, spilled from her overturned cup on the floor, drifted up. His loathsome kiss held memories of his last meal, roasted mutton and onions. Those many-ringed fingers gripped so tightly she could not move.

"What a curious specimen," he said breathlessly. "With proper nurturing you could become a gifted *cortigiana.*"

She gritted her teeth. Yes, far better to seduce many men for coins, she thought, than to be made your whore even for an instant.

The same whispering voice she'd heard earlier came again, from the darkest corner of the room. *Give your deadly gift to the dark man of the church. His words are lies. He will stake us all one by one, then torch the pyre and laugh.*

Still, she would give him one warning, to assuage her soul. "If you continue in this manner, I tell you, you will die!"

"Ah, a convent girl." He laughed. "Did the nuns teach you that? Well, I am the one here who speaks for God. Leave that worry to me."

So he had pronounced judgment on himself. It was not her task to save such a monster, but to condemn him. The heaviness in her belly surely meant the plague-smoke was gathering, preparing to infect him. It seized her just then with a terrible pain from belly to womb.

At the same moment, as the priest shuddered toward the final throes of ill-gotten ecstasy, all the church bells in Venezia tolled twelve times, as if for a funeral.

"Life is suffering," she murmured to herself. She did not want to die in the company of this holy monster. But she had agreed to the sacrifice. So she let go of the fear of what would happen after she died. Let go all worry about her soul. She would do this for the boy, for all women, for her sisters on earth. To avenge all the blood the other black crows had spilled, aided by such cruel, hypocritical, so-called holy men as this corrupt witch hunter.

But she would look in his eyes one more time, as he died. Curious to see if, at the last moment, he might repent.

Above her his pupils shrank to black pinpoints. He shuddered anew, but now the rictus on his face did not convey pleasure. With one last groan, the shrunken pupils expanded into a huge black discs. He cried out, "Deliver us from evil!"

"I have just done so," said Miriam.

She wrenched herself from beneath the priest and rolled away. Then rose from the bed and stood, as he fell dead on the sweat-soaked mattress.

The fire had died. The room was dark now, cold and silent. Through the window, she saw that colorful rockets, like those first brought to Venezia decades earlier by Marco Polo, were being ignited and launched over the celebration in St. Mark's Square. Constellations of red and yellow and blue lights shimmered in between the window's iron gratings, only to burn out and go dark.

Behind her, a half-dozen women burst into the room and surrounded the body on the bed. One was Rosa. She pushed up the long, embroidered sleeves of her chemise, pointed to the dead man, and said to the others, "Dress him, quickly."

His body faced the window, the beautiful dark ringlets tangled and damp. His face still distorted with fear and the knowledge of his impending death, unshriven.

Miriam picked up the gown he had torn off her and dropped on the tiled floor. As she dressed, rustles and whispers rose behind her.

"By dawn he'll be ready for burning," said Rosa, with great satisfaction.

Miriam turned to look at the bed. Already black marks, the swollen buboes were rising, to mar that perfect white skin. Infected with the plague her own body had cradled and distilled, Father Michel was no longer beautiful.

This face, she thought, suits him much better. And then something else occurred to her: The writhing of the plague-smoke, the cramps and pain in her belly. She no longer felt them, or the sick heat they had generated, furnace-like, within her.

She smiled and whispered, "Blessed Mary, Thanks be to you."

As the women finished their rites, Miriam slipped out the door. She felt strong, clean. Renewed. Quite well enough to walk all the way back to the City.

The following week, she and Amadeo stepped up into a cart she'd hired to drive them to Verona. She carried the lovely cloak Rosa had given her, and Amadeo's favorite toys in a willow basket. She'd left her shop and apartment as they were, for she would no longer have any need of those things. The two of them were on their way now to . . . well, not so much a new life, as simply the one they had always been meant to live. She and her strong, healthy boy.

While they jolted along in the cart she sang to Amadeo of the beautiful green woods and meadows of Verona, which he'd never before seen. They stopped overnight at an inn, then went on early the next morning.

The sun was setting when the carter finally stopped the next day at the long narrow lane that led to Zio Massimo's villa.

"We'll get out here," she told the man.

She climbed down, then helped her son descend safely to the dusty road. Though she wanted to run, she made herself walk slowly. Allowing Amadeo to stop whenever he wished to look at a strange leaf here, a rock there, an interesting insect crawling through the grass.

We are both alive, she exulted. I met a son of Lucifer, and yet escaped with my life. To dwell far from the beautiful, corrupt floating houses of *La Serenissima*.

It felt as if pure white clouds cushioned her feet as she strolled and sang. They would soon arrive and surprise her uncle. But along the way why not enjoy these golden meadows filled with bees and birdsong? Until they reached the glorious, rusted, familiar old gates, beyond which stretched the old family villa. And Zio Massimo's lovely, spacious gardens, full of all the herbs and flowers one might ever need in a lifetime. Beyond them lay the beautiful green woods of Verona.

Yes, Miriam thought. I did battle like Judith, for the whole sisterhood of Venezia, and in the end walked away. An indecent woman, bathed in light.

As you know, we denizens of the Night Bazaar are not confined by the annoying limitations of time or place. It is quite easy for us to slip backward or forward at will. In order, for example, to check on the fate of those who, at some point, either worked at or visited the Bazaar. Or, to again view objects formerly offered for sale here, in their present surroundings. In fact, it might be instructive and amusing to see what's become of a particular vendor, and all the specialized tools of that trade. Regard this striped silk fortune-telling tent before us. The painted sign announces its name: 'The All-Seeing Art'. Telling fortunes was the livelihood of this family for many generations, before they emigrated to a New World as yet unknown to the citizens of 14th Century Venice. Let's step forward a bit into the future, across a continent and an ocean. There, on the far shore, lives this same Italian family. I wonder, do they still keep up the old traditions?

TOWNIES

by Roy Graham

The bag is beautiful. That's what I think when I first see it, which gives me a weird feeling right away, because nothing in Mousetown is beautiful. Okay, that's not true, but the beautiful things tend to happen accidentally, like that time algae got into the shuttered Quickscrews Auto Shop down by the beach and grew into lacy green fractals across the walls. No one makes anything beautiful here on purpose. They sure as hell don't make beautiful bags.

This one is velvet, with little curls of golden drawstring running along the neck. The velvet is a shade I've never seen before, deep and dark, a blue people imagine when they think of the ocean. Which is to say, not the color of the actual ocean, or at least not ours. In the winter it's a dead gray. In the summer, snot green.

So the first thing I know for sure is that the bag is way too pretty. The second is that Vink found it while scrounging around in the attic of his grandparents' definitely-haunted home, looking for something to sell. The old couple died a couple months ago, within days of each other, and now his mom is trying to sell the house. They really need the money. A long time ago, according to Vink, his ancestors were rich. Sorcerers in Florence, he claims. Personal aides to the Medici family. Even though now Vink and his parents live in a trailer in Paradise Park, next to the worst, most trashy stretch of beach for miles.

"Nice sack, right?" he says, grinning.

"I swear to God and Christ if you dump out your grandparents' ashes or some shit from that, I am *out*." This from Marcus, the one black kid in our senior-year class. He is our accepted authority on the outside world, and it's solely thanks to his presence that Vink and I haven't been cast to the lowest possible rung on the social ladder. Marcus is cool. On him I can almost smell the Elsewhere, the having-been-places scent.

"Chill, bro. All that's in here is *magic*." Vink opens the bag and upends it onto the table. Marcus flinches back like something might leap out and bite him, but there's no spiders or cloud of grandpa-ashes. What does come clattering out is junk. Old junk. Little rocks, chunks of wood, coins, random shit.

I pick up a gray twig and turn it over. It feels weird and polished, maybe hollow. Oh. Not a twig, I realize, and drop it.

The little bone clatters across the table.

"Kind of creepy," I say, embarrassed.

Vink laughs. "It's supposed to be creepy!"

"You found a bag of garbage. That's what you wanted to show us?" Marcus shakes his head. Not so taken with it, I note.

"It's a *magic* bag. Full of *magic* garbage." Vink sounds frustrated now. "My *nonna* told me about this stuff. Reading the bones. You throw them and then, uh, interpret. You know. See what the spirits have to say."

"Harry Potter didn't live in Jersey, man. You gotta go to England for that wizard shit," says Marcus.

"I'll prove it. Ask me a question. That's how it works." Vink is already scooping the miscellaneous trash into both hands.

Marcus strokes his chin, miming thoughtfulness. "My grandma's coming to visit next week. What time's her bus getting in, David Blaine?"

"Her bus. Got it." Vink lifts his cupped hands and throws. The mess goes clattering all over Marcus's dining room table, some of it bouncing into the bowl of Doritos. When it all more or less comes to rest, he leans over the table, thick black eyebrows bunching in concentration.

He looks, I think, like someone trying super hard to shit.

"Waiting," says Marcus, fingers drumming the table.

"Hold on. I can't see." Vink stands up on his chair to get a panoramic view of the spread. I turn in my seat and look back into the kitchen, where Marcus's mom is washing dishes. She doesn't say anything about the chair-standing, or the guido magic happening in her dining room.

Meanwhile Vink is still squinting down at everything, trembling a little bit. Hands held out, palms down, putting on a bit of a show. Then, in the kitchen the phone rings, and we all jump. Even though this isn't real or serious. What we're thinking—me and Marcus and probably even Vink, if we're being honest—is that this old bag of grandma stuff will make for a funny joke.

Then the overhead lights, the cheap blue energy-saver kind, flicker and go dim for a moment. In the kitchen, Marcus's mom picks up the phone and closes the door. I can hear her talking to someone, muffled, on the other side.

"Ha!" Vink says at last. "Oh, I get it now. Good one. You almost got me, bro."

"What?" say Marcus and I at the same time.

Vink gestures down at the scattered charms and announces, proud and loud as a carnie barker, "Your grandma's dead! Right? It was a test. You're testing me. And my," he waggles his eyebrows, "mystical abilities."

"What the fuck are you talking about?" says Marcus, grinning but now looking a little uncertain. "I told you. She's coming to visit."

In the kitchen, something shatters. *Oh my god,* I hear someone say, through the door. Marcus's mom, still on the phone. *Oh my god, no.*

His mother hustles us all from the house before we can figure out what's going on. It seems like I'm just a casualty of the moment, a bystander—Vink, on the other hand, is radioactive fucking material, and the whole household wants him the absolute hell gone. He barely manages to collect his beautiful bag of garbage before they push us both out the door. One last look back, through the windows, and I see Marcus and his mother at the table where Vink had done his trick. Marcus's mom with her hands over her eyes.

We don't live close, by Mousetown standards, but everywhere is nearby in real world terms. Me and him head down South street until we hit Paradise Park. There we split ways, Vink to his parents' trailer and me up the dirt hill on the other side. The sun's going down. From here I can look down on the auto graveyard with its rusting hulks and the Walmart by the beach, already spitting phosphorescence out each window like the bait lights on some deep-sea monster. I slide down to the bottom, jump the gulch of broken bottles, and cut through an alleyway.

A dog starts barking somewhere. Everywhere else, more dogs start up in reply.

I'm home inside of ten minutes and there's nothing in the mailbox. "Did I get any letters today?" I shout after I walk in. "Maybe some big fat yellow envelopes?"

"No, Robert," says my father from the couch. He has his feet elevated on a pillow like he always does after work. It's supposed to help cut down the swelling. "No mail today. Of the non-junk variety, anyway."

"But it's April!" Technically, the first of the month. I had vibrated through classes all day, wondering. "College acceptances started going out in *March*."

"Zabardo is way down on the name list. Alphabetically," says my mom, also on the couch, my father's head resting in her lap. An old episode of "Scrubs" is playing on the TV. "They're probably still sending out letters, honey."

Harvard, Yale, Columbia, Brown, Cornell, Dartmouth, Princeton, and the University of Pennsylvania. Together, applying to all of the big fishes had cost us nearly five hundred dollars. I haven't heard a word yet, except from Anthem City College, which I had applied to only so my mother would stop bugging me about choosing a safety school. They want me, *obviously*, though personally I've already decided I would rather burn to death in a six-car pile-up than stay in New Jersey. I want to go somewhere with castles, turrets, fountains, and haunted gothic music buildings where the ghost of an old lady sometimes plays the piano. We're not rich, but I'm prepared to take out loans to have all that stuff. I'm prepared to do pretty much anything.

But no letters for me. Not yet. I suppress my disappointment so that it only escapes in little growls and yips, like steam from a kettle.

"Son," says Dad. "Will you please move? You're blocking my view of Mr. Braff."

"Listen to your father and move, Robbie," says my mother, stroking his hair. "We love you!"

The next day, Marcus is not in school. His family has to travel somewhere for the funeral. There aren't many details yet on the nature of his grandmother's death, but Mr. Pietsch in homeroom gets everyone to say a prayer, or at least pretend to. And Marcus is definitely going to have to talk to Hank the Guidance Counselor when he gets back.

At lunch, we all go out into the yard. It's a flat concrete plane, like you'd find in a parking lot or a prison exercise area, fenced in with net-free basketball hoops and decades-old paint marking out boundaries for some dead sport nobody remembers. That's all there is, usually. Today, though, there's also a small tent. Maybe left over from someone's Boy Scout days, though they sure as hell wouldn't still be Scouts now, judging by the tent's age. It looks like it might've been purple once but now it's the color of spoiled meat. Painted around the opening flaps, in white, are the words: *The Mystrious Vincenzo!*

The tent doesn't appear to be all that stable, up close. The right corner sags dangerously low. I lift the door flap and step inside. Even with my less than impressive height I have to bend my knees and duck just to avoid initiating a total collapse. Inside Vink is seated cross-legged on the floor, wearing a silk bathrobe a bit too big for him. His hair, slicked back and shiny, reminds me of a beetle shell. The whole tent reeks of whatever substance is holding that glistening black dome in place.

"Is Vincenzo actually your name?" I say. We've been friends forever, but I can't remember anyone ever calling him this. Even his family.

"What? Yeah. You thought my parents named me Vink?"

I shrug. "Also, you spelled mysterious wrong."

"Yeah, I know. But by the time I noticed, the paint was dry."

On the table is the pretty bag. Golden drawstrings cinched tight. Vink catches me looking a bit too close. "You want a throw of the bones, my man? Only five bucks. Since we're friends."

I think of Harvard, Yale, Princeton, and my throat gets a little tighter at the prospect of finally knowing. Or maybe that's from the chemical stench of Vink's super-hold hair gel. Then I remember I don't have five dollars. "Nah, I'm good."

"So get outta my tent, bro. I'm trying to run a business here. Oh, but when you leave, can you try and look kind of mystified? Like, whoa! I can't believe he knew all that about me!" He stretches his eyelids open with his fingers, demonstrating a properly mystified expression.

"Sure. You got it."

I leave the tent, and a few more people do look over. Curious, I guess, but no way is any high school kid going to shell out five bucks, even if Vink actually can tell fortunes. That business with Marcus's grandmother was probably just a lucky guess. A coincidence.

I sit through the rest of lunch and then chemistry class, where Tip Stevensson asks the teacher if the periodic table is the same in the fifth dimension. I gradually drift off, thinking about the integrated science course at Princeton. Maybe I will be a revolutionary brain surgeon. I'd settle for being a respected pediatrician, though. Or a lawyer, or maybe an edgy, brilliant screenwriter. Or even a hack screenwriter, whoever makes those infinite Netflix original rom-coms. I'd take anything with a future, away from Mousetown.

When I get home at four, there is *still* no mail.

Toward the end of the next week, Vink tells me he's made five hundred dollars. This seems impossible, but it's true; on Friday, he flashes a wad of bills as thick as our history textbooks. "We're going to the club tonight, bro!"

He says he knows one in Anthem where they don't look too close at IDs. Vink is so pumped up he can barely sit still in class. He has never held this many bills in his life, and neither have I.

"Vink," I say. "How could you make that much money? How is it even possible?"

He just shrugs. "People want to know what shit's gonna happen to them, bro. And they want advice, for what to do when that shit does happen."

"Shit doesn't happen to anyone here, though. *I* could tell their goddamn fortunes. Here's a reading for Donald Lurtz, all right? He's going to graduate despite being dumb as a rock because the teachers have all known him since he was a baby, and no one wants to personally fuck up his life. He'll start commuting two hours into Hoboken every day to work at the construction site where his dad is foreman. And he's going to marry Jennifer Blakowski when he breaks the condom by accident but thinks it's still okay to keep going for a minute."

Vink grins and nods. "Hey, that's pretty close. Wanna make some cash, Robbie? I could use a good understudy."

For a moment, I actually consider it. But Vink's already agreed to buy all my drinks for the night. So why bother?

After dark, the same Donald Lurtz drives us to Anthem in his dad's Thunderbird. Last time I tried to speak to Donald, he held me down and filled my backpack with garbage, but now he's just acting grateful to Vink. Deferential, even. He doesn't once call him a guido or a greaseball or a loser. He even lets Vink pick whatever Sirius station he wants while we drive.

We stop at a gas station on the side of the freeway so Vink can piss and buy Red Bull. Donald and I sit in the car listening to "Havana," me in the backseat, him drumming his fingers on the steering wheel.

"What did he tell you?" I ask. "About your future or whatever."

"Vincenzo? In the tent, you mean? Said I was gonna meet a girl tonight. A real freak, you know?" All smiles. Already proud, I guess, of this future freak adventure.

I imagine snorting, then imagine Donald lifting me into the air and pitching me over the guard rail. More carefully, I say, "And you, um, believed him?"

Donald blinks. Like he hadn't really considered an alternative. "I dunno, man. He had all these little magic charms. In, like, a bag."

"Yeah."

"And when he tossed them on the ground, the tent got super big."

"Yeah. Wait—what?"

"And there were like, lights. Off somewhere. And it smelled like girl in there all of a sudden. You know, flowers and shit? With something. . .weirder underneath. Like low tide."

Vink must have changed up the hair product.

And suddenly he's back, hopping into the Thunderbird, chewing on a Slim Jim. "Havana ooh nah nah," he says. "You guys talking about something?"

"The freak!" says Donald, and starts smiling all over again. Already forgetting whatever else he was about to tell me.

All I really want, for the rest of the night, is to talk to Donald a little more about his fortune-telling session—not the freak, extremely not the freak, just those other things he mentioned. But Vink's right there, absolutely banging out to "Uptown Funk", and then we're at the club.

THE WATERING HOLE, it says in big green letters over the rusted metal door.

True to his word, we get in just fine and grab a booth by the back, since it's still early. Donald is off to the dance floor almost immediately, prowling the perimeter like some big jungle cat on the hunt. At first Vink sits with me to one side, but after a while he gets tired of shouting over the music and goes to secure more whiskey shots from the bar. That leaves me alone with my thoughts. In the darkness of the club I try to envision what Donald might have seen in that tent. Could the multi-colored lights above the dance floor be what he was describing? I try unsuccessfully to categorize the sweat and booze on the air as "girl smells." All the while the bass throbs so insistently I feel it ripple the black leather of the booth.

"You're not from the college," says a voice to my right. It's barely audible over the electronic pulsing, but after a moment I pinpoint the source: a girl in a tight silver dress. She's older than me, but not by much. In the weird club light her hair looks blue.

"Sorry. What?"

"I said, you're not from Anthem CC." She says it just like that. *Sea sea.*

I make a face. "God no."

She laughs, and I feel like laughing too. Looking closer I can make out the dark roots of her hair, which I now realize *is* blue—it's not just the lighting.

"I knew it," she says. "There's something about you. A vibe."

"Oh. Yeah," I say, trying to feign awareness of my vibe. It was a good vibe, I hoped. A cool one. Unbidden, a series of inappropriate, impossible visions passes before me. Probably not visions of my future, but—

"I can pick out a townie from a mile away," she says.

Horror dawns on me, even through the whiskey daze. "What? I—no, I'm not from here. No way." And it's not even a lie. Mousetown is almost an hour's drive away.

She looks surprised. "I didn't mean it in a bad way. I like townies. They're not as pretentious as the other shitheads at school."

She says something else, but it's lost to the drone of the music. What about me tipped her off, I wonder? Is my shirt unbuttoned one rung too low? Can she make out the puffy cheapness of my Walmart sneakers even in the dimness of the club? Or maybe it's just an aura of nobodyness. That there's a thinness to me, like paper. Hold any Mousetowner up to the light and you'd see right through.

Vink sets down a whiskey shot in front of me, pulling me back to the world. When I look again, the blue-haired girl is gone.

"Bro, who was that hottie?" Vink practically yells.

"Nobody," I mutter.

"Think she wants a reading?"

I look up at him. Maybe he's had one or two himself at the bar, without me; he's swaying in place like a snake charmer. Did he really bring along that little bag of bones?

For a moment I consider asking for a reading myself. I still haven't gotten a single acceptance letter back. Then, in a curdling drunken wave, the fear hits me. What was a mere itch before is nearly a full body shiver now, as I realize what Vink and his little magic bag might show me.

Anthem CC.

I can pick out a townie.

"I'm good, bro," I manage.

He shrugs and slides farther into the booth.

By the end of the night, Vink and I fall asleep in the Thunderbird. The roof open to all three of Anthem's stars, drunk as we've ever been. That's where Donald finds us at dawn, his face all kicked to shit, swollen and bruised, with a red-brown crust of blood rimming each nostril. A dreamy expression plastered all over the damage.

"We gotta get the car back before my dad wakes up," he says, gently, almost like pillow talk.

I crash into bed as soon as I get home. This, I realize, is what a real hangover feels like. All I want is to be unconscious. Within moments I am.

Some time later, Mom touches my shoulder. She's being gentle. Weirdly cautious, which I might be wigged out by if I wasn't so totally asleep, and so mad about being woken up.

"Robbie. Honey?" she says.

Now, even in my muzzy half-asleep brain, I know something's wrong. She only ever calls me "honey" or "sweetheart" or "my little boy" when things are seriously messed up. Like that time the Walmart dumped a strange glowing substance into the tidewater, and no one could go swimming for a month.

I turn over to face her. "Did Dad fall off the roof again? Are we at war with Iran?"

"What? No. Sweetheart, your letters from college arrived."

I sit straight up. *Sweetheart.* Oh no. "Where are they?"

"I left them in the kitchen—"

And I'm up, dropping blankets and sheets in my wake, not exactly running but not calmly walking either. Once in the kitchen, I freeze. A stack of mail sits on the counter. Not big beautiful folders embossed with the sigils and regalia of institutions as old and storied as this very country—but plain and small white envelopes, the kind your aunt or your power company might send. No room in them for brochures about campus life, for bonus refrigerator magnets, for all the complex forms one might need to fill out, were one to be accepted there.

So of course I already know. But still, I have to know.

One by one, like a man expecting a tax bill, I open and unfold the small white letters.

Dear Mr. Zabardo . . . record number of applicants . . . extremely competitive pool . . . regret to inform you . . .

All at once, in a great glowing wave, it hits me: this sliver of trash-littered coast is my future. It will be my prison, then my tomb.

Behind me, Mom puts her hands on my shoulders. "Oh, honey. You still have Anthem City College."

I want to bite her for saying such a thing.

The next day is Sunday, and I will not be going to a prestigious institution many hundreds of miles from Mousetown, New Jersey. Instead, I am sitting in church. I didn't want to go, but Mom said it would be good for me. I think my strong reaction to the letters yesterday frightened her.

Vink's there too, with his whole sorcerous clan. Once, before he found the bag, I saw them as broke, a family of kindly beachcombers—his dad with those awful brown teeth, his mother's cheap spray tans and skewed wigs. Now it all seems like a cunning disguise. Vink waves at me when I come in, like everything in the world is fine. He's wearing a suit, and takes communion like a guy who hasn't been doing literal witchcraft all week.

When you're an Italian from Italy, it's okay to be mysterious. Maybe you have a cool accent, or a red Vespa, or five-hundred-dollar jeans. But an Italian from New Jersey has no business acting that way. Even if Vink can do real, actual magic, even if he's not just giving a bunch of kids heatstroke waiting for their turn in that stupid tent, he can't fool me. He's nothing but a poor kid hanging onto the American coastline like a deer tick. A townie on a ballistic trajectory toward shoeless beer-drinking, sitting on a porch just one damp, rainy autumn away from collapse.

Just like me.

I've known Vink forever, since we started forming memories. Since the plates of the earth cooled. When we were kids, we played in the auto graveyard, where semi-trucks with a terminal diagnosis made their final pilgrimage so they could die in sight of the ocean. As brave explorers on a far-off planet, we'd poke around under the hoods of those rusting behemoths, sifting through the guts of ancient alien robots. Tractor-trailers marked J.B. Barton or All-American Transport became, with a little rewiring, portals to other worlds; we'd climb into the darkness, shut the big doors and wait with our breaths held as long as we could stand it. We knew full well you couldn't breathe in the space between worlds.

Back then, Vink wanted to get away too. Which he doesn't anymore, obviously. Because if I had magical powers and could see the future, tapping into some strange world beyond the veil, I sure as hell wouldn't still be here to open college rejection letters. Or to sit in church pews in a new cheap suit, or stare at the Walmart as it pulses with light by the sea.

I'd be long gone.

At lunch on Monday, a line forms all the way across the yard from the entrance of Vink's little faded tent. Ten kids deep, sasquatches like Donald Lurtz and weirdos like Tip Stevensson and high priestesses like Lola Peretti all waiting to get their fortunes told. Unbelievably, near the front stands Mrs. Dollop, the math teacher, squished between two tenth graders. I watch from one of the picnic tables, which are all crusted over with fossilized seagull shit. Word's gotten around, I guess. Soon everyone in this town will know not just their ultimate fate, the big picture of their lives, but every insignificant detail along the way. A whole seaside community that knows what they're going to have for breakfast in ten years. What grade they'll get on next month's history quiz. Whose dad is gonna pull a DUI next fall. Like reading from a script, having the stage directions to your whole life.

It makes me sick to think about. Dizzy, like I'm watching the world from very high up.

"Robbie, Vincenzo wants to talk to you," a deep voice says, snapping me out of it. Donald Lurtz is hulking next to me almost like a bodyguard, hands folded behind him, making a broad wall out of his Devils jersey.

"I don't want to talk to him." Because it's all bullshit. Because I can't bear to know what he'll show me about my future.

"Well, but, he says you're *going* to go talk to him. Just, first I have to—"

That does it. I totally freak out. The punch I throw is neither elegant nor particularly destructive, but by luck one flailing fist crashes dead into Donald's nose.

He stumbles back, a stream of blood trickling from one nostril. "Yeah," he says, nodding. "He said that'd come first."

I howl and jump for him again, but someone grabs the collar of my shirt and I'm suddenly hauled back like a dog on a leash.

"Zabardo," says Hank the Guidance Counselor, who has caught me with all the dexterity of a lobster fisherman. "You better come to my office."

Hank the Guidance Counselor is wearing a tie printed with little yellow ducks. He used to be a marine, but now he grows out his thin blond hair so long, it's hard to imagine him ever having had a buzz cut.

"Zabardo," he says at me. "You're not really a puncher, usually."

"He had it coming. Literally. He walked over knowing he would get punched in the face."

"Hmm. I see." He writes that, or something, down on an oversized orange sticky note.

More of those have been plastered all over his office, but I can't make out what any of the scrawls say. Up close, his handwriting is totally indecipherable.

"Tell me, Zabardo. How're those college apps going? Heard back from any place yet?"

I say nothing. I am silent, Sphinxian. He wants to Guidance Counsel me, but I refuse to go along.

"Ah." Hank taps the tip of his pen against the desk. "Well, hey. Your mother told me you definitely got into that place down in Anthem. So that's something, right?"

I feel cracks forming in my worn, ancient-sandstone demeanor.

Hank leans in. "You okay, Zabardo?"

Which is when I crumple. My eyes go blurry. I drop my head into my hands, or try to, but overshoot and my forehead clips the desk on the way down. So from Hank's perspective it probably looks like I meant to whack my head on his desk like a psycho, and now I'm *crying about it.*

"Hey hey hey, it's all right, kid. Jesus. What'd I say?"

"Fucking *Anthem City College*."

He leans back in his chair, and laces his hands together over a slight paunch, seeming to really consider it. "Zabardo, there are kids here who didn't get into any college at all. There are kids who didn't even bother to apply. That boy with the purple tent, for one. Maybe this isn't what you want to hear right now, but you're one of the lucky ones. Privileged, even. It's okay to have roots in a place. To belong somewhere."

I wipe my nose. The pain in my forehead has dulled to a throbbing ache. "It would be okay if it was my choice. But it feels like something that was just *decided* for me." I can't articulate it in any clear way, but I recognize the feeling in nature-documentary form: it's like I'm krill before the great yawning mouth of a whale. Swimming without hope against an inescapable suction.

As if he's read my mind, Hank says, "Look, Zabardo. There are much worse places to be trapped than your cozy little hometown, all right?"

I don't say anything to that. Why bother?

After a moment, he jots something down on another orange post-it. "You can leave now. Just try not to hit Lurtz again, okay? 'Cause if he hits back next time I'll have to scrape you off the blacktop."

I get up, long past ready to be out of this orange-pocked office. Something stops me at the door, though. A nagging thought. He said, *That boy with the purple tent.*

"Mister," I say, then pause, realizing I don't know Hank's last name. "Hank," I start again. "Did Vink tell your fortune, too?"

He doesn't look at me. Just puts the cap back on his pen with an overabundance of care. "Yes, he did."

"What was it like?"

"Ridiculous. I mean, the kid wore a cape and turban from the Halloween superstore. But then." He pauses, blinking.

"Yeah?"

"I'd swear I saw something. Far behind him, where there should've just been the back of that moth-eaten tent. Buildings. Old stone buildings."

"But did he say what your fortune was? Are you going to win the lottery or something? Buy some big manor house?"

"No. Not that kind of building. Your friend said I'm going to die overseas," he says. "In a war."

"*What?*" I'm stunned by that. Hank isn't really my friend, no matter what he says in school assemblies at the beginning of each year, but he has been present and alive for as long as I can remember. I figured even after I went off to Harvard, he'd still be here, Guidance Counseling the weak and unwary. "But, couldn't you just not go? To war, I mean."

He smiles at me, then. "Zabardo, it's hard to imagine a world where I'd ever go back by choice."

When I find Vink, he's putting his tent away in the garage of his dead grandparents' house. Folded up and rolled into a creased, lumpy rectangle it may be small, but still looks pretty heavy. Clearly from an age before lightweight, hollow tent poles—all the supports are solid wood. Vink is sweating through his wifebeater, struggling to cram the rolled-up canvas onto a shelf above a wall of assorted junk. His latest fortune-telling outfit is folded, too, and stacked neatly in the driveway: a stiff gold costume-store turban sits on top of a purple cape and a pair of white gloves.

"Oh. Hey, bro!" His ink-black hair is pressed flat against his head, with a strange indentation circling his skull from where the edge of the turban pressed. "I was wondering when you'd get here."

I hadn't mentioned I was coming by. Actually, I hadn't even known I would until an hour ago. You could call it an impulse decision, but now I'm not sure such things exist.

I dig into my pocket and produce a five-dollar bill, wrinkled and mashed. My dreams are already crushed. What do I have to lose anymore? "Hey, Vink. Will you tell my fortune?"

"Oh, for sure. But it's after business hours, so you'll get the special one-time price."

"You mean…?"

"Yeah, it's free. Only problem is I already put away my tent."

I'm not sure why that matters, but don't say anything.

Vink considers a bit longer. "Why don't you come inside, bro?"

"Isn't your grandparents' place haunted?"

He shrugs. "Not *that* haunted."

The last time I'd been in the grandparents' house, I was maybe eleven years old. Even then, I remember the doorways and ceilings felt too close. Cramped—that's what I'd call it. Not helped by the fact that the whole place was packed to the gills with china knick-knackery and embroidered table shawls and brightly-patterned, mismatched furniture. Unwashed glasses and coffee cups on every available surface. A supremely lived-in aura everywhere you looked.

Clearly, things have changed. There are no coffee cups sitting around, first of all, and most of the furniture is covered with that special white cloth that stops upholstery fabric from fading or getting eaten by bugs. The effect is . . . okay, I won't lie: spooky. There's a draped armchair here, a covered end-table there, but some shapes are harder to identify. All of them loiter around the place like fat, old-fashioned ghosts. Along with something else.

Call it a bad vibe. Some houses, when left empty for too long, seem to get to liking all that quiet.

On the walls of the foyer, family photographs hang: a young, blurry girl holding a tabby cat, Vink's parents in white lace and tux on their wedding day, and—set apart from the others, in black and white—a woman who's seated and directly facing the camera. She looks perfectly serious, in the way that vintage-photograph people tend to do. Her clothes are a bit cartoonish, though, the collar of her dress enormous, the sleeves baggy. She's wearing a whole costume-shop's worth of necklaces and earrings and bangles.

From the kitchen, there's a sharp snap, as if from a pair of long-dead, bony fingers. I jump, but then Vink calls out, "You want a beer too, bro? My *nonno* left a fridge-full when he died."

I take a steadying breath. "I'm okay, thanks. Who's this lady here? The one in the old picture."

He comes out holding a Budweiser. "My great-grandmother! When she was young, back in the old country. She was, uh, a circus person or something. Okay, follow me. We need to be somewhere darker."

"Why?"

"It works better in the dark."

We go up the narrow, carpeted stairs. In the second-floor hallway, more pictures on the wall. Above our heads, a wine cork dangles from a string. Vink yanks on it and a trap door creaks down, along with a ladder. He goes first, impressively fast considering the beer in one hand. After he makes it up and steps off, I follow.

In the attic, it's almost impossible to see anything. I stumble over a footstool, then a bulging cardboard box. The only light is a dim halo coming from behind an oversized wooden crate. It's been pushed up against the one window, I realize. A brighter light flares in one corner as Vink activates the flashlight on his phone.

He's seated on a little leather stool. In front of him, on the bare floor, sits the pretty blue velvet bag, right next to his Budweiser. Even though it's still, I can somehow hear the bones and charms rattling ever so slightly. My mind playing tricks on me, maybe.

"This is where the real magic happens," he says, spreading his arms like he's hosting a video on MTV.

I sit on the floor in front of him, cross-legged. He picks up the bag and digs around inside. "Is there, like, something you want to know? Particularly, I mean."

"Is the bag magic, or is the magic coming from you?"

"Oh. Uh. The bag? Well, I couldn't tell the future until I found it. But, um, I don't think anyone else can do it, either. So, mostly from me. I think. Any other questions?"

"Why are you the one who found real, actual magic? You just use it to get beer money."

I think he rolls his eyes at me then, but it's too dark to be sure. "Bro. I meant, is there anything you want to know about *your* life."

"Okay. Sorry. Tell me, why does it feel like every individual moment I spend in Mousetown, I'm being suffocated to death? Or drained of all my blood? Even though I was never abused, and we're not that poor, globally speaking. Even though my ancestors crossed the ocean in a stupendously dangerous voyage before working themselves sick as, let's face it, basically slaves, all to give me the life I have right now."

Silence in the attic. The rustle of velvet, or the dry flutter of moth wings.

"Fuck, bro. I'm not sure a magic bag can tell you all that. But hey—let's try!"

Vink digs around in it again, then suddenly flicks out a hand. A moment later, I hear the pitter-pat of metal charms hitting the floor. He shines his flashlight on the spread and I lean over to see. If there's a pattern, though—my future spelled out in bones and wood and old coins—I can't make it out.

Vink points at a little piece of bone shaped liked an L. A tiny bit of a jaw, I realize. Maybe from a cat. "Okay, see how this kind landed of at the top? Above all the other shit?" Vink cocks his head. "For a while I thought it meant, like, you were gonna get bitten. Which would obviously be bad. But it's more about hunger. You want something really bad. College, right?"

Towers and ivy-draped turrets and haunted music rooms. Getting out of Mousetown, out of Jersey, into a life that matters. A big, grand existence far away, somewhere else. Finally losing this townie aura. "Yeah. Right."

I can't be sure, since it's almost impossible to see outside the narrow cone of Vink's phone light, but something starts to happen, then. The dusty, stale dark of the attic is replaced by darkness of a different sort. Thicker, like the smooth, heavy surface of a still pond on a moonless night.

"Okay. This." Vink points at a little wadded tangle of thread. In the light it shines back golden—just like the bag's drawstring, I realize, only it's been knotted into a ball. "This here is, like, all your big plans. But it's waaay far out, and sitting next to this little black rock. Which is . . . huh. Not a good sign. It's like—oh shit, bro. Is it . . . damn. Did you not get into any of those fancy colleges?"

I stare fiercely at the little golden lump of thread, furious it could just give me away like that. The edges of my vision are getting blurry, but I swallow the hot lump of shame and finally manage to keep from crying.

"Bro," Vink says, tenderly. "That sucks."

No, I can't bear it. "So what else does all this shit say? Because everything you said, I already know."

He waits a second, like he wants to say something else, then turns back to gaze at the spread on the floor again.

In my emotional state, with the pressure built up in my chest, and the almost-crying, I miss what's happening around me for a few moments. But finally I notice the crates and boxes and clutter are gone, swallowed by that soupy black all around us. Even the dim light from the covered window is gone now. There are other lights, though. Pinpricks shining impossibly far off, miles away but still inside the little attic, like this place runs on forever. Lights of yellow and red, like passing cars. Like traffic seen from far above. And I'm reminded, for some reason, of a freeway on-ramp.

Or maybe an exit.

Vink doesn't seem to notice any of this. He's concentrating on a misshapen copper coin sitting smack in the middle of everything, embossed with a dove in mid-flight. "Hey," says Vink. "Robbie, bro, you're not—"

But I'm up before he can finish, running away into the blackness all around us. Vink shouts something behind me, but I can't hear his words over my own pounding heart. I'm running for all I'm worth, running straight into the dark, expecting at any moment to slam into the wall of the attic or trip over an old ottoman and fall face first onto the dusty unfinished floorboards.

But neither of those things happen. Beneath my feet the ground goes from wooden planks to concrete, and still I'm running past it: Anthem City College, my shitty dorm, my first girlfriend . . . I see them all flicker by like old film, and then vanish. Soon they're far behind me.

The wooden floorboards underfoot change to sand and then loam and finally glass. I can feel it: I'm doing it. Going somewhere. Escaping from it all: Mousetown, my future, my fate, my stupid townie self. Everything is still dark, true, but I don't care, I'm just running. It doesn't matter where; only that I'm getting away. On the back of my throat I can taste a stranger air, something sharp and metallic, and it makes me remember huddling in the back of a dark and rusting ShopRite trailer with Vink.

You can't breathe in the space between worlds.

I inhale as deeply as I can, and keep running into the dark.

Now we shall detour to yet a different time and place: Paris, in the 18ᵗʰ Century. The object in this story was never on offer at the Night Bazaar, though its creation did occur at the very first one held in Venice. Unfortunately, I cannot actually let you gaze upon the item in question, this time. Suffice it to say, it's a most unusual oddity; the tanned hide of a creature more commonly found healthy and whole in churches, cathedrals, and monasteries. The artist behind this one-of-a-kind relic was a strangely-spoken, very demanding craftsman. He was with us for only a short time, but is still remembered with great awe, even among our own talented craftspeople. For his work is terribly beautiful beyond human imagining . . . which, I suppose, is the problem. For those viewers who have seen the hide are so shaken and overcome by this religious experience, their lives are never the same. That is, if they can manage to hold onto them, after that . . .

THE EXQUISITE HIDE OF BROTHER EDUARD

by Edison McDaniels

1: Saints Innocents

Mon Dieu. Paris, 1774.

The air of Parisian spring is rooty with the vile smell of the recently dead. The rains have come and gone and come again. The land is played out; the thin soil can't hold water. Cobblestone streets and muddy lanes are filthy quagmires where rats as big as terriers roam unmolested, and the stench of waste—human, canine, equine—is big and burdensome. The ancient buildings are unplumbed; their interiors dank and cold. Two or three or four stories tall, they wall the streets into dark, foreboding stone canyons where moss and lichen grow in the perpetual shadows. A continual sense of doom hovers, as if this land is cursed. As if the people—a burdened and afflicted lot of beggars, thieves, common folk, gentleman and ladies—expect the wrath of an unmerciful god to smite them in the manner of Sodom, at any moment.

Paris's soil is saturated with more than just water, however. Especially in the city's central acreage where the ground is hallowed and bones of a bygone era bob to the surface like gristle in a poor man's oxtail soup. Centuries in the making, Saints Innocents Cemetery is packed to overflowing with the mortal remains of beggars, fools, craftsmen, charlatans, priests, and the high born, all. The bones of a thousand thousand dead lie both atop and beneath the worn soil, their toxic effluvia leaching into the wells and rivers that supply the unfortunate population's daily drink. The ground offers up a festering stew of death and decay amid the leakage of putrid flesh and dry bones—an open sore on the corpus of le Cité itself.

Nothing grows amid the lime save a gray mold. In its poverty of color, unseen miasmas of the worst sort ooze from the ground like smoke off a fire, to contaminate everything. Birds do not fly over the cemetery. Meat left in the air rots before the eye, and local merchants tell of hung tapestries changing color overnight. Barrels of wine stored in nearby cellars yield only vinegar. A person caught within the walls of this boneyard, where only insects and even humbler creatures thrive, risks a violent, incapacitating nausea. Gravediggers complain of their hair falling out, of skin sloughing, of recent sores festering in minutes, and of a general derangement of the spirit. Incipient madness pervades all the diggers to the last poor devil.

The laws of both man and nature seem suspended.

2: Hôpital de la Charité

The thud of hoofbeats striking stone and wagon wheels grating across cobble-stones echoed off the walls of the *rue de Cabezon*. The wagon had been old when Monsieur Pierre first acquired it thirty years before. Its wheels had long since gone out of true under the weight of the dirt and bricks that were its daily burden, so it clunked rather than rolled. M. Pierre, himself also old and bent out of true, drove along the street as he had every night for over two-score years. His spine crooked, one shoulder higher, a dowager's hump bulging his threadbare jacket at the nape—the only part of him that seemed to be growing rather than shrinking away. Once a digger, he'd outlived his usefulness with a shovel. Now, to put food in his mouth, he rented out his mule and wagon for whatever work could be had.

He turned his cart onto the *rue de l'Université*, passing once again the black cinderblock walls of the *Hôpital de la Charité*. Its begrimed and sooty stone facade was an ugly place even amidst the blighted streets of central Paris. He had passed this very spot perhaps five thousand times in his lifetime, always with the same sense of dread. The *Charité* was a cursed place, attended only by those poor unfortunates who could afford nothing better. Its patients were the dregs of society: beggars and prostitutes, homeless waifs who so often fell under the wheels of a wagon or were found fevered in the back alleys. Those deformed by injury or made untouchable by disease, the ones who attended the dead, and those who were themselves condemned. This definition, of course, included most of the population of Paris.

The old man lightly flicked the reins, and like an automaton the mule turned the cart into the alley beside the old hospital. A few hundred feet along, the beast obediently stopped beside an old archway etched into the stone facade. The cart was only half filled with bricks and mortar, as heavy a load as the mule could pull these days. The man dropped to the cobblestones, hitched the animal to the post, and retrieved an iron key from his vest pocket. As he had done at least once a month for years, he fitted a skeleton key into the door's lock, applying great effort to turn it. The ancient, rusted mechanism finally gave with a reluctant screech. He pulled open the heavy, squat door. Inside lay black dark. A musky, disagreeable miasma wafted out. He returned to the cart, lifted out two bricks, and used them to prop the door open. Then stooped, drew in deeply a last breath of the better outside air, and stepped through the low portal.

M. Pierre was well acquainted with the bowels of the *Hôpital de la Charité*. He had in his possession a certain ledger that detailed the sordid history of this oldest of Paris's sick houses, passed down to him by his father. Who had in turn inherited it from his father, and so on, going back over a hundred and fifty years.

The flawed building had unexplained cold spots. Within its walls, lit candles gave no illumination—the bricks and stones seemed to absorb light as a sponge drinks water. A crooked place, it was built out of square so that doors frequently opened and closed of their own accord. Spilled water—even spilled blood—had sometimes been seen to flow uphill there. A sack dropped from the third-floor overhang took too long to hit the parlor floor on the first, and seemed never to fall straight. Worst of all—save, perhaps, for the deformities—was the way the cellar walls constantly wept.

The building was almost as old as Saints Innocents Cemetery, which occupied its backyard. Or more properly, the younger hospital occupied the older cemetery's front; a parcel once designated solely for the dead. That land was like a scar, upon which some saw hurt and others saw healing. The common ground between cemetery and hospital was a cellar wall, the oldest part of the structure. An imposing twenty feet high and built of piled red clay, it had been bricked over at least three times in its long history to counter an odd habit of bowing outward, like a penitent. Each time, more bricks had been added along the inside, so now the wall was very thick indeed. Yet still the stones wept a peculiar dirt-colored slime that had to be cleaned frequently. Otherwise the stench (M. Pierre found the nauseating stink of the day-old dead far preferable) would permeate the building. This slime sometimes contained—and this he thought worse than the smell, by far—the wiggling larvae of small flies.

M. Pierre had seen these maggots first hand. His earliest memory as a child was of wiping away that same fetid slime as his father, the hospital's brick mason, reinforced the wall with mortar and trowel. That was the year of smallpox, which had taken his mother and sisters. Once they fell sick, he'd known they would die. Not because of the fevers, or the terrible hallucinations, or even the horrific pustules which broke out everywhere until their skin was a mess of open cankers. But rather because of their charnel stink. They had smelled exactly like the wall in the cellar of the *Hôpital de la Charité*.

Twenty years on, his father had been the last workman to reinforce the cellar wall. He had fallen dead in the effort. By then, M. Pierre had been digging graves at Saints Innocents for a dozen years. It was no great thing to add his father's corpse to the mix. It was another, entirely, to inherit the old man's work at the cellar wall.

3: The Early Days

A 1596 engraving over the entrance to the *Hôpital de la Charité* reads "*Sad suff'rer under nameless ills… Whose soule art thou? Wantest thou suffrages, masses, or almes?*"

The history is a not a happy one. The original structure, built of wood in the waning days of the tenth century, was the first one lost in the Great Paris Fire of 1290. Though no reliable record of how that conflagration started remains, the fire was generally believed at the time to have broken out inside the hospital. After consuming all but the cellar, the flames turned outward to destroy half the city. They were said to have burned so hot, Paris itself became a crematorium. Saints Innocents cemetery survived, probably because there was so little left to burn in its thin soil.

Near a decade passed before the hospital was rebuilt, the exact year being lost to history, though it was substantially complete by 1302, the date of the earliest admission records, which are of survivors of the nocturnal massacre of the French garrison at Bruges in May. The Flemish insurrectionists sorted out the French by having them say the shibboleth "*schild en vriend,*" a phrase difficult for any native speaker of French to pronounce. The few survivors who escaped were brought to Paris in wagons smeared with their own blood and dripping with that of their dead countrymen—over two thousand perished in the nighttime slaughter. Many more died after arrival at the hospital, including every one of the first thirteen admissions. Citizens of the city still claim the words *schild en vriend* can be heard over the dying at *Charité* to this very day, the whispered moan of some disembodied presence.

The hospital was rebuilt over the remains of the original cellar, which survived the Great Paris Fire nearly intact. Indeed, the floor plan of the new structure was based on the dimensions of the original.

Problems surfaced at once. Parts of the structure were unnaturally cold. An effort was made to fix this by retrofitting fireplaces along several strategic outer walls. The result was a building with the odd accoutrement of many tall chimneys which littered the surrounding streets with ash, yet failed to warm the sickhouse. Windows were added against a claustrophobic interior darkness, giving the facade an unbalanced—most simply said ugly—look. The number of windows in the original plan had been forty-eight, four on each side of the three floors above the basement. After the renovations, they reached the unholy number of sixty-six.

Later, to counter this, in the year 1401 a sixty-seventh window was added by excavating a cellar wall within which to frame it, but the frame refused to hold glass. Invariably, new panes shattered within days. Always outward, as if something inside was intent on escaping. The cellar window finally was boarded up, but the problem of cracked panes spread. Soon no window in the building was left untouched. Several were replaced, again to no avail. Repairs were suspended because of the exorbitant cost of glass, made in small quantities by hand during that era. The windows, each and every pane marred by at least one crack, have stood thus for centuries.

Still, patients always came. It was a charity hospital after all, manned by priests, who were also physicians of the humble but learned order Brothers of Saint Paul the Divine. They treated the indigent sick and poor, including in that definition any person who dared to step past their wretched doors. Death was a frequent visitor also, for by some accounts the *Hôpital* was a place people only came to die.

In 1333, the first year of the Great Chinese famine which killed six million people on the other side of the globe, a certain Brother Eduard arrived. His name appears with frequent regularity in the ledger thereafter for the next fourteen years, usually in praise of his devotion to the sick and wretched. More frequently as time passed, he occasionally flogged the ailing, feeling encouraged that those who recovered were now free of their sins. Those who did not survive this treatment were buried in the unholy ground of Saints Innocents. Their sins bled into the earth, their mortal flesh turned to dust, and their tortured souls awaited possible resurrection.

4: The House Of Fortunato

The knocking that echoed through the home of Ognibene Fortunato was not unlike the hollow ring of a prayer issued inside a tomb.

After a minute or two, a fat, balding man dressed in a saffron-yellow robe opened the door. A tiny cross was tattooed in dark ink upon his left check.

"I wish to see the master of the house," said the traveler in awkwardly-accented Italian. He stood before the open door clad in the voluminous black robes of his order, a thin rope of bleached hemp binding his waist, a thin cross woven of willow hanging off the belt to his right. The man himself was also thin, having in the course of his travels given up the greater part of his meager food to the less fortunate. He had not recently trimmed his beard, so his mouth was nearly hidden. He carried only a bedroll and a book of prayer, though he considered only the book, and the worn sandals on his feet, to be essential.

The servant frowned. "My master is not within."

"I've traveled a great distance, all the way from Paris. When might you expect him?"

"Ah, you are French." The man smiled. "We are Umberto, humble servant to Fortunato. We are afraid the master is, or rather has been, detained. We beg you enter and wash the dust from your feet, weary traveler."

The traveler noted with a hint of smile how the fat man had seamlessly transitioned to French. The words perfect, without detectable accent. Though an odd habit, to be sure, was his use of 'we' in referring merely to himself. Perhaps he meant the entire household.

The traveler settled on a stone bench beside a wall fountain in the atrium. Soon Umberto returned carrying a salver of fruit and bread, as well as a carafe of wine and a copper goblet.

"That is an interesting sketch," the traveler said, after the servant had poured some wine and he'd taken a long draught. He pointed to a framed work above the fountain. At first, he'd merely thought it curious. But the longer he gazed, the more captivated he became. A face was somewhere in there, but was it that of a man, or a beast?

Umberto followed the traveler's stitched gaze. "It is said to be the likeness of Abdul Al-Hazred, poet of Sana'a. Our mistress came upon it some years ago at an Eastern bazaar. Exquisite, no? How infernally lifelike the eyes!"

That was it, exactly. They were those of a wildling. Large, but with lids darkly recessed beneath a heavy brow. The face itself bonier and more irregular than on than any visage the traveler had ever encountered. Neither pretty nor handsome, yet oddly attractive. Or rather, hypnotic. Whoever or whatever it was had clearly commanded respect.

Ah, the traveler thought. Heaven and Hell. The sketch displayed the disparity between the two perfectly. "My God," he murmured.

"They called him the Mad Arab," Umberto said. "The House of Fortunato welcomes priests and beggars alike. Which are you, sir?"

Without looking away from the framed sketch, he gave his bona fides. "I am Brother Eduard, devoted servant of the Brethren of Saint Paul the Divine. And of Our Lord, of course." The person before him did not need this list of his many teachers, nor a recitation of the several books he'd read, or all the monasteries he had visited. But he spoke of these things without hesitation, unable not to do so.

Umberto did not interrupt. "A priest, then. We shall take particular care," he said when the guest had finally exhausted his recitation. He knelt, removed Eduard's sandals, and began washing his dusty feet. "Even had you not answered, we should've known your calling. The simple robes might be those of beggar or priest, but these toes could only belong to a holy man."

Eduard frowned. "Are not the toes of one man much as those of any other?"

"Is the soul of one man as the soul of any other, Brother Eduard?"

"Hardly the same thing," Eduard said, sounding more arrogant than he'd intended.

"Oui, monsieur. We are but humble servants, the two of us. You know souls. We know feet." As he worked, the man sharply twisted Eduard's great toe.

The Brother winced and pulled his foot away. "You've been most kind. For how long will Fortunato be detained? I beg again knowledge of when he might return."

"I am sorry. We cannot say. In fact, many months have passed since he's been seen."

"Then I will take my leave."

"But perhaps…well, maybe not…" Umberto's voice trailed off.

"Do you play games with me, sinner? I've traveled many months. Does your head know more than your tongue reveals?"

"A thousand apologies, kind sir. We should not have presumed. Sometimes the tongue is a bastard. In truth, we possess no knowledge of when our master might return. Our mistress is conducting business in his extended absence."

"Mine is no business for a woman to deal with."

"Another thousand apologies. This stupid tongue of ours. . . . "

Eduard looked up at the sketch again. "The Mad Arab, you said. Yes, I can see that. This mistress of yours, where might I find her?"

"Signora Vera will be overseeing a bazaar, monsieur."

"A strange duty for a God-fearing mistress."

"Oh, it's strictly for charity. To feed orphans and widows. The Night Bazaar opens in a few days' time. In St. Mark's Square, at midnight."

"Well, I must speak with her now. Today."

"Quite impossible, monsieur. Our mistress does not receive visitors during the day, and her nights are occupied at the moment preparing for this bazaar nocturnalis. Such elaborate festivals do not come often, and they require, shall we say, exquisite planning. Would you like to see it? We can arrange this. The event is by invitation only."

"You know I am a priest. Why would God want his representative to visit such a sacrilegious pastime? Tell me, is your tongue a fool as well as a bastard?"

"I speak now not as a servant, but, well…as a fellow traveler. One who reveres His teachings." Umberto nodded vaguely toward the sketch. "Because, Brother Eduard, it is in just such places we can best serve our masters, don't you think? Or mistresses. We assure you, sir, whatever one's soul needs may be found at this bazaar. I'm privileged to know that its works shall be…" He glanced toward the sketch of the Mad Arab, "quite exquisite."

"Your tongue is a sly one, Umberto. I trust it labors in the service of your mistress even now." Brother Eduard smiled wryly.

And with that, he accepted the invitation.

5: The Bazaar

Tents, booths, tables, kiosks, even the occasional caravan wagon lined all four sides of the broad plaza, and spilled down the alleys. St. Mark's Square was filled to overflowing. How has this all been put up so suddenly, Eduard wondered. He'd visited the plaza the day before, and seen only the usual assortment of Venetians about—shoppers, peddlers, fruit vendors, artisans, the odd vagabond.

That servant was a fool after all, the priest decided.

But in the afternoon, upon returning to the House of Fortunato, Eduard was stunned to discover no palazzo there. Only a sty holding pigs, several lying dead in the mud. He had no better luck finding their owner than he'd had finding Fortunato. There was still the invitation, though, a curiously heavy piece of parchment with only four words inked upon it: *Bazaar Nocturnalis. Unum Fateri.*

Night Bazaar. Admits One.

A ticket, then. He did not want to believe the servant had gotten the better of him, and yet, here he was. Still.

Brother Eduard used the invitation, and saw many unusual sights in the dark aisles of the bazaar, but still could not find its mistress. There were others of interest about, however, varied and clever. Minstrels of every sort, shopkeepers hawking exotic wares he had neither heard of nor cared to try. The sweet, smoky scent of opium hung like mist in the alleys. He would swear a faint musky tang of fornication permeated the entire Square.

Eduard thought, If Hell has a distinct odor, this is it. He hoped it wouldn't linger on his clothing.

And yet, he couldn't bring himself to leave. The atmosphere was intoxicating. Around every corner, something unfamiliar. Under every sign, something beastly or forbidden or peculiar.

At one stall a little boy twirled a length of rope before him and smiled mischievously. Coming closer, the priest saw it was not a rope the child spun, but a length of his own innards strung in and out of his belly. Yet the boy smiled, and beckoned with a finger, whispering, "Come closer, sir."

Eduard shook his head and turned away, shuddering.

He drew back the curtain on another place and discovered within three ugly women, scantily clad, rubbing scented oil on a man. He was no younger than eighty, judging by his shriveled limbs. The old degenerate likely not been stiff in years, but was prodigiously so now.

A nearby cart offered trinkets from the Black Sea. "Suitable for gifting your enemies," the dowager proprietress said. "You have enemies, Holy Father, do you not? We all possess enemies."

Eduard actually could not recall ever having said of a man, 'He is my enemy.' But he didn't disagree, merely shook his head and moved on.

Around another corner, a fellow with smooth, glistening ebony skin tried to interest him in a concoction of scented oils and tar. "It will remove whatever ills you contract, now or in the future." The Nubian looked as strong as any man Eduard had ever seen, but one whiff of the eye-watering mixture convinced him to move on.

"A peacock feather, for good luck, that is all. We all need luck now and again," lisped a small girl with a twisted gold ring in her nose. Eduard did not believe in luck, though. He strode a path of prayer and repentance only.

"Fancy a lookin' glass, sir? No ordinary glass is this," bellowed a dark-haired gypsy woman. "Want to know what you'll look like in twenty years?"

Eduard did not.

A simple sign at one establishment read, MONEYLENDING HERE. ANY COLLATERAL. WE ARE NOT PARTICULAR.

As Eduard passed, a one-armed man climbed laboriously from the wagon upon which the sign was posted. "Were I you, sir, I'd pay attention to the clause about them not being particular. Nor sentimental, I vow." He hobbled away unevenly, his weight balanced between a crutch under the stump of one arm and his single remaining leg. Muttering, "Goddamned accountants."

The place hustled and bustled. Like a nest of rodents the people sidled and writhed about one another, in a jovial carnival atmosphere. This was no place for a priest.

And then he saw the dwarf.

The little man stood a mere three feet tall, wore a monk's robe, and was tattooed with a small cross on one cheek, just as was the servant Umberto.

"Hold, I say," Eduard shouted after him. "Little man!"

The diminutive monk stopped, looked up, and smiled. "I am Father Earl. Pray, how may I assist you?" His French was as perfect as Umberto's.

"I'm searching for Signora Fortunato. But in her stead the family servant, a man named Umberto, will do. Know you this Umberto, who has the same mark of the cross upon his cheek?"

"We know of whom you speak, foreign priest."

We again. The collective. It was damned strange. "Will you take me to him, then?"

"We can, if you are most sure that is what you wish."

Behind the short monk, an unnaturally tall man wearing a parti-colored outfit too short in the sleeves and trousers juggled several long knives. When Eduard looked closer, he saw the man's eyes were clouded the sanguine color of blood clay. The juggler was blind.

"Mon Dieu," Eduard mumbled, making a hasty sign of the cross. He nodded at the monk. "Take me there," he ordered, though he felt sure of nothing at this point.

Father Earl took his hand and wordlessly guided him through the crowd, moving up one piss-stinking alleyway and down another. At last they stopped before a worn canvas tent. UMBERTO'S INK was painted in large blood-red letters above the flap.

"I walked the same alley several times tonight and never saw this here."

"The bazaar is quite large, priest. Perhaps you are mistaken."

Eduard doubted this, but simply nodded.

"We leave you here, priest. Keep you well."

"And you as well, my diminutive Brother in Christ." Eduard inclined his head, then passed between the flaps.

It was humid and close inside. Overlaid with a thin stench of animal dung, and something else. Hide, Eduard thought. The beastly stink of curing hides. Tolerable in this case, but only just.

He waited for his eyes to adjust to the smoky gloom. Several other figures sat or lazed about, outlines indistinct. Men or women, he was not sure. One smoked a long pipeful of some aromatic herb. Others reclined on couches, sharing a hookah.

Fortunato's servant was crouched in their midst. He rose as Eduard approached.

"Umberto, have you misled me? You swore I'd find your mistress here."

"We do not believe we intimated this."

"You, Umberto, you. Not we. *You* mean, 'I do not believe I intimated this'."

Umberto grinned. "Brother Eduard, as a man of God, do you not feel His presence with you, always?"

Eduard frowned. "Of course."

"Then how to be certain, when you speak, it is solely your opinion and not His as well? Aside from the Great I Am, we are all we. Not merely I."

"Your tongue is too clever by far," Eduard muttered.

"A matter of opinion, sir. You have heard it, else you would not be here, in our business establishment."

Eduard swallowed uncomfortably. "You said nothing of this the other day."

"You did not ask, sir."

Eduard scowled at the portly bald man. "What game is this? Make that bastard tongue speak true, for once."

Umberto's grin was full of teeth and grit. A wolfish smile, long honed. "We are a simple businessman, monsieur. No games. You admired the sketch of Abdul Al-Hazred, the Mad Arab?"

"You know I did. Exquisite work. Though . . . unsettling in its aspect."

"We drew it," Umberto said matter-of-factly. Behind him several compatriots nodded.

"Now your tongue spouts rubbish. The sketch must be three centuries old," Eduard scoffed. "You couldn't possibly be its creator."

"He is a gifted artista, indeed," said one of the seated men.

Another chimed in, "Davvero, none better in the known world."

Still a third, "He has inked kings and queens. They wait on his pleasure."

"Three hundred years?" Umberto shook his head. "Twice that, actually. But we assure you, we drew it. From life. The poor mad soul died after the sketch was made. Very shortly after. Do you know why they called him the Mad Arab?"

"No, nor do I—"

"Nor do we. But you will agree the sketch caught the essence of madness."

Eduard nodded unwillingly.

"We can do the same for you, priest." That honed smile returned. "Capture your essence, that is. The very quality that makes you...unique. Would you care to possess such a portrait?"

Brother Eduard, to his dismay, realized he'd like it very much. "No, I . . . I . . . well, yes. Perhaps. What would such a rendering cost? I have no coin. I'm a simple servant of God."

Umberto curled his lip. "We do not deal in tawdry coins."

For the first time since taking his vow of poverty and donning priestly robes years before, Eduard perceived not just a need, but a great desire. "Please, tell me then. What will it cost?"

Umberto gave a dismissive wave. "In good time. First, let us begin. There will be no charge for canvas or parchment. We apply the ink to your skin. Then your essence will be on display for all to see. Forever." Umberto threw a brotherly arm around the priest's shoulders and walked him to the rear of the tent, then through a series of hanging veils. "We must begin before first light. The Bazaar lasts only a few more nights."

Umberto worked through the remainder of the night and into half of the next day.

Eduard alternately sat or stood as was necessary. He felt the pain in his feet, first. Tiny pricks of the artist's needles as Umberto worked at the initial inking, without even a preliminary sketch. Seeming instead to uncover the image within Eduard's flesh.

As a novitiate, he'd once watched a sculptor fashion a crucifix from granite. This memory came to him with the first needle-prick. It grew as his flesh filled with black lines of ink. The pain grew as well, making the experience all the more magnificent. It recalled to him Christ upon the cross, and the exquisite suffering the Son of God had endured.

How dare I compare myself to the Messiah, he thought. Still, the pain was . . . exquisite.

Umberto moved on to the priest's legs. "These will be covered and thus the least-appreciated part of my masterpiece." He worked his way up and down, inking Latin crosses of various sizes. At first, these appeared to Eduard random in their placement. But gradually Umberto's plan made itself apparent, as the smallest crosses coalesced into larger crosses, and those into still larger ones. Though this might be an illusion as exquisite as the pain. And as joyous.

His mind screamed with the joy.

At noon of the first day, the artist stopped. "We cannot go on."

"What? But it is so…beautiful. I can feel your work even in my bones."

Umberto sighed. "It is always so. But the work drains us. We need inspiration."

"I am a humble priest. I possess no—"

"Yes, so we have heard. No coin. But there is your left great toe."

"My . . . I beg your pardon?"

"For inspiration, we will accept your left great toe in compensation. To continue."

Eduard gasped. "What in the name of the apostles can you mean?" Yet he knew.

"It is only a toe." Umberto shrugged.

"Yes, but it is mine. A part of me."

"The toe of a priest. We said as much the first time we met. Do you not recall? Beneath the sketch."

Recalling the fine portrait of the Mad Arab, Eduard felt a deep longing. The marvelous painful joy of the past hours pulled at him again. This work must be finished. Anything else would be a sin. "Very well. I will give a toe."

He somehow managed not to scream as, with a small cleaver, Umberto hacked through the knuckle at the base. He then held up the appendage, viewing it from different angles before he tossed it away. Exactly as if it was nothing more than a toe.

The artist worked through the night and into the next afternoon. Eduard's legs swelled with the assault. Minuscule drops of blood covered the skin, obscuring the developing image. He caught a glance now and again of a small detail, a corner or a crosshatch in black ink, but not enough to make a coherent picture in his mind's eye. The pain was ever present, though, as if he were staring unceasingly into the noonday sun. He could not look away, though. He would rather be blind than do so.

The next evening, Umberto announced a need for further inspiration. "We must have the other great toe."

Eduard was feeling more blessed even than the day before. The thighs and calves of both legs and one arm were now covered in God's glory—a multitude of Latin crosses written into his flesh. He thought he glimpsed a face in there somewhere, composed of many tiny crosses. Or perhaps he only wished to see one. Each cross was exquisitely detailed. Some hollow outlines, some solid black, others various colors of ink. In each the vertical portion below the crossbar was longer than the other three parts. Every tiny cross was just that. And yet, together, so much more. Though unfinished, which seemed an abomination.

He stretched his unmaimed foot out and perched it upon the bandaged one. "Do what you must."

Again Umberto picked up the disarticulated toe from where it'd fallen on the bloody tent floor. Examining it from various angles, as if looking for something particular within the small bones. Then he tossed it away. A mongrel dog seized the morsel and ran off. And Umberto again picked up his tools: a quill, an ink pot, and a polished wooden handle to hold various needles.

Another day and another night passed. By then the priest's arms, legs, and back were a canvas of Latin crosses, various sizes and colors, though much was obscured by Eduard's own blood. Only his chest and belly remained virginal.

By now, his eyes were rolling in their sockets. He could not help gasping twenty times a minute, from pain and the sense his skin crawled with insects. How much more could he endure?

"We have gone as far as we can," Umberto said suddenly.

"But it is not done! What more do you need? I have thumbs. Or do you need my hands?"

"I beg you, priest, do not humiliate yourself. We care not for thumbs. And what good is a priest without hands? How would he bless sinners?"

"What, then? This great work must be finished."

"There is one thing. In order to finish, we must know you...in a biblical sense."

"You do not mean..." Eduard winced.

"We would be gentle," Umberto assured him.

But he was not.

When it was over, the priest lay bleeding anew, and Umberto went to work a final time. He moved more quickly, with renewed knowledge, it seemed to Eduard, progressing across chest and back.

"It is done, priest," Umberto said at last.

Exhausted, Eduard had fallen asleep. Now he roused to gaze at himself in a tall polished-brass mirror. Much as the artist had done with the toes, regarding himself from various angles, twisting this way and that. Finally he frowned. "You are sure it's finished? It is not quite the masterpiece I'd expected."

Umberto shrugged. "We are sorry, priest. We work within the limitations of the canvas we've been given. The work is as finished as any man could make it. If it does not look like greatness yet, we assure you it will yet. Greatness does not ripen in a few days. In time, it will be exquisite."

"How long?"

Turning his back to Eduard, Umberto sighed. "Who can know such things exactly? That is a question the Mad Arab asked us, as we recall. We gave the same answer we now give you." Umberto again faced the tattooed priest. "Unfortunately, long after you are dead."

6: The Brothers of Saint Paul the Divine

After his return to Paris in 1347, Eduard was a man living between Heaven and Hell, whose very skin was itself a living, breathing holy relic. He became a penitent, flogging and blistering himself ceaselessly at the bedside of frightened, vexed patients. At times he seemed almost mad, walking the floor a bit unsteadily, for lack of two toes. Scratching at his skin, chanting.

"I have defiled my body and soul. Oh Gracious Almighty, forgive this poor priest, though I am not worthy of Your mercy."

The ledger records these words exactly. Sometimes a servant named Umberto was mentioned. Sometimes the priest went so far as to damn this person, then left off to flog his back with all the greater zeal.

These details Monsieur Pierre read about repeatedly, in the old book. He removed his spectacles and cleaned them with a small cloth, then took a bite of the cheese that was his meal this night. Leaning closer to the candle, he turned to the next page in his father's ledger. More rightly it belonged to the hospital, or the Brothers. But he would never give it up, for the ideas it contained were blasphemy. Dangerous in the wrong hands. So he continued reading, evaluating and summing up the information. His body was bent, but his mind remained strong as ever.

On the sixth of June, 1366, Brother Eduard's penitence ended abruptly. He fell from a window on the fourth floor of the *Hôpital de la Charité*.

There is a discrepancy here, M. Pierre noted. This was the first mention of a *fourth* floor. When it had been added is unclear. Of more significance was why it had been removed. In any event, Brother Eduard's fatal fall happened in the middle of a busy, rainy weekday afternoon, yet somehow his plummet to the cobblestones of the rue de *l'Université* went unseen. His body, minus the great toes lost in Venice, was naked save for numerous Latin crosses tattooed upon him, neck to foot. In falling he struck an old beggar woman in the muddy lane, killing her.

A dutiful priest saw fit to record how her corpse, lying beneath that of dear, departed Brother Eduard, was quickly gnawed by rats, while Brother Eduard remained divinely untouched. After finding his body, his Brothers rushed upstairs to his room, where they discovered the door of the modest quarters blocked from the inside. After breaking it down, expecting to encounter an assailant, instead they found the window looking onto the rue de *l'Université* also closed. In fact, nailed shut. The room felt colder than anyone could ever remember it having been before, even in mid-winter. Eduard's clothes sat folded neatly below the sill of the nailed window—one pane of which was cracked, as it ever had been. A single naked footprint—the great toe missing—was plain in the damp dust outside, on the ledge of the window. Over the years, a legend grew around this footprint: How, on rainy days it would reappear. The more morbid accounts claimed rain washing over it turned pink, then blood red before flowing away.

Brother Eduard was the first priest to be laid in the crypt below the hospital, under a chapel on the first floor.

A certain Brother Richard would be the second.

He came to the charity hospital three years after Eduard's untimely demise, in the winter of 1369, and was assigned the dead priest's old room. The notation in the ledger are incomplete on this day. *Noting only, Arrived from Venice this day Brother Richard, replacing dear departed Brother Eduard. The new priest has been given Eduard's room on the third floor. May he ever rest in divine peace.*

Had the author of this cryptic entry actually meant to say the *fourth* floor? And what about the phrase, *May he ever rest in divine peace?* Did he mean Eduard or Richard? These things remain unknowable, for on the same night of his arrival Brother Richard passed away in his sleep, in the same bed Eduard had occupied until three years before—a bed which had apparently gone unused in the interval. The new priest had not appeared ill before he retired for the night. He was, in fact, the youngest ever to serve at the hospital. Though, of course, he died before actually serving even a day.

His death mask, the first but not the last made of a Brother of that unfortunate order, shows the contorted features of a man who died at anything but peace. The mouth gaping so wide it is almost certain his jaw had been dislocated. The startled eyes look lidless in their unholy stare. The mask has been hidden away for centuries. But his expression has been described, by those few who have seen it in recent times, as frankly hideous.

No records remain as to the fate of the cursed death-bed, or the straw that lay upon it. But according to the narrative, before the other priests left the room the newly-arrived Richard had fallen to his knees and prayed at the bedside, babbling in tongues (later translated into the ledger) about Eduard's "pious blood" which had stained the straw mat there.

Poor Brother Richard. So taken was he, either humbled or blinded by his predecessor's devoted sufferings, he insisted upon sleeping on the bare, prickling straw that very night.

"The sustenance every weary traveler seeks is here," he said, and pointed to the blood-speckled mat. His last words before the others left. Thus we shall never know more of his fate.

The room itself is modest in scale, though as to its exact size there remains some conjecture. After Richard's demise it went unused for over half a century except as a storage place. An anecdote from this period relates that once a boy was told to retrieve a book from 'the small room on the third floor.' The story, possibly apocryphal, claims the child was later found wandering on the *fourth* floor 'possessed of the Devvil in minde and body, with a burning fever. Also blinded, sans pupils, as seen in the face on a marble bust.'

Again, a storyteller has confused the third and fourth floors. Perhaps the child merely lost his way and was injured.

In 1399, a young surgeon, not a member of the priestly order, took lodgings 'in the fourth-floor room' while working at the hospital. After three weeks, he requested different lodgings, remarking 'I cannot sleep for the racket of noise. The sufferings of the patients on the ward below is all times loud in my ears.' And yet at the time there were no patients on the third floor, which was under extensive repair. Nonetheless, the surgeon insisted the sounds were 'distinctly unnerving.' He threatened to vacate his post if the request for new lodgings was not granted post haste.

His behavior became increasingly irrational, or else increasingly genius. He was called mad for pouring boiling oil on the open wounds of young lads run over in the street. He was too quick to cut for stone. He kept candles lit all night to ward off the spirits of the dead, but only on nights with less than half a moon. He had the single communal outhouse moved from one side of the hospital to the other, and afterwards the stench of the place was a bit less offensive. He disappeared for hours at a time, whereabouts unknown. He lost a good deal of weight, and at last began spending most of his time in the cellar, alone.

One day, when the Brothers went looking for him, they discovered he'd opened the crypt containing the bodies of Eduard and Richard, and then their vaults. If this was considered sacrilege, it wasn't recorded in the ledger. The priests reported Richard's remains were untouched. Except of course by time, which had not been kind.

Yet Eduard, a holy relic in life, was no less so in death. The doctor had torn away the dead priest's burial robes and vestments. He lay naked and exposed upon a slab of dusty granite. Perhaps in their grief the Brothers who had entombed him in 1366 had not recognized this holy relic among them. His skin, which should've rotted in the dank air of the cellar crypt—everything else certainly did—appeared as pristine as the day he had died.

"He looks younger, even," said the oldest among them, Gaspar, the only one of the Brothers who'd known Eduard in life. He knelt on the damp earth and held up a hand in the guise of the apostle Peter, thumb and first two fingers extended, the others curled toward the palm. He could not tear his gaze away from an illustration adorning Eduard's lifeless chest.

"I am certain that one was not there at his death so many years ago," he murmured. "I was his confessor, I washed his body myself. Mon Dieu." He wept. "Mon Dieu!"

The surgeon must've seen it too, the moment he opened the cellar crypt, pried open the vault, and lifted the burial shroud. In fact, he claimed to have seen it even before he'd opened the crypt. He was not a devout man, yet it had appeared for months in his dreams. 'The most beautiful, the most compelling vision I've ever seen,' he had told the Brothers more than once.

On the skin overlying the stilled chest of Brother Eduard there now appeared the most lustrous, exquisite image of Christ upon the cross any living being had ever laid eyes upon. The crucifix of Our Lord seemed to leap from the dead skin. At first glance, the wounds around the nails in the hands and feet were so brilliantly red, Gaspar thought they were actually bleeding. The crown of thorns was as green and vibrant as a springtime vine. And those gleaming tears upon the face—the face of Jesus—made old Gaspar weep harder.

So it had been with the surgeon. And so it was now with the Brothers.

And so it was all written down in the ledger, in 1401.

7: Monsieur Pierre

M. Pierre finished his meal and closed the old leather book. He removed small, wire-framed spectacles, and rubbed tired eyes. Reading the ledger always made his head ache. Still, he pulled the leather-bound volume off the shelf and read a few pages every month before going down to the cellar. A reminder of both what he had to do, and what he must always avoid.

The following day M. Pierre descended the steps to the cellar of the *Hôpital de la Charité* with difficulty. His bones and joints were not what they used to be and this part of the structure had long been unused, save by him. The steps were damp and worn, hollowed uneven from centuries of feet descending them. Lichen and moss grew in the cracks. The walls were a foot or more thick. If he fell, the place would swallow him. He could shout for days and not be heard.

It was a ritual, coming here. One he'd conducted every month for thirty years, since buried his father in Saints Innocents. He'd promised that much. Not to the old man in life, but to his stilled corpse as Pierre had lowered him into that poor, tainted soil. Just as his father had done with his father before him. Before them, there had been others, all the way back to the old priest.

What had his name been, again?

This is part of the aging, M. Pierre guessed. My mind is not as sharp as it once was. The past at times eludes me.

But the priest, the one who'd died falling out a fourth-floor window? Oh yes, Gaspar. He remembered now. He supposed he was now about Gaspar's age, somewhere between elderly and ancient.

Too old, he thought. I've been around too long.

Had Gaspar thought that, too? Perhaps that was why the old priest had jumped out that window four centuries before.

Of course, that wasn't truly the case. M. Pierre knew exactly why Gaspar had jumped. Same reason as Eduard before him.

Ah, Eduard—now there was a curious fellow. You might even say the man was cursed. The way things had turned out, that was putting it lightly. Eduard had jumped, and damned scores followed. He'd been first, but was not last.

"The last will be first and the first last," Pierre muttered as he descended the slick steps.

He crossed the cobbled stones of the dank cellar. The walls here were truly ancient. In fact, as a young man he had convinced himself he could still see scorch marks from that long-ago Paris fire, the one that had all but destroyed the city in 1290. One of the few structures that hadn't burned that day was this wall, which pushed back against Saints Innocents cemetery and its million buried denizens on the other side. M. Pierre more likely saw rot and mildew, not scorch marks, of course. Those would've certainly vanished long ago. Nothing lasted in the dank, dirty catacombs except bones. Not infrequently, he found bones down there. Usually near the wall, where they had somehow managed to work their way through from the poorly-consecrated soil of Saints Innocents on the other side.

No oil lamps down there, of course, so he carried a torch. His own son, Henri had been his name, had carried one for him, until. . . .

Why was it he forgot the things he most wanted to remember, and remembered the things he longed to forget? For five years he had been trying to forget that day.

First Eduard. And then Richard. Poor Richard, they had called him. Just out of boyhood. Beardless. Barely a man. Priest or not, he hadn't survived even one night under the unholy influence of cursed Brother Eduard.

Dear Christ, M. Pierre thought, and chuckled at the blasphemous irony.

Old Gaspar had been the third to go. A jumper, too. Probably mad as well. All those after him certainly had become addled. That is . . . except perhaps Henri.

No. No, he wasn't going to think about that. Not if he could help it. Please God, he thought, not today. Do not afflict me thus today.

The surgeon. The genius physician, he thought. The one who'd finally pried open the crypt. He must've been one strong fellow—in mind, if not in body. To have had the will to fight the compulsions all that time, to somehow not jump, himself. Only to realize, in the end, his life had been merely a single huge obsession. And that he had unleashed Hell.

In the end, he'd finally jumped, too.

Over the years, so had over a hundred others. No doubt more, whose names remained unrecorded. M. Pierre didn't know the exact number; no one did. Certainly not a small figure, though. Sooner or later, everyone who saw that cursed, beautiful crucifix on Eduard's chest went mad. Most then killed themselves, usually by jumping. He supposed it must've seemed the easiest way out. Or else. . . a way in?

Mon Dieu. He crossed himself.

Only Our Lord and Savior knew the answer to that. And of course the other one. The so-called Morning Star, the Bringer of Light. Out, or in. Heaven or Hell. Before or after. Life or death. Genius, or madness. The barrier between each seemed thin to M. Pierre. Far thinner than most people suspected.

He heard the wall creaking, so he was close now. Almost, he thought uncomfortably, as if it was breathing. A sort of groping moan he didn't like to hear. No man should have to listen to such sounds. Sometimes they sounded like screams. As if somebody—or something—was on the other side. Most often it seemed akin to scratching. Or perhaps gnawing was a better term. Faint, persistent gnawing. M. Pierre could picture the denizens on the other side clawing to get out.

There were the deformities; infants born with a split upper lip, or missing an arm. God's miracle of birth gone wrong. As a digger, he'd had to bury far too many malformed babes. He suspected the *Charité* had a higher rate of such births than other hospitals, but had no way to know. Maybe that was merely how the world worked. Perhaps diseased wombs were just the way of the poor. Most folks never saw, and so didn't know, that for every ten or twenty or thirty born with the proper parts, a few came into this world monstrous and ill formed. A truth too grotesque to think about. He'd once seen an infant with no eyes. In place of them, just lumps. As if a mad artist had pushed wads of unformed clay into the sockets. The priests had starved the poor creature. The worst part was how the thing, for he couldn't bear to think of it as a baby, had taken so many days to die.

He thought of the litter of kittens he'd once seen his father drown, when he was a boy. They too had emerged without eyes. Why hadn't the damned priests quickly drowned the baby and been done with it?

Pierre shuddered. He'd been forty years a digger, and had put those babes in the dirt, sometimes with one of the priests praying over them. At Saints Innocents, of course. Always at Saints Innocents. God, how he hated that place.

Almost as much as he hated this one, below.

There are thin places in this world, he thought. Spots so threadbare, the border between this world and the next is near nonexistent. Lose yourself in such, and likely as not you'll never get out again. Saints Innocents was like that.

The cellar of the *Hôpital de la Charité* was one of the thinnest places this world offered. Even its flies were a damned sight better than the maggots wriggling in the foul muck that oozed from the wall at the end of the passage.

He had to hold his breath now. Then he tripped over something, a huge thigh bone, and cursed it.

The wall itself was leaning heavily again, just as it had in the days and months before his father had last shored it twenty-odd years earlier. Had M. Pierre been even a little younger, he would've shored it up now. But his infirmities had grown too great. The muscles he'd built over two-score years of digging were gone. His body was as far out of true as a withered, fallen tree. He could no more fix the wall than he could put that ruined fruit back on its branch.

Dear Henri had been his hope. His boy had grown to a man under his tutelage, seeing the wall lean more with each passing year. Shoring it up had been his son's destiny, but the boy hadn't been as strong as the father. Not in mind, anyway. Pierre had warned him many times never to go near the crypt. To not listen to the muffled screams that seemed to emanate from behind the wall. And above all not to touch the muck oozing from it.

"I should've seen it coming," M. Pierre uttered aloud.

For Henri had not heeded all his warnings.

In the five years since, he hadn't found anyone to take his son's place. Now it was too late. Soon, very soon, there would be no wall to tend.

Now M. Pierre stood before the thing that had been the bane of his existence for as long as he could remember. A million dead lay behind that wall, a million denizens of Saints Innocents.

He closed his eyes. "All that stands between us is decaying bricks—and a tattooed priest 400 years dead."

He opened his eyes again. Here the old brick bulged to the point of bursting, like a pus-filled blister on the ass of wretched humanity. One blow could bring it down. The vibration from an overloaded ox cart on the *rue de l'Université* above might be enough.

Well, he thought, time to pay the piper. He turned his back to the wall, toward the massive twin doors wrought of iron and wood. Eight or ten feet tall, they'd once been whitewashed, according to the ledger back in his room. Now they stood dirty gray going on black. Merely looking at them made him shiver. He had touched them only once, and had never opened them.

But his son had.

Pierre cursed his failing mind. Why had it not yet failed successfully enough to spare him this memory? Five years before, young Henri's obsessions had led him to this very spot. He'd stolen his father's keys and unlocked the doors. Seen what was inside, what one of the *Brothers of Saint Paul the Divine* had long ago claimed was too exquisite for the eyes of man to comprehend, and so must be hidden away in this crypt. That, too, was in the ledger.

Henri, engaged to be married to his pretty childhood sweetheart, had nonetheless decided he wanted out. Of life, that is. And apparently into whatever Brother Eduard offered. Eduard, whom another priest had once called 'the bringer of light'.

If that was true, Pierre mused, it was indeed the light of Hell.

Henri had jumped from a bridge over the River Seine later the same day. The impact broke his neck. When M. Pierre discovered his keys were missing, he'd hurried to the crypt and found the doors flung wide. Without looking in—and this had been one of the most difficult things he had ever done in his life, he'd nearly broken his own neck in the struggle not to stare—he'd hauled the doors closed and engaged the lock.

Then had come the news about Henri.

But he would look now. He had to know what his son had seen. What all of them had seen. To know what they'd known. For what in the name of Beelzebub had been worth the risk?

He turned the lock and pushed the massive doors open.

Before him stood the marble vaults of seven priests, arrayed in line one after another. Their names were engraved in the stone of each rectangular box. Brother Richard. Brother Gaspar. Five more down the line.

And finally, at the far end of the crypt, Brother Eduard.

M. Pierre halted. The ground beneath his feet seemed to tremor. The air within the crypt, dank and warm, was a claustrophobic shroud. He heard something move, the faint grating of stone sliding against stone. And suddenly came the certainty he was not alone.

He looked up.

At first it appeared to be a body hanging upon the wall, perhaps put there to watch over Saints Innocents cemetery. To frighten away any trespasser who dared enter the crypt, much as a scarecrow guards a field of wheat.

But no—that wasn't right. The figure was far too flat, with no bulk to it. He stepped closer and lifted his lantern. The shadows of all the priestly vaults grew to shimmers on the walls around him.

The hide of Brother Eduard caught the dim light, and the whole crypt was suddenly, fantastically aglow. The thing had been flattened out in exactly the manner of a bear's cured hide, though that was where any resemblance ended. This skin was unfurred, and glinted as if flecked with gold. An array of Latin crosses adorned the extremities.

And . . . they moved.

Unable to avert his eyes, M. Pierre watched the ink come alive. The crosses dissolved, the ink suffused and coalesced across the hide of what had once been Brother Eduard. Moving with stunning speed toward the chest, which suddenly swelled. No longer flat and dead, what now occupied the wall above Pierre was a living portrait of Christ upon the cross. Blood dripped from his wounds. Tears leaked from his eyes and mixed with the blood oozing beneath the crown of thorns. His chest moved in and out.

"It—no, He," Pierre whispered, correcting himself, "breathes!"

More vivid than anything he'd ever seen in his life. Lustrous, and oh so beautiful. The tears on the man's face—the son of God?—looked as if they would continue on down to the ground. Pierre saw sweat bead above the Savior's brow. He thought he even heard him gasp.

"Mon Dieu." How could he have known it would be like this? He wanted to drop to his knees. No, he wanted to be part of it. He wept his own tears. Of course! It was all so clear now. Of course they had jumped. Anything to be a part of him. Anything to be with him. "I didn't know. Oh God, I didn't know. Please forgive me."

A thought came into his head. Or was it another's familiar voice?

"Henri? I'm here. Tell me what to do!"

The wall. Touch the wall. That's all you need to do, mon Père. Touch the wall.

The voice might've been Henri, or not. M. Pierre was beyond caring. All he wanted in the world at this moment was to join them.

He turned, still holding the lantern aloft, and walked out of the crypt, crossing the small distance to the wall. He stood before it, watching the bricks too breathe in and out. It truly was alive. He himself barely breathing as he reached out to touch it.

The bricks shattered into shards.

All the denizens of Saints Innocents poured forth in a tide of mud and old bones. The unholy slurry flowed first around M. Pierre, but soon grew in mass and submerged the old man. A huge, black, mottled wave swirled into the passage, flowed past the massive doors and into the crypt. It upended the burial vaults, dumping the bones of the priest unceremoniously into the malodorous stew. The slurry swirled violently, slopping up the far wall. It tore the flat hide of Eduard down from its perch, and ran like a river as it burst through the boards of what had once been the 67th window of the *Hôpital de la Charité*. From there, the charnel soup splashed and slithered into the streets of Paris.

The hide of Brother Eduard floated atop the muck. It finally came to rest on a side street, and lay there as if waiting.

A few minutes later a young couple, a man and his wife, spotted it while walking home from the marketplace. They paused to look, were instantly captivated, and took their rare find home to hang upon the wall.

Two days later the pair climbed all 387 narrow, twisting steps to the top of the bell tower at Notre Dame. No easy feat for a woman six months gone with child, but they lovingly encouraged each other the whole way up, pausing to rest as needed. Once in the bell tower itself, they held hands, stepped to the ledge, and jumped.

The following day, the sister of the pregnant woman called at the couple's dwelling. She did not find them at home. She did, however, notice an exquisite, lustrous image of Christ upon the cross hung on the wall of their cottage.

She knelt at the sight of it, and wept.

The next booth offers souvenirs of a particularly Venetian design. Here's a finely-carved and painted wooden prow of an old gondola, one handed down from father to son. For if Venice's streets are her canals, then the gondoliers are her drivers for hire. They ply their watery trade day and night, transporting businessmen to important meetings, students to university classes, lovers to secret assignations. These boatmen tend to be the most discreet and reliable of men. But even a gondolier can succumb to greed. The piece broken off this gondola's bow is part of a set; it's accompanied by a curious, painted mask with holes for eyes and nose, but no opening for the mouth. The third item in the set is a small wooden box banded with iron. Empty now, though at one time it held many coins collected over decades by a particular gondolier—though the money did not come from hard-earned fares. He found a different way to fill his household coffers. Though, in the end, since the money was not his by right, this scheme did no good. For, as we all know, that final boatman who ferries the dead to the Underworld always demands honest payment.

MASK MAKER'S BALL
by Carol MacAllister

Niccolò Forscari oars Venezia's deceased through the City's labyrinth of watery streets. And then, on their final trip across the Grand Canal to the Isle of the Dead, a hellish place filled with rotting corpses and lingering spirits. In that desolate spot despicable men scurried like water rats to strip the dead of clothing and valuables.

Greed had turned Niccolò, too, from an honorable oarsman into a rich *cittadini*. As he worked those calm waters, he stole the traditional coin families placed in their loved ones' mouths. Payment for the legendary oarsman, Charon, to carry them across the Goddess Styx's river. Without the proper fare, the deceased could not move on to their final rest in the Underworld.

Niccolò excused this cheating of the dead as a small indiscretion. *There is no such oarsman. Only a myth created by ancient pagans. Besides, who will ever know?*

Each night, he tucked the stolen coins into his overflowing money box, then went home to take his place at the head of the family table. As soon as he arrived, his wife went from kitchen to table, setting their supper out: bowls of pasta, platters of fresh fish, the occasional roast of beef. But Niccolò's favorite part came after the meal, sipping Chianti, watching his wife's graceful movements from fireplace to table and back. The familiar swish of her skirts meant the promise of another enchanting evening with the love of his life.

But when he arrived home on this night, the table was bare. No decanter of wine, no supper plate. And no Regina.

"Wife," he called. "Where are you? Where is my meal?"

"Forgive me," she called faintly from their bed. "I was too weak."

He rushed into their chamber, where Regina struggled even to raise a hand. The whites of her emerald eyes were shot through with red. As he drew near he saw black boils had erupted on that sweet face. The perspiring brow, the long dark hair damp with sweat, tangled and matted from her tossing with the fever.

"Niccolò," she whispered hoarsely, straining to sit up, to speak.

He shuddered. The familiar pallor he'd seen on so many dead before said the plague had entered his own home. "*Gimignano!*" he shouted, to call their servant. "Go collect the doctor."

An hour later he was still waiting. Every second of Regina's suffering pained him greatly.

"What is taking the old fool so long?" he muttered, pacing the chamber.

Nearly two hours passed before the *medico* staggered in. He drew off his cloak, face drawn, so tired he could barely stand. "What is it, Niccolò?" he sighed.

"Regina has been stricken. Tell me you can save her."

The doctor shook his head wearily. "Not many survive *le peste*."

"But you have known my family for generations. You must cure her! We are the only ones left."

The physician examined Regina, then turned away and sighed. "There is little I can do."

"But you must help her," Niccolò pleaded. "I can pay well."

"No one can buy their way out of death, though many have tried. But even holy dispensations have failed."

"Do something!" Niccolò shouted. "She cannot die."

"Very well. If you insist." The doctor pulled three live toads from a sack, and rubbed their secretions on Regina's skin. She moaned and cried as their caustic secretions burned her open lesions.

The second day, the doctor placed wriggling leeches on her arms and face as she shuddered with revulsion. "Give her wine to ease the pain," the *medico* said, as he went out the door.

On his third visit, the old man's quivering, age-spotted hand parted her smooth olive skin with the blade of a small silver knife. Regina's eyes were closed, though. This time she did not wince or cry out as the scalpel scored her arm. Her blood trickled sluggishly into a small silver bowl.

"Why do you torment her so?" cried Niccolò.

"Because you insisted! And to release the evil that has invaded her body."

On the fourth day, she lay on the bed nearly lifeless. The doctor examined her carefully as Niccolò paced the chamber.

"Make her comfortable," the *medico* said at last. "For in truth, I can do no more. Even the Holy Father's prayers are not answered these days. Bodies lay piled in carts waiting for burial. So many *cittadini* have been taken, there are not enough left to bury the dead."

Niccolò knew this already. He'd witnessed the growing number of corpses in the streets that lay cruelly unburied for days. The boldest rats darted from dark alleyways in broad daylight to feast on them. A shortage of gondoliers made it difficult to transport the decaying corpses.

The old man shook his head again. "So many lost. But rejoice in the knowledge that your *moglie* is a good and pious woman. Her soul will be saved. Clement, the blessed Holy Father, grants remission of all sins to those who—"

"Enough! Spare me the dogmatic discourse." He turned a deaf ear as the physician droned on, speaking the same words heard all too often in Piasa San Marco. His back to the doctor, he knelt at the bedside, and said to his dying wife, "Forgive me, Regina."

For he knew his own lucrative thievery had caused her illness, a punishment for his avarice and disrespect of the dead.

And indeed, though Niccolò sat vigil all that night, still the Black Death entered and gathered up Regina Maria Connestra Forscari in its cold arms.

But after twenty years of marriage, Niccolò could not let her go. Desolation pounded at his temples like the storm surges that sometimes battered his gondola. *"Amore mio. Amore mio,"* he sobbed. "My love. Do not leave me."

He dismissed their servant, then climbed into their bed, embracing her lifeless body. With neither children nor other family, he would now be alone, forever. He fell asleep, sobbing.

The next morning, he splashed water on his tear-swollen face and put on clean linen. Then he went about reluctantly preparing her for the final crossing.

He draped a woolen blanket over the table, covered that with their finest lace cloth, and laid out her still-youthful body.

Regina's peaceful expression might almost trick one into believing she was merely asleep.

He tenderly washed her with fragrant rose water, ignoring the terrible lesions on her fragile olive skin. He acknowledged only the familiar raised scar, a long-healed cut from the sewing shears. The cooking burns on her forearm from the fireplace tongs. And the heart-shaped birthmark he'd always teasingly kissed when they lay nestled together in bed.

From the cedar chest he chose her finest gown, green silk with a tight bodice and sleeves embroidered with white flowers. He had bargained with a Turkish trader for it. His fingers traced its square neckline and the satin-stitched roses that framed her sweet oval face. He lifted her ivory comb to smooth back her long dark hair, admiring the strands with auburn highlights. Recalling how she and a few lady friends used to sit on the rooftops to bleach their hair with the juice of lemons, spreading the wet strains upon wide straw brims to catch the midday sun.

He reached for his brass-bound money chest to take out the traditional coin, but then hesitated. How could his wife be dead? How could Regina need such fare for a final passage?

"No," he muttered. He could not bear to place it in her mouth. That would be admitting her death was real.

She will not need it.

Instead he slipped the fare for her mythical crossing into a leather pouch. Then lifted his wife from the table, cradling her like a child as he carried her through the dimly-lit streets to his moored gondola.

He laid her on a long tapestry cushion, her back propped against the wooden cross-arm. He tied her upright to it with a soft cord, covered her lap with a woolen shawl, then looked down and smiled. She appeared the same as on other evenings, when he had oared them at sunset through the watery streets of the city.

"*Amore mio,*" he whispered, shivering in a cold December breeze.

He took up the long oar and began the journey. A new moon offered no light, but that didn't matter. He knew the way through these watery passages in the dark. It was his trade, after all.

As they silently skimmed past tall stone buildings, Niccolò envied the lighted palaces and imagined the lavish interiors behind those thick-glassed, mullioned windows. Billows of soot rose as a thousand fireplaces struggled to warm the cold night. Walls of arched windows peered down at his passing, while within, Venice's wealthiest citizens reclined on linens as fine as silk.

The cold black water rippled sluggishly, wavering with few reflections.

He passed under the seven wooden bridges to the arched entry out into the Grand Canal, and then braced the long oar. The faint music of flute and drum touched his ear. A song that drew him back to the night of their wedding.

"Ah, Regina. Listen! Music, from St. Mark's Square. Can you hear it? The same tune was played at our first wedded dance." He imagined them once more whirling around the plaza. And why not? This would be their last evening together.

He could tie up at the waterfront. "We shall join the festivities one last time," he told her. In the dark, no one would notice her condition.

Lanterns flickered from the soaring bell tower as the gondola drew nearer to the cathedral.

"Look, Regina." Strange colors stretched across the lagoon like beckoning fingers guiding his way. Rows of billowing tents and fluttering banners filled the square. "A great bazaar forms along the waterfront, like some magical conjugation. Yet I heard nothing of its arrival."

The sight was strange, indeed, for with the spread of plague, the Doge had forbidden most public entertainments.

A sudden gust whirled about the gondola, billowing Regina's silk gown, tousling her long hair. And the thought came to him, *Now the cold air will serve her well.*

He choked back a sob.

Just then something small and white fluttered past his face, descending into the gondola like a bird alighting. He frowned to see a folded piece of parchment was now tucked into his dead wife's hands, as if she had been holding it all along. He snatched it up before the breeze carried it off again, and read the fine script: *For You.*

He broke its red wax seal and unfolded the parchment. "Why, it's an invitation. To the Mask-Maker's Ball. Tonight, at the chime of three." It was if his wish had come true. "Regina, my love! We shall have one final frolic in the square, before...."

He shuddered, closed his eyes for a moment, then looked down and read further: *A motley-clad fool will lead the way.*

A faint whisper touched his ear.

"What did you say, wife?"

He glanced at her sweetly composed, too-still features.

"Yes. We certainly will need masks. Though what a shame to cover that lovely face." He bent forward and kissed one cold cheek. "We will go first to Burano, where the finest masks are made."

I will make this night last as long as possible, he thought, as he oared away from the main island, up the center of the lagoon. Soon they passed the next island. Murano, where his deceased cousin Vincenzo had once worked fashioning colorful glass beads. Then he guided the boat out into open water, toward the island of Burano. The trip would be long, but the tide was right. If he quickly tied up and went directly in to purchase the masks, there would be time enough left to return for the festivities in the Square.

He whispered tenderly, "We will dance once again, *amore mio.*"

But the night was too dark to truly navigate. They rode the swift current until a rough patch suddenly shook the gondola. Niccolò lost his bearings as a surge swept them off course.

The windy squall finally ceased, but by then they were lost.

We should be at Burano by now, he thought, and looked for the torches which lit its small city dock. Seeing none, he oared on again, against what was now an oddly-shallow bottom.

Finally he realized he had passed the isle of mask makers entirely, and entered a narrow lagoon. The long oar got caught up in a tangle of water weeds. When he pushed hard against the bottom, the oaken shaft bent back, then snapped. The boat lurched forward, smashing against a rotted, collapsed pier.

Niccolò at first had no idea of where they were. But then he caught sight of a familiar, tall church spire. This was Torcello, a place deserted for many years. His boat had been drawn, as if of its own accord, through the narrow inland passage to *Laguna Morta's* rotting docks. Once, this island had been the bishop's seat, a vast center of trade. But over the decades shoals had blocked entry to its harbor. Merchant ships no longer plied the diminished, stagnant waters here. Malaria festered in the watery swamps. Desperate locals had tried to escape that disease by sailing across to Venice, only to be smitten by the growing plague of Black Death.

"Regina, we must go ashore. Wait here."

But when he climbed onto the fallen pier, the winds picked up again. He did not like to leave her alone in such weather, so he gathered his wife in his arms and carried her ashore. At last he spotted a muted flicker of light through the panes of Santa Maria Assunta's colorful stained-glass windows. Apparently a few of that order still maintained the ancient church. He decided to ask for shelter, and walked on toward the lights.

He paused, though, at the small arched foot-bridge spanning the narrow waterway to the church's entrance. *Ponticello del Diavolo*: The Devil's Little Bridge.

As a child, he had ridden along when his *papi* had delivered supplies to this cloister. Niccolò was always instructed not to leave the boat, nor to cross the bridge. Its frightening name was enough to keep him waiting quietly. Except, one overcast delivery day he'd grown bored, and sneaked off to brazenly stand at the foot of the bridge, daring himself to cross. But then he had glanced at the shadows underneath, and saw hunched, grotesque shapes clinging to the bridge's underside. He'd shrieked in fear and raced back to the safety of *Papi's* boat.

Now, that childhood fear stopped him once again.

"But what choice do we have?" he asked Regina, expecting no answer. He took a deep breath, stared straight ahead, and shuffled across. When he reached the church, he shifted her body to one arm, and hammered a fist on the church's massive wooden front door.

The hollow thuds finally drew a response: the door's peephole slid pen, and a crone wearing a rusty black wimple peered out. "Who is there?" she rasped.

"*Suora*, I beg of you. We need help."

The elderly nun opened a larger pass-through to peruse his disheveled appearance, and his burden. "No. Go, and leave us be."

"Please. My dear wife has . . . taken ill suddenly. I fear for her life."

Whispers came to him then, as if many others were speaking, or arguing, behind the door.

"*Suora*, may we enter, please?"

The rusted hinges finally squealed as they swung the door wide. But the hooded crone still blocked him from entering. "Why are you here, *messer?*"

"We only seek shelter from the weather tonight."

"No, I think not. Be gone." She shook her head and slammed the door again.

"Blessed Mary, Mother of Christ! Pray God, you must let us in."

More muffled whispers.

Just as Niccolò had given up hope, the door eased open again.

"Very well. You may enter. But only for this night. Follow me."

The robed nun held a tin lantern aloft as she led them down a wide musty hall paved with dirty gray flagstones. Cobwebs hung from the unused wall sconces like filthy gray veils.

The terrible state of the interior puzzled Niccolò. Surely holy sisters would keep a cloister cleaner, more orderly. Only a few sputtering ends of candles lit the sanctuary. He was puzzled, too, at the state of the works of art left within. Only a few statues of saints, but the noses and other parts of the faces looked as if they'd been hacked away. The paint of their robes, the gilding of the halos, had all flaked off.

Regina's limp body seemed to grow heavier as they shuffled slowly through a back hallway reeking of leprous blight and decay. They passed under a crumbling archway to a narrower hall, lined with rows of vacant cells.

The crone dragged open a door with rusted, squealing hinges.

Niccolò was relieved to at last lay his wife on the narrow cot inside. The robed woman lighted a yellowed, half-burned candle set on a marble-topped chest, turned again to look at them, then crossed herself and gasped. "*Mio Dio!* She is so very quiet."

"What?" Niccolò feigned a look of shock. He reached for one of Regina's hands. It was far too cold, the fingers stiff. "No, no! I am so sorry, my love."

The elderly woman stared down at them. "I fear your wife has the pallor of death. Perhaps I should call Father Castiglioni for the last rites."

"No! She is only very ill." Niccolò still did not want to admit his lovely Regina was no more. Perhaps very ill, yes . . . but then, if she did enter into death without the last rites. . . .

The nun interrupted his thoughts. "I shall bring wine and a loaf of bread, at least. Some olives as well . . . to what place do you travel?"

"Burano, to buy masks for tonight's ball. My dear wife's wish on her sickbed was to dance as we did on the night of our wedding feast. I know then my Regina will come back to me, well and whole."

The sister frowned. "And where is this ball?"

"Piasa San Marco."

"Ah, a blessed place. And who is your host?"

"The Mask Maker himself. He sent us an invitation. But I fear now that we have been delayed, we will not be able to attend after all."

The woman shrugged. "Only Our Father knows the answers to such things. Now, I will bring your food." She closed the door behind her.

Niccolò dragged a heavy wooden chair over next to the bed, to be near his wife. A few minutes later, three sharp knocks sounded.

"Come in," he called, expecting the promised meal.

Instead of the elderly sister, a tall man dressed in dark vestments stood out in the hall. "I have come for you," he said.

Niccolò gaped at him. "For us? I do not understand. Who are you?"

"I am called Charon." He paused, as if waiting for some word of recognition.

Niccolò stared incredulously. That was a name from ancient myth. Was this some sort of joke?

As if sensing his confusion, the man smiled. "My little joke. It is a very old name, yes. Not a common one. But I am the Mask-Maker, on my way to Piasa San Marco. To my Grand Ball, tonight, in Venice."

Niccolò gasped, "Why, this is unbelievable! We have your invitation!" Then he frowned. "But why are you here, now?"

The man shrugged. "Foul weather has detained me."

"I see. As it did us."

"I heard you were here, and so thought to introduce myself. I expect you still plan to attend?"

The man's odd grin was disturbing, but perhaps its crooked cast was just an illusion created by the flickering candlelight.

"Yes," Niccolò said. "That is still our fervent desire. But I fear we cannot do so, now."

The man looked surprised. "And why is that?"

"We have no masks, and too little time left to travel the long distance to Burano, then back to Venice."

"Time is ever fleeting." The strange fellow cackled, raising shivers along Niccolò's spine. "But have no concerns on that score. You will ride with me to Venice."

"A generous offer. But the way is dark as pitch, and the tide runs against us."

"No matter. My craft is swifter than most."

Niccolò felt reluctant still. "Many thanks, *signore*. But we . . . we possess no masks."

"I carry many with me to sell at the Night Bazaar. You may have one for your wife, of course."

"You are most generous, but…" Niccolò hesitated, not wanting to seem greedy. "I too will need one."

The robed man nodded. "*Nessun problema.* Two it shall be."

Niccolò's eyes welled with tears. Even though this fellow acted strangely, how generous he was! "*Grazie.* How can I ever repay you?"

"You already have. For it is my great pleasure to be of assistance."

"And when will we depart?"

"At the bell tower's next strike. Meet me at the foot-bridge. The other side, across from the church, on the unpaved path."

Niccolò knew he could carry Regina to the boat, but once they boarded, the Mask Maker would surely see how silent and still she was, how devoid of life. Then he might refuse them passage after all. Perhaps he could pass her condition off as deep exhaustion, and claim she was merely deeply asleep? In any case, this was his only means of leaving desolate Torcello. His oar was broken, the gondola damaged, and Regina's stiffening body was becoming more difficult to explain, and to handle.

Nonetheless, when the bell tower struck the half hour, Niccolò left the church carrying his wife. He stopped midway across the bridge to look around; the Mask Maker was nowhere in sight. Just as he stepped off onto the path, though, a voice from behind said, "*Bueno Sera.*"

"Oh! Good evening." Niccolò spun toward the shadows, but saw no one there.

"I see you have chosen to join me," said the same voice.

Regina was slipping from his grasp again, so Niccolò shifted the burden, turning away to hoist her more securely. When he turned back, the cloaked Mask Maker stood before him.

"Perhaps I can help to carry your poor wife?"

"No!" Niccolò snapped. "That is, many thanks to you, but I require no assistance."

As they neared the lagoon. Niccolò gazed in admiration at a long, slender gondola tied up at the old pier. Lanterns hung on tall poles secured to the gunwales shed flickering rainbows of light onto the inky, sluggish waters. Golden tassels swayed on the awning. Red banners unfurled, rippling from poles, fluttering on a breeze now fragrant with lily, carnation, and rose.

"Please, step aboard," the Mask Maker cajoled. "Come, come." He extended a hand toward Regina.

Niccolò drew back. "No! She is asleep. I do not wish to wake her."

"Are you certain?" The Mask Maker reached out and touched one of her embroidered sleeves. She shifted then in Niccolò's arms. In his great surprise he nearly dropped her.

"Why, it seems she has awoken, *messer*."

A miracle! Niccolò was speechless. He had prayed she would somehow yet live, but . . .

How can this be?

He gently set her on her feet. Regina staggered for a step or two, then straightened and stood on her own, shoulders back, looking alive and quite well.

The Mask-Maker took her hand to help her aboard.

The doctor was wrong! Regina lives, Niccolò exulted.

Or could it be merely a cruel trick, something strange that might happen with the rigor of death? Yet, as he hesitated, the cloaked man helped her step down onto the cushioned bench.

Niccolò followed, supporting her as she leaned back against a silk cushion. "Are you feeling well again, *cara mio*?"

She nodded shyly, as if embarrassed by such a fuss made in front of a stranger.

The Mask Maker grinned. "So, we are all happily off to the grand ball."

Niccolò sat back too, as the gondola glided into the Grand Lagoon, its bow pointing toward Piasa San Marco. He glanced at his beloved wife from time to time, to be sure she still sat upright and full of life beside him. The dark night sky was full of stars now, and it revealed that they were both happy, alive, and well, and would soon dance at the Grand Ball.

He sighed and closed his eyes, relieved.

A tap on the shoulder woke him some time later.

The old man's voice whispered, "We have arrived."

Niccolò yawned, then blinked at the great festivities spread out before them, up in the crowded square. Was he dreaming, or was it an illusion? Pierced brass and tin lanterns illuminated rows of wooden stalls full of goods, standing side by side with billowing striped tents. Violins and flutes played as an organ-grinder cranked out tunes while a tiny monkey wearing a red vest capered and danced.

Costumed singers strolled, motley-clad jongleurs juggled plates, balls, vegetables, even small animals. Dancers in exotic costumes dipped and whirled, while acrobats contorted, flipped, and tumbled in the open areas. All of it reflected in wavering double off the shimmering Grand Canal, as laughter and happy shouts skimmed the rippling waters.

Niccolò's empty belly growled ferociously; the old nun at the cloister had never brought the promised food. Among the more exotic scents of black pepper, ginger, nutmeg, and anise, he inhaled more homely aromas: roasting chicken, garlicky vegetables, the briny tang of mussels, the smoky, meaty smell of seared pork and beef.

A goblet of Chianti would wash it all down nicely, he thought, followed by grappa to soothe the gut.

"I have your masks," the Mask Maker said suddenly.

"Oh?" Niccolò was startled out of his gustatory dream. "Why, yes. Thank you." He glanced at Regina, who smiled faintly at him.

"But you are early," proclaimed their host. "There is time to rest, or to stroll the Bazaar and shop. The ball begins when the clock tower strikes three."

"It all looks so grand," Niccolò said. "We can hardly wait. Where is the entry?"

"At the far corner of the plaza you will see a narrow passageway. Just beyond is the bridge."

Niccolò frowned. "I see. But, after that, how do we …"

"*Per favor*, do not worry. Your guide will appear." He handed over a linen sack. "The masks. And now I must tend to my booth. Other guests will need costumes as well. There are so many tonight!" he said with obvious delight, and then stepped from the grand gondola onto the stone pier.

Niccolò opened the sack and pulled out a painted full-oval mask. Jet-black glass beads trimmed the eye holes. Swirled designs in gold leaf swept from the chin out to the cheeks. The eyes of peacock feathers softened the edges.

He held it up. "Look, Regina. Do you like it?"

The black-satin ribbon ties dangled as Niccolò's fingers traced its red, heart-shaped lips. He was reminded of Regina's soft, plump rosy mouth, in her youth.

She took the mask from his hands, then held it in place as he tied the ribbons behind her head, taking care not to tangle them in her dark, sun-streaked hair.

He pulled out his own, a simple design made for a man: a half-mask of black leather, with a bulbous nose. Something else remained in the sack. "What's this?" he murmured.

A bycocket, a fashionable hat for a dandy. Its peaked brim projected out-landishly, well past his forehead. A small ostrich plume was tucked into its ribbon band. "*Fantastico!*" he exclaimed, flicking the feather and laughing.

Then he held the mask over his face and peered through the eye holes. "How wonderful!" Somehow, through it the bazaar appeared even more lively and sprawling—a phantasmagoria of lanterns wheeled kaleidoscopes of color through the surging crowds. Shifting mirages of undulating tents and spinning stalls layered upon each other and then. . . .

What in blessed Heaven

. . . thronging around them he saw deformed creatures, some with nodules of horns, others dragging long scaly tails, backs hunched, mingling with the crowds of Venetian revelers. Red and green-skinned demons, serpent tongues lolling, were sidling up to the infirm, touching drunkards' arms, leading *cittidini* into the shadowy alleys. Small furry things tugged at the hems of women's lovely gowns as the rich material brushed over sewer drains filled with water rats, while misshapen long-taloned lizards skittered underfoot.

Aghast, he shuddered and lowered the mask.

Regina reached out and touched his arm, looking concerned, as if to ask what was wrong. But she did not speak.

He glanced up again at the festival, which now appeared just as it should be. The horrifying, yet strangely beguiling sights he'd seen through the mask drew him back to see more. Again, he peered through the eye holes, this time at the city's rooftops. Grotesque stone gargoyles rose from their usual crouched positions on drainpipes and cornices to skitter up and down the stone and stucco walls. Winged griffins bounded along the edges of tile roofs. It seemed that different worlds were layered there before his eyes. Or perhaps within his unraveling mind?

A burst of loud laughter nearby broke the spell.

He shook himself and reached for Regina's cold hand. "Come, Wife, let us join the others." But as he set down his mask on the bench, in order to climb out of the gondola, the clock tower suddenly struck twice.

Two o'clock, so soon?

"Oh dear, time is flying away. We need to prepare for the ball, my dear."

When he touched her arm, though, it felt limp, lifeless. He lifted her from the seat and she rose, then slumped against his side. "You are still weak," he said.

But how could he walk her safely along the narrow finger-pier? Fearing they would be late, he smoothed out her gown, tied the lovely mask more snugly, then tenderly stroked the curve of its painted cheek. "Rest here, dear *moglie*. I will find someone to help us."

As soon as he crossed the sea wall and entered St. Mark's Square, a reveler dressed in colorful motley, with green-striped leggings and a white ruffled collar, approached.

Niccolò pushed past him.

"Sir, hold please." The motley-clad man grasped Niccolò's sleeve. "I am sent here to help you."

Niccolò glanced back and recoiled from the entertainer's ape-like snout, and the bump of a devil's horn on his forehead. Both appeared too real to be merely part of a costume.

"Sir, I am your guide," the stranger insisted. "Is she ready for the grand ball?"

"She? Oh, you mean my wife." Niccolò pointed to the gondola at the far-side of the pier. "Yes. But she is ill and cannot walk any great distance."

He feared her miraculous return to life, which seemed somehow connected to the masks or the Mask Maker, might fade away once more. But he could not tell this to anyone, not even a doctor. They might be disbelieved, even accused of witchcraft. "I simply cannot carry her off the gondola by myself," he added.

"It is my pleasure to assist. Show me the way."

Niccolò pointed out over the seawall, where so many boats rocked on the incoming tide. "Let's see . . there. It is that one."

The fool squinted. "Oh yes, the Lady Regina."

"Why, yes. That is the name of my wife. But, sir, how do you know this?"

The jester shrugged. "My master knows everything." The bells on his shoes jingled as they headed down. As they neared the large gondola, a woman seated inside stood abruptly, and smiled up at them.

Niccolò gasped. "Regina! But—"

The fool grinned. "Is this not your bride, *messer*?"

"Why, yes. Of course." He stared at his lovely, rosy-cheeked wife, clad in her rich velvet gown and glittering porcelain mask. "Dear wife," he whispered, "You are very much stronger now. You look so . . . well. *Fortuna* has decreed we may again start our lives together."

Obviously that useless old quack of a doctor had mistaken a grave but temporary illness for death. How many more has the old bastard cheated of life? Niccolò thought angrily. *Orrore!* How many has he consigned to a coffin before their time? Well, he would leave a message for the Doge in one of the *Bocca de*

Lione receptacles near the Palace. Then the old pretender, the so-called *medico*, would be arrested for malpractice. Or worse.

The fool cackled. "It appears she can manage quite well on her own."

"Yes." Niccolò nodded, thrilled over Regina's growing strength. "I suppose she can."

"I will lead *her* through the plaza," the fool said firmly. "You may return on your own now."

Niccolò frowned at him, puzzled. Return where, and why? "No need. Surely, I can find *our* way."

The guide tapped Niccolò's hand. "Have you an invitation, then?"

He winced and pulled away, hand smarting as if a hot poker had grazed his wrist. He withdrew the parchment from his pouch and handed it over. "Yes. Here it is."

The jester peered down at it a moment, and finally said, grudgingly, "It is my pleasure, then. We will both walk with her."

As Niccolò and the fool helped his wife step up onto the stone seawall, he still feared something was amiss with all of this. But if he could have his dear Regina back . . . he would accept her return without question, and push any doubts from his mind.

"Come along, *Signori* Forscari. Others wait on me."

Niccolò shrugged. "Feel free to step aside, then, and go about your business. I am able to manage *our* attendance." He nudged his lovely bride and whispered, "Regina, *amore*. Do you truly feel better?"

She nodded.

He tilted his head lower to catch a glimpse of her emerald eyes behind the mask, but it was too dark. So he led her on, and they entered the plaza milling with *cittadini*. The jester's bells faintly jingled as he followed a few paces behind.

Niccolò pushed through the crowd, past rippling tents and stalls full of attractions: fortune-tellers, time-venders, dancing whores. Revelers perused stalls selling carved ivory, fragrant sandalwood figures, fringed shawls adorned with fine beadwork. He admired colorful, screeching exotic birds brought from distant lands.

Once, Regina lost her balance and nearly swooned to the paving stones.

The fool pushed forward, touched her arm, and she stood erect again. He then snapped at Niccolò, "Sir, I am charged by my master to walk with her to our destination." He pointed ahead, to a small arched foot-bridge. "Ah. See? Here we are."

The bridge recalled to Niccolò the old childhood panic he'd felt at Ponticello del Diavolo. Of course it could not be the same bridge. Still, the very thought slowed his steps.

The jester pointed to a set of tall wrought-iron doors on the far side. "There is your entry, *Signora*," he told Regina.

"Entry?" Niccolò shuddered, trying hard to master his fear. Then it struck him. "Oh, dear…I've forgotten my own mask. Regina, wait here for me."

The bazaar seemed to spin about him in a riot of bright colors, sharp smells, hoarse shouts . . . and from somewhere, a faint mocking cackle. He raced on, swift as a *bravo* coursing his steed at Siena. When he reached the pier, though, the Mask Maker's boat was nowhere to be seen. He scanned all the others tied up there, but the fancy gondola they'd arrived in was gone.

The clock tower rang out the half hour.

It's nearly three!

He pushed his way back through the bazaar, bolting down the narrow aisles, nearly tumbling venders' carts full of silk scarves and leather boots, disrupting puppet shows and startling half-naked dancing girls. At last he caught sight of an over-sized mask hanging from a rod. Below it a painted sign read, *Mask Maker*.

Niccolò stopped abruptly at the table which blocked the entryway of a fringed, green-striped tent. He shouted, "*Signore*, please! Where are you? I must have a new mask."

No answer.

He leaned over the table and peered inside. *Oh, no. It's empty. All the masks must be gone.*

Just then a finger tapped his slumped shoulder. "The tent is closed, *messer*."

"But I need a mask, and quickly. The ball starts soon, and my lovely Regina awaits. Where is the Mask Maker?"

"Oh, *Signore* Forscari. I did not know you. It is I." The man threw back his hood and with a flourish of one hand, pointed to the table. "There is another, just for you, see? Over there."

Niccolò saw now there was still one mask left on the table. How odd. He snatched it up. "How much do I owe, *signore*?"

"Indeed, nothing, sir. It is my pleasure."

"*Mille grazie!*" And he raced off again, back to the bridge crowded with beautiful costumed *cittidini*. Now a throng of masked invitees pressed against the closed entry doors. Niccolò searched wildly for Regina but only saw the backs of unfamiliar heads. He tied on his new mask. Hoping, as he had before, to see things more clearly. Shouting, "Regina! Wife, where are you?"

But this new mask was full-faced and it covered his mouth. It must be muffling his cries. His hands fumbled to untie the black ribbon so he could call out again. Feeling panic, he groped for the knot without success. When his fingers scrabbled for its edges, to tear the thing off, he cried out in pain.

The mask had somehow fused to his skin, become one with his face.

What sorcery is this? Where are you, wife? Wait for me. Come back, amore mio!

The sea of invitees turned slowly toward him then, as if they'd heard his panicked thoughts. Their true faces were revealed, under masks turned translucent. Distorted visages with sunken eyes, emaciated cheeks, festering patches of rotting skin. Corpses! Like those he had so often robbed of their promised rest in the Underworld. He searched desperately to spot Regina's lovely green gown, but saw only a host of emaciated figures bound up in dark shrouds.

The entry doors groaned open slowly. The crowd turned back and shuffled forward. Niccolò stepped onto the bridge to join them.

A hunched, stocky figure with ram's horns and cloven hooves stopped him midway. "You are late! Where is your invitation?"

"My...my wife has it."

The toll-keeper grunted skeptically, "Is that so? And her name?"

"Regina Maria Connestra Forscari."

"Oh, yes . . . but that was only to admit one, the deceased. The lady has paid her fare and moved on. Why are you here?"

"To dance, of course," Niccolò protested. "The Mask Maker himself invited us. Ask him!"

"Mask Maker? To dance?" The cloven-hoofed toll-taker sneered. "Perhaps on to the *eternal* dance. But you are far too late." Then, as Niccolò gaped in horror, the toll-taker dwindled in size. He shrank lower and lower, until he became one of the water rats, and scurried under the dark bridge.

"Come back!" Niccolò shouted. "I can pay, I swear it." He dug into his pouch for Regina's silver coin, but felt nothing there.

No! Where did it go?

"Please! Let me pass. My wife awaits my return. She will be frightened."

The clock bell tower echoed three loud strikes as the shuffling dead slowly entered.

Finally Niccolò was close enough to peer through the open doors, but he saw nothing lying beyond them. When at last he stepped through, he stood on an odd shoreline of gray mist—no ocean breeze carrying the clean bite of salt air, just a faint cloying whiff of sweet flowers, with an undertone of sulfur.

Crowds of milling dead lined up to board one of the grand gondolas. Hunchbacked oarsmen hurriedly collected fares as the passengers took their places, facing forward, ready to reach the Underworld. But there was no river to cross here, only a huge body of brackish water that boiled up from below like a cauldron on a cooking fire.

All the grinning boatmen's pockets bulged fatly with coins, though.

Niccolò knew this was all a sham, nothing more than shameful trickery. The oarsmen were unholy deceivers, for the old pagan myth had made clear there was only one true ferryman who oared the dead across the River Styx.

But then, what is this terrible place?

He shouted, "Where am I?" and kicked at the ebbing waves of time lapping around his feet. Was this the demonic place below, which the church had so often warned of? That did not seem right, either. Perhaps it was all simply the workings of his cursed, enchanted mask.

The harsh shriek of a seabird startled him. He looked up and saw, leaving from the pier, a gondola which carried a woman whose dark hair bore familiar reddish-blonde streaks. Her boat was slowly moving away from the shore with all the others.

He cried out, "Regina!"

She must think the Holy Father's remission of sins cleared her way . . . or, somehow she already collected the coin from my pocket.

No, he told himself. The church, the old myths . . . all lies to frighten children and fools. Regina must get off that boat. My sweet wife cannot be heading to her final rest.

"Come back!" he screamed.

She turned her sallow face to gaze back at him. Then raised one hand in farewell and closed her sunken eyes.

Time, the swiftest passage, swept her far out to sea. And slowly the gondola sank into the boiling swell of dark water.

Now there was nothing Niccolò could do. His tears flowed in such a copious tide of grief it loosened and washed the mask from his skin. His false face whirled away lightly as a dead leaf on the outgoing winds.

No use to shout or curse or damn the gods. Regina was dead. Thrown with all the other innocents into an existence of endless gray misery in the Underworld. There would be no happy rest, no rebirth into a new life.

Jesu, what have I done? The Mask Maker has deceived everyone.

"Regina. Please come back to me," he sobbed.

The massive entry doors were slowly creaking shut. He bolted up and squeezed through the remaining gap, then ran across the collapsing bridge. The haunting notes of a lute and chiming finger-cymbals tried to draw him back to the bazaar. But when he looked over one shoulder, the square was empty of tents, stalls, and revelers. Rosy fingers of morning sun stroked the familiar worn paving stones, which held no more young couples, old men, noisy children, or stray begging dogs. Where had reality left off, and illusion begun?

"*Regina!*" His tortured cries echoed off the surrounding buildings. His head throbbed, his heart pounded, his empty arms ached for her.

Across the Square the church's grand doors stood open, as if to welcome him back. To offer comfort and sanctuary.

I will find and bring her back, somehow. Even if I must demand it of God himself.

He stumbled across San Marco Square, and traipsed inside the church, down the stone aisle paved with clerics' graves. Bracing himself on a wooden railing, he paused to stare up at the painted saints smiling down from their places in the promised afterlife. Then ran past the altar laden with the golden relics of salvation, and scurried down the wooden staircase into the rotting basement.

An open cask of communion wine offered a brief respite from pain. Then he slumped senseless in a damp, cold corner staring at the massive old timbers his ancestors had driven deep into the marshes to create this false island, the piers to support her heavy stone buildings.

That was when he saw them again: chittering creatures like the horrors that had clung to the underside of the old Devil's Bridge. The misshapen grotesques peered down at him with beady red eyes as they scurried across the ceiling beams and crawled along the columns and cracking foundation, clinging with sharp black claws, lashing long scaly tails.

"Niccolò," a familiar voice whispered from the shadows. "Come, *mi amore.* Let us dance, as you promised." A soft hand reached out in the dimness to stroke his cheek. "Join me."

Stupid with drink, he closed his eyes and slurred, "Regina. Have you finally come back for me?"

"Take my hand," her voice cajoled.

As he reached out, three sharp knocks sounded from above. A breath of cold air raised shivers as it rushed over him. A rank smell like that of Torcello's ancient, mildewed cathedral drifted to his nostrils. A black mist lowered from the rafters, coalescing into a dense, dark orb before his eyes.

He squeezed them shut and crouched, arms folded over his head, rigid with terror.

Regina's voice whispered again, "Join me."

He dared to look up at last, hoping to see her.

Instead a horned creature with eyes like banked coals stood glaring down. "I need more gondoliers," it grunted. "At least, so long as this profitable pestilence lasts."

"Who . . . who are you? Who speaks to me?" Niccolò stuttered.

The apparition smiled. "Who indeed? It is only I."

"Speak your name!" Niccolò shouted, still dizzy with too much sacramental wine.

"I will not. But if you please, you may call me Mask Maker."

Niccolò crawled toward the familiar figure. "Mask Maker? You, who once called yourself Charon! But I know your true identity! The Deceiver. He who comes in many forms. You cheated me of my wife. And she of her rest."

"Ha! Who are you to accuse me?" The demon's forked tail lashed under his cloak, tumbling several ancient stone saints to the ground. "You have cheated even more than I, my greedy friend. For mere coins! Until your coffers overflowed. And like yours, so have mine!"

Niccolò drew back. "What are you saying?"

"Regina's soul is tainted by your acts, though her innocence is even more loathsome to me. Perhaps I will release her, in time. But there will be no redemption for you! You may rot for eternity in Hades. Or," his voice lightened, turned cajoling, "perhaps you will join us? For we are Legion."

"Not unless you take me to her first!" Niccolò scrambled up the steps and burst from the sinking basement. He staggered back down the aisle of the church, which was paved with the graves of phantom clerics who chortled and grabbed at his ankles with ghostly fingers.

The short winter day was at a close by the time he reached home. A gust of cold wind pushed him, like a pair of cold hands, into the dark, empty house. He reeled into the main chamber, lighted some candles, then stumbled to the table.

His chest heaved with weariness. He braced both hands on the wooden tabletop, and called out, "*Gimignano!*"

No answer. Then he remembered he'd dismissed the servant, after Reginia passed on.

He looked down at the table, and gasped, "What is this?"

His fashionable bycocket hat and the leather mask from the bazaar sat on the lace cloth, as if waiting for him.

Has the Deceiver been here, as well?

Hoping to catch a last glimpse of Regina, he lifted the mask and peered through the eye holes. His own familiar wood-shuttered windows faded. He saw nothing but a misty grayness.

A lingering scent of his wife's fragrance, the delicate perfume of rose water, came to him, though. He threw himself across the table, head in hands, and sobbed. His heart gave one last great heave, shuddered, and then seized. And his own spirit passed from his body.

The sweet chirping of spinks and sparrows woke him. He lifted his head, and saw beneath one pale, lifeless-looking hand a square of parchment. Addressed only, *For You.*

"She has come for me!" he exulted. Now he only need take a coin from the box, and—

But at that very moment his evanescent spirit rose, lifting with the birds to float above an ebbing shoreline layered with faint impressions: the fantastic Bazaar, its grotesques skittering lightly as dandelion fluff upon a river. Scenes from his own life, far more prosaic. Three bright stars pulsed above a spiraling portal lined with fangs like a mythical dragon's open mouth.

What is this place?

Off in the distance, the dark silhouette of a small craft glided on an unseen sea. In seconds, it shifted so quickly through time its outline blurred, before it halted bobbing before him.

So I am indeed dead, Niccolò thought.

He held out his invitation to the oarsman, but with some hesitation. This frightening wild-haired figure wore only a loin-cloth, and grimaced terribly as he motioned for him to climb aboard. Perhaps the Deceiver had returned yet again?

Nonetheless, Niccolò insisted, with only a slight quaver, "I am come to join Regina."

He stepped down into the ancient-looking black vessel.

They traveled quickly for a short distance, but soon the funereal craft slowed, and the boatman set down his oar. "I am Charon." The huge oarsmen held out an oar-callused hand. "Your fare."

Niccolò knew then that the ancient gondolier did indeed stand before him—the old myth was real. He pretended to search through empty pockets. "I . . . I fear I haven't any coins with me, at the moment."

"Really, *signore*? And yet you stuffed so many of mine into your own money box." The oarsman chuckled grimly. "The Goddess Styx must be paid, or you will never cross. Like so many of the poor dead ones you once carried."

"Why, of what terrible crime do you pretend to accuse me?" Niccolò blustered. But of course he knew. "I pray you, move me on," he begged. "I do not need to pay. I hold an invitation!"

The ferryman roared, "No pious soul here receives such a thing! You are dead. Invitations have no value."

Niccolò stood abruptly, rocking the small craft. "Row me on to my wife!"

"I cannot. I may only ferry souls across from life to death."

Tremors roiled the waters, as if the quaking Earth herself rumbled deep below, shaking the boat.

"The Goddess Styx rises from the depths," said Charon. "If you have no coin, she may toss your miserable corpse into the bowels of the Underworld, the great pit called Tartarus."

"No! The Holy Father has granted us all remissions!" Niccolò lied, for he knew he surely had not passed away simply from the pestilence. And that, even if remissions did matter, they would surely not be enough for his salvation.

"What Holy Father?" Charon snorted. "Of whom do you speak?"

The waters all around the vessel boiled, swirling into a whirlpool that threatened to swallow the craft whole. The boatman calmly toppled sideways. His oar slipped into the maelstrom as he shouted, "She demands payment, now!"

The Goddess' outraged cry wailed and keened over the water. Her breath was as hot as the sirocco winds off Africa.

Niccolò clutched the gunwale desperately as the craft heaved. "What can I do?"

"Nothing but wait here in the Between," the oarsman said, floating beside the boat he normally piloted. "Or perhaps risk a swim back to shore. Though few survive that ordeal."

"But I cannot swim at all!"

"No matter. It is certain the Goddess will cast you down in the end. After toying with you as a cat does with a mouse, for a time." Charon laughed. "An offering may be made by a relation or a kind friend. Then you might move on someday."

"But I have no one!" Niccolò wailed. "They've all passed on."

Only the lap of waves against the gondola's sides answered him this time. The oarsman was gone. He had moved on to ferry others, as he must.

Niccolò still drifts in silence on the stagnant waters of nothingness. There is no end to his well-deserved anguish, and no one left to care. Forever he is cursed to sit in the Between and cry out, "Regina, *Amore mio!*"

Some nights, his faint cries carry inland on the sea winds. But no amount of moans or wails will ever release him from this purgatory. The sounds only disturb, from time to time, the restful sleep of *cittadini* who lie on silken sheets, dreaming of their own gracious lives. And of course the dead, who are busy preparing for their own, more peaceful crossing to the Underworld.

A caravan cart of the sort favored by the traveling Romani is parked on the outer edge of the Night Bazaar, its wooden sides and wheels painted with bright colors in fanciful, flowery, fairytale designs. One wall unfolds, opening up into a real theatrical stage, complete with backdrop, draperies, and various acrobatic equipment. And who performs in this portable theater, you ask? Why, only the most entrancing—and entranced—carved and painted wooden dolls. Though all different, each is of a most exquisite, lifelike, and singular design, magically strung to pirouette and cavort and perform fantastic acrobatic feats. Their creator, the old madam who oversees the traveling theater, is a singular creature as well—though far less comely than her poppets. But step closer, why don't you, and take in a show? The curtain rises every evening, promptly after sunset . . .

WELL PLAYED

by Corinne Alice Nulton

It was the marionette, not the madam, who first captivated Litty. Stringing her along, until she, too, was strung up. Just as the madam had done with the rest of the pretty puppets who dangled together helplessly, noosed to the back wall of a moldy, miniature stage in a painted, donkey-drawn caravan.

Litty had been a mere child back in 1348, wandering ghost-like between open carts heaped so high with plague-riddled bodies, the wheels would barely turn. These conveyances were loaded daily and taken to the burial pits on the island, the barges laboring beneath their burden swallowing wave after wave, struggling to stay afloat outside Venice's more sedate canals.

In those days Litty, too, had weaved around as she tried to avoid touching people. To avoid looking up at the big, oozing black boils on the faces of sickly strangers who staggered and cried out in pain, or in grief. She slept in corners, or in empty buildings, left alone in the world after the same illness took every member of her household—mother, father, sisters.

The doctors were the worst. They carried bags of sharp instruments and wore black cloaks. Most were skinny old men with long hooked noses like the beaks of ravens. Carrion birds. She always feared these old bird-men were looking at her. If so, what could they possibly want? To drain her of blood, perhaps, while prodding her flesh with little shining knives. If the surgeons did see her, they must've been the only ones to notice a child so small she could slip unheard and unseen down crowded streets, beneath the concealing red rays of the sinking sun. A numb pattern of unfeeling movement through death-filled alleys and squares, back to her orphan's nest in the latest empty house.

She'd felt more ghost than mortal in those terrible weeks.

Until the voice had called to her.

A sweet, seductive melody, the happiest sound she'd ever heard. It drew her down an alley and well away from the city's boundary, into a nearby wood. To a little puppet-cart set up beneath a canopy of rustling, whispering leaves. Litty was so small, she had to crane her neck and tilt back her head to look up at the compact wooden stage where a marionette performed.

Kat the Acrobat was the beautiful puppet's name. As soon as their gazes met, Litty was as good as noosed.

But Kat was no mere toy. Rather, a particularly dainty doll who flew up to perch in the rafters of the miniature covered stage. Then down, down, past floorboards and footlights, swooping out into the audience with lightning-fast twists and turns that coiled and knotted her silver strings violently. Impossibly. Only for the doll to gracefully straighten and land on tip-toes in a perfect, seductive pose, giving an all-too-cheeky grin over one coffee-colored clay shoulder. If not for those same shining strings, Litty would've believed the acrobat was no puppet, but a midget, a diminutive near-woman. Her black ringlets held caramel highlights. The long, thick hair sprouted straight up from a widow's peak and cascaded down her lean-muscled back. Large oval irises of the same toffee cream shade, set in milk-white orbs fine and pure as any glass made in Murano, stole glances at Litty in between moves.

Kat's pink lips pursed and then opened slightly, as if the puppet had danced herself breathless. Her short, exotic red-silk skirt flared out on the turns, only to cling tighter to her curves as she spun. A mere doll, perhaps, but still the most beautifully-carved and crafted human form Litty had ever seen.

She danced frantically, deliberately flailing, falling, only to land in fouettés that shot her up abruptly into the air again. Like a butterfly trapped in a jar, she flew around the small stage's confines violently. As if mere wood and clay parts would not break. Though clearly that was not the case, for as Litty leaned closer she spotted spiderweb cracks just beneath the puppet's painted curls, in the crevices of her jointed knees.

Even broken, she was beautiful.

Litty was enchanted *then*—before the witch had even uttered a word. As soon as the puppet flirted and entranced her, Litty had already gone from living girl to dummy. She just didn't know it yet.

"That's quite enough." The voice of the old *signorina* cracked like a whip.

An ancient creature, she was draped in a yellowed-lace dress spotted with black stains. Slumped on a little stool against the side of the cart, as if waiting the return of her own puppeteer. But the withered old lady was very much human. Her layers of skirts and petticoats reeked of a swamp-like decay, as she lifted a hand to pick at a bulging black boil on one cheek. Her stringy silver hair had been raked back into a twisted, braided bun. Even so, strands spilled out all over the place, like snarls in a dingy gray ball of yarn.

The madam snatched the puppet off the stage before Kat could even enjoy a final bow.

The children standing in a huddle around the stage had sighed, and together let out a sad little, "*Aww. . .*"

The old woman only scowled. holding Kat carelessly by her lithe torso, letting her strings drag behind on the ground. Then she seemed to think better of it, and cradled the stunning little toy in her arms like a fussy newborn as she bore her offstage. Mumbling under her breath, as if in a heated conversation.

But with whom, Letty had wondered. The puppet? Even as the old woman turned away from the crowd, Litty had felt she was still being watched. Not by the madam, but by the gigantic bun centered at the back of her skull; the wad of hair knotted and woven with cloth and strange trinkets and buttons. It looked like a small, grotesque second head.

"Oh? What's this!" The madam's drooping head perked up then, as if a great secret had been revealed to her. She twisted her neck around to look directly at Litty, who'd been leaning her cheek on the edge of the splintery stage, disconsolate, while all the other children slowly wandered off. A few other stragglers lingered, too, staring up at the empty, dark stage where the beautiful doll had danced. Running their own fingers through the air as if to practice. So they'd be fast enough to touch her, next time.

"Come here, child." The madam nodded at Litty and licked her lips, smacking them as if a most delicious snack had just arrived. She animated Kat with one hand to make her wave. "Would you like to play with my little friend?"

More than anything, thought Litty. "Y-y-yes, *Signorina*." She held out both arms.

"Call me Madam." The woman snickered. She waved Litty around to the back of the cart and up a narrow set of steps.

Litty cautiously stuck her nose past a long, faded velvet curtain drawn across the narrow doorway. Inside the caravan, a closet-like space was tucked behind the stage. Gaze circling the room, she tried to memorize each of the beautiful marionettes who hung there: a fairy with translucent butterfly wings, a clown with a bright red collar and elongated nose, a princess with a jeweled tiara, a mermaid with shiny scales and tiny white seashells tucked into her pale-green braid, a pair of matching masqueraders, a soldier with a blood red jacket, and a knight with metal armor so highly polished Litty could see her own ear-to-ear smile.

She wanted to play with all of them at once.

She could barely see the fine pale strings they hung from, thin as a hair and in varying lengths, crossing the ceiling like a gigantic spider web.

"Katarina." The madam nodded to the puppet still nestled in her arms. "Now, she is much too fragile for clumsy little hands." She sat Kat up right, centered between the arms of a rickety oak chair. The slippers that shod her arched, carved pine feet did not even reach the edge of its seat. The doll's amber eyes stayed fixed on Litty as her owner reached up into the rafters for a piece of unmolded clay. The earthen lump was clad in a feathery ballerina bodice and tutu, but still hairless, eyeless, rough. And rather scary, its form prickling with sharp little silver pins that held the white feathers on straight.

"This isn't finished yet, so you can't break it." The old hag put the barely-human object into the child's arms.

"Ohhhhhhh . . ." Litty heard her own longing whine before she felt the breathy hiss of it leave her lips.

She traced the lumpy figure with small, stubby fingers, pretending they could shape the clay, all the way up to the pink rosettes blushing its cheeks. The cool glass eyes she rubbed with the tip of one callused thumb, roughened from years of weeding and hoeing and raking seeds into dirt in colorless rows of grain on her parent's farm outside town. She held the puppet's blank face at eye level, trying to imagine just how beautiful it would soon become. Perhaps with her hair in a braid, like the mermaid's. Or would this one have a little silver tiara like the princess? Oh, and what about delicate pink slippers to leap around in?

The beggar girl could not pull her graze away from the unformed ballerina dressed like a majestic swan.

Just then, from the corner of one eye, she saw Kat's head slip slightly sideways against the chair back. The puppet dropped her hinged jaw, letting out a faint, dry hiss. Like a distant scream carried on the back of a cold winter wind.

The child froze, trapped in that single background note. Its high, dry pitch made her shudder, yet she couldn't run. For Litty's hands were suddenly clamped down hard on the clay puppet in her arms. Her body seized, trembling yet rigid at the same time.

The witch looked down, smiling, lips moving, though no words were uttered aloud.

Trapped, Litty stared into the musing eyes of the faceless, unformed ballerina, watching in terror as her own mud-brown hair, pinkish-brown freckles, and clear green eyes began to bleed through the surface of the blank white clay. The features became more prominent with each little tremble of her hands. She understood, then. The beautiful puppet's high note was no longer a gasp in the background—now it was her own shrill scream!

By the time she managed to drag her gaze away from the toy, her ragged wool skirt was already turning to pure white feathers against her legs, her filthy canvas bodice twisting into spotless, beaded lace. She rose slowly, helplessly, on tiptoe, pulled by strings that slowly poked out of her joints and grew longer, until they twisted around a pair of crossed wooden sticks clenched in the extended fingers of the smirking witch.

With a flick of one wrist, the madam made Litty spin and take a little bow.

Only when she lifted her head again, did Litty notice just how sad all the hanging puppets looked.

On the chair Kat closed her hinged mouth and shook her head sadly behind the witch's back. Even though it had been she, the marionette, who had really bewitched Litty with her eternal beauty.

The witch cackled as she strung another soul up backstage, to hang from the rough rafters of the cart. Damning Litty to centuries as a mere plaything.

One evening, about a hundred lifetimes later, Kat gave one of Litty's strings a gentle jerk. "Hey, you."

But Litty swung away, dangling from an upper beam, hiding her glass eyes from the dwindling rays of the sun. She didn't want night to come. She didn't want to keep waking in the evenings as a human girl, only to sleep away the days as a mute, inanimate marionette.

"Come on, now." Kat, too, swung forward, until her pink-painted lips grazed an ear hidden in Litty's hair, pulled back into a ballerina's perfect bun.

"Grrrrr . . ." Litty pushed Kat away. Knocking her gently into the mermaid puppet, who flicked her tail, still in deep slumber.

"Come on, the sun is setting. It's time to wake," Kat insisted, gliding along gracefully, grasping the spare strings like vines to cross the ceiling and slip around to the other side of Litty. Cradling her gently in both arms, lending a shoulder on which to hide her sleepy eyes. She gently ran her fingers through the few renegade strands that escaped Litty's tightly-pinned bun. Until, slowly but surely, her friend reluctantly blinked wooden eyelids open.

"Hey," Litty mumbled, and leaned forward to press her painted clay lips against Kat's.

"Morning." Kat smiled, pulling her lover gently forward by the stings so that they could press their foreheads together. "It's a new night."

Ugh. So it was.

Litty could already hear the stumbling steps of drunkards, and smell the sweaty must and mothball scent of old men. Johns, the puppets called them. Gathering outside, impatiently waiting for the madam to pull back the curtains, and reveal her expensive, enchanted performers.

For the last few centuries or so the caravan had traveled with the Night Bazaar, tempting the desires of desperate mortals with their seductive little show. Tonight, they were camped on the outskirts of New Orleans, though the rare and costly marionette collection was still housed in the same old wooden caravan, its bright paint peeling. The cart was parked in the foyer of a sinking hotel at one end of a narrow canal, off a bayou. Gentlemen in seersucker suits came to gawk at puppets of all ages, eras, and genders. Or, for a hefty sum, to play with the dolls as they pleased, once the sun set and the puppets became human again. As eager hands stuffed bills into the witch's coin pouch and grabbed a porcelain beauty, the toys turned to flesh beneath the rays of the setting sun. Dutifully performing whatever sort of entertainment their outfits suggested—belly dancing, ribbon twirling, juggling, singing . . . and when the performance ended, when the rising sun glistened again over the water to illuminate the dark, trash-choked canal, their bodies stiffened and shrank back into the puppet forms they were forever enslaved to.

But what if a toy refused to play along?

Litty had wondered about this, early on. Until one morning she saw a less-than-accommodating fairy's wings ripped off, her fragile wooden spine cracked in half while she slept on helplessly in puppet form. Toys like her who rebelled were broken beyond repair, unable to turn human again. The witch liked to display their remaining pieces in a shadowbox in the back of the cart. A warning to any other toys who might feel reluctant to cooperate.

"Tell me again," Litty said, burying her head in Kat's chest, "about when we run away."

"Of course. But quickly." Kat gestured at the sleeping princess who was just stretching out slim wooden arms. So far to each side one fist socked the sleeping soldier, who yelped in pain. The entire caravan was starting to wake.

"We'll sell flowers?" Litty pressed.

"Yes. We'll live somewhere out in the country, where it's quiet and clean. Far, far away from everyone and everything that could hurt us. And we'll grow fruit trees and vegetables, and—"

"The most beautiful sunflowers in the world. So beautiful their faces wouldn't need to follow the sun. It will orbit nearer just to bask in *their* beauty." Litty sang out the familiar, beloved phrases as if they were part of some hex that would ensure their eventual freedom from bondage.

Kat laughed. "Yes! Fields and fields of them. Though, of course, we'd also grow the usual roses, lilies, tulips, pansies. . . every petal, of every color. To be cut, arranged in a vase or bouquet, and sold."

"Quietly, simply, and all so lovely."

"While in love." Kat winked at her.

Litty wrapped her arms around her partner's shoulders and closed her eyes. She loved pretending the two of them were actually waking inside this cherished dream—lying out in a vast field of flowers, their tiny thatched cottage a pale blur in the lush green distance. Waking only to each other, and to a quiet farm, instead of all this, this—

"Get up, my pretties! We have customers! Up! *Up!*" The witch's grating voice held the dry crackle of dead, crumbling leaves. Like her, it too carried a sort of earthly decay. All the marionettes cringed, though with hope in their big glass eyes. For sometimes, the hag's horrendous, deadly-sounding coughing fits thrust her about helplessly, as if determined to kill her on the spot. One such fit came now, until she coughed blood onto a stained sleeve for several moments before pulling down the curtain to douse the last few rays of setting sun.

One by one the puppets sighed and drifted to the floor, strings sucked up and into their veins, clay surfaces rippling, then softening into skin. Clacking wooden joints replaced with strong tendons and smooth muscle and bone.

Litty blinked, wincing a little as her hard glass eyes jelled into white-mucus orbs framed with dark fluttering lashes. Ahh, to be human again. She loved holding Kat during the transformation. Feeling the grained, dry wood of her lover's hands melt and soften into warm, satiny skin. Moist as a freshly bloomed petal, like those on the flowers they so often dreamed of.

The cart was tiny. The puppets always woke tangled in a pile on top of each other. The fairy princess, still groggy and drooling, landed between the mermaid and the solider, who both roughly threw her off. But, in doing so, the solider bumped his head against one moldy wall, and cursed in pain.

Little love was lost between the toys. Only that which had grown between Kat and Litty.

But there *was* a game they all shared. As they left the little cart and lined up so the audience could feast their greedy eyes, each puppet would pick out a john in the crowd, and then whisper an imagined backstory to the others.

"There," the soldier began, pointing to a young lad in uniform. "A member of the infantry, like me. Used the uniform to run away from home. Probably just a private. Clearly closeted."

"Also like you." The mermaid rolled her eyes. "Let's see. . . him, next to that fat one. Wealthy, of course. Probably about five ex-wives. Three of which he murdered."

"More like four, but his comrade there looks pretty poor," the male harlequin narrated. "He's just a guide. Brings rich old fools to disreputable places, but pisses away the money he steals the moment it touches his hand."

His motley-clad, masked female counterpart giggled. "The want-to-be pirate will definitely go for the ballerina. Dirty, drunken sea-men pretenders always choose fragile, clean, and beautiful."

"And that lady there," Litty chimed in. "She's a run-away tattoo artist, looking for someone who'll drown all the waves of sorrows in a drink with her—"

She stopped suddenly when she noticed the same small, chubby-cheeked child she'd seen several nights in a row. The boy ran to the back edge of the crowd, ducked beneath a black cape, then emerged again as a tall, sharp-nosed young man in his teens or early twenties. His gaze was aimed directly at Kat.

"Oh no," muttered Litty.

No need to guess the shapeshifter's back story. He had already sobbed it out into Kat's bosom far too many times. He took this form mostly—a twenty-something with long, scrawny limbs and shaggy auburn hair—but the shifter had many shapes. He had come to the witch a few years back, hoping her skill with magic puppeteering string might help him control all the other beings inside him. Some were male, some female. Some outright monsters. The witch had given him the power to choose his form, in exchange for his services—she'd tied the magic strings in little knotted bows around his wrists. Not giving him complete control, but allowing *her* to control the forms within him. And thus had come her price: he must guide lonesome strangers to her little wooden cart every evening.

"Ah, yes. My regular." Kat sighed. "I hope those strings are tied good and tight tonight. Last week he was transforming in between thrusts." She leaned in close, breathing hotly on Litty's neck, imitating his panting, "—a child, *ugh*, an old woman, ugh, a meaty body builder, uuuugh, and—ahhh! An awful monster with rows of needle teeth." She snapped her own white canines to punctuate the end of the sentence.

Litty took her hand. "Please don't go with him tonight. It's dangerous."

"Hey, now. After centuries of this same work night after night, it's nice to have something a bit different," Kat joked, bumping a hip against her girlfriend's, obviously trying to lighten the mood. "Besides, we'll need him to help us defeat the witch. Well, maybe not Asher himself. But one of his other monstrous forms could definitely take her down."

"We don't need him." Litty hated Asher. "He likes you a little too much."

Since the first time she'd met the shapeshifter, the mere sight of him made her afraid. He was much too fond of Kat, utilizing her services at least twice a week. And he had this absurd notion the three of them were *friends* or something—that when the time came to run away, they'd all walk out the door together holding hands, singing a stupid pop song. He always greeted Litty with an over-enthusiastic hug and tacked on degrading little phrases at the end of every sentence, like, "There's my girls! My daring duo! Two doting dolls. How's it hanging, puppets?"

Gross. We are not *his*, Litty thought fiercely. He's just an escape route.

"But we *do* need him, love." Kat touched her lover's face with soft fingertips. "We're so close to escaping. And if he likes me too much . . .well, he'll also trust me too much."

"No whispering now," the madam hissed. "You all know the plague was spread in whispers, on the contaminated breath of the infected. Hold your tongues, or I shall hold them for you!"

That was her favorite threat. The dolls had heard it a hundred times, but still all bowed and curtsied as their mistress stumped past, inspecting them for any infractions or shoddy attire.

The madam waved a hand for the customers to come forward and choose their partners for the evening. The pirate, as predicted, pushed eagerly toward Litty. When he opened his mouth, she almost grew tipsy from the strong fumes of alcohol that gusted out.

"Let's see how high and fast you can really spin!" he told her. He grabbed at the cloth and feathers of her tutu and jerked her up close, until their bellies touched, then ran his fingers up the backs of her thighs.

Litty stole a look at Kat, who gave her a wry little smile over Asher's shoulder. Something about her warm caramel eyes could always settle Litty's soul. So that, with a faint sigh, she could submit to the pawing and pinching and poking. Close her eyes and disappear into their field of flowers while the john did as he pleased.

"Are you need in need of a new *danseur*, miss?" The thunderous voice ripped Litty's daydream in two. Her flower-fields vanished in a confetti-hued shower of petals.

A skeleton-like figure was ambling towards her, face shadowed by the brim of a top hat. He'd apparently stepped out from behind the other johns, for she had never seen him before. His glowing yellow eyes, the extreme height, and the angular bones of his face made her feel astonished none of the puppets had noticed him before.

He slid a long, slender ebony walking stick between Litty and the overly-enthusiastic pirate. Then with one long fingernail lifted Litty's chin, raising her face, drawing her gaze up to his. "For I'd love to serve as your gentleman for the evening," he added.

The witch gasped, and all the puppets froze in place. She was not one to ever show fear, so the very sight of her trembling made all her toys shrink back in terror.

"Master." The witch bowed to the skeletal being. "I am here only to serve you."

He was breathing hotly now on Litty's throat, moving his cold lips slowly across her smooth bare shoulders. "Just passing through." And then the man—*was* it even a man?—shrugged, pausing long enough to tip his hat at the witch. "I heard you've created quite an establishment here, since those many years ago, when I found you in a heap of plague-rotted bodies. I see you're making good use of that doll, and the string I gave you." His gaze shifted to the huge bun at the top of the witch's head.

"I never fully recovered from the plague," The witch snarled, pointing to a black boil on her face. "You didn't save me. You cursed me to an eternity of its horrible symptoms."

"But you only asked to *survive*. It pays to be more specific with one's wishes." The skeleton man grinned, exposing long yellow teeth. "I mean, I can always take it back, if you'd prefer?"

The witch blanched, and quickly cut him off with, "How may I help you tonight, good sir?"

"Just here for my cut." The demon pulled Litty a little closer, forcing one long thin leg between her trembling thighs.

"Oh, you will be quite happy with that one!" The witch spoke faster now, stumbling over her words. "She's one of our best! And all yours, to do with as you will, of course!"

"She'd better be." Twisting the top of his cane, he drew out a short, thin knife and delicately glided the sharp edge along Litty's neck, then down one shoulder. A thin trail of red bubbled up in the blade's wake.

Litty closed her eyes and tried to imagine a field of sunflowers. But nothing came to her. The cutting stung like fire.

"Stop it!" Kat's shriek bounced off the crumbling plaster walls of the listing hotel. Every john froze in mid-grope. The puppets stilled, too, as if someone had just jerked their strings taut.

"Relax!" The witch coughed into a fist. "She can't *die*. And whatever he breaks, I can glue back together at dawn."

He pressed the knife deeper, cutting paths along the veins of Litty's arms. She bit her lip so as not to scream. All she could summon of her dream cottage now was the blood-red roses, crimson petals falling around her.

Kat leaped from Asher's embrace and ran towards the sadist gripping her girlfriend.

Asher caught up and grabbed one arm, holding her back. Still Kat screamed in an endless loop, "Stop it! You monster! *Stop!*"

Litty made herself smile at Kat, hoping that would calm her. They both would live, no matter what. This pain was only temporary. This particular sadist would be gone in the morning. She'd be back inside the cart, daydreaming with her lover, in no time.

But Litty's weak smile seemed to enrage the skeleton man. He took hold of her other arm and twisted it up sharply behind her back until she screamed. A loud, sickening crack echoed off the damp walls of the sunken foyer.

Kat went crazy then. She clawed her way out of Asher's grip and went for the witch's head, crawling up the old hag's back, encircling her neck with one wiry arm, her legs clamped around her waist.

The skeleton laughed. He forced Litty to the ground, then ripped her feathered tutu down the middle. He climbed on top of her—apparently planning to take her right there, in the foyer, in front of all the other johns and toys.

Litty couldn't see what was happening to Kat any more, but the witch shrieked when she finally broke free of her grasp.

"You wretched doll—you know you can't kill me!"

There came a hollow thud, then a crack and a thump. Kat. Hitting the floor hard, like the pile of wooden joints and glue she was during the day.

"*No!*" Asher screamed, as if he had just seen a beloved person turn into a doll that was all too easily broken.

Light from the hotel's huge marble fireplace cast the evil madam's shadow into a dark silhouette, as she pulled Kat's strings, making the beautiful, disobedient marionette dance right towards the fire roaring there.

And then, made her leap in.

The flames flared up as they devoured the acrobat.

Was it Kat screaming then, or was it Litty? Impossible to tell. She sobbed as the skeleton thrust into her, again and again, but didn't feel that particular pain.

Later, when the sun rose, the witch pressed one of Kat's scorched wooden arms into Litty's bruised human ones. "A reminder, my pretty, that you're just a plaything."

Litty lay on the plank floor of the wagon as blank-faced and limp as a puppet, though still human. Clutching Kat's pitiful remains in one fist held tight against her heart—the splintery wood of the right arm. Sharp enough to prick Litty's palm, but she couldn't feel it. Nor anything else, really. For hours, then nights, then weeks, she lay there. Watching the witch clean and mend her torn, blood-stained tutu. Watching the sun rise above and fall below the flat dark water of the canal, lifelessly rotating from human to doll to human. The witch gave her a kick here, a curse there. The other puppets sometimes tripped while trying to step over her.

Still, Litty did not budge.

Asher came one night, poking his head through the curtained doorway of the cart. His eyes were red and puffy. He kneeled beside her. "Come on, Litty. You have to get up, or the witch will kill you, too."

So what? She didn't care. At least she wouldn't be here anymore. At least she would no longer feel this horrible gaping numbness. So she lay still and mute as a fallen statue on the damp, warped floorboards.

"*She* wouldn't want this, you know," he added, sniffling, wiping his nose on one grimy sleeve.

Litty wanted to roll her eyes then, but even that would take too much effort. Asher didn't know anything. He was a dumb, clingy John. Another, smaller monster. A mere tool Kat had failed to properly harness before her death.

"She told me things," he insisted, as if reading her mind. He pulled a small, crushed sunflower out of his jacket. There were deep creases in the petals where it had been folded in the pocket. He dangled it before Litty's face, her ghost-like stare.

Tears welled before she could blink them away. She slowly reached out to caress the bruised, wrinkled petals with her fingertips, sobbing softly. Imagining it was the skin of her lover as they transformed together at dusk.

"I'm going to take you away." With his fingers, Asher gently combed the tangled locks that spilled from her frizzy, unkempt bun. "We'll leave the Night Bazaar and go to some other land. I'll carry you around as a doll during the day, and you can keep me company when you transform at night."

Mid-sob, Litty broke into a bitter chuckle. When the laughter calmed, she jeered, "Until the witch uses the strings to make me return. Or until you get bored and leave me on the side of the road. Or turn into a monster and kill me."

Asher flushed, clearly hurt. But the mood passed like a breeze. He again focused his attention on the near-ghost lying before him, and snickered sarcastically, too. "Yeah, well, what should I do, then? Kill the immortal witch? Or kill you to extinguish your pathetic misery?"

"She's not a witch. She's a puppet."

For Litty had been thinking about this in obsessive loops as she lay limp on the floor. She'd replayed all the skeleton-man's words: about a doll, about the plague, and had come to the same conclusion again and again. "Just as I'm a puppet. As Kat was a puppet. As they are all puppets. As you're pretty much a puppet. She . . . is . . . too."

"Bullshit. I've never seen the old lady turn into a doll." Asher shook his head, though his gaze zigzagged around the closet-sized space as if he expected to see a miniature witch strung up in the rafters. "And I've seen her in daylight," he added, "So—"

"A different sort of doll, perhaps. But she's a doll all the same." Litty's eyes were also searching the space for some sort of humanoid toy. A horrible, musty, antique puppet. "That's why Kat couldn't kill the old woman. That must be how she survived the plague."

Litty dragged her hand away from the already-wilting sunflower and extended it to Asher, who gently pulled her to feet. But she didn't let go of his wrists. She held them tight.

"I need you to make a distraction so I can search for her weakness, her doll, without getting caught."

He shook his head. "She's too powerful. She'll know."

Litty swayed slightly from exhaustion. Asher caught her in his arms as she staggered, holding her upright until she found her balance. She was betrayed by a loose floorboard, which gave a high-pitched, warning screech.

"Shhh," he said. "She'll hear."

"Litty, my pretty, are you ready to entertain?" the witch called through the doorway.

Litty dug her nails into the knotted strings around Asher's right wrist. The puppeteer's strings that allowed the witch to help him choose which one of his-selves he would be at any moment, to keep all his different forms under control. She ripped out the largest knot, then viciously clawed, yanking free the rest of the string from one of his wrists and quickly backing away.

He gaped down in horror. "No, no, *no!* Fuck no, Litty!"

Too late. His body was already folding inward like an accordion, morphing into another shape.

"*No!*" he screamed at her.

Litty was already stumbling backward down the rotting steps, out of the little cart and into the foyer of the moldy, sinking hotel.

She hid behind a marble column and saw the witch curse and scream. She saw Asher fall off the steps to roll and thrash on the ground, gradually turning into a serpent-like beast with dead-branch limbs, and rows and rows of needle-shaped teeth. The same monster Kat had once described to her.

Only then did Litty dash back inside the caravan, eyes reeling and zigzagging all over the small interior space. Where was the witch's doll? This was the only place it could be hidden; the place where the witch had always kept her belongings. Litty flung musty leather account books off the shelves in handfuls, dumped vials of paint and piles of cloth and wooden spools of thread from the work table, then moved on to the dresser before the last bottles shattered. She tossed all the drawers, emptying each before yanking the cushions off the only chair, then lifted and smashed it against the wall.

Outside the cart rose screams and shouts from the other Johns. From some of the marionettes, too. The pitiful little yelp of the fairy princess. The melodic cry of the mermaid, the flip-flopping thump of her fish-tail striking the stage floor.

Should she go out and help?

No. Let them die, as Kat had died. At least their deaths would be a useful distraction, so Litty could finish searching the cart and find a way to destroy the evil bitch who'd enslaved them all for centuries.

But there was no witch-doll, no puppet version of the madam, anywhere.

"*Where is it?*" she screamed, starting to doubt her own theory. She yanked down yards of cloth remnants, then the old tapestries that lined the walls in onion-skin layers, until she was down to the bare, unvarnished antique wood.

All the shelves were empty. Every crevice searched. The broken chair lay in pieces.

Desperate, Litty stood on tiptoe and reached up to the ceiling, feeling through the rows of unformed dolls, the clumped knots of extra string. Praying her fingers would graze the cool grain of an unfamiliar wooden torso, the frayed-yarn hair of a puppet she'd never seen before.

But she found nothing new up there.

"*You beast!*" The witch yelled at Asher, outside. "Ungrateful demon! I gave you those strings! I gave you control. How could you!"

The shapeshifter hissed at her like a deranged snake.

"My dolls! All my beautiful dolls!" The witch sobbed. The cart swayed as she scrambled up its steps. The beast slithered after her, scales rasping over wood.

Trembling, Litty wrapped herself in the dusty curtains still draped across the door, just before the witch burst in.

"My beautiful, beautiful marionettes. My pretty little things. Gone! All gone," the old women moaned, raking broken nails over her boil-pocked face.

The shapeshifter turned briefly into a small boy with brown curls, laughing manically at the witch. Then into a beautiful teenage girl, who taunted in a cockney accent, "Prettier than me, were they?"

"And dead like them you'll be!" The witch shot up an arm, catching the end of a snarl of string hanging from the ceiling, and whipped it down like a net over the shape-shifter. He transformed into a fierce body builder, then into a tiny girl-child. Then back into the same demon, gnawing on the string with needle teeth. Raging and shifting, raging and shifting, until finally he settled, exhausted into just Asher. Red hair sweaty and tangled, pointy nose poking through a cocoon of strings.

The witch raised her big pair of sewing shears high in the air, poised to slit the shapeshifter's throat.

That's when Litty saw the doll. It *was* there, but not hanging from the ceiling or in a box or drawer. Its face was on the back of the witch's head, looking right back at her. Peering through the disordered silver hair, which was really magic puppet string braided and looped and growing from her scalp. Loops and whorls of string held the doll in place, exposing only a few patches of a twisted, wrinkled face made of age-darkened rags, black button eyes peering out from its folds. The cloth body was bent and twisted back, concealed inside the thick, coiled braid.

That was where she'd kept her own ancient puppet all these years.

Litty lunged, leaping onto the witch's back. Snaking an arm around the crone's skinny neck, digging the nails of her free hand deep into the old woman's scalp.

The madam bucked like a roped bull, tossing her head and screeching. Litty yanked her hair back, biting down on clumps of the braid with her teeth, gnawing until the wrinkled doll broke free. Then slid down the bony back, choking the ancient puppet with one fist while they reeled around the small space. Groping for something, anything sharp.

The witch swung around, aiming her scissors once again. This time the shiny, honed edge was pointed at Litty's throat. "What now, little ballerina?" The madam smiled, watching her scrabble away over the floor in search of a tool to cut or stab with: a shard of glass, a paring knife, a stray darning needle.

The witch took three big steps forward, cornering Litty. And still no weapon in sight. "Now give me the doll!"

Litty shook her head, gripping the stinking, moldy puppet tight against her chest with one hand, pulling the jagged piece of her lover's remains from her dress pocket with the other. "Who's the puppeteer now?" she jeered.

Then she plunged the splintered length of wood right into the center of the rag doll's body.

The witch dropped as if she too had been run through. She curled into a ball on the floor, writhing and screaming.

Litty stabbed the puppet again, in the face. And again, harder, in the back. Once, twice, three more times. With every blow the witch shrieked and wriggled like a hooked fish. Until gradually her twitching slowed. Finally, she lay silent, still, and limp.

Litty continued stabbing the toy until every bit of stuffing had oozed out. At last her arms dropped to her sides. The witch was dead.

But so was Kat.

The unbearable numbness remained. She considered lying down again, to wait for death. Instead, she knelt, took a deep breath, and shuffled through the debris on the floor until she found the creased sunflower Asher had brought. For a moment, she cradled it gently in both hands, as one might a newborn. Then tucked it behind one ear for safe-keeping.

She climbed out of the cart, stepping over the gory remains of Asher's monster-feast—a human arm here, a mermaid fin there, a quarter of the princess' skull lying on a moth-eaten Persian carpet, broken like an egg-shell, next to a heap of several dead, blood-smeared johns who had been regular customers.

Oh my, so much blood.

She walked out of the foyer where the caravan had been set up, and out into daylight. The sun's rays warmed her bare limbs. How great it felt to be human again in broad daylight. She took the sunflower out of her hair and twirled it, imagining she was with Kat, walking in their endless field of flowers.

Asher crawled outside too, on all fours, back to his usual shape. "Ohhh," he moaned, gripping his head like a man recovering from an awful, blood-induced hangover. He looked over one shoulder at all the dismembered bodies, and gagged. "What a mess. What do we do now?"

"Now?" She sighed. What *could* she possibly do now? A woman who knew nothing of the world outside of this moldy caravan filled with hanging puppets, moody shape-shifters, and skeletal monsters. And what good was being human if she was still without Kat? Anyway, what did she know about raising flowers? Planting and growing and cutting them, arranging bouquets—except for this small sunflower, she hadn't touched or held a real blossom for centuries. And it was already wilting.

She let the drooping bloom slip from her fingers, and watched it sink into the dark depths of the canal. Gone, along with her dreams. She did not know how to live in a world without Kat. A world that had taken everything, ripping her only love away.

Although . . . puppets. She knew *all* about them. Painting on pretty, forced smiles. Sewing elaborate wardrobes. Stringing them up. Playing with them. As the world had played so heartlessly with Kat, and with her.

And no one had ever bothered to care.

Who will be the monster now, she thought. And abruptly turned back to Asher, who still stood nearby, anxiously waiting, wringing his hands.

"Stop dithering!" she scolded. "We need to find some new puppets. An acrobat, I think, and a princess, and . . . oh, yes. A mermaid, of course—"

Litty broke off, breathless with her vision of this new role. A respite from mourning Kat. She smiled, then cackled, much as her predecessor used to do. Though her laugh was still high and shrill with youth and beauty. She was healthy, her body strong. Many years of soul-plucking and puppeteering lay ahead.

And so, on that day, the marionette became the madam.

One famous story, by a certain Mr. Edgar A. Poe, 19th-century Master of the Macabre, is unique in literature. For "The Cask of Amontillado" consists not of the usual beginning, middle, and ending, but only the story's final events. The last act of a tale of long-suffered outrages, for which the injured, grudge-holding party finally takes revenge . . . in a very concrete manner.

In a quieter, less accessible aisle of the Bazaar, stands a deserted stall littered with faded signs. Its goods seem little more than jumbled bits of iron, broken fittings, or discarded hand tools. A hodgepodge scattered across plank trestle-tables: bent drill bits, rusty files, peculiarly-curved wrenches, an ancient hammer, assemblages of screws and pincers, rulers marked in ells and lines, dull saws, axes with loose heads. But amid the junk gleams an ancient-looking trowel that nonetheless appears new, for its fine steel blade shines. The handle, crafted from a dense, expensive wood, is intricately carved. Perhaps it was made more for ceremony than for actual use? Yet, along those still-sharp edges cling hoary grains of crusted mortar. . . .

THE THOUSAND INJURIES OF FORTUNATO

by David Poyer

I suppose this will sound strange, but Fortunato and I were friends in our youth. As boys, we both attended the academy of old Doctor Guarino, in an obscure quarter of Venezia. *La Serenissima*, ruler of the waves, bastion of liberty, mistress of empire, and the greatest, most beautiful city below Heaven. He and I were classmates; yet not of the same social class. Ognibene's family had been prominent ever since the ancient Romans, fleeing invading barbarians, refounded their republic amid these swampy islets. The Fortunatos were members of the *Signoria*. One great-grandfather had governed as Doge.

My family, the Montresors, were patricians once, as well, but during the Crusades paying ransoms destroyed our fortunes. We retained only our pride, our coat of arms, and an antique palazzo in the Rialto, the oldest quarter of the city.

A stonemason, my maternal grandfather had arrived from the *terrafirme* forty years before. The towering splendor of St. Mark's, the skyward yearning of the

Campanile? My grandfather barged that sugar-white stone, of which our city's glory is wrought, from our quarry at Rovigno on the Istrian coast. We owe the towers, basilicas, sumptuous palaces which line our serpentine canals to artisans like him. Not to those whose names adorn books of history.

When I inherited the family business, I devoted myself to expanding our holdings and, above all, to executing work of the highest quality. This duty he had impressed upon me again and again as the creed against which craftsmen should measure ourselves.

Thus, as we grew, young Fortunato's path and mine diverged. His *destino* led to important posts in diplomacy, the archives, and the administration of our overseas territories. Mine to the teeming wharves, the quarries, and our family's noisy, hustling construction sites. The bulwark of our eternal Republic is that all men are free to work and build, each for his own profit, yet uniting in defense of the common good.

Still, in the narrow alleys of our great town Fortunato and I would sometimes come face to face, and seldom did our meetings end without adjourning to a wine shop. A connoisseur, he favored that nutty, aromatic sherry called Amontillado. Imported from Spain, it was rare even when the riches of the Mediterranean flowed through our hands.

Our first disagreement began at a time when all seemed otherwise well. War with Genoa had been averted. Each day our galleys moored at the Mole, disgorging silk from China, pepper, cloves, dyestuffs from the Indies, wool from England. Intricately-woven carpets from the deserts of Araby. And, as merchants prosper, they send for builders. The chest in the catacomb beneath my palazzo grew heavy with gold. I purchased a brickyard and clay pits on the mainland, rebuilt the kilns, and sold fine red and gray brick and terracotta roofing tile stamped with the family crest: a man killing a serpent whose fangs are embedded in his heel. I began to lend money, too, screening my usury by using the services of an old Jew. I suspect Heshamet abstracted more than the one part in twenty that was his due. Yet I made no complaint, for so skillful were his manipulations, my capital multiplied like the rats that scour the wharves by night.

But with wealth also came the sin of pride. I began to look above my station, yearning to reclaim the honors that had once made our name respected.

Encountering my old friend in St. Mark's square one day as I returned from crossbow practice with the city militia, I took him to a *taberna* overlooking the

Bascino. The black gondolas bobbed at their moorings. The island of Giudecca and the spires of San Giorgio wavered across the water like a fever-dream.

I revealed my hopes over cups of a Greek pressing. "The passing of old Sesendolo has left a vacancy on the *Maggior Consiglio*. Is it possible I might secure his seat?"

Stroking his chestnut beard, my former schoolmate gazed out upon the glittering sea. At last he murmured, "The Great Council? It would cost many of those golden *ducati* you love so well, dear Micheletto, friend of my youth."

I spread my hands. "It is true I love gold, but to forward the interests of our city is my dearest wish. I believe God has given me good fortune for a reason."

Fortunato cocked his head, as if harking to the song of a distant *sirena*. "You would commit your private funds to *La Serenissima?*"

I nodded. "When yet a boy, I wished to become a captain-general. My grandfather insisted business came first. But perhaps I can add to the glory of the Most Serene Republic in some other way."

When Fortunato smiled, his sharp-nosed features resembled a rat's. Gesturing to the attendant for more wine, he leaned in. "To qualify, one must be patrilineally descended from a former Counselor. Yours is an old bloodline, though now sadly obscured. No doubt the Archives could find one among your ancestors. But do you truly wish for such responsibility? You were never the most brilliant ornament of old Guarino's academy."

"His lectures bored me." I shrugged. "I hated Greek."

"Truly? I found it fascinating. Did you know he is dead?"

I shook my head.

"I purchased his entire library from the widow." Fortunato smiled. "In any case, you are a respected businessman. Trade has not the stigma here that it carries in Florence or Milan. And you are young, but some complain our *Signoria* has grown too gray." He let that hang in the air a moment, then murmured, "How much are you willing to commit to a campaign?"

I hadn't actually thought my offer to be for a 'campaign,' but rather a donation to be applied for the good of the city in some way. The dredging of a pesky shoal, or another bridge across the Canal Grande. "What would you suggest?"

He proposed a sum that reared me back in my seat. "By Christ's body! Such a commitment would absorb my entire profit for this year."

Fortunato flicked his fingers as if they were wet. "For what one truly desires, why count the price? And remember, once you don the golden chain of nobility, your heirs too will be *gentilhuomini*. It is not an expense, but an investment."

We met again two days later, in old Heshamet's counting-house. Fortunato refused a bill of exchange. "Gold would speak more ardently."

I handed over minted coin in hempen bags, weighty enough that he whistled his gondolier in to carry them to the boat.

Yes, I felt a pang as the fruit of my toil vanished. But when someday I married, my children would sit among the mighty at the Feast of the Sea, as the city pledged its troth anew to Oceanus with a tossed golden ring.

So I eagerly awaited the next session of the Council of Forty. As everyone knows, after names are placed in nomination the balloting is secret. Still, everyone had a rumor to pass on, and the chatter along the waterfront was this: Of all the candidates put forward, none had yet achieved the twenty votes necessary for election.

The next morning a crier below my palazzo announced, "Salvatore Pisani has been elected!"

I dashed my wine cup to the floor. It shattered, sending my orange cat clawing frantically up the window hangings. I called for my boat, and set out to confront my friend.

He was just leaving a small apartment near the Archives. Where, one of his servants had informed me, he spent hours each day with his collection of rare manuscripts. I drew him into a doorway, glancing up to make sure no chamberpots were being readied to empty.

"You look upset, *amico mio,*" he chided. "Truly, you must master these choleric humors. They may lead to a sickness."

I gripped his cloak and pressed an arm to his throat. "Piss-Anus has been elected to my seat, you fornicating liar. A *gente nuova*, without even a distinguished ancestry!"

Choking, he tried to push my hands away, but the strength of a scholar was unequal to that of one who daily handled stone. "Stay, Montresor! You were ahead until the final ballot, and many compliments were voiced on the floor. Such exposure will not hurt when it comes time to award this year's business."

"But you promised me the election. And your breath stinks, pus-mouth!"

"Dear sir, the Doge himself could make no such guarantee. I lobbied, I cajoled, I leaned my thumb on the scales." He gazed heavenward. "I swear by Saint Mark, you could've had no more earnest advocate. The competition was simply too stiff. However, another member is often absent, and some say he is a dotard."

"Where is my money? I will have it back, since you were unsuccessful."

Fortunato rolled his eyes and huffed. "Am I dealing with a fool? You know where your gold went! Still, as I explained, the money is not wasted. Campaign again, and start a step ahead."

I allowed him to placate me with soft words and promises of a minor post. "As for your proposal that I stand again for the next vacant seat, perhaps committing a larger donative, I will have to take that under advisement."

We parted, still friends. Or so I thought.

Some weeks later, from a random remark repeated in earshot of an engineer at the Arsenal, I learned my nomination to the Council had in fact been black-balled. One member alone had crossed me off the list. No one could say, of course, who my enemy had been.

A year later a messenger arrived at my door, bearing an invitation sealed with Fortunato's crest: a horseman refusing a crown that a man on foot was offering. I'd heard Ognibene was engaged. Not to a local lady, but one from our eastern dominions.

On the appointed day I dressed and perfumed, and gondola'd to the Church of San Polo. After the incense and vows, Fortunato led his bride down the aisle. She threw back her gold-brocaded veil, revealing a swarthy, black-eyed visage. Inordinately tall and slender, she had the swaying gait of one who spent much time riding horses. Her nose was proudly aquiline, but I could not say for certain it was Greek. She was no Italian, is all I can swear to.

As the couple passed, headed down the aisle, our gazes crossed. I caught my breath as a mutual appreciation passed between us. She nodded regally, then turned away, smiling down into the flushed face of her much shorter new husband.

At his palazzo, Fortunato and his wife already stood welcoming guests as we stepped from our boats onto the wooden landings that floated with the modest tides. He took my hand eagerly, and turned to her. I noted again how very smooth, though dusky, her skin. How enchanting the rose tint warming her cheeks, how sweetly promising those ripe, pursed lips.

And how very noisome the breath that hissed from between *his* rotting teeth as he squeaked, "Vera, meet one of my oldest friends, a respected builder. Monty, this is the Lady Vera Kryptikos, of a very old family in Crete."

"*Signore*," she murmured, her accent not quite Greek, but perhaps from even farther east. Only one word, yet freighted with more than acknowledgment. Her searching regard took me in, from my new red leather boots to the plumes in my hat, and approved. Perhaps even . . . invited.

I bowed deeply and kissed her hand. "Signora Fortunato." Then I passed within.

Later Ognibene sidled up. After I complimented both palazzo and bride, he gripped my shoulder like a brother. "And when will you marry, Montresor? Is there no pretty fawn who catches your fancy?"

I shrugged. "Perhaps. One of these days."

"May I suggest a fair one? Ideal for you. She will bring an excellent dowry. I can arrange an introduction."

Lucrezia Cracco was the youngest daughter of a trading family that dealt in lumber, resin, and coral from our colonies in Dalmatia and the Aeolian Islands. Plump and healthy, neither overly intelligent nor doltish, blessed with a hearty laugh and a forgiving nature. Which I admit to later sometimes taking advantage of.

We were married that fall, and then it was Fortunato's turn to compliment me on my home. Less grand than his, of course, but in a high and healthy quarter of the city, with a view across into the Ghetto where the Jewish population lived. At one point I encountered Lucrezia and Signora Vera with their heads together in earnest discussion. When they caught sight of me they exchanged glances, and both softly laughed.

Our first child came early, as many are wont to do, six months after the wedding. The babe was lusty, sucking greedily from the teats of its wet nurse. My little Camilla of the chestnut hair grew quickly, and how I loved her! A year later, a son arrived as well. Named Vittorio, after my father. Praise God, both survived the childhood fevers and thrived. After which my still-attractive but now broader-hipped wife fended off my advances, saying she needed time to recover before bearing more children. This was less a strain than tacit permission, as I'd had my eye on a girl from another district. I soon set up Maddelena in her own apartment, near my studio. And for a time events jogged along, and all were content.

Then, one day in late fall, the lady Vera stepped from the Fortunato gondola in a dizzying sweep of silken robes, shining hair, flowers, and perfume. She marched upstairs to Lucrezia, and stayed all afternoon.

At dinner, when I asked what all the talk and giggling had been about, my wife said, "She recruited me to help stage a charity. For the benefit of the unfortunates in Constantinople."

"Why are they so unfortunate in Constantinople?"

"The people suffer from earthquake, famine, and renewed assaults by the Turk. On top of which, a pestilence of some sort drives refugees west from the far Orient." She sighed. It seemed India, Tartary, and Armenia were covered with corpses.

"As to the charity, we will be expected to contribute," she added.

To this I readily acceded. Business was brisk; old Heshamet expected excellent profits from a new project.

Through Fortunato's intercession, the city had contracted with me to dredge a canal at the end of the Rio San Lorenzo. My Hebrew had purchased some close-by, low-lying marshland at an astonishingly low price, and artisans were enclosing it with stone bulkheading from our quarries. Thus, we were charging the city for spoil disposal, while using the dredged silt, mud, sand, and shells to create new land which we could then either sell or build on. An opportunity I congratulated myself on seizing, while supervising the erection of the shears—for if these are not properly set up, workers will die. I even helped manhandle the two-ton blocks into position, so the seawall would present a uniform, graceful appearance, and maintain the integrity of the new land behind it.

The promised charitable bazaar held that Christmas of 1348, on St. Mark's Square, was not quite what the priests had expected. Signora Fortunato had stocked it with the dregs of society: astrologers, alchemists, palmists, crystal-gazers, peddlers, pardoners, quacks, minstrels, artists, fortunetellers, tooth-pullers, dice-gamers, and fools. Not content with these outrages, she'd scheduled it to stay open all night, lit by flambeaux, to close only at daybreak.

The single time I went, on a drizzly evening, the torchlit stone flags were covered with trinket-stands, gaudy banners, victual- and drinking-booths. Sailors, workers, and the rabble of the *populo grasso* squandered their pennies, thronging tents and booths featuring monsters, freaks, and contortionists. I did enjoy the bear-baiting, but felt troubled. Should we really tolerate, in the very burial place of the blessed Evangelist, displays of unspeakable vice by dancing girls from the storied island of Lesbos and kohl-eyed boys from Alexandria? Jews in locks and tassels one could put up with, so long as they bore the cloth badges to mark them out. But it seemed we were now expected to welcome Musselmen and Parsees in turbans, and bowlegged Tatars, not to mention strange yellow and black faces from even more remote, questionable lands.

Add to this the drunken, spewing dregs of our own stews, pawing respectable matrons and *puttane* alike. Others in the crowd murmured imprecations as well. But, observing the loudest protesters furtively ducking into the booths which promised delights beyond the imaginings of the godly, I understood. Man is born to sin just as sparks must fly upward. Those who think to wipe it out would fain end in extinguishing Man himself.

The bazaar only lasted for a week. Vera had intended it to run until after Christmas, before shocking news swept the city. A Lesbian girl had daggered an archdeacon. Why he was in range of her blade was not discussed—nor what he'd done to merit the stabbing. Enough that one of the clergy had been attacked.

That evening marines from the Arsenal mustered in the streets. Led by mounted officers, they cleared the bazaar with halberds, knocking down any who dared object, setting fire to the remaining red-and-white-striped tents with torches. Bruised and terrified, the motley of mountebanks and musicians scattered to the winds. Suddenly, the exotic fair was no more.

Lucrezia told me later, "Lady Fortunato cursed them all roundly. The priests, the *Signoria,* even the officers. Calling them whited sepulchers and worse." My dear wife smiled. "And vowed that one day she would bring the bazaar back, to entertain and bewitch."

A little after the New Year I was summoned to court. An annoyance, but one in my business is accustomed to legal travails. Generally all that's required is a few silver *soldi* tucked into the right purses. A tariff which I'm happy to pay for the privileges enjoyed as a citizen of the Most Serene Republic, esteemed in all the world for her freedoms and her wealth.

I arrived to find standing against me one Vincenzo di Friuli, a public prosecutor I knew to be a tool and client of Fortunato. Thinking this augured well, I answered up when my case was called, and was surprised to hear myself indicted for making unwanted improvements upon the property of another. Only with difficulty did I penetrate the legal Latin to understand Friuli was asserting I did not own the land I'd been dumping spoil on.

At my turn to speak I said respectfully, "I must correct the learned prosecutor. The land was purchased and the deed recorded."

"No such record has been found in the Archives," Friuli shot back. "*Title nulla, re nec terram.* No deed, no land."

I begged more time to hale my witness into court. "And that will be . . . ?" Friuli asked.

"The Jew called Heshamet."

The prosecutor turned to the judge, smiling. "As Your Honor knows, the oath of a Hebrew has no weight in a Christian country. Without written evidence, you must find Signor Montresor guilty. The property then reverts to the original owner, who may or may not decide to accept the improvements the defendant has adduced. Which he did at public expense, but obviously intended for his own enrichment."

To that I had little to counter with, and humbly argued for a stay of judgment. "To inspect my records. Obviously the deed has gone astray, lost at the Archive. Or was never recorded."

Perhaps Heshamet could produce a receipt, so I could persuade the court some mistake had been made.

With a sour pout the judge granted the stay. "But for one day only," he added.

After calling Heshamet to me, and gaining no satisfaction, I set off for Fortunato's. He was at home, feverish and in bed. Sitting beside him, I recounted my problem and begged advice.

Ognibene ruminated for a time, stroking his beard, then coughed into a fist. "Absent a deed, my old friend, I fear you are up the canal of shit."

"But my factor assures me the deed was properly sealed and submitted. You are an official at the Archives, are you not?"

"Part time, to benefit the Republic. There is no *salarium* involved."

"This cannot be a simple matter of a mislaid document. Why would the *Signoria* even think to *look* for a deed? How would it have come to their attention?"

Fortunato avoided my gaze. "Possibly a denunciation was handed in."

I sat back, brow furrowed. The *bocche de leoni*, the slot-mouthed stone lions found on the side of the Doge's Palace, and on the walls of several churches, were always open. Any citizen could slip up in dead of night and stuff in an anonymous note denouncing another of a crime, a trespass, or a heresy. Depending on their content, denunciations were investigated either by the Inquisitorial Office or an arm of the secular government. And the *Quarantia Criminale* tried an accused in secret, undefended by counsel.

"But Ognibene, who would indict me for an innocent error, one not even my own mistake?"

He shrugged. "I cannot say. But I will urge Di Friuli to request the smallest possible penalty. Other than that, my hands are tied," he murmured sadly.

In the end I had to plead guilty. True to his master's word, Friuli asked the court for leniency, and the fine was trivial. However, I lost title to the land and all my investment in it.

When next I boated over that way, several men were raking the spoil, turning it over with spades to make it consolidate more rapidly. In a year or two it would be buildable. I glared with fury upon the lovely limestone my masons had laid into neat courses. I coasted past, then turned back and hailed the rakers in the rough, friendly manner of a fellow *cittadini*.

"*Amici,* brethren, how hard you're working! Though I see no supervisor. Who is your master, that I may compliment you?"

They replied with the name of a labor team supplier I sometimes dealt with. I tracked him down, then traced out the man who'd hired him. After employing *bravos* from my district to apply rough persuasion, I listened dumbstruck to a bruised, weeping man utter the name, "Jiulio Fortunato."

Ognibene's younger brother.

I considered my next move for some days. Ognibene stood far above me in the Republic's hierarchies. A member of the Signoria with important connections and enormous wealth would not easily be struck down. Yet my family motto was explicit. *Nemo me impune lacissit.*

No one insults me without retribution.

Fortunato would not have to die, for he'd merely cost me gold and damaged my reputation. Still, I must be revenged . . . yet not too suddenly. My retribution had to be understood by its victim to have come from me, yet also leave me immune to retaliation. Such subtlety required study.

Meanwhile, plague rumors from the East grew more ominous. The bishop led processions and litanies, imploring God to withhold His divine anger. Prelates abjured those whom prosperity had made complacent. They reproached careless judges, nobles who lived in pomp while cutting the grain dole, counselors who legislated to benefit friends. They condemned our widespread blasphemy, sodomy, scandal, and gaming. They also rebuked the young, who had taken up French dances full of lecherous and sinful gestures.

In response, our churchmen actually reformed themselves. Those nunneries turned bordellos were closed; clerics who fancied young boys and girls were removed. These developments were truly sobering, and convinced us all the city was in mortal danger.

After long debate, that winter the Signory closed our ports to commerce from Constantinople, Rhodes, and the Levant. "The plague's ravages have been gravest among the Turks and Mohammedans," a priest told me. "A clear sign God sent the pestilence to punish them for denying Christ. He will protect us, His people, if all repent and make restitution."

Soon, many were the masses endowed. Beggars and lepers in our alleyways grew fat on the alms cast into their bowls.

Still, ever and anon the names of afflicted cities grew closer, more familiar. So the Council of Ten proclaimed the interdict. Our merchant galleys were laid up and their crews discharged. Arriving ships were quarantined off Lazzaretto Vecchio, fumigated with sulfur and antimony. No one was allowed ashore until certified free of sickness. Our once-noisy wharves lay silent, save for the chants of priests swinging censers, praying for the whirlwind to obliterate foreign heretics instead of us.

One night, heading home from my mistress Maddelena's house, I noticed a blackness looming off the embankment of the Riva ca' di Dio. I clutched my dagger, trusting to my strength and size to deter footpads. Not a fingernail of moon, nor faintest star gave guidance as to where was safest to tread. Only great caution kept me from pitching headlong into a canal.

I halted as a rancid, rotting stink swelled in from seaward, on a breeze that moments before had been fresh and clean. Yes, the canals stank, as did much else about our city. But this stench was more loathsome and repulsive; somehow *evil*. A corrupting reek beyond anything I'd ever scented.

A dark ship was ghosting on that breeze. I paused transfixed, and heard water rippling at the prow of a galley. She coasted in unlit, only the luffing of sails betraying her, and hove to. A spark kindled. Muffled voices gabbled in a strange tongue. I pressed my back to the wall behind me as wood thunked and boomed. I sidled along it, then ran toward the glow of a distant torch until I encountered a pier guard. He was bundled against the wind, shivering in his shack.

"A ship," I gasped. "Breaking the interdict. Making for the landing."

To my surprise he shrugged. "Cleared for entry, *Signore.*"

I frowned. "Pardon? The quarantine states—"

"It is licensed to pass. This single ship. Tonight."

Increasingly puzzled, I retraced my steps to the landing, where a dark bulk lay close alongside the mole. As I felt my way, tripping over one of the dock lines, something bumped my ankle. I kicked out. A satisfying thump was followed by a hiss, a muffled squeak. The rat I'd just booted scurried off into the night.

Amid the scrape and thud of boxes rose a familiar voice. I strode forward, gripping the hilt of my weapon. "Fortunato!"

"Is it you, Montresor? What an unexpected pleasure."

My friend threw back a cowl as someone kindled a torch. Its guttering illumination showed crates stacked on the pier. A horse-drawn cart, and two bravos engaged in loading it.

"What is this?" I demanded. "No ship may enter our harbor. That is the law."

"The *Signoria* made the law. They may also grant exceptions."

"What in these crates is so important you would risk the same fate as Constantinople?"

He bent and prised up a lid. Beneath it were coiled and layered dozens of scrolls and codexes. Even by torchlight it was clear they were ancient.

"Works of classical literature, sold by the dying monks of Byzantium." He brushed one with a reverent finger. "Macrobius, Ptolemy, Pomponio Mela, Psellus, Dioscorides. And others, unknown to us for a thousand years or more. Philological studies, commentaries, orations—a treasury of wisdom! Treatises on medicine, alchemy, geography, magic. Visit my library one day, old friend. Gold is not the only treasure to store up. And ignorance not the virtue the Holy See assures us it is."

He hoisted the last box into the cart. I stood bemused as it rattled off. A mate called down to cast off, so the ship could depart. The darkness returned, and at last I resumed my homeward way.

The onset of Venice's own disaster was signaled by a violent trembling of the earth, as the bells of St. Mark's Basilica pealed out a harsh, discordant chime.

The deaths began near the waterfront. At first grieving relatives carried coffins in traditional processions to our churchyards. But the contagion accelerated, until the tolling of bells was forbidden, so monotonous and unending had the clangor become. Hundreds fled into the *terrafirme*, as if Death could not follow one to the country.

The course of the disease was this. A man, woman, or child would wake healthy, but overcome by melancholia. Within hours they were seized by fever, which in a day or two led to delirium, a racking cough, difficulty breathing, and bloody sputum. Sweat, blood, tears, urine, vomitus all turned black and fetid.

Soon even the sufferer's closest relatives were seized with disgust and fear, turning away, abandoning the victim to his fate. Perhaps more terrifying still was a second form, which began with the discovery in groin or armpit of a small black carbuncle. These *gavoccioli*, as the commons called them, multiplied up and down the limbs, accompanied by intolerable pain. This too soon progressed to death.

The contagion continued week after week. Priests fell in the very act of lifting the Host during Mass. Physicians prescribed aromatics, but died in their turn as the wretches they attended breathed the miasmic vapor upon them. The taint drifted along our narrow, twisting canals. Day by day each citizen anxiously examined his body. Dreading the fatal stigmata, they all too often found it and, gripped with despair, renounced all hope. Abandoning their final hours to frantic drunkenness or fornicating as the greatest city on earth defecated its dead into charnel pits.

Even so, the bakers who escaped death continued to turn out loaves to sell. As I owned several barges, the *Signoria* asked me to arrange an emergency grain importation from Istria. Though also stricken, that region did not seem to have suffered as badly.

The evening before we were to sail I received another note from my old friend, requesting I visit at his scriptorium. Jesu be thanked, my own house had been spared. My little daughter and infant son were fretful at being prisoned indoors, but day after day had passed and our anxious inspections of their ivory limbs detected no signs. Leaving Lucrezia burning spikenard-scented candles to keep out the diseased air, I wended my way through deserted streets, cloak wrapped tightly, holding a sachet of ground cinnamon beneath my nose.

The door creaked open. Despite a fire smoking in a brazier the room was shrouded in darkness, and thick with an indescribable stench. A taper guttered on a table littered with unrolled parchments, their corners held down by tarnished brass and clay figurines or idols. Queer distorted shadows writhed on the walls.

At the table, bent like a hunchback, sat a cowled figure. It took me some moments to realize it was Ognibene Fortunato. Something glittered on his face: reading stones, beans of clear glass set in a wire frame, which some affected to improve eyesight. His head was lowered, and through thinning hair gleamed pale scalp. He glanced up, then was seized by a sudden fit of coughing. "*Ugh . . . ugh.* Is that you, Montresor?"

"*Si.*" My voice was too rough, so I adopted a more emollient note. Until the time of my revenge I must present a smiling face. "In these dark days, I rejoice to see you in health. What wouldst thou have of me, old friend?"

He gestured at the scroll before him and croaked, "Read."

One hand on the hilt of my rapier, I peered down.

"It was in one of the boxes from Byzantium. You can see?" he muttered.

I moved the candle closer to the smudged lines of ancient text. A coldness ran up my back, but not because of anything I read. The parchment was indecipherable, just meaningless squiggles. "You paid good money for this nonsense?"

"Ignoramus!" he snapped. "It's Arabic script. This manuscript is what we scholars call a ghost book. Men have argued for centuries over whether it even exists. I've seen a few references in murky works of alchemy, but never expected to hold it in my hands. Here. I've copied out the opening sentences into something more accessible to one untutored in the Semitic."

The next sheet he pulled over was in Greek, lettered in his own calligraphy, to judge by the scant fluid in his inkwell. I bent closer, catching my breath as the stench assailed me. It smelled as if he were rotting where he sat, dissolving into corruption. "By Christ's bowels," I muttered, "You had best see a tooth-puller."

"Shut up. Read."

"I'm trying to, but you know I was never—"

"Then listen! *Alithos, apokalepteta, EE aoinia zoe then katike sta heria ekeinou pou norizoume os Theo. EE alithinithename brisketai se mia Allee sphaira, pio skoteenon kai poli palioteron thenamion. . . .*"

Just as he'd always done in school, the bastard was showing off.

I spread my hands and shrugged.

He rolled his eyes, heaved a sigh, and gave it to me in Italian. "Truly is it revealed, eternal life resideth not in the hands of the one we know as God. True power lives in another realm, far darker and far more ancient. Some call them demons. Others style them the 'Old Ones.' But their real names must only be pronounced with exquisite precaution."

I recoiled. "Blasphemy! What heathen fabrication is this?"

Fortunato explained, "It purports to be an instruction manual by one Saracen named Abdul Al-Hazred, called by some 'the Mad.' Its Arabic title is Al Azif, which I take to mean something like 'the howling of demons'. If I interpret this introduction aright, it will provide trustworthy instruction for attaining or bestowing eternal life."

"Christ alone is the path to eternal life." I glanced toward the brazier. "Let us immolate this foulness, before the Inquisition hears of it."

I snatched the papers up. A sudden chill like a fistful of snow burnt my fingers, then a razor-edged icicle of infinite cold penetrated the length of my arm. It froze my bones to iron, up to the shoulder. There it hesitated for the fraction of a pulse-beat, then darted downward, searching for my heart.

I nearly dropped the thing into the coals then. But even as my fingers loosened, suddenly I no longer wished to destroy it. Why, the very idea seemed insane. Indeed, I realized I would die to protect the scroll.

My grip tightened, snatching it from the flames at the last instant.

Simultaneously a new thought uncoiled within me. A knowledge suddenly discovered, like placing one's hand on a poisonous viper in a place once thought safe.

Anyone could drop a denunciation into the Mouth of the Lion. And the mere possession of a document such as this would doom the owner to the attentions of the *Domini Canes*, the Dogs of God. Their penalties ranged from confiscation of goods to grimmer pains such as the stake. I desired revenge; perhaps the instrument had just been vouchsafed into my hands.

I set the papers carefully back. "Truly, you intend to translate this. And do what with it?"

"All knowledge is useful," Fortunato observed, as he had on the quayside the night his ship arrived. "When we dispel the darkness, Man may truly see the universe about him."

"Or discover yet deeper darkness. Yet worse horror."

His sneer was like a suppurating wound. "Deeper than that which afflicts us now, in our terror and helplessness? Trusting to the intercession of the saints . . . who are all, by the way, themselves dead. In short, are we not already in the grasp of the evil one?"

This question I found myself unable to answer.

He tapped the scroll angrily. "If what the introduction says is true, this offers the ability to master the dead, and bring them back to a state resembling life. Obviously, it is too dangerous for translation into the vernacular. But it might be safe in Greek. The original title is overly obscure; I would name it something more direct. Why, soon we could even be printing copies!"

Fortunato's nails scratched in erratic spasms at an ink-blotch on his throat. Or perhaps it was something else, black and swollen. The rotting stench grew stronger.

"What is 'printing'?" I asked. "No, never mind . . . you summoned me here. What is it you want?"

He sat back. A cesspit foulness welled up from his garments until I could scarce breathe. He muttered, "I value the advice of an honest man."

"Go on," I urged, while in my heart I brooded on his destruction.

"You are right, this may be dangerous. On the other hand, it may simply reveal why its author was called The Mad."

"There would only be one way to find out," I said.

And the snake uncoiled in my soul.

"I trust you, Montresor. In some ways, you're a better man than I. Badly lettered, and without imagination. But still, possessing a certain peasant integrity." He lifted the manuscript with a sigh, weighing it. "What say you, old friend? Preserve . . . or destroy?"

The insult stung like a wasp. How dare he call me peasant, with generations of Montresors entombed beneath our ancient palazzo?

"No," I said, and the serpent lifted its head. Its tongue flicked out, the eyes blazed lapis fire. "You must translate it, Fortunato. Essay its spells. And tell me what you discover."

I sailed for Ischia the next dawn. We coursed on a fair wind, alone on the sea, and for once feared neither pirate nor Saracen. Fourteen rowers died during the voyage, though.

Others fell ill too, back in our city, though I did not yet know. And I was not with them.

Our return was delayed by contrary winds. It took a week to beat back by sail, but we were too short of hands to row. Flying the flag that proved we had clearance to land, we put in to a ghostly-silent Arsenal. But no linehandler came out to berth us. The shiphouses were vacant, the hulks deserted, the stone quays littered with dead rats and dogs. I went ashore to seek out those to whom the grain should be delivered, but found their offices untenanted as well.

A shudder shook me. Had the pestilence left me, alone, alive in the city? I ran through deserted, echoing streets. Jumped down into a drifting gondola, and sculled desperately for home. At last I stood before our palazzo, unable to speak. Staring at sloppily-laid bricks and mortar built up to block our front door. A black cross was painted over the masonry.

Someone cackled behind me, and I turned.

A crone out in the street leaned on a bent stick.

"What means this, old woman?" I demanded, gripping my sword-hilt. "In the name of the blessed Saints, what happened here?"

"They are entombed." She cocked her head like a crow. In her great age, she was clearly touched in the head. A cretin, a true child of God.

"Entombed," I repeated stupidly.

"By order of the *Signoria*. Where the plague enters, that house must be walled up."

Entombed. Now the word echoed like the boom of a prison door. "But there was no plague here," I protested. "We were free of sickness!"

"Perhaps when you deserted them. But now they are vomiting black bile. Pustules cover their breasts. They cough blood, writhe in their shitty sheets—"

She shrieked as I knocked her down into the gutter. "Sick, deformed hag! The Devil speaks through your rotting tongue."

She cursed me back, forking two fingers in the sign of witching. "I lie not, and may dog-worms devour your festering cock!"

Ignoring her babble, I stared at the masonry blocking the door. God help me, the bricks were impressed with the Montresor seal. *A foot crushing a serpent, whose fangs are embedded in its heel.* I hammered with my dagger's hilt, but the mortar had set hard. I succeeded only in breaking my weapon. I called out then, circling the house.

The upstairs windows were open, but no voice gave reply.

I must've lost my head for a time, because the world seemed to go dark. Some time later I found myself arguing frenziedly with the warden of the *sestier.* Pushing gold into his hands, which he thrust back as violently. Finally I threatened him with my rapier.

"Put that away, *signore,*" he kept repeating. "It was an order. I had to obey."

A new blaze of darkness. I came to again slamming a bronze knocker on a familiar door. At last it creaked open, and I was face to face again with the man who had forestalled my election, cheated me of my land. And now, walled up my family alive.

"Stay," he commanded in an iron voice, though not to me. I turned to see a trooper in armor behind me, sword half drawn. "It is only a friend, bereft and lost."

"As are so many," grated the man-at-arms.

"Quite true. Come in, sweet Montresor. Take a glass of Medoc. You're here about your house. Your wife and child."

"*Children.* They've been entombed! Walled up like corpses."

He shook his head sadly. "By order of the Council of Ten, on the advice of the most learned physicians. The only way this plague may be contained."

"They don't answer. They may already be dead."

"They may yet live. Only your daughter was visibly infected. No one is walled up without being provided bread for many days. We are not Turks."

My little girl, my beautiful Camilla of the chestnut hair. I sank to my knees, weeping. With shaking hands I offered him ducats. They fell from my fingers and rolled ringing across the marble floor.

Noble Fortunato only looked away. For the first time I noticed his skin was spotless now; that he stood erect and hale. But . . . surely he had been very ill, when I left?

He patted my head. "You must take this stroke like a man. God has forgotten his servants. I lost my Vera, as well."

"Your lady wife, dead?"

"She lies lifeless, all her beauty fled." When I squinted up, grief was graven into his visage.

He began to speak, as halting as a stammerer. "What . . . price would you give, good Montresor, to have them back? Your dear Lucrezia . . . your daughter, your son?"

"Anything, Ognibene! All I have."

"As would I, my friend. But God has forgotten us." He shook his head. "Abandoned children, we wander crying out for whatever power may yet send aid."

What power is that, I might've asked then. And perhaps even gotten an answer.

It took most of the night to dig through into my wine cellar, hewing a tunnel beneath two of the colossal supports of the catacombs. Wending my way with a candle through galleries strewn with the bones of Montresors past, I emerged at last at the archway that led up from the vaults. Here, in the suite of rooms where the laughter of my children used to echo, all was hushed save for the skittering claws of a rat. Across the threshold lay the decaying body of our orange cat, mouth a rictus, stretched out in rigid death-agony. Pools of black fluid seeped from its tail and mouth. Stepping across, I shouted for my family.

The only answer, a rhythmic reverberation I slowly realized was merely the beating of my own hideous heart.

They were dead, all dead. Twisted together on the same great bed in the same darkened room. Lucrezia's face, though swollen and empurpled, looked the freshest. She'd clung to our children even after their passing. The stench was a solid thing, walling me off from them with such terror I dared not enter. Only crouch, groaning, tearing out my hair, cursing myself. How could I have abandoned them? They'd died alone, without even being shriven. Walled up alive, condemned by order of a man who had so often called himself my friend.

Seizing a heavy chair, I kicked and battered down the brickwork at the front door from within. Then staggered forth to see ragged lepers with cloths tied over their mouths carrying corpses from adjoining houses. A sickly nag swayed between the shafts of a cart into which they threw shrouded bundles. A smoky pall hung over the nearest canal.

I lifted my fists to the sky, and the evil uncoiled, like a basilisk emerging from the egg. For it was then I swore to obtain the ultimate degree of revenge.

The night had shielded me from the worst sights when I'd landed, but by day it was clear all litanies and processions, promises and precautions had been in vain. Bodies lay stacked five deep in the squares. Bloated corpses floated in the canals. A few emaciated men straggled by, some carrying heavy wooden crosses, others lashing their bare backs with knotted cords as they staggered and chanted. The youngest one dropped even as they marched, gripping his throat. His eyes rolled upward. He gagged out blood, convulsed, and rolled into the canal with a splash.

I staggered along, numb under the blows of Heaven. A bird dropped from the sky into my path, and I stepped around it. Wailing rose from the doomed city like that of the condemned falling to the Inferno imagined by the Tuscan poet.

I emerged into another square where barges were being loaded. Masked workers tossed corpses in to sprawl on one another. The last landed atop the heap and rolled down, sheet unwinding, revealing a tumble of blond curls above a blackened face.

My mistress, Maddelena.

I flinched as someone grasped my elbow. "Signor Montresor? So you yet live."

I turned from the barge with a shudder, recognizing one of my masons, a cloth tied over his nose and mouth. "Benedetto. What is this? These are our barges!"

He glanced about warily. "Yes, signor. It is the only business to be had, now. We take gold for burials in consecrated ground. But instead we must pole out into the lagoon, and dump the bodies at sea."

I could not believe my ears. For decades the name Montresor had stood for honest dealing. Value for value. "What chicanery! Who has put you up to such wickedness?"

He turned his palms upward. "The Signor from the Council. Your friend Fortunato. He said your family were all dead, and showed us a paper. It stated he was your heir."

I began to say we would dump no more corpses into a sea that provided us sustenance, trade, wealth. Then thought again. Had not Heaven itself abandoned us? The snake writhed in my heart, and I shouted, "He lies, for I still live. The gold will go to me, not to Fortunato!"

Guidecco knuckled his forehead. "As you say, *signore*." He paused, frowning, staring at my neck. Then bowed, crossed himself, and backed a few steps away.

"What is it?" I blinked, and the world suddenly swam. Feeling faint, I touched my fingers to the spot where he had stared. There it was: the first hard, knotlike pustule.

I do not recall how I made it home, but somehow I did. To lie for long days alone in the soiled bed wherein my family had died. I screamed and cried, to think my life was ending. And how, since I was unshriven of so many sins, only Hell awaited.

I do not know how or why I lived, either. But at length the horrible buboes burst, oozing corruption onto the sheets, accompanied by stabbing pain. I wept and screamed again, cursing God. Perhaps only the thirst for vengeance kept me alive. But after many days I was able to stagger from the bedroom, gnaw a crust of hard cheese, and drink off a bottle of sour wine I found in the pantry.

At long last, after weeks of horror, the deaths slackened. Perhaps the miasma had drifted on. Or perhaps enough had finally suffered to sate an angry God. Who can say? But gradually men voiced a tentative hope, glancing fearfully at the sky. The Bishop announced a high Mass to celebrate our deliverance and renew our vows. Heaven had seen fit to show mercy at last. Venice vowed not to forget; to henceforth walk in sobriety and virtue.

I was taking a gondola to Cannaregio to see if Heshamet had survived, when my eye was caught by a cantering horse. A white one, on which a veiled woman rode, a guard trotting close behind. The steed looked familiar. Was it not one of Fortunato's? As we passed each other, she threw back her veil.

I stared dumbfounded at sparkling black eyes, a bold gaze, and a swarthy, surpassingly lovely countenance. Then the veil twitched back into place, and she rode on.

Lady Vera. But . . . Ognibene had told me she was among the dead. With my wife, my children, my mistress, and so many others. So how was it that Signora Fortunato could be well and hearty, riding a pale steed?

I ordered the gondolier to circle back, but he was slow and clumsy. By the time we retraced our course she'd turned a corner and vanished. I stared after the apparition, with wild surmises. Could it be true, what I suspected?

Two more weeks passed, and the sickness did not return. Had perhaps burned itself out, like a fire in a grainfield meeting bare ground. And, like mice after just such a storm, the people crept out from their homes. Perhaps only half the citizens we'd counted before. Shaken, dumb, we wandered the empty streets, avoiding one another. For in days past even to grasp a hand meant inviting the embrace of Death. The Council announced a public day of thanksgiving, followed by our traditional Carnevale, held as usual on Shrove Tuesday. This year the wine and sweetmeats would be funded by the treasury.

I understood; a celebration was necessary to restore the spirits of those who'd survived.

Yet my own spirits needed no kindling, for an inferno still burned in my breast. I would be avenged! Yet how, when, if my suspicions were true, the one who had done me so many injuries had ferreted out the secret of frustrating Death itself?

It was after dusk, that first evening of the masking and dancing, that I finally encountered my friend once again.

Ognibene Fortunato accosted me with excessive warmth, for he had drunk much after being appointed Lord of Revels. He wore motley; tight-fitting parti-colored dress, and on his head the conical cap and bells.

I was so pleased to see him I thought I should never be done wringing his hand. "My dear Fortunato, you are luckily met. How remarkably well you look today."

And it was so. The black stains on his skin I'd noted earlier were gone. The thinning hair had come back thick and dark. His unlined skin looked fresh as a girl-child's. Thus were my darkest suspicions confirmed at last. He'd spoken the dread words that consigned his soul to the demon, but his body to youth and everlasting life.

"'Tis true," he slurred, staggering so with inebriation that I had to catch him. "I *am* looking remarkably well."

"Do I mistake myself, or did I not see the Lady Vera out and about some days ago, too? Looking for all the world as lovely as the day you married."

Fortunato bent and produced a cough. "*Ugh—ugh—ugh.*"

"A nasty catarrh you have there," I noted.

"It is nothing. Mold from my manuscripts, I think. Yes, my lady is well now. Very well indeed."

Neither by word nor deed did I give him cause to doubt my good will. I continued to smile in his face. Of course he could not perceive my smile *now* was at the thought of his immolation. "Yet you told me she was dead, old friend."

He drew me aside, and in a low voice asked once again, "What would you give to bring back your daughter, your son, your wife?"

"I mourn them still. But their souls are now God's."

"So the priests say. But if they lie?"

"Then still it is better they be dead than alive, if their souls are the Devil's."

Fortunato laughed, and coughed again. "Yet think on it, *amico mio*. What could one not do with unending life?"

I smiled again. "Perhaps the question should be, what would *you* do, my oldest and very dearest of friends?"

"Why, read the books," Ognibene said. Some of the wine-vapors seemed to lift then. He looked past me, blinking as if close to tears. "*All* the books, in every tongue. What else would be worth the sacrifice of my soul? I'd translate them, then condense all I have learned. I would create . . . an encyclopedia. Containing all knowledge, all philosophy, natural history, rhetoric, mathematics. Make it available to all. You ask, what will *I* do? Free mankind from ignorance forever, Montresor!"

I was barely listening to these drunken mutterings. Free mankind, indeed! I had long since determined to kill him, to avenge the thousand injuries suffered at his hands. But, how to murder one who is no longer mortal? What revenge could be taken on such a monster?

This puzzled me. Until, pondering, I understood at last what I must do.

I seized his shoulder, bent close, and murmured with surpassing charm, "My dear old friend. I have received a pipe of what passes for Amontillado, and yet I have my doubts."

Many years from now in some far-off country, perhaps another pen more skillful than mine will take up my tale, casting it as a fiction. Recounting how I tempted the drunken Fortunato to my home, and led him beneath my palazzo, through nitred passages of great antiquity, chaining him in a niche cleared of the bones of my ancestors. And therein bricked him up, with the trowel and mortar I had left earlier to accomplish the deed.

Yet all is not yet told. For as I abandoned my former friend Ognibene Fortunato there, entombed alive much as he had entombed my beloveds, a faint jingling still echoed from within. For he lived, of course, and would live on and on.

"For the love of God, Montresor," he cried out, then laughed like a madman.

"Yes," I agreed, turning away. "For the love of God."

And through the gift and curse of his evil book, I do not doubt but that he liveth inside there still. No mortal has disturbed him now for fifty years. I filled in the staircase with solid stone, and led a pipe from the canal to conduct water into the catacombs to fill his living tomb.

Alas, I have no heirs, and my palazzo decays. When I pass away it may be torn down, and some new edifice reared upon its foundations. I shall be shriven, take to my grave, and abide with God. While Fortunato will rave tormented and alone, choking and drowning eternally, through endless centuries, until Christ himself descends at the End of Time.

And what of the work he called the *Necronomeikon,* the Book of the Imaging of the Dead? A mysterious blaze broke out in his scriptorium during the carnival. Sadly, his manuscripts seem to have vanished, down to the last scraps of Plato and Averroës.

I do know now what 'printing' means, though. A German has lately set up a press in our city, and advertises for manuscripts, so he can make their writers famous and rich.

I saw Lady Vera several times after that, over the years. She remained perpetually fresh and young. I smiled in her face, and flattered her, feigning affability. I doubted she misses her husband, though she sometimes wonders aloud what befell him that night of Carnevale. Of course, I have never told her.

And for the love of God, I never shall.

The scarf hanging from a hook on that antique hat rack looks so soft. Such an amazing variety of colors in the weave . . . like the shifting tones of a restless body of water. Now watch: unfold it, and the fabric is somehow much larger than it first appeared. There's a reason for that, and it's not only because we Italians know how to arrange any sort of clothing to stylish perfection. No doubt you've heard of the mermaid of myth and fairytale? A sea creature who appears in infinite incarnations all over the world. Venice's canals and bays also host such legendary sirenas. A few once had a connection to the Night Bazaar. But when the time came for us to move on to new cities, new times . . . these lovely creatures balked. Tied by family and tradition, most chose to remain in the waters of La Serenissima. Sometimes their songs drift from the canals at night. Occasionally one may still be glimpsed by the very observant late-night wanderer who lingers by certain bridges. But take care, gentle guest, ti prego. Don't stand so close to the stone edging just above the dark waters. For sometimes, that liminal space between our two worlds is uncertain, and has been known to move.

SIREN SONG

by Rebecca Lane

Maybe it was raining on this damp, gray day in Venice, but Ellie couldn't feel the drops. Had it been snowing, she wouldn't have cared. Today, like every other for the past year, she stood at the foot of the Bridge of Spires and watched the sunset, as sobs choked her lungs and stole her voice. Scooping her hollow, curved miserably in upon herself.

How can I still be standing? she wondered.

Carlo had slipped through her fingers, like a handful of water scooped from the Cannareggio Canal, below.

Faintly, from several streets over, a song drifted across the water. Though she couldn't make out the words, Ellie shivered and reached up to grip a ring strung on the silver ball chain around her neck. The heavy gold band had been Carlo's. Though ancient, its warm glow hadn't faded, despite scratches, dents, even hints of engraved words on its outer curve. But the ring was too big for her fingers by far, so she kept it on the chain. Afraid even to use a brass sizer in case it slipped off and rolled away, lost forever in some dark Venetian alley.

When had she started walking the city again? And why, of all the bridges in Venice, had Ponte delle Guglia become her place of vigil? They'd rarely come here together, yet for some reason this place *felt* like him. Maybe it was the old bakery around the corner that made the brioche and the hazelnut coffee he drank each morning. Or the pleasantly rough feel of the seawall's stones under her hands. The singing gondoliers, or the hollow knocking of the moored boats bumping the docks. Something here was more like him than anywhere else in Venice.

If Carlo were to rise from the dead, surely this would be where he'd do it.

The dark water below shimmered and rippled as if spattered with rain. Farther out, the Grand Canal spread like an ocean. Each day she came to watch the tide flow out past her, into the tumultuous *bacino* where shallow waters mixed with deep, hoping to feel a little grief flow away with them. But the ache and agony only deepened. Her cheeks were always wet, her hands icy. But then, she no longer felt warmth or life, so why would she notice the cold?

Someone touched her arm. "Drink this. It'll warm you."

Ellie blinked and looked down. Her eyes widened. Suddenly she was cradling a white china mug of steaming coffee. Its heat through the ceramic was shocking at first, but she welcomed the pain. How wonderful to able to feel something!

A young woman stood next to her, looking expectant.

Ellie blinked. "Sorry. Did you say something?"

The woman's brown eyes twinkled as she smiled. Her damp brown-black hair was pulled into a braid that draped over one shoulder; a small watermark stained her shirt there.

So it *is* raining, Ellie thought, and reflexively tucked a blond lock behind one ear. But the strands felt dry.

"I said, looks like you need some coffee." The young woman's Italian accent was faint, somehow a little off. Another transplant who'd stayed so long she'd almost become part of the stonework.

Ellie gazed down again, as if the mug was a foreign object. "I . . . thanks. But I don't remember—"

"Oh, I got it for you. Had to pry your hands off the railing to make you take the cup. You're half frozen, honey." She took Ellie's arm and led her toward a café a few paces from the bridge. "It's warmer in there. Come on."

"But I don't know even you." Ellie reluctantly took a sip as they walked.

"*Non importa.* I know you. You've come here every day the past two weeks just to watch the water." She drank from her own cup. "I'm Rosa. I work here."

She jerked her head toward the brightly-lit restaurant.

"Caffe del Doge," Ellie read aloud, staring up at the painted sign above the door.

Rosa grimaced. "Sure, not the most original name. But the coffee's good and we have a great baker." She opened the weathered, blue-painted door. "And it's warm inside."

The aromas of yeast and cinnamon, butter and sugar woke Ellie's stomach. Which commented with a growl loud enough to wake the gargoyles on the Guglia bridge.

"Wow. When did you eat last?" Not waiting for an answer, Rosa stepped behind the glass case, and set an orange cranberry scone on a thick white saucer. "Sit down. Sit!"

Ellie reached for her wallet, but Rosa waved her off. "Nah. On the house."

The still-warm scone crumbled as Ellie took a bite. Grated orange and cranberry tasted sharp and sweet at the same time.

Rosa grinned. "Good?"

"Very good. Thanks again." She hadn't meant to talk with her mouth full, and patted the crumbs away with a linen napkin.

Rosa sat, too, and picked up a glass shaker of cinnamon. She sprinkled some into one palm, and poured that into her own coffee. "So," she said, without looking up. "What happened to you?"

Ellie tensed and took another sip of latte. It always hurt to say the words. "He . . . died." She pointed at the café's front window. "Right over there."

"Gods, I'm so sorry." Rosa patted her hand.

"He . . . he had something . . . maybe an aneurism . . . while leading a ghost tour. He fell into the canal. They never found the body. I guess the tide . . . there wasn't even a funeral."

"Oh no! I'm so sorry."

"Thanks, but why do you care?" It sounded harsher than she'd intended. "Sorry. I meant, well, you don't really *know* me. Oh, I'm so bad at this. It's been... a long time since I talked to anyone. I may have forgotten actual manners."

Rosa smiled. "No worries. It's OK." She looked thoughtful. "I care because . . . hmm. Well, you seemed nice and looked sad. It's cosmic, right? Or maybe karmic. We're connected and all. I mean, pain and loss shouldn't go unacknowledged. No one should have to mourn alone. Especially . . ." She glanced down at the ring on Ellie's necklace.

Ellie frowned. "Especially what?"

"When something could be done about it." Rosa gave a casual shrug, took another sip, and made a face. "Ugh. Cold coffee. Freshen yours while I'm up?" She crossed to the counter for a refill, and brought back two sugar cookies. "I hate to pry, but was that his? The ring, I mean."

"Yeah. He said it looked better on me. It's been in his family for a long time." She absently spun it on the chain. "Carlo collected stuff. Rings. Books. Lost girls." She tried to smile, but her lips trembled.

"May I?"

Ellie reluctantly handed the ring to Rosa. She hadn't taken the chain off since Carlo died.

"Feels familiar, doesn't it?" Rosa turned it over, tracing the markings. "Oddly . . .warm. Like you're still wearing it." She handed it back.

Ellie slipped it back on the chain. "Never thought about that before, but yeah. It's always warm. Especially right around the engravings."

Rosa looked up again. "If I could help, would you come?"

Ellie frowned. "What do you mean?"

"Look, there's this place. Really, it's a smaller version of an old medieval bazaar, but I'm thinking maybe someone there would recognize your ring. And consider it, like, your free admission. The people who run it . . . they like oddities, rare stuff. And that looks like the rarest of the rare. Whatever you want, whoever—alive or dead—well, you could probably ask for it there."

Ellie stared at her, incredulous. "Are you saying I could actually *see* him again?"

Rosa nodded. "Maybe only briefly. But it's worth a try, right? Meet me here at midnight, I'll take you. Make sure to wear the ring."

Ellie swallowed hard. And without any more thought, blurted out, "I'll be there."

Back at her flat, she squinted against the light in the foyer. It's too bright in here, she thought. Even though it was overcast outside.

When she sank into Carlo's old overstuffed armchair, dust clouds puffed up around her. She no longer had the heart to clean. There was too much of him still here. At first, she'd tried to go through his things. Empty the closets, give his clothes to the mission or one of the other charities in the city. But whatever she touched—a sock, a shirt, a sweater—his smell of lime cologne and leather lingered. He'd held and used that toothbrush; how could she simply throw it away? So even a year later, the flat still looked like two people occupied it. Each morning she put on the coffee, and set out two mugs. Hers with a Manet painting, his with a map of Verona.

Then she'd sit at the table, drink coffee, and attempt once more to read the book on meditation her well-meaning friend Lyssa had sent. "Give it to God, Ellie," she'd said on the phone. "Send your grief out into the universe. Don't keep carrying him around. You have to move on."

But the book mostly remained unopened. Seed catalogs still cluttered the side table. They'd planned to start a garden in window boxes, but hadn't been able to agree on exactly what to grow. So they'd browsed until the season passed, then she'd given up and bought a planter of hanging wisteria. That'd died too. Her aloe plants and African violets withered in the windows; neglected, forgotten.

It was a small place, just two tiny bedrooms, plus bathroom, kitchenette, and parlor. The spare room had doubled as an office since there weren't many visitors. Ellie had lived in Venice now for three years. Her first year abroad turned into a second, then a third. Last Christmas her parents had posted her gifts from Connecticut, with a note saying they'd put all her things in storage. Whenever she asked for something, they mailed it over. But that was her old, past life. Venice had become the real one.

At first friends offered to visit, and some even made good on it. But her college roommate had written to her afterwards: *Wow, I barely recognized you! Living in Venice with such a handsome guy. So exotic. Jealous!*

If you grow to resemble the people you live with, Ellie apparently had begun to look like Venice to them. Strange, even 'exotic'. When old friends did visit, it was usually the last time she heard from them. They'd all acted uncomfortable around Carlo. Their visits less a hello, more a final goodbye.

He'd been a graduate student and TA at University Ca' Foscari, housed in a Venetian Gothic palace. She'd taken his history class there, then gone on one of the ghost tours of the city he conducted every week. That had been her first Halloween in Venice, and she'd marveled at the costumes and fantastic masks. He had worn one too; a fox face that looked so real and expressive she'd gasped. He loved to walk the city telling obscure anecdotes about things that'd happened centuries ago on some particular corner. Or old ghost stories attached to some ancient bridge or palace. "Playing tour guide lets me share the colorful bits of history I've collected. Every bridge has a romance, every canal its fascinating tragedy."

When the rest of the ghost hunters went home after the tour, Ellie had stayed on. They'd walked the city until dawn. Something they continued doing the next two years; crossing bridges, checking out narrow, winding alleys, looking for more stories. On one infamous corner, where a 14th century *bravo* had died in a sword fight, Carlo had suddenly proposed. Without an engagement ring—there would never be time to choose one of those, as it turned out—but the question had been raised, and she'd said yes.

"I can't wait to introduce you to my family," he'd said, and pulled her to him for a kiss.

So it was all unofficially official. Until suddenly it wasn't, and she was left alone in a nameless limbo: No funeral. No body. He was just . . . gone. And she remained in this familiar but still foreign place, drifting without an anchor.

Perhaps she'd feel different tonight, though. Less lost. On a ghost tour of her own devising.

Like every city, Venice each night slipped out of its cheerful, practical, everyday dress, and into something a little more revealing. More mysterious. Floral prints and ballet flats were traded in for sequins, black dresses, and tall high heels. Shops whose windows lit up like smiling eyes in the daytime were closed, dark, even scowling. People spoke differently too; voices quieter, more intimate. Save, here and there, for an occasional loud burst of laughter, or a heated argument in an alley echoing off the ancient stones.

After wondering what exactly one wore to a secret bazaar, she'd pulled on a sweater over her T shirt and jeans, and tied on a pair of old sneakers over bare feet. "Always opt for comfort and function," she'd muttered, knotting the laces. Then, if things went south, she could run. High heels got caught between cobblestones. Sequins and silk weren't the warmest in November.

She arrived back at the Ponte Della Paglia at a quarter to midnight. A sleepy, distant accordion was wheezing slowly through a waltz : *1* . . . *2* . . . *3, 1* . . . *2* . . . *3*. A dancing couple glided across the stone platform near the bridge.

A red-haired woman draped in scarves and bracelets sat hunched near the entrance to the Caffe del Doge. "On your way for the evening, *bella*?" she called.

Ellie smiled and nodded, in the polite way she'd been taught at her mother's side, back in New England. "Yes, I am. But…."

The crone smiled, revealing one gold tooth. "But you don't know where you truly go."

"N-no." She stammered. "I mean, yes. I think I do."

"No, you don't. I see what you wear." The woman looked her up and down, gaze settling on the ring around Ellie's neck. "I know what *that* is too. But you, my dear, have no idea. Come, sit. We can trade tales. I will tell your future."

Ellie glanced at her watch. Rosa wasn't due for another ten minutes.

The fortune teller smiled and knotted her long red hair into a loose bun. The silver, bronze, and gold bracelets stacked on her arms chimed like tiny bells. "Let's see your hand." She turned it palm up, so moonlight lit the lines and creases.

"It's a bit dark here." Ellie peered down, too. "Does it say anything interesting?"

"It shows possibilities. Darkness reveals things that otherwise go unseen. And it's the best light to see someone by, the moon." The fortune teller leaned closer and turned the hand until moonlight and streetlamps highlighted the lines and grooves of her palm so starkly they looked like crevices and ravines.

Out on the canal, the same moonlight danced across the surface in bright broken shards. A gondolier rowed past. And . . . wait a minute. She frowned. A pale face had surfaced alongside the boat. Then it disappeared again. A scalloped fish-tail easily a three feet across slapped the water.

"Is something wrong, dear? What did you see?" The fortune teller murmured, though she never looked up from Ellie's lifeline.

"N-nothing! I mean, I thought for a second, but . . . no." Suddenly she wanted her hand back. "Sorry, I'd better be going. My friend's a little late. But you said you knew where I was headed? Like, you recognized me?" She pulled away and shoved her hand in one pocket.

"Not you, *Cara*. The ring. Centuries ago, it would've been an invitation to enter a secret marketplace."

"Someone else told me the same thing. What do you know about it?"

"That was very long ago, in 1348. And the real Night Bazaar only comes once, to any place." The woman flapped a hand dismissively. "Now there's a small festival here, of sorts. A borrowed version. Hardly the same thing! Still, they like to say whatever you want, whether you know it or not, will be there." She pursed her lips skeptically.

Anything I want, thought Ellie. Anything at all. . . .

"It's over that way." The fortune teller inclined her head towards a narrow alley. "Between the gargoyles. But watch the edge of the canal. It moves sometimes, you know."

Ellie turned to look that way. "It *moves*. You mean the stones? What does that mean?" But when she turned back, the woman was gone.

At the entrance of the alley, the carved gargoyles' toothy gray-stone smiles looked so devious, she didn't even want to walk between them. But the trilling of a flute drifting down from the other end lured her in. Soon she was surrounded by a whole tapestry of sounds: breathy accordions and shrill violins whined a slow love song. Conversations whispered from dark alcoves. The smells were so numerous she couldn't place them all. Myrrh, amber, sandalwood, Patchouli, Cinnamon. Foreign and mysterious, exactly the way the Silk Road must've smelled. Mingled with the murky, salty, slightly fishy scent of some nearby canal; such a heady, intoxicating mix, soon Ellie felt a bit drunk.

Then the alley suddenly opened up before her into a *palazzo*: a walled town square. Decorated with so many colors they seemed to explode like fireworks in the dark: burgundy tents, violet buntings hung in doorways and windows. Green and blue caravan shops crowded the edges, as vendors and barkers hocked their wares.

No one else seemed to have come alone, though. She caught snatches of conversations from couples and groups as she strolled past. One vendor called out, "What do you want, *molto bella*? Jewels for your pretty neck?" A harlequin contortionist dangled gems knotted on threads—diamonds, rubies, sapphires—the glittering strands dripping, cascading like water to the cracked cobblestones. "Or silks for your dresses?"

Ellie reached out and a Mandarin-style dress appeared, hanging from an ornate hook on the beam of one stall, its vivid plum-purple ripe as the fruit. The fine, thin fabric slipped through her fingers like water.

"Beautiful. But I'm just looking."

The harlequin's smile faded when he glanced down at her ring. "Ahh. Special night for you, then. I give special price to go with it."

She hesitated. But where would she wear such a dress? To water her dead plants? "No, thank you—"

Someone bumped into her from behind, and she stumbled back into the flow of the crowd. Every place she looked, things were happening. Love, sex, food, drugs, drink. Bacchus would be proud. Proud? He'd be smack in the middle, king of all the revelry.

She paused beside a fountain, feeling overwhelmed.

"You look lost," said a man sitting at a tall cafe table near the water. Beneath his ink-black jacket the collar of a snow-white shirt was unbuttoned. His dark hair looked tousled, as if he'd just gotten out of bed. And in his hair . . .

She looked more closely, and flinched. Were those *horns?* The tiny curved protrusions almost concealed in the coal-smoke curls. Part of a costume, she decided at last. Everyone else was wearing one.

"Greetings, *bella.*" His voice floated easily above the noisy chaos as he waved her over to the table. "Please, sit."

She nodded and took the tall cafe chair opposite his, relieved to escape the stifling crowd for a moment. "Thanks. I was invited here, sort of, but . . . my host never showed. Anyhow, I'm pretty sure. . . ." She looked around again, and swallowed. "Pretty sure I don't belong." A tear trickled down her cheek. "It was foolish to come. I should've known better."

"*Triste piccolo.* Sad little one, what makes you say that?" He passed a burgundy silk handkerchief across the table and smiled again, his teeth very white, the incisors slightly pointed. "Sit and talk a while. Wine, coffee?"

Why not, she thought. Where else do I have to be? "Water. No, wait please . . . how do you say it? *Acque minerale gassate.*"

He raised an eyebrow. "Mineral water. That's all?"

Ellie sighed. "See? Even my drink choice is wrong. Boring. I don't fit in here." She turned away and looked out over the canal, where ripples congregated at the surface. The water shivered like the skin of a living creature; like a horse's hide shooing a fly. "The edge moves, you know," she whispered.

He frowned. "*Scusi?*"

She shook her head. "Just something I heard once."

"So, who did invite you? We like to keep track of such things."

Rosa, thought Ellie. Who stood me up. For some reason she didn't want to admit she'd been fooled into this. Whatever *this* was.

The waiter arrived with a tray. He set a tall narrow glass of water in front of her, then served her companion one full of a thick-looking scarlet liquid.

The man sipped daintily, closing his eyes, clearly savoring the taste.

"It was Rosa," she said reluctantly. "Who works at the Caffe del Doge. She said I looked sad, that maybe coming here could help."

"Rosa, Rosa. . . ." he mused. "Ahh, yes. She's new. May need more training."

"So I am in the wrong place. I really don't belong here." Ellie bit her lip, fiddling with the ring on her chain, turning it over as the lamplight made the worn gold glow warmly. She took a sip of water, then scooted her chair back. "Thanks for the drink, but I should be going."

"*Aspettare.*" He held up a hand. "By the looks of that ring, you do belong. May I see it?"

Ellie sighed. "Why's everyone so interested?" She unfastened the chain and handed it over. Even this close she couldn't tell if his horns were tied on or somehow clipped into his hair. Whether they were porcelain, plastic, or... "Is it valuable or something?"

"Or something." He turned it over in his palm. "You don't know its story?"

"No. It's not really mine. I was supposed to get married, but . . . he died. It was his. Passed down from his mother or grandmother, he didn't remember exactly. It wasn't a real engagement ring. We never got to choose one of those."

"Oh, but it *is* very special. Worth more than all the blood diamonds in Africa. One of only seven crafted by the Honorable Kazim Ali, who learned from the metalsmiths of Venice's first Night Bazaar. The rings were given to some of the company's original . . . well, performers, you might call them. Your beloved's ancestors must've been one of them. These rings weren't bestowed lightly. Most have been lost over the centuries, but certain privileges are afforded if you possess one." He handed it back. "No, you are supposed to be here, *cara*. You just don't know *why* yet."

"Oh great. Another lost cause."

He shook his head, looking faintly amused. Then stood and stepped behind her chair, to clasp the chain around her neck. Now the ring hung near her heart again.

"What is your name?"

"My parents named me Eleanor. Just Ellie to everyone else."

"*Mi chaimao* Giancarlo."

"That was *his* name. Well, Carlo, I mean." She shrugged. "Of course, it's common enough here."

"*Sì.* Still I'm sorry to have reminded you of your grief. I've always thought Carlo a good name."

"I liked... like it very much." She blinked hard. "So, you've been with this bazaar a long time. What do you do here?"

He laughed softly. "Quite a while, yes. And I do whatever is *necessario.*"

She drew back. "How vague. Sounds a bit ominous, don't you think?"

"No, no. It is merely *flexible.* My task is to read people. To make sure they have a good time, are being seen to."

"Ah. Like me. So you're in customer service."

"Not quite. More a Master of Ceremonies. Or a concierge. Making sure things run *properly.* Yet I have not succeeded in this case. What're you looking for, *cara?* What do you *want?*"

This she did know. "To be able to sleep without nightmares. For the ache in my heart to go away. I want to feel peace..." She hesitated. "To be honest, I really just want him back."

"*That* I can do."

Before she could laugh or argue, he snapped his fingers. Three things appeared. A tapestry chaise longue, close enough to the canal's edge to dangle a hand into the water. A soft blanket with golden tassels. And a low table, which held a white cup and saucer, a wisp of steam hovering over it like a miniscule ghost.

Giancarlo took Ellie's hand across the metal tabletop, pulled her gently to her feet, and led her over. Smoothly as a dancer, he lowered her to the lounge. "Lie here. I'll tuck you in. Even sing a lullaby, if you like." He winked. "When you drift off, there will be no nightmares. Only sweet dreams. Only *peace.*"

He said nothing about bringing Carlo back, but she obeyed. Giancarlo handed her the warm cup full of thick hot chocolate.

She laughed. "Cocoa. Really?"

"To summon the sweet dreams, of course. My own recipe. Very old."

The chocolate was richer than any Ellie had ever tasted before. She quickly drained the cup, and handed it back. "Sorry." Her face felt hot. "I drank it too fast."

"*Nessun problema.* Now lie down." She obeyed like a biddable child. He spread the blanket over her, tucked in the sides, and covered her feet. "There. As you might say, snug as bugs in rug."

The weight of the blanket felt comforting, familiar. "You promised a song," she murmured sleepily.

His amber eyes glimmered. "*Certo*, I did." He stroked a lock of hair from her forehead, and she drifted even closer to sleep. "Any particular song, Eleanor?"

Her eyelids felt pleasantly leaden. Her mouth moved slowly to answer. "Just . . . something . . . nice."

"One of my favorites, then. By Yeats."

"That was . . . his favorite, too." Her words slurred slightly.

Giancarlo sang in a clear tenor, voice lulling her further into sleep.

> *To and fro we leap*
> *And chase the frothy bubbles,*
> *While the world is full of troubles*
> *And anxious in its sleep.*
> *Come away, O human child!*
> *To the waters and the wild*
> *With a faery, hand in hand,*
> *For the world's more full of weeping*
> *Than you can understand . . .*

The last line faded away. "Sleep well, Eleanor." His lips brushed her forehead. "I must go back to my work."

She didn't watch him go, feeling simply too tired to move. She only wanted to sleep, dreamlessly, curled under the blanket. Or better yet, to dream only of Carlo, alive again.

Sometime later she opened her eyes. The canal water below was stirring. Giancarlo's lullaby seemed to echo back from a long distance away. The watery ripples below opened like dark flowers as faces emerged, breaking the surface. Black eyes, pale blue skin, hair that flowed down long and straight as a wet veil, draping shoulders and chests.

It wasn't a dream.

Ellie gasped, and blinked. The apparitions submerged, vanishing with a flick of webbed, jagged fish-tails. One stayed a bit longer though, staring up. Smiling from beneath a familiar tangle of dark hair.

Her eyes widened. "Carlo!" She struggled to rise from the chaise, to reach for him.

The man in the water smiled, and pressed a finger to his lips. And then, as if he had hold of her shoulders, pressing her gently down, she sank back onto the chaise beneath the blanket.

"Good night, Carlo," she whispered. And thought, *Sweet dreams indeed. Let me never wake.*

A hand was gently shaking her shoulder. "Dearest *ragazza*, time to wake. Someone will miss you."

"No," Ellie moaned as a cold draft penetrated the warm blanket.

"It's still early. You can return to your apartment before anyone sees."

But why would that matter?

Ellie's eyes opened to a misty dawn. An older woman, hair streaked white and red, pulled a shawl more tightly around her shoulders. She was backlit by rosy morning light, a silhouette against the dawn. Her wrists chimed with jingling bracelets.

"Oh. Thanks. I didn't mean to actually fall asleep out here." Ellie's head was full of cobwebs. And music, and chocolate, and . . . mermaids?

"Of course. Who would ever mean to sleep out in the cold? But someone took good care of you. This is no trifle of a blanket."

Ellie looked down. Its heaviness surrounded her like a vast cocoon. Shards of colors were trapped in the fabric, which felt soft as a kiss. Her first good sleep in months, drifting off with Giancarlo's song in her ears.

"I fell asleep looking out at the water. And thought I saw... mermaids." In the light of dawn, this sounded totally ridiculous

The woman nodded. "The canals are hypnotic, are they not?"

"Wait." Recognition dawned on Ellie. "Weren't you here last night? You offered to read my palm." Yes. The scarves, the jingling bracelets, the thick red hair still straggling out of its loose bun.

"No, dearest. We haven't met. People do say I just have one of those faces."

Ellie combed her fingers through her own tangled hair, not sure she believed that. "Well, thanks for waking me." She stood, stretched, and folded the blanket over one arm. It smelled of spices and chocolate and smoke.

"*Un momento.* Before you go." The old woman touched her arm. "This is for you." She held out a Tarot card.

"Oh, I'd hate to take that and ruin your deck."

"Not mine. It was left here for you."

Even as Ellie touched its faintly damp edge, she knew the handwriting, the heavy black strokes scrawled across the back of the light blue card.

At Midnight –Carlo.

She turned it over again. On the verso a body was falling toward a moat from a tall castle turret.

"Where'd you get this?" Ellie's voice shuddered in her throat.

The woman shrugged. "I saw no face."

"Are you serious?" she snapped. Then took a deep breath, trying to calm herself. "Sorry, sorry. That was rude. But could you please tell me what it means? My Tarot is pretty rusty."

"Does a baker know how to read a recipe?" She leaned forward and studied the card. "It's The Tower, you can see. It means change is coming. Chaos. And of course, to be careful."

"Thank you," she said reluctantly, gazing down at the disturbing colored engraving. "And you're sure you don't remember where it came from? Who left it?"

But the old woman was already gone.

"What do you think happens after we die?" One of those questions everyone asks at some point, of a friend or lover. The kind whispered in the dark, when you are afraid perhaps to see the expression on the other person's face, or how more light might change the answer.

Ellie had asked it their first week living together in the apartment.

"Do we reincarnate on the wheel of life and hope we don't end up as an earthworm or a cockroach?" she'd asked Carlo. "Or become stardust and float off into space? Or maybe close our eyes and just sleep forever. I wonder if we'd still dream, though."

"I don't know what happens, Ellie."

"Would you want to come back?"

"Sure. Why wouldn't I?"

"Because you'd be in heaven with angels and harps. It's supposed to be so much better."

"Better than you?" He'd laughed and stroked her cheek, and she'd blushed. "I'll make you a deal," he added. "If I die first, if I can, I'll try hard to come back."

She frowned. "But how?"

He'd snorted at that. "Think I know? Who knows if there's even a place to come back from. Still, I swear I'll try. That's a pretty good deal, don't you think?"

She'd squeezed his hands. "And if I go first?"

"Then wait for me there. I'll catch up."

"But how'll I know it's you? If you're reincarnated, or whatever."

"Here." He'd pulled the heavy gold ring off his finger and pressed it into her hand. "This was my great-great-grandfather's, or maybe grandmother's. Anyway, passed down through our family for centuries. No one remembers exactly where it came from. But my mother always told me, 'Wherever you go, someone will know this ring.' "

He got up, rummaged in a drawer of his desk, and took out a thin, silver ball chain. He strung the ring, and hung it around her neck. "Consider it our password."

She still remembered that night, and the promise he'd made. And yet he'd left her, and not come back.

But tonight, I'll see him again.

An hour before midnight, she could wait no longer. Wrapping the blanket around her like a cape, she left the apartment and walked toward the bridge. At last she spotted the two gargoyles, and went down the alley, to the narrow dark entry to the little bazaar.

It was all the same: the booths, the people, the smells, the music.

"How'd you sleep last night?" Giancarlo was at the same table, drinking the same stunningly scarlet liquid. A glass of mineral water sat across from him, waiting for Ellie.

"Wonderful, thanks. I wanted to return this." She folded the blanket and held it out.

He held up both hands, warding her off. "No, no. It's yours now. Maybe you'll get cold."

She laughed. "I can't walk around Venice wearing a blanket. People will talk."

He laughed. "You Americans. So helpless when it comes to fashion." He took the cloth and folded it so quickly her eyes could hardly follow the movements. Soon it was the same length and width as a winter scarf. "There." He wrapped it around her neck, the fabric still soft as water, the weave as fluid.

Her fingers teased the fringe. She impulsively leaned forward to kiss his cheek, but paused halfway.

He smiled at her hesitation. "So, Eleanor. What shall it be tonight? Thrilling moments of sin? The safety of anonymous love? To see what your future holds?"

She shook her head. "Just to see him again, even for a moment. But you knew that."

"To be fair, I did. But it's proper protocol to ask. I've a place already set up." He brushed back his curls, exposing the horns for a moment. Small and curved, dark brown, scored with rings like a tree.

She followed to the edge of the canal, where a gondola bobbed at the pier. The music and laughter of the Bazaar sounded muffled the moment she stepped down into it.

"Now then, let's tuck you in." He unfolded the scarf again, covering her as he had the night before. "And this, to warm you from within." He handed down a mug of Murano glass, the Garden of Love pattern, filled with hot chocolate. And a small basket of grapes, as well. "I take good care of my favorites."

Ellie looked around. "Where's the gondolier?"

"You worry too much, Eleanor." He untied the line, grasped the tall curved stern, and pushed the gondola into the canal. Beneath his hands the lacquered wood there glowed red gold for a moment. "Only say where you want to be, and it goes to that spot. But ask nicely. We don't like rudeness."

She frowned. "Who is 'we'?"

He merely smiled and waved her off. The gondola glided on, oarless, unmanned, to the center of the canal. Giancarlo called, "See? You're safe in my hands, above or below. I won't be far."

Above or below. What did that mean? Ellie leaned back on the upholstered bench. Water lapped the painted hull, chuckling, whispering to her: secrets, songs, snatches of poems. The liquid world was never really quiet. *Hush hush, shh shh*, it murmured. The mug was so hot it almost burned her palms, but so what? Let it sting. How wonderful to feel things again! She'd been numb far too long.

Let this night wake me up for good, she thought.

"Is this seat taken?"

She turned toward the voice and gasped. "Carlo!"

"It's good manners to invite a guest in to sit. Somehow all your American etiquette never taught you that." He stood next to the gondola as if they were out on the street. But how was that possible? Was there some sort of ledge or platform under the water?

She was too scared to lean over and look down, for fear of tipping the boat.

He wore what she'd seen him in last: a black T-shirt and sodden blue jeans. His hazel eyes glinted in the dark, his brown hair curled damply at the neck and temples. She'd often run her hands through those curls, catching her fingers in the tangles. "Elf locks," she used to scold. "You're hopeless at grooming." She'd known every inch of him so well.

"But you can't be here. You died, and left me!"

"I can, Ellie. Because you *asked* me to come. Because I promised. Even death can't separate us, for long." He drummed his fingers on the gunwale, as if impatient.

It really was Carlo. Why hesitate over a few strange questions, when so many other stranger things had already happened? "Please, yes. Come on, climb in." She leaned toward him. The gondola rocked alarmingly, but righted itself quickly, as if steadied by invisible hands.

She grabbed Carlo's hands once he was in the boat, and pressed them to her cheeks, to soak up the feeling of his *realness*. They weren't icy cold, but not warm either. More like a spring evening, like staying in the pool too long, just before your lips turn blue. She kissed the palms whose lines she had traced a thousand times, the fingers she'd intertwined with hers. "It's you. Oh Carlo, it's really *you*."

A pale line interrupted the tan on his ring finger, the same width as the gold band hanging around her neck. He lifted her chin with two fingers. "Of course it's me, Ellie."

She wiped away tears and whispered, "I got your note." She handed him the Tarot card with a shaking hand. "What's this supposed to mean?"

"The Tower? Well, maybe you've gone a bit Rapunzel, and need to get out more. Or a transformation, perhaps." He shrugged.

"I saw you last night, before I fell asleep."

"Of course. I wanted you to." He leaned forward and kissed her forehead. "I've missed you, Ellie."

They talked all night, the dead and the living. Reclining side by side, watching the stars wheel like pinpricks in a swinging tin lantern, as gray clouds skated across a darker velvet sky.

"What was that song I heard last night?" she asked.

He sat abruptly, and so did she. "You *saw* them?"

She hesitated, then admitted reluctantly, half-jokingly, "I thought it was a bunch of mermaids, to be honest."

He smiled. "Yes. My friends."

She almost snorted. "You're acquainted with mermaids who live in the canals?"

He shook his head. "Call them *sirenas*. It's the proper term, the name they prefer. They even taught me their songs."

He leaned over the gunwales and opened his mouth. A clear tenor rang out over the water. But the words were not any language Ellie recognized. She shivered, even though the blanket was still warm. The song made her ache and yearn for things that had never been—and yet somehow, it seemed, still could be.

Four shapes rose from the water on the starboard side, with the long sleek hair and steel-dark eyes she'd seen before. *Sirenas*. Sirens. Their arms were a smooth greenish blue. Their slender webbed fingers ended in curved nails that shimmered like mother of pearl, and looked sharp as razors.

"Carlo," she whispered. "I don't . . . what's going on?"

He kept singing and did not answer.

Their melodies wove in and out, as fluid and dark as the water. Screeching, crooning, then smooth and lulling. The song sighed like a faint breeze at sea, then rose to a stormy shriek.

Ellie leaned farther out, gradually enchanted by the music. Each word drew her closer to the water, like links in a chain thrown from a deck.

"Here now. Careful!" Carlo gripped her shoulders and pushed her down on the bench again. "You're freezing. Better wrap up!"

She curled against him, shivering. "Th-thanks." Her teeth were chattering.

"I'll tuck you in. You need the blanket more than I do. I'm beyond the reach of the cold." He rubbed her icy hands. "That's a good girl. We have all night to listen."

At sunrise, a gondolier's hoarse singing woke her.

She sat up and looked around. Her gondola still floated in the middle of the canal. The morning sky was pinking across the horizon.

"What do you do out there?" the boatman shouted when he saw her. He oared out, tied a line to the prow of her gondola, and slowly towed it back to the pier, scolding her in angry Italian all the way.

"I'm sorry, I . . . had special permission to take it out last night."

"Alone?" he scoffed. "*Pazza!*"

She shook her head. "No, I'm not crazy. And I wasn't alone. He was right here." Ellie tapped on the bench, as if Carlo might magically reappear to defend her.

"You are alone now. That is what matters," he growled, scowling. "Lucky for you I don't call the *carabinieri*."

Ellie gripped the prow as she stepped up onto the seawall.

"Now look at what you do. You'll pay for that!" The gondolier shouted, pointing at the prow.

"What do you mean?" She bent to inspect the spot. Two clear handprints were scorched into the wood, blistering the paint. The same spot where Giancarlo had held the prow to push her out into the canal.

"Show me your hands, *strega!*" The man grabbed her wrist and forced one hand down, but the blackened print stretched too long, well beyond her own fingertips. As if she were wearing a man's too-large glove.

"See? It wasn't me!" She pulled free and stepped back from him.

A few other boatmen gathered around the gondolier. Two quickly crossed themselves.

"*Spiacente.* I'll just go now." She lowered her head and walked quickly away from them. Wrapping the blanket tightly around her shoulders, she headed back home. The sirens' eerie song still echoed in her mind.

Golden light tilted across the wooden floor of her apartment, the sun's glow dimmed with each passing hour. This was the room she'd gathered all her mementos in. "The scattered wrecks of my life," she muttered, having read that line somewhere, about debris left over after years of living. Maybe it was a poem by Browning? Pictures, books, photos, ticket stubs. . . .

A year ago her heart would've swelled, her eyes overflowed at what it all represented. She'd have wrapped herself in memory like a comforting blanket. Add a nightly cup of tea or wine, and her part-time work at the antique store, and that would've seemed enough. And someday, maybe, room for another love. But now, all of it was nothing to her. The photos were of someone else wearing her face as a mask. She couldn't remember which movies or concerts they'd seen together. Couldn't even bring to mind the last book she'd read. All she could think about was Carlo, and seeing him again.

He'd kept his promise. He had come back.

Now it was time to keep hers.

She checked her watch. It was far too early, but she couldn't stand to wait another minute.

Past the gargoyles, past the coffee shop, past the fortune teller. Ellie rushed on, arriving a full hour early. At the end of the alleyway, though, Giancarlo met her, blocking the entrance to the square. Looking bemused, shaking his head. Other bazaar performers and vendors hovered in the background, paused in their work, as still as if frozen. Watching her with puzzlement or pity.

"Eleanor, we aren't yet open. It's only eleven. See, no one else is here." He waved a hand at the deserted square. No tents, no booths. No music. Just an empty plaza with café chairs stacked near the canal.

"Sorry. I just couldn't wait any longer." She smiled hopefully. "And what's an hour, really? I mean, you said the ring gave me special privileges." She babbled on, desperate to convince him to step back. She had to come in. To once more see *him*.

He looked gravely down for another moment. Then, as if deciding something, he nodded nonchalantly. "Very well. If you insist on early admission, we can spare a little magic for you. One of our honored few, after all."

Ellie tried to sidle around him, but again he stepped in her way.

"Giancarlo, let me pass." She craned her neck to look behind him,.

"My dearest, for such a great privilege, one must pay."

"Pay? But that's never been an issue before." She tapped the ring on the chain.

"It doesn't cover an early opening." He sighed. "To demand payment is an awkward thing. Business in a place of pleasure. It feels . . . indelicate. Still, I must insist."

She gazed up eagerly. "Sure. What do you want?"

"One drop of blood. And for you to have a drink with me."

She raised an eyebrow. "Blood. Like, *my* blood?"

"An essence, so to speak. One such as I can taste your dreams, your sorrows, your whole life story in a single drop." He smiled self-deprecatingly. "Best mixed with wine. A nice red brings out the memories more clearly, I've found."

"That's . . . really strange. But OK." She nodded and stepped forward.

This time he let her pass.

She sat in her usual seat. As if on cue, a waiter appeared with two glasses of red wine, and a small, sharp-looking knife on a tray. He set it all on the table, and disappeared again into the darkened café.

Giancarlo took hold of her left hand. "The heart side," he murmured, and with the point of the knife stabbed the tip of her index finger.

Ellie winced, but did not protest. What did it matter? Soon she'd see Carlo again.

Giancarlo held her finger over his glass, pinched tight. One shimmering drop gathered at the tip and fell into his wine, disappearing in the crimson liquid. He followed suit with his own finger, letting a thick drop fall into her glass. "One for me, one for you."

They raised the glasses to their lips slowly, watching each other's eyes, and drank at the same time. Ellie completely drained the wine, and set it back on the table next to his.

"Not so bad, was it? Did you learn anything interesting?" asked Giancarlo.

"I can't put my finger on it, exactly, but I feel like I know you. From somewhere, long ago." Her voice trailed off and she shook her head, feeling as if she'd just walked through a mass of cobwebs.

"Well *your* essence, my dear, tastes delicious. Though I already knew that, truth be told." He winked. "Ask me how."

"How did you know?" she repeated dutifully, impatient to get to Carlo.

His lips curled into a wry smile. "You'll soon find out, dear Eleanor." He leaned across and kissed her cheek. "Now then, a promise is a promise. Hmm. So very many promises."

He raised an upturned hand like a symphony conductor. The square shimmered, then glowed golden, as if filled with candlelight. "Now, you mustn't tell anyone I bent the rules."

"No, I swear." She kissed his cheek in return. He smelled of wine, with a coppery undertone. "Thanks for everything." She turned to look out at the water. No sign of her Carlo. "He said he'd come," she murmured. "He promised."

"He did not lie," said Giancarlo. "Look. Over there."

Across the canal, on the opposite bank, stood a figure, face pale in the moonlight. Several sirens surfaced below the spot where he stood, singing and splashing.

"Carlo!" She waved. "I'm over here!"

"He can't hear you," said Giancarlo.

An apron-wrapped server came to the table and took away their glasses.

"I got caught last night, out in the gondola," she confessed. "Almost landed in jail, but the gondolier let me off."

"That's good." Giancarlo got up and went over to hunker down by the edge. He called to one of the sirens, "Rosa! Come here, please." With a slap of her powerful green tail, she swam to the wall, and pulled herself out of the water, elbows propped on the stone edge.

"Is that Miss Eleanor's beloved?" he asked, pointing at the man standing across the canal.

"Rosa!" Ellie called to her, smiling. "From the bridge! You gave me coffee."

"Sure. You were cold." The siren grinned, exposing sharp white teeth, then turned to Giancarlo. "He's just over there." She pointed a long, curved nail.

"I have to see him again," Ellie insisted. "Please. What will that cost?"

Giancarlo smiled. "Oh, Eleanor. Have you learned nothing? The real price always comes later." He kissed her hand.

Ellie winced. It felt like a sharp nip, almost a sting.

He released her hand, licking a drop of blood discreetly from one corner of his mouth. "Of course. Be with him forever, if you like. He's waiting for you."

Ellie felt like a puppy on a leash. "But there's no bridge here. And it's so deep. I'm a terrible swimmer."

"The sirens will assist. Won't you, Rosa?" He patted Ellie's cheek. "I loved meeting you. A truly special young woman. I shan't forget you."

"Yes. Me either." She nodded absently, still watching Carlo. He seemed to be walking on the surface of the canal, slowly making his way to her. "I really have to go now."

"You are sure, then? Very well, take your leave."

Giancarlo grasped her hand and led her to the edge. He helped her descend a crumbling stone stairwell which led down into the canal, until the water reached her waist. He kissed her hand again, lingeringly. "Hang on to that kiss for me. I'll be wanting one last payment." He turned to the sirens now clustered around them.

"Of course," Ellie said, looking at the sirens clustered around her. Like a school of fish, she thought, and almost giggled.

"Ladies, take care of our honored guest." Carlo stepped back then, retreating up the stone stairway.

The sirens swam closer, and the water churned as it used to when, as a child, she'd thrown stale bread into the duckpond back home. The fish had always jockeyed for scraps, too, splashing and leaping.

As the sirens' frenzy roiled the water around her, she was grazed by cold spikes and jagged tails. A sharp fin slashed her shin. "Ouch!" she cried, and a cloudy thread of blood wound to the surface like red smoke.

A green-haired siren rose, sharp teeth pink with blood. Rosa.

Ellie jerked back in panic. Did they mean to devour her like hungry fish?

"We come to help you swim to him," the siren crooned. When she took Ellie's hands into hers, though, they weren't the warm dry ones she'd felt last week at the café, but roughly scaled and deathly cold. "Come along. We'll lead you to him, pretty lady."

"Yes. All right." Ellie nodded. Giancarlo had said there'd be a final price. So be it. And really, what was a little bit of blood?

Carlo should be getting closer. They'd meet in the middle, it seemed. But how could he stand so tall, above the water, when all she could feel was its depth rising, rising, all around her?

More hands gripped her arms, all cold. Some were smooth, some scaly. Some even had tiny barbed spikes that dug into her skin like miniscule fishhooks. "We'll take you to him," they all sang. "It's only a little farther."

Ellie wanted to turn and wave one last time at Giancarlo, to thank him. To watch the world she'd known slip away. But the sirens held her fast, leading her deeper. And yet . . . somehow Carlo seemed farther away now, not closer.

Ellie slipped and lost her footing on the slick stones of the bottom. She kicked, trying to tread water. The sirens held her afloat, though, and she pushed down panic. *Just let me get to him, then I'll be fine. I'll let go of everything else. They're only . . . things. And then we'll be together.*

All that mattered was he'd come back, as promised. And *I'll live with him, happy, just like before.* "Let go, I can swim now," she ordered and tried to pull free.

"Very well. We won't be far," Rosa whispered, releasing her arm.

That ululating siren song began again, unfamiliar and foreign, but this time she could make out the words.

> *Come away*
> *Come away*
> *Into the belly of your dreams*
> *Come away come away*
> *There's no time for screams.*

Fear tightened her throat, as if she were about to be sick. But she was almost there! So close now.

"Carlo," she whispered, "I'm coming, I promise."

But her legs ached now. They felt so heavy, so tired. Her kicks slowed beneath the surface. The shawl floated, tangling about her arms. The more frantically she thrashed, the more it twisted, clinging to her like a drowning swimmer. Twisting around one arm, looped like an eel about her wrist.

"Here, Ellie. Let me help you."

She looked up from the knot of fabric she'd been struggling to untie. Carlo stood in front of her. "I'm stuck," she gasped. "I can't get loose."

He pulled the shimmering length of fabric free in a single fluid motion. It floated away, down the canal. "There. Better?"

"Much, thank you. But I'm . . . really tired," she panted. "Is there someplace to rest?"

"Lean against me." His voice was smooth, soothing, yet discordant against the sirens' song. She laid her head against his chest, and he kissed her forehead. "Just rest. Let go. You'll be fine."

She gazed up. "Look. The stars are watching us," she whispered, and closed her eyes on darkness. The scissoring of her legs against the current slowed. The water felt warmer now. Why was she still so cold?

She shivered, and sighed, and let her head slip beneath the surface. Even there, the sky's diamond eyes still penetrated to watch her. It didn't matter.

She closed her own, and drifted off to sleep, shrouded in starlight.

As Giancarlo waited by the water's edge, Ellie's shawl floated past, headed downstream to the Grand Canal and open sea. The sirens' song that'd keened over the canal, echoing underneath the bridge, was fading away in the dark.

Rosa swam up and set the dripping gold ring on the stony edge. Giancarlo knelt and picked it up. He dried it carefully on a white handkerchief, then turned away from the ink-dark water.

Immortals had always lingered at the bazaar. We gather here with those of our own kind, he thought, as he took his seat again at the table. Those who understand us, as human beings cannot. The mermaids, the magicians, the fortune tellers . . . some have seen centuries pass.

He too would be here forever, tied to the secret little square at the end of the alley guarded by twin gargoyles. As emcee, as ringmaster, until the Bazaar chose to release him some day. Until then he must be its eyes and ears, alert to everything.

Especially the weaker mortals. The ones who flitted like moths drawn to fire. Some always came too close, and singed their wings. These would never fly again, but still might live. Others, even more heedless, flew straight into the candle's flame, fueled by hope and desperation, only to dance on to a flaming death.

The dance is still beautiful, he thought. Sad, yes, but always beautiful.

All he could do was watch until they fell to the ground, flaming, to smolder into darkness. It was merely his job to hold out the light, and then bear witness as they burned.

The Midnight Bazaar was just opening; foot traffic already picking up. Harlequins, fire breathers, and tea-leaf readers called out to the Invited. Giancarlo sat back in his chair near the canal's edge, eyeing the newcomers.

A server arrived at the table and set a tall fluted glass of crimson liquid before him.

"And a hot chocolate, please," Carlo said. "I'm feeling nostalgic tonight."

The server nodded, "Of course, *Signore*." And he turned away, disappearing back inside the tiled café.

A hundred years from the time of this first Bazaar, Europe will see the beginning of a more enlightened era. Still, in the alleyways, rural cottages, damp dungeons, and unschooled minds of many, wonderment and superstition and a belief in magic will still reign. Appearing as truth to those who believe, as clear and certain as daylight.

This is certainly the case in mid-15ᵗʰ-century Flanders, where any unmarried woman must fear the close, constant scrutiny of her neighbors. Any threat to her good name must be avoided, or public censure follows, swift and sure. Sometimes even fatal. The risk is far greater if the woman is a healer; one who works with medicinal herbs to physic the sick. In the minds of Bruges' citizens, it is a short step from brewing willow bark tea for aches and pains, to enchantment via a love philtrum . . . or a deadly poison the truly desperate might seek.

All sorts of decoctions will still be decanted into small, decorative flasks, in this near future. Some look much like the small pottery one displayed on a table at this antiquities stall. See? Please, hold it, turn it over. Very plain, almost homely, no? And yet once it was powerful enough to initiate a love story that ultimately spanned time—though in a most unexpected way.

IN BRUGES

by Mau VanDuren

The harbor at the Zwin, in Damme, was filled with ships, their masts rising straight and tall as if in hope of receiving riches from a benevolent deity. A three-mile canal and road connected the docks to the wealthy city they served. Bruges was a member of the Hanseatic League, a trading association of cities that reached into the Baltic Sea in the north. Trade with Mediterranean powers such as Venice had made Bruges the hub of commerce. Everything that moved between north and south saw its harbor and markets.

The magnificent St. Salvator Cathedral dwarfed everything else, its tall spire eager to touch Heaven. Perhaps a reminder to the Almighty to bestow His blessings in this world, along with His welcome to the next.

In contrast, the city merchants' richly decorated, three-story offices looked down their long noses on the ordinary working people in the cobblestone square, certain the fortunes behind their doors were the true signals of divine approval.

And, it must be said, some folks heretically though silently favored a philosophy which promised worldly wellbeing also predestined one to a place in Heaven.

A late sun was just clearing red-tiled rooftops, burning frost off the rows of stalls that filled the Great Market. Wisps of steam shimmered and rose, disappearing into the deep-blue sky arched over the city. Melt water plinked off the edges of canvas-roofed stalls.

The winter of 1447 had been a bit colder than usual. Clothilde Peeters shivered, whisking a stray drop from one hand as she took in all the goods clamoring to attract her eyes and nose. Some aromas were familiar: mustard, parsley, red and green meat. The odor of decay from the latter was particularly potent. But it was cheaper, and some liked the strong taste and pungent smell. Others of a more sensitive nature, though, had found the stench to be instant grounds for separation.

Many of the smells Clothilde detected were not local, though. Spices from faraway places like *Ottomans*, *Misr*, and *Ynde* especially intrigued her. She'd read about them in books at the Beguinage, as well as fabrics more exotic than homely Flanders wool; Egyptian cotton and linens, patterned Ottoman rugs. And strangely-shaped, colorful fruits that grew in even farther-off lands. Yet here those same fantastic items were stacked all around her.

She closed her eyes, inhaled deeply, and smiled.

In a dark corner of the market, where the sun's rosy spokes had not yet penetrated, she came upon a table still patched with frost. Instantly her gaze caught on a small flask, and instantly she knew she must have it. The vessel's narrow body of brown ceramic was quite ordinary. But the incised ornamentation and exotic inscriptions around the top looked strange, even alien. It appeared out of place, possibly even out of time; a bit forlorn sitting between other flasks of glass, clay, brass, and wood. Only the glass vessels revealed their contents of colorful herbs. All of them were capped with wooden stoppers. All, that is, except the little brown glazed one. Its short neck had a shiny reddish stopper made of wadded cloth, out of which four strands of twine led to a thin leather strap. Nor did it have the usual wax seal meant to preserve contents that were highly perishable, poisonous, or otherwise dangerous.

She reached across the other wares to pick it up.

"Heed, *gyrle*," a gruff voice muttered.

She halted, hand in midair, surprised. She was old enough to no longer be called 'young lady', let alone 'girl'. But did the voice intend flattery, or insult?

A lanky man emerged from the shadows at the back of the stall, breath crystallizing before him in the frosty air.

"Oh. Pardon," Clothilde stepped back a pace. "I only sought to. . . ."

She trailed off as she took in his appearance. The ragged clothes, the deeply-carved lines in a sun-bronzed face, the thin, crooked nose, obviously broken more than once; all betrayed a hard life.

He stepped closer to her, and to the object of her interest.

Clothilde straightened and caught a whiff of strong body odor. Not unusual, of course. Her Uncle Sem used to claim he took a bath once a year, "Whether I need it or no." Most folks believed that a layer of greasy dirt on the skin protected one from illness. For those who were still alive after a plague or two, it certainly rang true. The Flemish, as did all Low Landers, held the belief that "what doesn't kill ye makes ye stronger."

"This . . . very *singular*," the merchant hissed, tapping the top of the flask with one black-rimmed fingernail.

She couldn't place his accent, even though she was familiar with Dutch, French, English, German and, of course, her native Flemish. His speech carried none of those inflections. He rolled his Rs, and the consonants were stronger.

His hands, in grimy fingerless, undyed-wool mittens, moved over the small flask, but he didn't touch it, as if showing a sort of reverence. "Ye peep close, no?"

The odd choice of words amused Clothilde. She nodded. "Well, master, I mind not." She hid her grin, imagining the man was sizing her up to gauge the best price he might get.

"Yes, confident. Peep close." He motioned stiffly with one arm. "But no feel!"

"Oh, I durst not." Clothilde made a show of clasping both hands behind her back, then bent and brought her face so close it almost touched the flask. Her nose tingled a bit. She peered at the design: circles and squares with tiny squiggles inside. Several rows of scribbled characters encircled the neck. A foreign text of some sort, or just decoration? She'd never seen anything like it. A real puzzle. What did it contain? The design looked too fancy for mere cooking herbs. Medicine, perhaps? Alchemists from the East were renowned for their skills and potions; in her world of healers, midwives, and hedge witches, anyway.

She looked up again at the vendor. "Well, I thank ye. Good day." She turned as if to walk away.

"Ye not fancy, then?" The vendor said quickly, as if trying to delay her.

"Oh . . . it is a right artful flask." She feigned shyness and looked down. "But I have scarce enough coppers for daily fare." She paused and looked up through her lashes, to see the effect of her words.

The man gave a Gallic shrug. "So?"

"So, my master would beat me if I came back and scanted his meals." She took another hesitant step away.

"Half schelling," the vendor offered.

Clothilde shook her head.

"Three stuivers."

When that still got no response, he added, "One stuiver, then."

Clothilde turned back tentatively. Five penning was a good point from which to bargain.

"I appreciate that ye take great pains to meet me, sir. But still I dread to see my master wroth."

"Two penning?" He flung out both hands, palms up, as if to imply only a fool would ignore such a magnanimous offer. His gaze shifted to catch and hold hers.

She looked down and sighed, as if it was a terrible decision. Then lifted her head again, biting her lower lip. "Well and good. Mayhap I can parlay one penning against his terrible wrath."

"Hold, sir. I'll offer two penning!" A short, rotund man was approaching the stall. He wore a long, light-blue robe and a cap adorned with two odd bumps like short, round horns.

The vendor briefly glanced his way, but did not acknowledge the newcomer. Instead he smiled covertly, revealing a few lonesome, brown teeth. To Clothilde it appeared the vendor was pleased with the man's arrival, as if he had expected it. And yet, he chose to ignore him.

"It is pact, then." The vendor took her penning. He rummaged beneath the stall table, pulled out a fairly clean rag, and used this to cover the flask before picking it up and wrapping it in a neat little bundle.

"May I eye that flask a moment?" The newcomer pointed at it. "The thing is quite exotic, I expect."

The vendor nodded, but still didn't look at the man. Instead he handed the bundle to Clothilde, spat on the penning, and rubbed it between both hands before tucking it into a worn leather purse. "Ye have happy," he mumbled to her.

Finally acknowledging the short man, he muttered, "Yer chance come later."

How odd. But indeed, Clothilde was satisfied, for her favorite bargaining ploy had worked. She tucked the purchase into her basket, smiled at the vendor, and briefly glanced once more at the short man. Then she turned away, to continue on through the market, for she needed bread, cabbage, and meat for the day. Perhaps even an apple, if she could find one. These victuals were not to feed a master, for she had none.

She'd lived on her own ever since leaving the nunnery at the convent a decade before, while still only a postulant. The Beguinage's books had been a great source of knowledge, but before a year was up she'd exhausted the old Greek and even the Arab texts recently translated into Latin. Beautifully-decorated but boorish religious tomes had been all that remained. By then the mind-numbing discipline, repetitive chores, frequent waking for nighttime prayers, and servitude to the church's haughty, woman-hating masters had disillusioned her.

She walked swiftly away from the booth, back into the heart of the marketplace. An hour later, basket heavy with good fare, she was headed for home. As she passed the same dim corner she noted the foreign herbs vendor and his exotic wares were already gone.

But in contrast, as if he had never even stepped away, there stood the same short, rotund man with the funny, horned hat on his round head.

Clothilde returned his polite nod.

"My dear lady, please be not afeared," he said anxiously. "I was merely awaiting ye."

"Awaiting . . . me?" She frowned. "But why?"

She wasn't afraid, in any case; merely intrigued. Bruges had changed rapidly with the increase of southern trade; strangers were now a common sight. The novelty of their origins still excited her curiosity. That same curiosity which had driven her into the Beguinage at *Ten Wijngaarde,* in order to have access to its many books. She was a free woman now, but curiosity still had her roaming the markets in search of the unusual, along with daily victuals.

"I had . . . a hunch, no more. It is the flask I seek." He gave a tentative smile, his large eyes squinted. Disarming laugh lines radiated from their corners.

Clothilde looked down at her basket, and the wrapped flask. "Indeed? What about it?"

He nodded at the basket. "If it is what I *thenk* it is . . . well."

"Aye?" Her curiosity was most definitely aroused now.

"It may have led ye back here," he added.

Most people would've laughed at the preposterous suggestion, out of disbe-lief or in fear. But Clothilde the healer understood. The man was talking about magic. "Pray tell, then," she challenged.

"Yes, of course. Later in the day." And with that, he turned away. Before Clothilde could ask where it was he meant to meet and talk with her, he'd disap-peared into the maze of stalls.

Solomon de Suavis came from a long line of Venetian bankers who had arrived and set up shop in Bruges a century earlier. Back then, trade arrangements between Venice and the Hanseatic League had opened opportunities in finance that Venice's Hebrew businessmen were keen to exploit. But de Suavis wasn't just financially canny; he was also a romantic soul who loved the modern arts. Especially the new technique of oil painting that had originated in Bruges. A consummate wheeler-dealer, he also spoke enough languages to deal with most any party.

The morning's encounter at the market had greatly intrigued him. The odd little flask looked so familiar. Not that he'd seen this particular one, or any like it, before. He'd only read about such an object years ago. The treatise mentioning it had claimed that, once opened, the little brown pottery vial had vanished, taking along with it those who were nearby. Of course it could've merely been a sort of fairy tale; a folk story about magic. But suppose it was true? Or even partially true.

It struck him now that the woman who'd purchased the flask hadn't been wary of it, or of him. On the contrary, she'd been openly curious. The glint of sharp intelligence in those sky-blue eyes—he smiled at the recollection—had shown she had spunk. He wanted to behold their gaze again. He'd even followed her home, at a discreet distance, so that such a meeting might take place. But how and when should he attempt it?

Certainly not in broad daylight. Hebrews were not supposed to mingle with gentiles, and most definitively not with those of the opposite sex. But he had to examine that flask! The urge was bewildering. Had he felt this driven before, this . . . propelled?

He tried to shrug it off all day, as he worked in his office on the ledgers. All to no avail.

At dusk, in the late afternoon, he set out to pay the woman a visit.

After a simple evening meal of boiled meat and onions, Clothilde sat at a small pine table near her kitchen's brick stove. She'd already washed and put away on the shelf the wooden plate and spoon, and now cradled a warm pewter mug full of *pepermunt* tea.

Finally, hands sufficiently warmed, tea drunk, she set down the mug and picked up the odd flask again.

Her fingers tingled as she held it; a feeling a bit like that in her funny bone when she'd badly bumped her elbow on the door-frame last week. And yet, also not the same. For she felt it only in the spots where her skin touched the cool pottery surface of the flask. She turned it over and peered closely at the engraving. Was it a sort of text? Not Latin, nor even Arabic. Not that she could read the latter, but she'd seen both in some of the nunnery's books. And like them this script, if script it was, seemed divided into distinct bits, like words in sentences separated by tiny spaces.

What did it say, though?

A soft knock on the door startled her. Who would come calling after dusk? Her neighbors were not in the habit.

She rose and peered out through the small window beside the table, but saw neither lamp nor torch. That calmed her a bit. As an educated, single woman, she was leery of drawing undue attention. Lately, the increased gossip about witchcraft had put her on edge. She knew her neighbors were suspicious of her, as they had been of her mother, from whom she'd learned the healing arts. The benefits these folks received from her medicinal services had thus far prevented them from reporting her to the city's authorities. Or worse, to the church. The Papal Inquisition of 1231 had given life-and-death powers to the Dominicans, who used them to viciously guard the faith against heretics.

Or rather, she thought angrily, against any competition from scientific, scholarly work. Thus healers were now automatically equated to witches and sorcerers.

Another knock sounded, this time a bit louder.

She couldn't ignore the noise any longer, or someone might notice. Quietly she stepped to the door, one hand folded around the hilt of a small dagger she kept in a pocket sewn into her skirt. A woman alone never knew where danger might lurk. "Who goes there?"

"De Suavis," a soft male voice replied.

"I ken no one by that name."

"Aye, ye do. We met just this morning."

She frowned. The odd man at the stall? "He with the horned hat?"

"Yes. At the market, mistress. I suggested a meeting?"

Mistress? So he knew her to be a single woman. Yet she knew aught of him. But the longer he stood outside, on her doorstep, the more likely neighbors would notice. She needed to send him away quickly, but quietly.

She unbolted the door. "Come in. But only for a moment." A risky move, for inviting a man into the house of an unmarried woman was bound to incite outrage and talk. But any conversation between them had better take place in private.

"I thank ye, mistress." De Suavis, in a dark-colored cloak, followed her gesture at the table. He went over to sit there, on one of the two chairs with woven-rush seats.

She stood squarely in front of him, hands on hips. "A fine time to come knocking at my door. Now we both be compromised."

"My sincere pardons." He did *sound* sincere. "We Hebrews are restricted in our movements, as ye know. I thought it more discreet to meet private-like, after dark."

She nodded, but still worried, couldn't help scolding him. "Excepting that my house is often watched by neighbors."

He frowned. "But why?"

"On account of me being both a woman alone, and a healer."

His eyes widened a fraction. "Oh?"

"Or, as some would have it, a witch." She rolled her eyes.

"We didn't have those in Venice," he informed her.

She doubted that, but decided not to remark on it. "I am not a widow, but a spinster," she added for good measure.

"We did have those," he said, in such a deadpan tone she nearly laughed aloud.

He sat stiffly, with hands on thighs, looking up trepidatiously as a schoolboy being lectured by a master.

Well, she thought, he should've done better at his studies regarding my situation. Women who dared to educate themselves or show their intelligence were viewed with as much suspicion in Bruges as were Hebrews, and considered nearly as undesirable. For the mere existence of such women made great men feel inferior and insecure.

She realized then he was no longer wearing his distinctive horned hat. So he'd taken some precautions, at least, donning the long, hooded cloak instead.

"Very well. This is a good instant in which to elucidate yer purpose," she ordered, folding her arms and tapping one foot.

De Suavis nodded. He pulled back the hood, and opened his mouth to speak.

Just then came a loud banging at the door, followed by a deep-voiced shout. "Devil!"

"Sorcerer!" screamed another, higher-pitched voice.

"Now ye have done it. They glimpsed you!" Clothilde spat. "Swift, rise and follow me."

The Hebrew only sat there, mouth still open, frozen. Well, no doubt he'd heard terrible stories of how such mobs treated their victims. But inaction would not do; it would get them both killed.

She snatched her cloak from the wall hook, whisked the flask from the table and into her pocket. Then grasped his sleeve and dragged him up.

In panic he stumbled over his chair, but she towed him on, relentlessly, to the back of the house. There, she carefully opened the back door just a crack. The alley appeared empty, so she drew him outside, softly closing the door behind them.

She led the way through the narrow passage, which stank of feces, acrid urine, and rotting cabbage. It curved around the building next door and led them back out onto the street. Then, from several houses away, they stood near the wall. Observing a small mob of men and women in front of her house who carried torches, hoes, and pitchforks.

The banging on her door stopped abruptly when one man kicked it in. An ugly mob, indeed.

"Swift," she hissed. "We lope now, or we expire!"

De Suavis, who'd apparently not run anywhere since childhood, seemed to suddenly recall the use of his feet.

At least the back streets were deserted this evening. But Clothilde wasn't sure what to do next, or where to go. The city square, perhaps? On Saturdays the market was still open late, and crowded with shoppers. That should provide some anonymity, for a time.

"Follow me," she urged. Once they were lost in the crowd, she'd think of something.

"Perchance, mistress!" her companion protested, panting. "Why not flee to my house now, and surer safety?"

She didn't have to consider the offer for long. Hiding thus would provide shelter until the mob dispersed. And she would get answers about the strange flask all the sooner. "*Ja, ja.* Now, stir shanks and lope!"

They ran for perhaps half a mile. Then he pointed her to a wide alley at the end of the long main street, and she ran through it after him. Leaping over a shattered chamber pot, two stacks of firewood, and a chair with only three legs.

The Hebrew stopped midway down, at a planked double door, and pulled out a brass ring heavy with keys. He chose the largest and jammed it into a rusted iron lock. After what seemed an eternity of scraping and jiggling, the tumblers clicked and the door swung wide. He stepped back and waved her in ahead of him.

The entry was pitch-dark. Clothilde froze, unable to see where to safely step.

The Hebrew grabbed a fistful of her woolen cloak and pulled her deeper into the gloom. "We duck heads here," he murmured as they passed under a low doorway. After some shuffling and muttering, he struck a flint and lit a small lantern hung in an alcove. The flame flared, dimly illuminating a windowless room.

"I regret to have put ye in this predicament, *gentile signorina*," the short man uttered, as he pulled off his dark blue cloak.

"So do I, seigneur," she said fervently. Yet she felt oddly attached to the stranger by then, a sort of friend met in adversity. She must rely on him now for . . . well, who knew how long, though such dependence had not been her choice. The idiotic timing of his visit had forced her to accept his protection.

A man's protection! For a woman, a state she'd always judged to be an uncertain quandary, at best.

De Suavis held out a hand for Clothilde's cloak. She slipped it from her shoulders and gave it to him. "Ah, well. Nowhere else to go now," she added.

He hung the cloak next to his on nearby hooks, then turned back to her, one dark eyebrow raised. "Pardon?"

She rolled her eyes. "Ye are a Hebrew, *nee?*" His distinctiveness was obvious. Her words had come out like an accusation, though, which she regretted. Frustration and anger had made her momentarily want to hurt him. Yet she'd never had any quarrel with his people, or their religion. *To each his own wisdom . . or folly.* That was her motto; an acceptance of others passed on by her departed mother.

"Yes. I am of that faith," he said brusquely, shoulders stiffening. "As I told ye."

Well, of course he would be wary, even prickly on the subject. The people of Bruges, for the most part, admired Hebrews for certain things, like their talent for business and banking. But did not, as a rule, actually *like* them, for much the same reasons.

"Well, then . . . how will ye be able to get me out of this muddle?"

He pressed his hands together before him, as if in prayer, a disarming gesture of politeness. "If ye please. May we be seated now, and speak of the matter?"

She nodded. Stuck here, she might as well attend to the cause of it, as well: that *verdoemde* flask. "*Ja.* And now ye'd better have some good answers."

"My dear *signorina*, truly ye do not squander words. Have you the flask upon you?"

"*Natuurlijk.*" She felt it, still safely tucked into the secret skirt pocket, though her hand gripped not the tiny bottle, but the hilt of her trusted blade. A precaution, until she could be sure of her host's true intentions.

"Please then, accompany me." With a grand welcoming flourish, the banker led his reluctant guest into a larger room furnished with fine tapestries and thick, soft rugs from the East. He lit two oil lamps and set one on an inlaid desk, the other on a long oak table. Atop it, many open books and scrolls were held flat with Venetian glass weights. Eight oak chairs with arm rests and high backs circled the table.

They sat down across from each other. Clothilde produced the flask and set it halfway between them. De Suavis reached out to touch it, but blinked and quickly withdrew his hand.

"Droll, eh?" She chuckled. "The clay has a certain life to it."

He tried again, slowly drawing it closer, studying the surface. "A rare script. How quaint." He turned the flask over and then back again. "Remarkable, really." He looked up at Clothilde.

She was aware of his scrutiny, but her own gaze had been drawn like a lodestone to due north, as she scanned the wall lined with tall shelves of leather-bound volumes. *Mijn God.* So many books! Her heart beat a little faster.

He pointed in the same direction. "Ye take pleasure in reading?"

Clothilde nodded absently, reading the titles. "You have a notable selection."

"Ye be most unusual in my experience of the people here. In fact, in all of Flanders."

"Indeed?" She pursed her lips thoughtfully. "There be more volumes here than on all the shelves of the Beguinage."

He frowned. "What is . . . Be-guin-age?"

"The place where the Holy Sisters reside."

"Ah." De Suavis had heard of those stubbornly single women who, if they did leave the walls of their cloisters, went about clad in crow's-wing black. "The ones devoted to God as husband, for they do hate men." He sat back, clearly waiting for her reaction.

Clothilde shook her head. "*Nee*, not precisely. They only abhor ignorant ones."

The banker nodded. "Do ye ken many ignorant men, yerself?"

She rolled her eyes. "Oh, *ja*. Do Hebrews all-times ask so many questions?"

He raised his eyebrows and spread his hands. "What be amiss with asking questions?"

She smiled. Having tasted his intelligence, she wanted to probe further. "Ye do hark me back to Matheolus."

"Aye." De Suavis nodded at his guest. "I know of the man." He laced his fingers on the table top and gazed up at the rafters. Which, to his dismay, were thickly draped with dusty cobwebs. "Let's see how much I recall," he said, quickly looking down again, lest she follow his gaze and discover the poor housekeeping.

"As I recollect, '*Women can sing to more than one tune. What good were the Periher-meneias, the Elenchi, divided into several branches, the Prior and Posterior Analytics, logic, or the mathematical sciences to Aristotle? For a woman surmounted all of these in mounting him, and conquered the master of logic. She placed a bit and headstall on his head and he was dragged into solecism, barbastoma, and barbarism. The hussy used him as a horse and spurred him on like a female ass. She lifted her crotch far too high when she rode the male. The governor was governed and the roles of the sexes reversed, for she was active and he passive, willing to neigh under her. . .*' "

He folded his arms. If she knew the diatribe, she wouldn't be shocked. "Now *ye*, mistress. What do *ye* ken of him?"

"Huh!" She rolled her eyes. "His *Lamentations*. Matheolus was a bombastic ignoramus. All those tirades about women, yet the fool priest was never married.

Not because . . . or *only* because he hated women. Mayhap he hated his own impotence, or an unfed hunger. Or both!"

She smiled, as if well satisfied with her response. "Now tell me, be Hebrew men just as ignorant as Christian ones?"

"We are not as dissimilar to them as we ought to be," he admitted, deeply impressed. She was comely, as well as intelligent. And . . . unmarried, as he'd surmised earlier.

She nodded. "Whatever the religion, it seems men refuse to fathom that a woman can be more than cook or housekeeper or . . . " She paused, then blurted out, "Why not friend or partner or teacher? Or merchant or artisan or banker?"

"Hmm. Much has been written on the subject. Heard ye also of Maimonides?"

She snorted. "Aye. Another great misogynist! His contempt for my gender is legendary." She scowled as if the very thought of this particular philosopher enraged her.

"Aye." De Suavis nodded. "In many ways he was that. However, Maimonides was quite divergent on the matter of a woman's place in matrimony."

She only looked skeptical, and said nothing to that.

With her temper already high, he didn't want to provoke her further, and yet. . . .

Clothilde's original annoyance was subsiding. Now she felt a growing sympathy with the Hebrew. But why in the world should that be?

We are in no ways alike, she thought.

"Maimonides defined three categories of amity within marriage," he was saying. "The first being an affiliation dependent on mutual utility."

She grimaced and slapped the table. "He would, though, would he not? Mutual utility! She cooks his meals. She cleans his clothes, and his house. She comforts him in bed. And, oh yes, she bears the babes and tends to the brood. And what does *he* do? Pays for it all. Ye ken, now, what she's forced to be? Maid, washerwoman, harlot, wet-nurse, and nanny."

His thin smile looked a tad defensive. "When the utility evaporates, the bond of love dissolves."

"*Love*," she scoffed. "More like, When she becomes an equal, the bond of love dissolves. Some love *that* is."

The banker did not seem to take her challenges amiss. Perhaps he knew how it felt to be valued only for what could be gained of him.

"The second is, with the sharing of sorrows, troubles, and also joys," he said. "Joy becomes double joy, and sorrow becomes half sorrow."

She frowned, but did not protest that observation.

"And the third is a commitment to shared goals," he added. "Both dream of attaining great ideals, with a readiness to sacrifice for the achievement of all." He peered across the table to see how she weighed those words.

"As long as *her* ideals are attained in the home," she scoffed, crossing her arms.

De Suavis sat back, as if disappointed. "I'd hoped you would come back with something more than vexation."

Clothilde noticed the banker's stare, but she was still busy thinking about those categories. All three important enough, surely, but …

Suddenly, she grinned in triumph. "Ah! But the *order* is wrong. The first should've been the last, since it should be supported by the other two."

De Suavis raised an eyebrow. "Mutual utility last. Hmm." He nodded. "Depending on how ye interpret the three, that could be an ideal cohabitation, aye."

"Hmm. And they . . . they are . . ." She trailed off, biting her lip at a new realization. She took a deep breath, gathering courage. "And they, who have all three. They are the lucky ones."

They each looked away, as if suddenly shy. Men and women of short, or even of lengthy acquaintance, did not have such discussions. Men and women did not talk together this way, at all. The idea was ridiculous, if not scandalous. No doubt also ungodly. But she couldn't help it; she'd felt bound to respond. Which had felt . . . well, not so much challenging, but more an extraordinary meeting of the minds. This man, whatever his beliefs might be, was anything but ordinary.

"And . . . have ye ever been so lucky?" he asked hesitantly.

"I never wed," she said softly. "And yer . . . lady wife?"

He shook his head. "I have yet to become acquainted with that woman."

She tilted her head, thinking of his wit, his great wealth. His modest yet not unpleasing form. That seemed hardly credible. "Truly?"

"Aye, I ken your meaning." He shrugged ruefully. "And at my age! Though my community in Venice pressed me hard." He turned up both palms. "But it seemed . . . there were no suitable candidates for one such as I."

She could not suppress a skeptical look. Men were always masters in the marriage game. How could he not find a woman to suit him?

"I . . . suppose I am too demanding," he admitted. "Wanting not just cook and bed-warmer. Nor to be sure, a pure scold. Which is why I am come to Bruges, to escape the yoke. The endless matchmaking. And so many . . . community-dictated traditions."

She grinned. "For there are no Hebrew women here," she guessed.

"Oh, a few. But all, it seems, blissfully wedded." His lips quirked into a minimal smile.

"And so ye have given up."

Had he given up? Or merely reconciled with reality? "Better to be alone than wedded in misery," he observed. "Though who may ken? I might find the right lady, yet. Mayhap one learned, intelligent, adventurous, and . . . er, comely, as well."

"*Oh jee.* All of that?" She smiled back wryly. "Then we be both unlucky . . . and yet lucky, all at once."

A blush heated his face. "Ah, but we've strayed from the topic at hand!" He abruptly turned his gaze from her, back to the flask. "Remarkable, no? The engraving is in Avestan. A religious script from Persia. Zoroastrians, a sect in India and Persia, once employed it."

"I have read something of them. But can ye make out the words?"

"From right to left. Just as with Hebrew." He turned it around and, without thinking, giggled. "Why, what do you know? There *is* real magic inside!" He looked up. Then, seeing her astonished expression, flinched. "No, pray ye. Heed this. It reads something like, *I am the light in the dark, miscellany in monolithicum, asylum in a tempest, a where and when of sovereignty.*"

"Hmm. Harks of help for a friend in need," she murmured.

De Suavis nodded. "It certainly intrigues."

The homely little bottle has forged a bond of sorts between us, Clothilde mused.

But there was no future in a connection. He was Hebrew. She, Christian. And at this point, perhaps an accused witch. Witches had no future at all, except in the flames. Regardless, in Bruges, no matter how well read, a woman dared not be drawn to a man not her own kind.

She rose reluctantly and scooped up the flask. For to stay here any longer was danger, too, though of a different sort than that which awaited her at home.

"I . . . well, must discover what has become of my house." She winced inwardly. What a poor excuse. Quite possibly she could never go back there. Once the title "witch" had been assigned, it was very hard to shake off. Should one even live long enough to try.

"Oh, but think, mistress." De Suavis stood abruptly, too. "There may yet be great danger!"

She was already pulling on her cloak. And there could be no question of him escorting her home.

As Clothilde walked back the way they had come, she mused on their odd conversation. Marriage was a closed subject, she'd long ago decided. Her mother had married a brutish man who'd beat them both. One day he'd simply disappeared. Run off somewhere, she'd always assumed. Or else . . .

But no. Surely her kind, gentle mother would not have used her talents in so dark a way. Even though there was little other recourse for a woman chained to a violent man.

So Clothilde had sought to avoid the risk altogether by joining the Beguinage. And once she'd left, still refused to consider being yoked to anyone but herself.

Yet she'd willingly discussed the married state this night. As if she'd forgotten its evils, or as if her very will had been compromised. But she'd enjoyed conversing about philosophers she had read of while in the convent, and had felt something else stirring.

Not nostalgia, for she did not yearn to return to the nuns. Rather, the joy of talking to someone as an equal. Even to spar and argue. And she couldn't disagree with everything Matheolus and Maimonides had written. Many women she knew *did* act willfully ignorant and troublesome, even when their subservient roles had been of their own choosing. Perhaps a few simply preferred it that way. After all, from those with little power, little responsibility could be expected.

Still, it irritated her that those two men, members of the boorish sex, sometimes had a point! But she also admitted something else: the rotund, learned Hebrew could not merely be dismissed as another misogynist. And that . . . well, that was the scariest revelation of all.

Clothilde walked the cobblestones now aimlessly, fearing to return to her own neighborhood too soon. It was dark and cold; few folks were still out. Perhaps she should've stayed at the Hebrew's, after all. It would've been safer than going to a place where she might be dragged off by city *schutters*, or, worse, the Inquisition.

She had friends, but most were married and did not live alone. She would not expose them to the dangers of associating with an accused witch.

Back to the Beguinage, then? She doubted they would take her now. She had left many years ago, but memories of betrayal fade slowly, if at all.

Her hand slipped into another pocket of her dress and emerged with a small leather pouch weighted with a few silver and copper coins. That made up her mind. There was plenty for a bed and some breakfast. She would have enough left for fare to Damme, where she might board a ship and flee for her life.

The inn, located close to the *Minne Water* near the walls on the east side of the city, was an old establishment and priced accordingly. But its fire was warm, the victuals served hot in large wooden bowls, and the wine not too vinegary. The foundation had settled unevenly, so the stucco on its red brick walls was crumbling off in spots, and the timber floors slanted like a ship's decks. Fat tallow candles in brass holders provided light too dim to reveal most of the cobwebs draped like dusty lace between the heavy oak ceiling beams.

Upstairs she had to share a cot in a communal room. It was warmer that way, but the smell of unwashed bodies and chamber pots was potent. And the one window was firmly shut to keep maladies from entering with any fresh air.

Sleep mostly eluded her. Normally she relished questions, but she also liked them answered. Too many had popped into her head this day, after purchasing the strange, tingling flask that was again burning in her pocket. How odd, in retrospect, that the vendor had let it go for a single penning. Then the Hebrew had come along, twice. They'd talked of philosophy, partnerships, matrimony. Even love! Perhaps there was indeed magic in the flask, as he'd claimed.

After what seemed many sleepless hours she heard a rustling noise over the snoring all around her. A tall figure rose from a bed across the room. Illuminated by the dim light of a waning gibbous moon it passed the window, and she recognized the beaked silhouette of the flask vendor! On softly squeaking timbers he slowly approached her cot.

She held her breath and didn't move.

His shape knelt beside her. "Hush," he whispered. "No harm."

Oh, she had no intention, this night, of causing a ruckus that would bring the innkeeper and possibly the law, or worse.

"Here. Note from banker." The vendor slipped a small piece of parchment under her hand. Then rose, tiptoed to the door, and slipped out.

It was too dark still to make out the scrawled words. But at dawn she sat up in her cot and hastily unfolded the parchment.

Dear Mistress Peeters,

Please forgive my earlier impertinence. I beg you come to my office at Damme on the morrow. I have vital information to share.

No signature. But who else might also have an office at the harbor? She ought to resent his current impertinence, too, on top of the previous. *Come to my office at the harbor* was not even a proper invitation.

She pulled the flask from her skirt pocket, thinking to simply dispose of it. But how? Where would be best? She could throw it in the canal. Or break it to pieces on the cobblestones, and take the fragments to the rubbish heap.

But, she thought with a shiver, think what might then come out. A demon? A Jinn? Foreign poison? Or even a miasma to cause dire maladies. The thing she had wanted so dearly that morning seemed a curse, now.

But the banker . . . he was a nice man, really. Smart, knowledgeable, interesting, and . . . with vital information to share. Her heart lifted. She felt . . . lighter. Almost joyful. A journey to Damme was necessary, in any case, for she must seek passage on an outbound ship to escape this place with her life intact. She still had questions about the flask, as well. How fortuitous that her great need to leave Bruges also created an opportunity to discover some answers. Her journey could strike two birds with one stone.

Those were the only reasons she would admit for the journey, even to herself. She tucked the flask back into her skirt pocket, tied on her cloak and, shoes in hand, headed quietly for the door.

After a hasty breakfast downstairs of bread and ale, Clothilde boarded a wagon near the marketplace. The cobblestone road from town to harbor started at the Koolkerke Gate in the city wall, and followed the narrow remains of the old canal to Damme on the Zwin. The air was chilly, though there wasn't much wind. Every now and then a pale winter sun peered out from between sheepish clouds. Large horse-drawn drays growled past, their wheels groaning under heavy loads, on the way to market from the country.

In the open wagon Clothilde and two other women kept warm under a wool blanket provided by the driver; it smelled only faintly of horse sweat. The passengers' condensing breath drifted behind them as they chatted, becoming one with the frosty air. The iron-clad wheels rumbling over the cobbles played counterpoint to the rhythmic clatter of the horses' hooves.

Half an hour into the ride, tall masts began to show through the leafless trees lining canal and road. None were dressed in sails to head out, for there was as yet no wind to power them.

As the last trees dwindled, the harbor of Damme came fully into view. Ships large and small were being loaded and unloaded along the timbered quay. Others had anchored all along the Zwin awaiting their turn for the stevedores, or for a favorable wind and tide. Even in deadest winter the quest for wealth did not relent.

The driver reined in his two dappled *trekpaarden*, and the wagon rolled to a halt before an aptly-named inn, the *Noordster*. No sailor dared navigate the open waters without the guidance of that nighttime beacon in *Ursa Minor*.

Clothilde and her companions descended and made their goodbyes. Then she looked up and down the main street for a sign of the Hebrew's office. "*Verdoemenis,*" she muttered. Why had he not described the building, at least?

"My dear lady," said a pleasant, Italian-accented voice behind her.

She whirled. "Seigneur De Suavis!"

His smile was warm beneath the now-familiar horned hat. "Mistress Peeters, I am pleased to have noticed ye riding in."

She felt happy to see him, and not just because now she needn't search him out. But 'happened to notice' her? Hmm. "A fortuitous convergence," she suggested.

"The tavern." He gestured behind him at a low timbered building. "It would be a pleasant meeting place at this hour. Alas, their victuals are not cooked in accordance with my religious customs." He shrugged apologetically. "So, if it pleases ye, I've had something prepared at my office."

Clothilde's stomach rumbled. "Show me the way!" A meal and a new experience. Why not?

Side by side they walked from the quay into Damme. Many of the buildings near the water were constructed of wood, signaling the temporary nature of any booming harbor town. But farther in, stone and bricks gradually replaced raw planks.

They stopped before a narrow two-story redbrick house with a Gothic façade of lacy, carved stonework. A brass plaque set into the heavy oak door read, BANK VAN VENETIE. Its three large keyholes were only prudent for a bank to have. No doubt a goodly sum of gold was locked inside.

De Suavis applied his key to one lock, then opened the door and led his guest into a bright room with a large bankers' desk in the middle. A tall lectern stood in one corner, and a narrow table with two chairs was positioned under a row of windows. These had decorative iron bars, and faced the street. The opposite wall's fireplace was tiled with Portuguese *azuljeos* depicting bright blue cherubs and saints on a pristine white background. Small as it was, the fire somehow warmed the room comfortably. A wall of bookshelves hugged an iron-clad strong box with two heavy latches, each closed with a large, ornate padlock.

"Let us sit here." De Suavis carried two chairs closer to the fire.

Clothilde stepped closer to the fireplace and took a closer look. "Oh, how ingenious."

He flinched, looking faintly guilty. "Beg pardon?"

"The hearth." She pointed to a bundle of parallel pipes that entered the fireplace at the bottom, ran up at the back, and came out again at the top.

"Oh, I see. Merely that." He sounded oddly relieved.

Such a strange fellow!

Solomon watched Clothilde point to the various pipes as she spoke. "The fire heats them. Warm air rises up and out, while cold air is drawn in at the bottom." She looked up again. "It is Archimedes's theory of gravity, applied! Yer own idea?"

He nodded. She was so observant, so smart. So unusual, and yet pleasant. So . . . accepting, even complimentary. He straightened his shoulders, wishing just then to appear taller. "Mistress Peeters, forgive this impertinence. But it would please greatly if ye called me Sol."

She frowned. "But that is the personification of the sun. A god in Roman mythology. Bestowing such a name on one's babe seems presumptuous, indeed. It must surely give a child foolish notions. Sol, truly?"

"It is short for Solomon, which my parents named me," he explained a little stiffly, dismayed. "After the ancient king of Israel."

Clothilde's eyes widened. "Ah, yes! I see. But here first names are meant to be used by close relatives. Or old friends, or . . . or spouses." She paused, frowning. "But ye and I . . . what are we, if we are not any of those?"

"Forgive me," he mumbled. "I move too hastily."

"Too hastily for what?"

De Suavis shook his head helplessly. "Why, to ken ye. To become, well, friends."

Now, why did I say that, he thought. It wasn't truly what he had in mind, but mayhap friendship was a safer thing to mention, at this point. More ambiguous than love.

Oh dear. Was he in love?

"Friendship between a man and a woman? I have never heard of such a thing." She looked not so much taken aback as thoughtful. "Though it does put me in mind of the French abbess, Héloïse, and her long relationship with Pierre Abélard. She once wrote to remind him of the Ciceronian model of friendship in marriage. Saying, *The name of wife may seem more sacred or more binding, but sweeter for me will always be the word amica.*"

Sol nodded. "The nun was educated and outspoken. A prime logician, Abélard had been a worthy match for her."

Clothilde laughed. "Yes, reading of them always gave me a glimmer of hope. But . . . Abélard. . . . " She paused, blushing.

"I recall." Sol winced. The priest had been punished for the relationship with castration.

"Sol," she murmured slowly, as if tasting the word. "It has a nice ring to it." She smiled. "But then you must call me Clothilde. If you like, that is." Before he could respond, she added, "Or, I suppose . . . Clo."

Her bright eyes, so filled with questions about the world and the unknown. Youthful still, as if adolescence had not left her.

"I would be pleased to do so . . . Clo," he said hesitantly.

"My mother called me that whenever she embraced me," she told him.

The intimacy of that confession emboldened him. "I like that image, Clo," he said more confidently. Imagining her mother, a kindly person, an older version of the woman before him, hugging her daughter.

How he longed to do the same!

Instead he reached across the table, past the little flask, and gravely took her hand. Feeling a little resistance before she gave in and relaxed. "And ye surely perceive that I . . . er, look upon ye with some fondness," he said softly. "We ken each other barely a day, but it feels as if I have done so for years. Ye think directly. And are so . . . cogent. Why, Master Matheolus would have found more than his match in Mistress Peeters." He chuckled.

"Oh, do not mind Matheolus. For ye appear a lot more agreeable."

"Aye?"

"Though ye have lived alone for a long time, have ye not?"

He nodded and sighed. "I see what ye mean." She was gently telling him it could not be; reminding him of how impractical their situation was. "Yes, Clo. It is folly. There can no-times be anything betwixt us."

"*Nee.* For I'm a Christian and ye be Hebrew." She looked away and sighed, though she did not withdraw her hand. After a moment she turned back again. "I recalled something else of Heloise, though. The nun and Maimonides lived in the same times. Mayhap they read each other's writings. And what of his three categories of amity?"

"Ah!" He felt a stirring of hope. "Indeed, you are right. Though of course as spiritual friends we could never attain all three. They pertain to matrimony and the, er, physical bond it contains." His turn to blush. "And that," he raised his eyebrows, "is not written in the celestial firmament."

"Ha!" She grinned. "And who said aught of matrimony? Isn't it mostly done to gratify the community? So its members may feel the security of a worldly bond made between others. And the couple, are they not sanctioned by the community to be together?"

De Suavis nodded, puzzled.

"*Thenk* about it," she insisted. "A bond between a Christian and a Hebrew possesses no community to bless it. So who or what, then, would require a marriage?"

He was impressed, though her logic held a flaw. "In our case there are *two* communities, Clo," he reminded her gently. "And they would unit in great denunciation of such a bond."

Clothilde weighed the meaning of Sol's words with growing sadness. Oh, why did life often seem so ridiculously hopeless? She laughed bitterly. "*Beste me*, I can sight pyre and gallows already." She looked down at her hands on the table. "Then what do ye put forward, instead?"

He took a deep breath. "This subject is precisely why I bid ye to come here. It is regarding the flask, of course. For I did remember a strange, yet pertinent occurrence of some one hundred years past. In fact, one century ago, in Venice."

"Ah yes. Ye said that was yer home. And so, do tell me. What happened there?" she said eagerly.

"About a hundred years ago, in 1348, there was once a midnight bazaar," he said. "Or at least there is a story of one. A fable, mayhap, which claims it was an exotic marketplace so strange and sudden, no one in the city had ever eyed anything like it before." He swung an arm out, as if this wonder lay before them. "Set up in the plaza they call San Marco."

She frowned, confused. "Were there previously no markets in Venice?"

"Yes, of course. But this one was nothing like. It appeared only for a week, and in several locations. Once even below the ground, or so they say, and anyone who knows Venice will ken that is not possible. Only mud and water down there. And yet . . . here it comes: one moment nothing. The next . . . a Night Bazaar full of all one could desire, but merely dream of."

"Truth be told?" She looked doubtful.

"Well, in the manner they related the thing, it sounded most outlandish. Strange speech came from boxes. Musical in a fashion, but with strong rhythms. And very loud. And there were large, well . . . paintings in frames, and in them, the subjects moved about!"

She blinked. "But paint on canvas cannot move. Was it witchcraft?"

He shrugged. "I know not. They say the scenes were capricious. Changing swiftly, much faster than in a Greek drama."

Clothilde snorted. "Interesting. But how does such a wonder relate to us?"

He held up a finger. "In this way. The tale also cited a small flask of some renown."

"Like this one?" She tapped the bottle on the table between them.

"Aye. It had the power to vanish, and take along people who held it, too."

"*Lieve God*," she breathed, horror struck. "But where did they *go*?"

"Exactly. Where indeed? Which is why I wanted to eye that flask, from the outset." He raised a finger. "For what if we too might discover the answer? And with it, a resolution to both our dilemmas." He hurried on before she could object. "Do ye recall the meaning of the inscription, which I read out to you?"

Clothilde hesitated. "I believe so. It said . . . a light in the dark? And . . . asylum in a tempest."

He nodded. "And a where and when of sovereignty."

"That does not sound like a bad place," she admitted. And if they did go there, and survived the journey, at last she would learn the truth of the mystery the flask contained.

"Do you think—" de Suavis began.

But Clothilde raised a hand to stop him. "Hark. Do you hear that?"

For she had noticed a most dreaded and familiar sound. The shouting of many voices, the stamp of many feet. Sounds that always heralded the approach of a mob. Sounds she had heard the night they came for her mother. And the more recent night when she, herself, had almost been taken. Those flickers of light out in the darkening street, beyond the windows. Was it not the flaring of torches?

She rose so abruptly the chair toppled behind her. "Come, we must flee!"

Through the windows, outside the house, though the sun had not yet set, all was dark as midnight.

Clothilde understood now. She reached out and closed one hand around the little flask. *A when and where of sovereignty . . . a light in the dark.* These could be her fate! Instead of the other one, which she knew all too well ended in imprisonment, torture, and flames. Her fingers tingled. Did a friendly genie truly dwell inside, now that there was a great need?

Her other hand reached for the thin strings holding in the stopper.

Take me in! The flask seemed to urge.

"If you wish to save us both," de Suavis whispered, "open it now!"

"Oh yes, Sol. That is just what I will do," she said softly. For indeed, what was there left to lose? Everything, and nothing. And the one penning fare she had paid? It was less than a pittance, compared to a new life somewhere. "Anywhere else," she whispered.

When and where in sovereignty. Was that right? Surely those were not words merely popping up in her head like the panicked flight of startled birds. She looked at her friend for confirmation, but he only nodded, as if eager for her to proceed.

She tore at the tiny straps until she held the torn strings in her fingers. Which, with the hum and tingle of the flask beneath them, had gone quite numb. She felt magic in it, and surely only magic could lift them up now.

Someone banged hard at de Suavis's heavy front door.

In one swift movement she pried out the wadded cloth stopper, lifted the mouth of the flask to her lips, and threw back a swig of the contents. On her tongue it tasted sweet as the first honey of the season. She swallowed and handed the tiny bottle to her friend. "Now ye do so," she said.

He took the flask from her, looking a bit uncertain.

Oh Sol, she thought, do not fail me now, when we have come this far.

At last he raised it to his mouth and took a gulp of the same syrup that was still sliding down her throat.

The pounding at the door grew louder, more demanding.

Clo barely noticed. In the midst of a frigid Bruges winter, she felt a warm breeze at her back. Vaguely she heard a faint clatter as Sol dropped the flask on the tabletop. It fell to, and then somehow *through* the polished wood. A deep rumble that was no longer a human fist hammering on a door's panels shook the house's very timbers. The floor beneath them shuddered and heaved. Objects rose all around them; the tapestries on the walls flapped like crows' wings. Books took flight from the shelves. The table bucked like a spring colt.

"Come," she said, reaching out to Sol. "We must leave now."

Without a single backward glance at his fine furniture, or even at the iron-banded safe, he took her hand and followed, pausing only briefly at the closed front door.

The pounding, the raised voices, had fallen silent.

He took hold of the heavy brass pull, and opened the door. The silence abruptly ended. As they stepped out into the street, all around them the quay was thronged. People talking, laughing, strolling arm in arm.

A plethora of market stalls held such wares as she had never seen before in Bruges. There rose the mingled scents of Eastern spices and exotic fruits, musky civet and flower perfumes. The vivid colors not of silks and cottons and wool, but of even stranger goods hawked by merchants, praising their quality, professing the bargains that could be found. But this market was still changing, shimmering and wavering, like one painting made on top of another. The confused-looking stevedores, dock workers, beggars, market women, traders, sailors, and captains of Damme were fading away too.

Clo squeezed her eyes shut in terror and clutched Sol's hand, thinking, Will we too simply disappear, as in the legend of the flask, never to be seen again?

When she finally dared look again, the market was gone. Replaced by a spacious park, shrouded in twilight. The air now was not just warm, but hot as a *midzomer* day.

On a knoll in the middle distance stood a tall spire, lit as with a thousand lanterns. Off to the side rose huge stone buildings, all gray save one; a beautiful red sandstone castle, also lit as if it were day. And farther in the distance loomed an even larger white building, its huge dome crowned with a robed soldier holding a sword aloft, as if to ward off any threat concealed in that darkening sky.

Just then a series of thunderous explosions, one after another, tore at the very air. Clo shrieked and flung her arms around Sol. Who clung to her even more tightly.

Colors lit the sky as the heavens filled with bright sparks much like the Chinese rockets she'd seen once on a festival day, in Bruges.

"Sol," she whispered. "We are not in Bruges anymore."

This was a new place, its humanity an odd assortment of features, skin colors, cultures, religions, races, clothing. Odder still, they all milled about in close proximity as if they didn't notice this strangeness. As if they had lived all their lives together in some unfathomable, unnatural harmony. Yet it looked so natural. How was that possible?

Clothilde glanced at her companion, perplexed.

He turned to her and stretched out an arm towards the mêlée of motley civilization. "*Sovereignty*," he said, quoting the flask's text softly.

Its meaning only now dawned fully on Clothilde. "It is . . another word for freedom."

Sol nodded. His joyful smile warmed her heart. "I was right." He chuckled. "It did contain a cure! For a very bad ailment. That of the old human condition!" He took her hand and patted it. "And now, ye and I . . . shall we approach this new adventure intellectually, inhabiting this *when and where* with the shared joys of new kenning?"

She smiled, and nodded. "Of course. All the while heeding Maimonides's three categories of *amicitia*."

"And . . . of love?"

But it wasn't truly a question any more. She felt confident of that. "Yes. And love."

A woman strolled past, wearing a tight pair of pantaloons—pantaloons, in public!—their hems so short Clothilde blushed after a single glimpse of them.

"Hey!" the woman called after them. "Great costumes!"

"Happy Independence Day!" said the man accompanying the scantily-clad woman. He wore short, baggy leg-coverings, exposing lean shanks and bony knees.

After a second glance, Clo's mouth fell open. For now she clearly recognized that beaky profile: the market vendor from Bruges. Much cleaner now, though, and wearing a strange blue cap with a brim like a duck's bill.

Before she could speak, however, the lanky fellow had walked on, out of sight.

"Is aught amiss, Clo?" asked Sol, as they headed deeper into the crowd, their way lit by the colorful glare of Chinese rockets. "Are ye feeling unwell?"

"*Nee.* All is quite well now." She tucked her arm more securely in his. "Why, just look about! This will be a far more perfect union, for us, by far."

And so, filled with hope and anticipation, they entered the sparkling magical Mall and merged into the crowd, becoming one with the many. Ahead lay untold marvels, and the *amica* only an innovative society purged of prejudice, preconceived ideas, and predefined notions, could hope to offer them.

The tiny glass vial displayed on a shelf in this booth may strike you as unimpressive, yet it perfectly exemplifies the true nature of human hypocrisy. For, while witchcraft has long been prohibited here both by law and by religion, some Venetians tend to shrug or even thumb their noses at the dictates of the Holy Father in Rome. For instance, a well-known priest on the island of Malamocco is said to happily engage in sorcery along with his regular church duties. He's rumored to be on such good terms with the Evil One, he keeps him close by in the shape of a large white dog. Still, from time to time, those higher up feel a need to make a show of cracking down on witches, real or imagined. At least, to persecute the less influential practitioners of the darker arts, and even simple healers—especially if they happen to be female. In times of great trouble and few solutions, it's always useful for the ruling class to have a scapegoat on which to lay the blame. Sometimes, though, such blame can rebound darkly, as if glimpsed in a haunting dream . . . as it did, once upon a time, for the former owner of this innocuous-looking little vial.

POSIONE D'AMORE
by Dana Miller

Boot heels clacked across the gritty stone tiles of Piombi prison shortly before sunrise; iron chains rattled along the inner walls. The stars blinked down from a dark sapphire sky as if peering curiously into the single small window of each cramped cell, for no shutters prevented December's chill from freely gusting in past the iron bars. Those prisoners chained inside trembled incessantly, and not solely from cold. When a confession was necessary, so were brutal tortures.

For some held captive in Piombi, their time on earth was nearly over. And the burnings always commenced at dawn.

Sabina Boverelli, a respected midwife, had been arrested the week before on allegations of witchcraft, after the last half-dozen babies she brought into the world arrived stillborn. Shortly thereafter, each of the mothers had contracted plague, suffering fevers, headaches, and chills followed by seizures, vomiting, and, bloody black flux. In a state of delirium, one young woman had accused Sabina, insisting, "The midwife is to blame!"

The disease spread rapidly. Soon all six mothers joined their children in Heaven.

Rumors had circulated rapidly through Venezia: Sabina *must* be a witch, though she'd sworn her innocence, and fervently declared her love for God. "The mothers and babes must've been tainted by some miasma prior to the births," she'd told the church fathers. "I am a good midwife. One who loves and worships the Holy Father."

Still they'd conferred, shaken their heads, and placed her under arrest.

Now she prayed on her knees, hunched on the cold flagstones in one corner of her cell, no longer able to feel her frostbitten feet. Pleading with God to deliver her to His Kingdom, and free her from the disgrace of being branded a heretic.

The boots halted outside her cell, followed by a jingling of keys. The iron door creaked open, and two guards stepped inside. "Get up!" one ordered.

Weak, hungry, and cold, Sabina was unable to rise alone. Grimacing, each guard took an arm and hauled her to her feet, stuffed her battered wrists and ankles into irons, and dragged her out. She was the first to be loaded into the ox-cart waiting outside.

Sabina silently prayed while the other five condemned climbed up, pitifully sagging as they took their seats. As the open cart rumbled over the cobbles some prisoners sobbed, a frosty haze puffing from their gaping mouths. But she had resolved not to show weakness.

Let the flames consume me, she thought. It will be painful, but quick, if I inhale the smoke deeply. No more shame, hunger, or cold. I will finally be at peace.

She glimpsed the rising auburn sun between olive-tree branches. Farther on, in a vast field, stood rows of tall wooden stakes. At the base of each were heaped piles of wood. The sweetish stench of charred flesh lingered, from the ashes of those burnt the previous day, in the still-cooling embers.

Dread washed over Sabina as the oxen halted before six freshly-hewn stakes. Yes, her agony would soon end. But for many others, it was only the beginning.

No matter how many arrests had been made by Sir Amatore Ferrante, Commander of the League of the Chosen, the disease-laden winds still blew. Black

Plague was seething through Europe, claiming thousands. Showing no mercy, even to those who devoutly believed God would protect them. Some said it was divine punishment, a manifestation of His wrath against sinners unworthy of His love. Venice's doctors claimed the Black Death was caused by miasmas floating on the air. Though some believed neither of these official explanations, though it would've been dangerous to say so, aloud.

Andrea Dandolo, the Doge of Venice, had recently entered his fifth decade, and carried all the hardships of his people on broad but weary shoulders. Though his habitual expression might appear sullen, he cared immensely for those he ruled. And he firmly believed plague was caused by forbidden magic. So, he sent forth a decree to burn any heretics found to be witches or sorcerers, or any who dabbled in the dark arts.

The task was great, but the reward would be greater. "If we rid Venice of all dark magic, God will protect us again," he told Ferrante. "We must gather a league of godly men to see this task to the end."

Ferrante was eager to prove himself, for he had two desires in life. The first was to become a member of the Council of Ten. He'd quickly climbed the ranks while in the military, retiring as a commissioned officer, a Marshal of the Venetian Army. Then he was elected as one of three leaders of the Council of Forty, known as *La Quarantia*. Impressed with Ferrante's military knowledge, the Doge charged him with arresting all suspected witches and sorcerers. He was given a small army, and made Commander of the *Lega del Prescelto*, the League of the Chosen.

Ferrante's second great desire was to marry, for he had neither wife nor child. He'd come close to matrimony twice, but never experienced the besotted feeling of true *amore*, even with those two ladies. The first marriage agreement had been broken after the maiden received a better offer from a minor count, one which would raise her higher in society. The other engagement was cut short when Ferrante's future bride died one night of a sudden fever. She'd been buried two days before the nuptials were scheduled to take place.

Believing he was incapable of finding love, if not cursed, Ferrante had thrown himself into the work of serving God—and his lord on earth, Andrea Dandolo.

During the day, Ferrante slept. At night he and his squad of witch hunters knocked on door after door, and conducted interrogations, gathering evidence. They haunted the streets, alleys, and canals, as well as the outlying woods, hoping to infiltrate covens. Everyone knew midnight was the hour when true witches and sorcerers woke to practice their craft.

After just a fortnight, the Lega had made many arrests. The prison was overflowing. Trials came even swifter, the burnings just as frequent.

Sometimes, though, Ferrante felt uneasy. He'd actually had doubts, in a few cases, as to whether some of those arrested were truly guilty. These dark notions most often tormented him in the early morning hours. Sometimes he was unable to sleep after returning from a raid. The faces of the accused came to him in the dark, declaring their innocence. But he could not dwell on such weak musings. He'd sworn to use all his military expertise, and trust in God. Better to sacrifice a few innocents than to let one heretic go free. The innocent, after all, would receive their reward in Heaven.

It was his sacred duty to purge Venice of witchcraft.

Early February was bitterly cold. At the cusp of dawn, the square near the Doge's palace lay silent. Dandolo woke at the clatter of hooves on cobblestones: his men returning from a nightly hunt. Blinking owlishly, he rose to peer from the doorway of his chamber just as Sir Ferrante trudged down the corridor, wearily rubbing his face.

"Well?" Dandolo came to the door, tying a crimson sash around his velvet dressing gown. He frowned at the dark circles beneath Ferrante's eyes. Though he was just past thirty, the Commander's dark brown hair showed streaks of gray around the temples.

Ferrante knelt, inclined his head, then rose. "Six more arrests, my lord. All locked in separate cells at Piombi prison."

Dandolo cleared his throat, and took a step closer. "And have those imprisoned confessed?"

"Only to their innocence, my lord. As they all do, at first. But I will have their confessions with the encouragement of Massimo, the chief inquisitor. That is a promise." Ferrante laid his right hand over his heart.

"You've done well. And worked so tirelessly! It has not gone unnoticed or unappreciated." The Doge smiled.

"Thank you," Ferrante blearily croaked.

Dandolo's eyes narrowed. "I wonder, though, will the success of these hunts suffice to make you happy?"

Ferrante stiffened. "Of course, my lord. I serve at your pleasure, and that of our Lord."

"It has not escaped my notice, either, that you return night after night to a cold, empty bed."

"No matter. It brings me great happiness to serve you, and this holy cause. There are more important things than finding a wife."

Ferrante's true feelings were quite different. He wanted nothing more than to spend each night in the arms of a loving spouse. A pious, comely woman waiting to welcome him home. A partner to confide in and, someday, to present him with a child to love, as well.

Dandolo rested a hand on Ferrante's arm. "You never complain, but I see the loneliness in your eyes. Understandably, you might be cautious about another attempt to wed, as Fortuna has not blessed your matrimonial endeavors, in the past." He stroked his beard thoughtfully. "But I wish to express gratitude for all you've done, and continue to do, by *insisting* you must marry."

"My lord," Ferrante protested, "I truly don't need—"

"No more objections! This, I command: Find a good woman, and find her soon. Waste not a single moment. Only God knows what tomorrow may bring for each of us."

"*Si*, my lord," Ferrante muttered, bowing his head. "I will do as you say."

Dandolo nodded, and returned to bed.

True, there were suitable women at the palace, but none fueled a fire within Ferrante's heart. He would rather live alone the rest of his days than marry without love. But now the Doge had ordered it.

He groaned and ambled to his chambers, to crawl under the blankets of that cold, empty bed.

Just before noon Ferrante's eyes flashed open. He rose and peered out his single window. Based on the sun's position, it must be near noon. The blazing fire that had driven the chill away earlier was now mere embers. He shivered as a cold draft flushed the remaining warmth from the room.

His nightclothes were sodden with sweat. A racing heart had jerked him from slumber. Normally he never recalled dreams; exhaustion plunged him into the deepest of sleeps after the night hunts. But this time he remembered every-thing. Or was this memory, not a dream?

No, surely it wasn't real.

Yet the woman . . . he'd never seen her at court, or on the streets of Venice. How could he dream so vividly of someone he'd never met? Her sky-blue dress, its tattered hem, the wild, disheveled auburn hair . . . he was sure he'd never seen this woman in the palace halls. Her eyes were the same electrifying blue as the gown. Each time their gazes met, he'd felt drawn in deeper. He could not forget her now, thanks to those piercing eyes.

In the dream, he'd followed as she trudged through a foot of freshly-fallen snow, with only a thin brown shawl to keep her warm. Hardly enough protection in deepest winter, yet she'd not seemed bothered by the chill wind.

Icy air had burned Ferrante's throat; his breath formed white mist with each exhalation. As he'd slowly gained on the woman, she stopped to glance back with a strangely twisted grin. He remembered calling, "Stop! Wait!" But no sound escaped his lips. He'd been determined to know where she was going, though, and kept following.

Of course he had known, even asleep, that it was folly to pursue such a strange, mysterious woman through a dark wood. But some unholy force urged him on. He could not resist, no matter how he strained to stop, to turn back. Then again, what real harm could result? It was but a dream, after all.

At last she'd turned to face him. "You must marry, *Messer* Ferrante, but have not yet met the one you will adore. Find me, and I will lead you to her."

"What? I . . . I don't understand," he'd stammered through chattering teeth. "Where do you take me? Where are we going?"

"Find me," she repeated, her words trailing away. Then she'd slipped between two gnarled oaks and vanished deep inside the dreary woods.

That was the moment Ferrante had jolted awake. Now he wondered: could this strange dream have been brought on by a fever?

But his skin felt cool. "No matter," he muttered. He must push the mysteri-ous woman from his thoughts. Perhaps the dream had merely been evoked by his marriage conversation with the Doge. Apart from conducting hunts, he now must choose a third bride, and he feared leaving the task too long. Dandolo might take it upon himself to find a woman for him. Then Ferrante ran the risk of being displeased with a choice not even his own.

Flinging the quilt back, he rose and stretched, pulled the damp nightshirt off, and called his manservant to quickly dress him for the day.

To shake off the eerie dream, Ferrante fell to plotting a route for the upcoming hunt. Around one, Carlotto Velluti, a member of the Council of Ten, rapped on his chamber door. "A written accusation of witchcraft has been sent to the palace," he informed Ferrante. "Claims of a mysterious woman walking alone in the woods, late at night."

"Hmm," said Ferrante.

"It is suspicious and improper for any lady to behave in that way." Velluti's voice was somber. "The accuser claimed he called out, but she simply vanished like a spirit, into the trees. He dared not follow, for everyone knows the Devil works there after dark. The Doge demands an investigation."

"Of course." But a burning tingled in Ferrante's gut. It intensified and spread to all his limbs, as if a terrible spell had been cast on him. "I . . . I will leave at once." He sprang forward and snatched the statement from Velluti's hand.

Carlotto looked surprised. "Shall I summon your men, Signore Ferrante?"

"*Non necessario.* Let them sleep. There's a long night ahead. I'll conduct a quick investigation myself. Should arrests be required, we'll ride out again at nightfall. I shall return shortly."

Of course it was not wise to go out alone. His men should always be in attendance during such dangerous missions. But the desire to leave unaccompanied had flowed from his lips like quicksilver. He'd had no control as he spoke the words, and knew in his heart they were not his own. At the same time, he felt powerless to reveal this to Velluti. For then he'd have to try to explain the dream, and would only sound like a madman.

At the stables he ordered his gelding, Bova, be saddled. The day was overcast, the air cold and lifeless. A perfect day for burning witches, Ferrante thought, as he veered off the cobblestone street to follow an unpaved road into the woods, which lay about a half-hour's ride from one of the burning sites.

But three hours later, dusk was falling early, and he was lost. The sun had sunk so far behind the trees, he now could not find the right path back to the palace.

The air had grown colder, too. He shivered as he scanned the trail he was on, in search of suspicious footprints. There came then the squeak and crunch of boots on fresh snow. Not an animal, for panting human breath accompanied them. Someone was out there.

"Hello?" he called. "Show yourself!"

The footsteps halted.

"Who is there? I've . . . I've lost my way. I beg you, direct me out of these woods."

The footsteps resumed, with no answer. But he saw a figure passing along the tree line a short distance away. The slight silhouette of a woman.

"Follow me," came a breathy whisper.

Again Ferrante felt the strange pull inside, compelling him. The urge to advance all but consumed him. Could this truly be the mysterious woman he'd been sent to find? "Of course," Ferrante called after her, heels nudging Bova forward.

Snaking through the trees, reins in one hand, he guided the horse toward a line of deep footprints in the snow. With the other, he clutched the collar of his cloak against the cutting cold. It would do no good to invite a fever.

"Slow your pace," he shouted, teeth chattering. "I must ask a few questions."

The woman was too far ahead to hear, or else simply ignored his request. She continued for perhaps a half-hour before Ferrante felt Bova was gaining on her at all. Strange! How could a person traipse so swiftly through deep snow, when he was unable to keep up on horseback?

"Quite impossible," he muttered. At this rate, he would be late to join the Lega for the nightly hunt. His men would be concerned, perhaps even search for him. It seemed unlikely, however, that they would suspect he'd ventured so far.

At that moment faint beams of light pierced through the trees, as if from many lifted lanterns. And was that . . . music? Ferrante leaned forward and squinted, trying to make out what lay ahead. A celebration of some sort?

"Welcome," a woman's voice sang out from the dark.

Startled, he nearly toppled from the saddle. He reined Bova in, then swung a leg over and dropped to the snowy ground.

The woman he'd followed stood just off to the left, waiting.

"Have we met before?" he asked, trudging to her side.

She smiled. "Am I familiar to you?" Turning her head coyly, she tossed long curling red hair over one shoulder. "Perhaps from a dream?"

Yes. It was she, the blue-eyed one. And yet . . . no, the idea was absurd. He grimaced in consternation. "Perhaps, but who are you?"

"You may call me Vera."

"And why have you led me here, Signorina?"

"Because we both desire things which we can only achieve together."

He touched the crucifix that hung from his neck. "But *where* are we? What is this place?"

She smiled. "Follow me, and see."

"I will not take another step until you answer," he growled. A woman he'd met before only in a dream now stood in the flesh before him? A sorceress, then, undoubtedly. It had been more than unwise to ride out alone. Now his life, even his soul, might be in danger.

She shrugged. "As you wish. Welcome to the Night Bazaar. Follow me, and find the answers you seek." Turning away, she sauntered off through a pair of garnet brocaded drapes that had been incongruously suspended between two stout pine trees.

But . . . surely they had not been there before? Ferrante frowned, but pushed on through them for fear of losing sight of her.

Past the draperies a crowd milled in a clearing. Everywhere his gaze fell he saw marvels. Inexplicable, forbidden sights. Row after row of red- and green-striped tents had been erected so closely they pressed up against one another. Colossal torches staked into the earth lit the entrance to each. As Ferrante passed one he saw, through the open flap, a table displaying rings, necklaces, and brooches set with odd, glowing rocks and moonlike stones. Another tent offered unfamiliar bottled herbs on shelves, and bunches of strange-smelling plants hung suspended from tall willow arches. Smoky spices, myrrh, and sandalwood incense perfumed the air. Throngs buzzed from tent to tent, talking loudly, laughing, singing foreign songs.

In fact, Ferrante was unable to make out what anyone was saying. As if they all spoke no Italian, and conversed only in alien tongues. The air felt warmer, too. As though he'd been transported to a different place. Or . . . a different season?

The next tent he passed stopped him in his tracks. Two women sat inside, facing each other. The one to the right was clearly far along in pregnancy. The other chanted while dangling a silver charm on a chain, swinging it before the pregnant woman's face.

"What evil is this?" Ferrante shouted, crossing himself and dashing inside. Neither woman looked up, as if they hadn't noticed his sudden appearance.

A sharp tug on his arm. It was Vera. "Please, *Messer* Ferrante, leave them be." She led him out of the tent.

"But what sort of Devil's work was that?"

"The young woman who's with child is simply seeking advice for a safe and healthy delivery."

He shook his head, baffled. "But that is trickery! To lure in the naive and innocent, then make promises beyond anyone's control, save God's."

"We do offer many services not found elsewhere. Our tonics contain healing concoctions that even the best Venetian doctors are unaware of, as yet."

"None of that sounds very godly," he said, looking around. "This place is unnatural!"

"Not at all. We merely help those who suffer ailments, or are in pain. Or who wish to improve their lives. You seek a wife, *signore*, do you not?"

"That is not your concern. What could a den of unholy charlatans have to do with me?"

Her fingers felt hot as they curled around his cold-numbed hand. The torch flames reflected in her entrancing blue eyes. Her touch had an instant calming effect, though now he feared he was no longer in control of his body.

"What could we offer you? Why, everything." From a leather pouch hung at her waist, she pulled out a tiny, twisted glass vial with a cork stopper, half full of a pale pink liquid. A small parchment scroll wrapped around its neck was scrawled with a strange symbol.

He drew back, frowning. "What is that?"

"The contents will provide the thing you've always longed for—true love."

"God in Heaven, you *are* a witch!" He threw off her hand. "This is a coven. Witches, all! By the power granted to me by Doge Andrea Dandolo, everyone here is under arrest!"

"Really. And what is *my* crime?" she snapped, as if she had no fear of the Doge, nor of him, or indeed not even of heavenly disapproval.

His eyes widened. "Why . . . for . . . for bribing me with a sinful love potion!"

"Ah." She sneered. "*The Pozione d'Amore?* A mere *philtrum d'amore* that might be found in the possession of any lady at your court."

"*Basta!* I arrest you, then, for . . . for harboring other witches. For creating a secret demonic society filled with evil and forbidden practices! All are the work of the Devil."

Her laugh was as beautiful as shaken silver bells. "*Molto comico*, Signore Ferrante. But I have done none of those things. And I certainly do not work for the Devil. I simply help those in need, for a small payment."

"And what's the nature of that payment?" he demanded. "Tricking innocent souls into making a pact with evil? Signing their names into the Dark One's book of souls?"

"Hardly. I possess no such book. We travel the world to find medicines. Remedies to cure ailments. We provide solace to the brokenhearted. Simple mixtures to help those unable to sleep, or in the grip of nightmares." She stared at him then so boldly he fidgeted and had to look away.

"Even tonics for men who struggle to properly bed their wives," she added. "We seek only to help and heal, like any doctor in Venice."

"And you propose to supply me with a wife if I simply drink a potion?" He sneered. "Do you think me a fool?"

"I'm only offering the means to make your most cherished desires come true." Again she held out the bottle.

"You know nothing of my desires," he replied, teeth gritted.

"Oh, but I do. A loving wife is something you have long wished for."

"A loving wife is every man's desire. That makes me no different."

"I would agree, if all men desired the same things. Some are motivated by money, power, success, or independence. You do desire success in your career, but would gladly give it up should you find the right woman. You only wish to be a member of the Council of Ten because your life lacks happiness elsewhere."

He gaped at her, then scowled. "How would you know such things? Have you been following me?"

"That was not necessary. I am skilled at intuiting such needs. Every life force has a particular color, sometimes more than one. Each shade means something different, and changes based on a person's thoughts and feelings. You may not believe in such abilities, yet they exist. So...you may now turn around and leave the Bazaar. Find your way back to the palace, then try to return and arrest us all. But you will not find us again, I assure you."

"You dare—"

She held up a hand to silence him. "Should you leave now, you will venture on with your mission set forth by the Doge, and work hard to become a member of the Council of Ten. But you will still live alone, filled with regret. A great void in your heart. That is, of course, your choice. But why? For before me I see a man with so much to offer. What a shame if so much love should be wasted."

Ferrante felt her artful words drawing him in. Could the contents of that tiny vial truly have the ability to give true love? He longed to possess the potion, a feeling which intensified the longer he stared into Vera's eyes. *Yes.* He *must* have it. He wanted nothing more in the entire world.

"And what sort of . . . payment would you expect for such a . . . medicine?"

"Only that you open your eyes and see the harm your work for the Doge is causing. You seem to believe it a noble thing to burn innocents convicted of witchcraft. Those you have not even given a proper trial before condemnation."

"There is no time for trials! The plague is upon us, the proof clear at the time of the arrests. That's enough."

"No. That is only seeing what you wish to see, rather than what is truly before you. Many innocents have been sacrificed for your misguided cause! Do you not understand that each blameless life taken will turn your soul darker? We seek to help people here. Not commit sanctioned murder, as you do."

Ferrante tore his gaze away from her bewitching blue stare. "I am no murderer!"

"Can you prove it?" she challenged.

"I needn't prove anything to you, or the other sorcerers hosting this . . . this . . . obscene Bazaar. A den of iniquity which goes against everything I believe in."

"Have you shown your deity's famous mercy to any of those arrested? Or were they simply thrown into a cold cell until the day their name was called, then led away to be burned?" Now she sneered at him. "Tell me, how can a mere man aspire to play God?"

Ferrante stared, unsure of how to answer. The fear that sometimes he'd made the wrong choice in those arrests had been gnawing at him for some time. But duty forced him to repress such concerns. Should he question his methods or his conscience, the Doge would view him as a traitor to the holy cause.

She stepped closer. "I see curiosity in your eyes. Unlike most, you wisely came searching for answers. Just as the Pope did when he visited us."

"The . . . His Holiness was *here*?" He gasped, then shook his head. "Bah! Lies."

"So you say." She lifted her chin. "Don't you see things must change, Signore Ferrante?"

"The plague is here. I must do all I can to stop it. To protect innocent lives against those who bring doom upon us."

"The plague comes whether you burn a thousand, or no one. It will claim life after life. Yet you have no idea why it is here in the first place. Fools such as yourself attempt to eradicate disease and death based on false claims of witchcraft as the root cause. You've been told what to believe by men claiming to have the answers—God's answers. In reality, the machinations of the corrupt to mislead the credulous. *That*, Sir Ferrante, is the real evil on earth. Killing innocents heals no one. You must end this persecution."

The motion of so many people passing by was making Ferrante dizzy. He looked at her once more, and warmth washed over his body. Again, her words twisted in his mind. Again, she held out the potion.

With a groan, he snatched the vial and tucked it into his cloak. He withdrew a purse filled with silver *grossi*. "What is the price?"

"Your coins do not interest me. Instead you must reason with the Doge. Call off the raids. Convince him to order a stop to hunting down the innocent."

"He'll view me as a traitor. I'll be arrested myself."

"Drink that and you'll find the woman you've always dreamed of marrying. But if the raids do not end, its effects will not last. You have two weeks to bring the torture and burnings to an end. Otherwise you'll lose everything the potion gave you."

"No. I can't do this." He pulled the vial out again and thrust it back at her.

"*Per favore.* Take it with you. Only think about it," she said soothingly. The fire reflected in her eyes burned brighter. Gently cupping both hands over his, she pushed the bottle back toward him. "You have until dawn to decide."

Unable to sleep after returning to the palace, Ferrante paced his chamber, replaying the night's events. I should return to the woods with my men and arrest them all, he told himself. What shocking, sinful sights! Devilry, trickery. Yet . . . how had the woman known all about him? As if she had a secret passageway into his heart. His desire to find love, the constant turmoil endured each night after the raids . . . things he'd never revealed to another soul.

Dandolo would never agree to stop the raids. But, what if after all the arrests and the burnings, plague still afflicted Venice? Ferrante would not only have failed, he might even be held responsible.

Perhaps this truly was his one chance at real love. Should he turn his back on the thing he'd wished for so long? Perhaps it would not hurt simply to *try* the potion. If it was useless, a hoax, he'd be no worse off. And if it actually worked . . .

He would think of how best to deal with the witches at the Bazaar, later.

He held vial close to the candle at his bedside, peering at the writing on the scroll fixed to the bottle. Beneath the words *Pozione D'Amore* was inked a symbol shaped like a trident. The center prong extended farther, with an encircled star sitting upon its sharp point. The base of the symbol curled oddly into a spiral, like a whorled snail's shell. He'd seen it before, a mark known as the "Forbidden Symbol". So Vera was part of the secret coven being hunted across all of Europe—for crimes of witchcraft, and for being the force behind the plague.

And he, Ferrante, had discovered them here.

But when he recalled her fiery, spellbinding gaze, he was again frozen. Again overwhelmed by the reassurance he'd felt simply looking into her eyes.

"Bah, foolishness," he snapped. With his thumb, he popped the tiny cork from the neck of the vial. It dropped to roll around at his feet. He threw the vial back and, in one swig, let the bittersweet pink contents slide down his throat.

While waiting for some effect, he decided it best to hide the evidence. No one must ever stumble upon bottle or scroll. But they could be useful later, as evidence in a trial.

He retrieved the cork, then stepped around to the other side of the bed and stomped hard. A loose tile popped up. He bent and shoved the vial deep into a space beneath, then carefully pressed the tile back into place.

He paced his chambers for a while after that, feeling a slight queasiness. But was that due to the potion, or merely worry and exhaustion?

The next day the palace was in a flurry of anticipation. Duca Donatello de Amalfi, a widower at only thirty-nine, would soon arrive in search of a new wife. The duke's only daughter, Lady Ardita Amalfi, who had celebrated her seventeenth birthday the week prior, was accompanying him. All the noble unmarried ladies at court were in a flutter at the prospect of becoming the new Duchessa de Amalfi. But men were not immune to the excitement either. Having heard rumors of Ardita's tantalizing beauty, her dainty foot, and beautiful voice, they too swooned—but with hopes of sweeping her into bed. These lustful desires were shattered, though, upon hearing the Lady was so deeply pious, she had once contemplated entering a convent. Then the men glumly agreed that such a devout one might not be so easily swept.

As Ferrante half-listened to some gossiping noblemen, he was approached by Carlotto Velluti. "I rejoice to see you safe after your expedition, by God's grace," Velluti began. "Your men were concerned when the sun set and you had not yet returned. The Doge in particular was quite distressed. He insists you always be accompanied on future investigations."

"Of course," Ferrante replied. "I apologize for causing alarm. I simply lost my way in the woods."

"And . . . the investigation, was it fruitful?" Velluti wrung his hands eagerly.

Ferrante wondered what would be the best reply. He didn't want to invite further questioning. "Unfortunately," he began, sighing, "I have nothing new to report."

"Ah, that is truly a shame." Velluti shook his head. "*Non importa.* Surely tonight's hunt will yield an abundance of arrests."

"Yes," Ferrante nodded, feeling shaken. "No doubt it will."

It truly did happen in an instant. The moment their gazes met across the palace's elegant Audience Room, Ferrante was taken hostage by Lady Ardita's ethereal beauty.

Her form was indeed both elegant and delicate. Waist-length brown hair, worn loose as she was as yet a virgin, glimmering with streaks of deep red. Eyes warm as polished amber. Flawless skin, smooth and creamy as purest eggshell. And, perhaps because she had just stepped inside from the cold, two lovely spots of rose warmed those porcelain cheeks.

"Might I trouble you?" The Doge turned to Ferrante. "Please escort Lady Ardita around the palace. Introduce her to some of the more suitable nobles."

Ferrante inclined his head. "Of course, my lord!"

He crossed the room and bowed to her. "The Doge sends his regards. He has given me the honor of showing you the palace. Would you grace me with your gentle company?"

Lady Ardita nodded. Her blush deepened.

The duenna, Ardita's governess, was a short, plump woman in a black gown, veil, and wimple. She followed close behind as Ferrante led them through the halls to the Shield Room, where Ardita nearly collided with Gemma Sassoli.

The Duchessa was strolling arm-in-arm with the widowed Contessa Stella Finucci. This catty pair traveled everywhere together, for their shared avocation in life was gossip. No doubt they knew of the arrival of the Amalfis, and were hurrying to catch a glimpse of the legendary beauty and her very eligible father.

"Oh, Signore Ferrante! We nearly had an accident," Duchessa Sassoli gushed, narrowed gaze shifting to Lady Ardita, then quickly back to him.

"Ah, but such a fortunate one!" He bowed, glad to be a buffer between the two old cats and Ardita. They wouldn't dare step out of line with him at her side. Otherwise she might've been cornered and, mouse-like, swallowed alive by incessant questions, as they devoured every detail of her life. Even now their eyes held a feline glitter, an urge to sink their claws into new prey. "Duchessa Sassoli and Contessa Finucci, I am pleased to present the Lady Ardita Amalfi of Catania, Sicily."

The women uncoiled their arms long enough to curtsey and simper.

"Such a pleasure," Contessa Finucci said. "We have been *dying* to meet you, Signorina. We must talk later and become better acquainted."

"You are too kind. That would be lovely." Lady Ardita's dimpled smile seemed to say she would quickly forward the hours simply to join them again.

Once the women had swept off, out of earshot, Ferrante leaned in and whispered, "Steer clear of those two."

"I beg your pardon?" Ardita looked up, eyes wide.

"The duchessa and the contessa are not trustworthy. They don't want to be your friends. Only to use whatever you say or do against you, later."

"I . . . I do not understand." Her lower lip quivered. "Who would act so dreadfully?"

Ferrante sighed. "You do not yet know palace life, my lady. While some here are noble and pious, others find joy in treachery, lies, and deceit."

The duenna sniffed disapprovingly.

Ardita paled. "Oh dear. Perhaps I should not remain in such a place."

"I have heard of your character," he began. "You are pious and innocent. Thus I will make sure to introduce you only to those I believe worthy of your company."

"Oh, please do!" she cried, laying a hand on his sleeve. "I am in your debt, *signore*."

Just then a short, stout woman turned the corner. Her brown hair was coiled in an elaborate coif. As she approached them her hands fluttered. "Oh! There you are, Signore Ferrante."

"We're in luck," he told Ardita. This is the lovely, honorable Nencia Ghiselli. I was hoping to find you, Contessa, in order to present the Lady Ardita Amalfi."

"So wonderful to make your acquaintance, *cara mia*."

They both curtseyed.

"Lady Ardita has just arrived from the country. She has no one to guide her in the ways of court life. We just encountered the Duchessa Sassoli and Contessa Finucci . . . "

"Oh, them." The Contessa rolled her eyes. *"Due gate vecchia!"*

"Yes, as I explained." He glanced at Ardita, who smiled back. "But I believe you ladies have much more in common."

"Say no more." She turned to Ardita. "I will come find you a bit later."

"I pray the time flies," Ardita whispered, but she was gazing raptly at Ferrante.

When they were alone once more, she thanked him. "I fear I've no talent for seeing faults. When I was schooled at the convent, the sisters taught us to believe everyone holds goodness within."

He nodded. "I see. But you are one of the rare few who holds goodness in their entire being."

"Oh, *sì?* And what about you?" she playfully chided. "Are you not a proper gentleman, filled up with goodness?"

Now he could not meet her eyes, though he flashed a lackluster smile. "There are those who say so. Sometimes I'm not certain it is true."

She laid a hand on his arm. "How can you say such a thing?"

"As Commander of the Lega del Prescelto, I lead the night raids. For a noble cause—to stop the spread of plague—but sometimes wonder if it is right I decide whether another person lives or dies."

"Oh, but it isn't up to you," she said fervently. "This is God's plan. *He* decides. You merely carry out his work. Witchcraft is evil, no? So my own priest says. The *streghe* go against everything God teaches. You only labor in His service."

"You are truly a devout and wise young lady. I'm inspired by your devotion," he said, as they passed through a set of carved double doors and into a dark, narrow corridor. The portly duenna hobbled a few discreet paces behind.

"And I admire *your* honesty and openness. Most men do not speak of what is truly in the heart. How will I fare, though, when you're not with me? Or know who to trust?"

A good question. He sighed as he guided her down an even tighter passageway. Its tapered columns and arched, carved wooden ceiling hovered less than a foot overhead. The hallway curved left, then right, then left again.

Ardita looked alarmed. "A mythical labyrinth. Where does it lead?"

"My lady," the Duenna interrupted. "I advise we turn back. It is not proper to venture so far with a gentleman you have only just met."

Ardita turned to her governess. "Do not be alarmed, Marta. Signore Ferrante is regarded highly by the Doge himself. And you will not leave my side for a moment." She turned back to him. "Would you be so kind, Signore, as to reveal our next destination, and ease my nurse's mind?"

"Of course. One of the extraordinary things about this palace is the maze-like halls and secret passages. Something at this end you must see. Whenever someone visits for the first time, and I am their guide, I always make it the final stop of interest."

A few more curves and turns led to a dead end. A single torch flickered in an iron bracket on the wall ahead. Ferrante lifted it high. A carved stone image of a lion's face, centered on the wall, leapt out as if to charge them.

"*Mio Dio!* Those eyes." Ardita crossed herself. "As if it stares into my soul. But what…what are the fearsome jaws for?"

"There are such *Bocche dei Leoni* not just here, but in several parts of the City. People come to submit accusations against those they believe have committed a crime. You see?" He pointed to the open slot of the mouth. "Here, notes may be slipped in. If you know someone has broken a law, it's your Christian duty to report it to the Doge."

She laid a hand at the base of her throat. "But would that not put me in danger? If the criminal discovered I wrote the letter."

He shook his head. "That will never happen. See the inscription below? *Per Denontie Segrete*. Your name would be kept secret by his eminence, in gratitude. For he abhors wrongdoing, and rewards those who do the righteous thing. One devout as you will always know right from wrong. And this is the place to report a crime as safely as under the holy seal of the confessional."

As he spoke, the events of the previous night crept into his mind: his own sin in not speaking up about the coven; the obtaining of a magic potion; the lie he'd told in claiming the journey to have been an unsuccessful investigation.

"Who else knows of this place?" Ardita's fingertips brushed the snarling muzzle of the carven *leone*.

"All who live here. Some won't enter these back halls, though, for fear of never finding their way out. But I want you to feel safe anywhere in the palace."

She blinked up through a shimmer of tears. "You are terribly kind, to take so much trouble with me."

Ferrante smiled, racked the torch onto the wall, and led the lady and her duenna back toward the main corridor. He nearly jumped when a small, soft hand slid secretly into his, entwining their fingers. He glanced back, but the old duenna appeared oblivious. Was Ardita merely frightened? Or did she feel what he did? That is, a growing love . . . and great desire.

"Will you capture all the witches before the plague kills more people?" she asked, voice echoing in the long hallway.

"Unfortunately, the future is still uncertain."

"You must rank highly in the Doge's approval. After the hunts are over… will he favor you in some way?"

"I've hopes his Excellency will see me as a desirable candidate for the *Consiglio dei Dieci*."

"The Council of Ten?" She nodded. "You would be a wonderful member. A god-fearing man whose will to succeed is strong. I can sense it."

Not until they reemerged into the main corridor did she let loose his hand. And as he led the way to the grand golden staircase, to show off the Square Atrium, he not only felt the heat of desire, but as if he had known her all his life.

Lady Ardita's eyes glimmered as she peered up at the ornate gold and ivory ceiling decorations, one hand pressed to the wall for support. As if she too had felt the world shifting beneath her. "How exquisite," she whispered, pointing up at the gilded relief of clouds and cherubs. "Like a glimpse of Heaven."

As she turned and started up the stairs, Ferrante blurted, "If you would please linger a moment, Lady." His heart thudded. She was the one. The woman Vera had promised. Here with him now only because he'd drunk the potion. He could not simply let her leave.

"I . . . I understand your father has brought you here to broker a suitable match. So I feel emboldened now to profess my feelings. From the moment I saw you across the room, I knew that . . . that God has called you to me. Every single event in my life has happened because I was meant to find you. The one who is everything I ever wanted, and more. Please, may I speak to Duca Amalfi regarding a match between us?"

The Duenna gasped and crossed herself twice.

Ardita's surprised look turned slowly to a joyful smile. Yet she did not answer.

"And so I, uh . . . " Should he withdraw the offer now, and save face?

But just then Ardita delicately laid a slim white hand upon his forearm. "I am greatly honored, Signore Ferrante," she warmly answered. "Please *do* speak to him."

They were married on a cold, sunny day the following week in St. Mark's Basilica. Ardita walked toward Ferrante on her father's arm, wearing a midnight-blue embroidered gown, her hair intricately braided and pinned up beneath a lace mantilla threaded with gold.

Ferrante was unable to think clearly as the priest droned on. He pinched his own arm, fearing to awaken and find it all a dream. But no. Ardita still stood beside him, veiled and lovely, and now his wedded wife. He thanked God to have made it to the altar this time without something going terribly amiss.

A lavish wedding feast followed immediately after, in the palace ballroom. Wine flowed, and silver platters of baked fowl and venison roasts, crusty bread, fine cheeses, and sweetmeats were constantly replenished throughout the afternoon. Later, the wedding night brought more bliss than Ferrante had ever imagined possible.

But at midnight he was yanked from a deep sleep. Someone was calling his name. Propped on one elbow, he bent to behold his bride, still asleep. Carefully he rose from bed, frantically searching behind curtains and furniture, following the drifting murmur of a husky female voice.

"*Follow me, Ferrante,*" it chanted. "*Follow . . . follow . . . follow.*"

First she seemed to speak right behind him, but when he turned there wasn't a soul. Then the floor creaked by his chamber door, and the melodious voice drifted in from the hallway. Swinging the door wider, he slipped into the hall. The voice spoke again, farther down. Soles chilled by cold flagstones, he tiptoed down the dimly-lit corridor toward the Compass Room. Only a few of the torches mounted at every corner were still lit, so he stumbled now and then in the dark.

Soon he realized no guards were stationed at their normal posts. Aside from his shadow on the stone walls, no one witnessed the awkward pursuit. But how could this be? Where were the Doge's men?

"Please, wait!" he begged. "Where do you take me?"

"*Follow . . . follow . . . follow,*" whispered down the hall.

"Stop!" he shouted, voice echoing. Heart racing, clothes damp from sweat, he shivered but ran on.

At the door to the Doge's apartments, Ferrante paused, panting and trembling. Fearing the voice would lead him there next.

But it had fallen silent.

Torchlight tinted the hallway as red as the witch's hair, and the air felt unnaturally chilly. His breath condensed in white clouds before him.

The one called Vera had told him to speak to the Doge about stopping the night raids. He had drunk the potion, then met and married the woman of his dreams. But to keep his new love, he had also agreed to hold up his end of the bargain.

Cold, exhausted, he fell to his knees, hands clasped. "Please, just a little more time. I swear, all will be settled. Let me return to bed with my bride. In the morning I will appeal to my lord. In a week, the raids will stop."

He held his breath, waiting. The silence lingered.

Finally, Vera's voice floated to him like a summer breeze, so close he felt a warm exhalation on his cheek. The hairs rose on his nape as she uttered one word.

"*Go.*"

He exhaled, slumping in relief.

A draft swept through the hall, extinguishing the remaining torches one by one. Ferrante was left to feel his way in the dark back to the safety of his bed. Where Ardita peacefully slept on, while all night Ferrante's mind churned with anxiety, foreboding, and fear.

The next day he requested an audience with Dandolo. The Doge sent a messenger with apologies, citing pressing matters of state, promising to see him soon. Unable to explain the urgency, Ferrante could only nod and send the boy away.

For the next three nights Vera tormented his dreams, springing him from his nuptial bed, sending him on a fruitless chase through the palace, as each day passed without a halt to the raids. Ardita always appeared undisturbed when Ferrante returned to bed.

Still, she had detected his unease. "Why so troubled, husband?" she asked as they prepared for bed the following night.

She'd think him mad if he told the truth. But she was his wife. He ought to share his concerns, at least partly.

"I'm afraid," he began, sitting beside her on the silken coverlet, "that the nightly raids may need to stop."

She stared at him incredulously. "But why?"

"What if I'm sending innocents to the stake, when they swear no guilt even under the direst torture? Could some accusations be false, or at least mistaken? I worry for my soul. Surely God will punish me."

"But you are carrying out God's work! Why do you think He sent the plague in the first place? He's angry we allow heretics to commit satanic acts." Her voice trembled with righteous indignation. "What if you call off the raids and the witches continue to practice dark magic. Why, then *I* may contract plague, as the wife of he who hunted them. What then becomes of *me*?" She gasped, gripping her nightgown just above the heart. "Please do not send me to an early grave, husband! I have joined my life with yours. Do not tarnish our union in the eyes of God."

Ferrante wrapped his arms around her. "Hush, *carissima*. I would give my own life to prevent any ill befalling you."

He waited until she was sound asleep, then left the bed chamber. He would not wait for Vera to haunt his dreams again. No, he must speak with Dandolo, even if it meant disturbing the great man's rest.

The Doge's chamber guards knocked to rouse him from bed.

"*Santo Vergine*! What is it?" Dandolo stumbled to the door, nightcap askew. "What brings you to my chamber at this hour, Ferrante?

"My lord, I do apologize, but I must speak with you. On an urgent matter of . . . morality."

Dandolo flapped a hand impatiently. "Go on, then."

"I can no longer, in good conscience, conduct the witch hunts. I fear our Lord does not approve."

Dandolo frowned. "Has this something to do with the Lady Ardita? Perhaps her soft female heart has softened you as well?"

"No! I mean . . . yes, my lord. In some ways. She is so very pious, yet hates to see blood spilled," he lied. "So, well, I think—"

"I do believe," Dandolo interrupted, "your bride will come to see this as a just and noble cause. These raids will ensure the safety of Venice's citizens, and also bring you closer to becoming part of my Council of Ten. A goal you have sought for quite some time, no?"

That was before Lady Ardita, though. "My lord, plague decimates the city no matter how many arrests we make. If God was pleased, would he not show it? And perhaps it's impossible to capture every witch and sorcerer, in any case."

"True. But we must do all we can. Do not disappoint me! You'll have nothing to fear from anyone once you are part of my Council."

"But my lord, must we—"

Dandolo held up a hand. "No more."

Ferrante hung his head. "Yes, my Doge."

"You shall do my will. *That* is what is expected." His tone was sharp with contempt. He turned back into his chamber, leaving Ferrante alone in the hallway.

The following night would be the first Lady Ardita had spent alone since her marriage. She could join the rest of court in nighttime merriment, but the notion of drinking, dancing, and playing cards among so many worldly strangers felt sinful.

"I will stay in for the evening," she told Ferrante.

Her husband had introduced her to a great many nobles, but she did not yet know any intimately. He would not be there to protect her from vultures like Duchessa Sassoli and Contessa Finucci. The last thing she wanted was to associate with unpleasant women who wished only to flirt and gamble and divert themselves. Thus far, whenever she refused to join in, they'd mocked and taunted. She wanted nothing to do with them.

So, after a solo dinner in their rooms, she put on a dressing gown, enjoying the warmth of the blazing fire. Pouring a small glass of Amontillado, she browsed through some leather-bound books Ferrante had bought for her.

Eventually settling on *Lives of The Saints*, she skimmed the first few pages. But her mind drifted. She worried about her dear husband's safety. And about where he stood on the subject of the raids. Why the reservations? Witches and sorcerers were the bane of Christianity. Demons intent on bringing forth an evil in this world so horrific God had extended his hand to intervene. Would any true Catholic hesitate? What would Ferrante gain by going against God?

Perhaps she'd leapt into marriage too soon, tying herself to a man she knew little about. She had felt such strong affection at first, but now . . .

She closed the book and laid it on the bed.

A distraction was what she needed. Ferrante had said she might have some space in the large cabinet in his library. So she removed the contents from the shelf he'd designated, and laid them out across the top of his desk.

The first document was the deed to a plot in Cremona. She noticed quite a bit of correspondence from the Doge, and many letters as well from someone named Jacopo Alighieri. Could this last be related to the famous Italian poet, Dante Alighieri? Ardita didn't mean to read the letters from Jacopo, but she was intrigued. Such a noteworthy association! They were written in a casual, intimate tone, so the two must be close. Then she discovered something exciting. The letters *were* written by the son of Dante Alighieri. Answering Ferrante's correspondence about his enjoyment of the *Divine Comedies: Inferno, Purgatorio*, and *Paradiso*.

In response, Alighieri the Younger had written:

Especially now, with plague ravaging the country, I understand your great desire to read my father's works. If anyone else had asked, I would surely decline, as some of the poems are not yet published. But for you? I will do my best to send copies of each.

It was signed, *Your good friend, Jacopo Alighieri.*

A final letter, dated a fortnight ago, was from Jacopo's sister Antonia. Her brother had contracted a sudden illness, possibly related to plague.

He has joined the angels and his sacred father.

Saddened for Ferrante, now Ardita felt ashamed. She returned to organizing the former contents of the shelf into neat stacks. Then set a leather-bound journal, a stack of fresh parchment, a pot of ink, and two of her own books there.

Then, satisfied, she decided to pray before turning in for the night.

When she knelt beside the bed, something shifted beneath one knee. A loose tile.

Dear me, she thought, what if my exhausted husband trips over this in the dark? Unable to push it firmly back in place, she lifted and set the tile aside, to see if something was lodged underneath. She held a candlestick from the mantle over the spot, and discovered a dark, shallow nook.

"Oh!" she gasped, as something faintly twinkled there. She felt around, discovered a small object, and scooped it up. An empty, twisted glass vial. She held it close, squinting to make out the scribbled words on a tiny scroll bound to it.

Pozione D'Amore.

Ardita gasped. A love potion?

And the odd symbol below the words. It looked familiar.

Yes . . . now she recognized it. While traveling across Europe with her father, she'd seen the same mark posted on a parchment broadside. First in Paris, near le Hôtel Saint-Pol. Then again when they'd stayed at the Orso Grigio in Innichen Town. The Forbidden Symbol, displayed on the Pope's warnings to all good Christians: *Avoid any who bear this mark.* It represented the secret society of witches responsible for bringing plague.

She fell against the side of the bed, heart thumping painfully. Her own husband, in league with witches? She thrust the vial back into the hole, set the tile in place, and scrambled to her feet.

I have been lied to, betrayed by the man I trusted!

Clearly he must have connections with a witch to obtain such a potion. Then a new thought struck her.

Has he used it on me? Could this be why I was so suddenly captivated with him? Did he drink the potion, or slip it into my wine? Oh Jesu, he is no god-fearing Christian after all, but a sympathizer with those ensnared in the dark arts!

Or worse.

Is he, too, a sorcerer?

She lay awake the rest of the night, tormented. Wondering what to do.

As the stars wheeled in the heavens, gradually giving way to dawn, Ardita made up her mind. She got out of bed, rushed to the cabinet, and retrieved a blank parchment and her pot of ink.

Ardita made certain to leave their chamber well before the time her husband normally returned from night raids. Spotting Contessa Nencia Ghiselli just after breakfast, she stayed by her side the remainder of the day, hoping to avoid being alone with Ferrante. She shuddered now at the very idea.

"You seem distressed." Nencia frowned with concern as they walked in the formal garden. "I recognize that unease in your eyes. Such a look always has to do with a husband."

Ardita stiffened, but said nothing.

"Don't fret, little one. Whatever we speak of will be kept in confidence."

Ardita twisted a silk handkerchief hemmed with gold thread. "Do all husbands keep secrets from their wives, at the palace?"

"Undoubtedly they do, *cara mia*. For some it is their duty to do so. Others cannot trust their wives with delicate information. Or any information, for that matter. Some here take great pleasure in gossip, as you may have learned."

"Oh, yes." Ardita sighed. "That, I am well aware of."

"Do not let trifling matters weigh on your conscience. Signore Ferrante is an honorable man. Should he keep secrets, I'm sure it is only to protect your virtue. He wouldn't wish you to hear about immoral, ungodly transgressions."

Ardita bit her lower lip. "But . . . what if a wife suspects her husband is concealing something truly terrible?"

Gently resting a hand on Ardita's arm, Nencia smiled sadly. "Why, then it is even more essential you know as little as possible. To ease your worries, why not turn to God?"

"Of course." Ardita forced a smile. "I will do just that."

Dandolo requested an immediate audience upon Ferrante's return. "I hear no witches were brought in last night," he said sternly. "How can this be?"

Ferrante nervously cleared his throat. "We, ah, did not encounter anyone I had reason to suspect of the practice, my lord. Perhaps this is progress. Thanks to much diligent work, there are now fewer of the guilty to be found."

"Is that so?" The Doge raised an eyebrow. "Well, I trust that, above all others, you would know how to spot a heretic. I also expect, based on our last talk, that you would never be so careless as to defy my orders."

Ferrante nodded. "Indeed not, your eminence."

"Get some rest, then. Let's pray tonight's raid proves more fruitful."

Ferrante bowed and excused himself. He hoped the witch Vera would notice the lack of arrests, and spare him a bit more time.

After Ferrante left, Dandolo ordered Colonello Baldi be brought to him.

"You were at Signore Ferrante's side during the witch hunts, correct?" he asked the portly soldier.

"Yes, my lord. Every night."

"And what is your opinion of the last raid? Was it well conducted?"

Baldi blinked and looked away. "There were . . . moments during the night when we stumbled upon individuals who seemed suspicious. I urged Signore Ferrante to make arrests. It seemed apparent, after questioning, that they must be guilty."

"Did he give a reason for not following through?"

Baldi shrugged. "He argued there was a lack of evidence."

"And was that true?"

Baldi sighed, turning his hat around in his hands. "The evidence was before us, your eminence. The other men could not understand his change of heart. He seems altered. Even . . . frightened."

"How so?"

"Strange herbs and potions were found in some cottages near the forest. The inhabitants refused to reveal how they came to own such items. In one home was a small wooden coffer bearing the Forbidden Symbol. Still, Ferrante let them go. Yet it was blatantly clear these were not godly folk."

Dandolo praised his honesty, then dismissed him.

As soon as Baldi departed, a messenger appeared in the doorway, holding a folded square of parchment.

That night the red-headed witch drifted into Ferrante's dreams again. "Your time is up. You have failed me and yourself, and must now face the consequences. You . . . are . . . not . . . worthy."

Ferrante gasped and bolted up from his pillow just as the door to his chamber flew open. Ten of Dandolo's guards rushed in. Two pulled him from bed and hauled him to his feet. The others scattered around the room, ransacking the cabinet, the linen chest, everything.

"What is this? How dare you!" he shouted. "I am—"

"You are under arrest," Dandolo said firmly. The Doge stood glaring from the doorway.

"*Arrest?*" Ferrante gasped. "On what charge?" He scanned the chamber but saw no sign of Ardita. That was a relief. Then he noticed one of the guards pulling up the tiles near her side of the bed. "No, wait!"

The guard knelt for a closer look. When he rose, the vial that had once contained Vera's potion was clamped between two fingers. He handed it to Dandolo, who held it up to the pale dawn light filtering through the leaded windows.

"What would your response be," the Doge asked, "if I were to say you are under arrest for procuring love magic?"

"You believe *me* to be a sorcerer?" Ferrante gaped. "That's a lie! I'm innocent!"

"Did you drink this potion, or did you make it?" Dandolo demanded.

Ferrante's mouth tightened. Why bother to answer? Whatever he said would condemn him.

"How did you come to possess such a vile thing? I must say, I'm deeply disappointed. Not only in you, but in myself. I believed you loyal, but was mistaken. You evil, selfish heretic!"

Ferrante fell to his knees. "My lord, I have ever been your faithful servant. I would never—"

Dandolo cut him off, voice tight with anger. "Is it not odd the leader of my witch hunts, a man deemed honorable and out to prove himself, suddenly questions those very raids? And when ordered to continue, returns the following day with no arrests. I then receive a written accusation dropped into the *Bocca de Leone*, alleging you to be a sorcerer, a sympathizer with those dabbling in dark magic. Further, the accuser reveals the exact location for proof of these claims." Dandolo twirled the vial between his fingers. "Would you say there is enough evidence for an arrest *this* time, Commander?"

Ferrante shouted, "Who is my accuser?" He repeated the plea as his hands were shackled. Nobles looked on with horror as he was dragged from his room, bootless, still in his nightshirt, his protests echoing down the halls.

Ferrante still argued as he was marched from the palace, until he grew hoarse from screaming. Winter wind nipped his skin. The snow beneath his bare soles was so cold he could believe the guards on either side towed his feet through a fire.

No use shouting, though, or putting up a fight. He knew well enough where they were taking him—to rot and freeze in a prison cell in Piombi, until his time came round to be tortured, forced to confess, then burned at the stake. Like all the souls he'd sent to suffer the same fate.

Lifted into the cart, he dropped heavily onto a wooden bench. The iron shackles clanked as his hands shook.

No, the raids hadn't been stopped, as promised. And yes, it had been two weeks. His time was up. But no new arrests had been made! Why couldn't that be enough for the cursed witch, for now?

Hearing the murmur of many voices, he lifted his head. A crowd had formed outside the palace. Faces peering up at the wagon, eyes wide with curiosity.

Lady Ardita stood among the crowd. Ferrante started to call out to her, but something halted him. Her expression. The only face that did not show surprise or shock or horror. She did not even look sad . . . but rather, relieved.

Could his own wife have made the accusation?

Then another figure caught his eye. Behind Ardita stood a taller woman in a sky-colored gown, her long auburn hair wild and unkempt, dazzling blue eyes full of scorn.

Vera.

Their eyes met. She folded her arms and stared, that cold blue gaze cutting into his soul like the heated iron wielded by the head inquisitor.

Her lips did not move, yet her contemptuous whisper rode the wind as the cart jolted forward. Slithering through the rusted bars, pouring like hot lead into his ears.

"You . . . are . . . not . . . worthy."

Ferrante sobbed and clenched his fists. Now he would pay the ultimate price for his betrayal. There was no way out, not even for the witch hunter in chief.

He gave a last despairing scream as the carriage rumbled down the unpaved road to Piombi prison. Carrying him toward the same poor unfortunates he had once condemned to burn. Making him one of them.

The long-nosed proprietor of Tengu Ghost Ink is only one of many who create permanent body paintings at the Night Bazaar. In his home deep in the mountains of Japan, Tengu's true form was that of sacred bird monster. Here at the Bazaar he wears a human guise in order to ply his traditional trade of irezumi—for birds have no thumbs, after all. His many satisfied clients—those still living, that is—bear testament to his incredible skill with needle and pigment. Indeed, Tengu has illustrated the skins of many famous individuals, including several Doges and, back in China, the honorable Marco Polo. One such tattoo plays a part in the next tale. Why do you hang back? Wait! Don't hasten away until you've seen all the designs . . . so cunningly wrought as to make one believe they could indeed move, and even speak. Why do you step away? Ah, I see. Afraid of all those needles, eh? Well, should you change your mind, Tengu will be here all night. And most happy, I am sure, to make a living masterpiece of you.

CINNABAR AND STONE
by Naia Poyer

Marina Nakazato jolted awake at the clear bell-tone of an incoming email. The weak afternoon light didn't illuminate the corners of her tiny studio, but even its faint sparkle on drifting dust motes made her eyes water. The bedside clock showed three P.M.

She clasped her head and groaned, remembering Happy Hour in the drab, ramen-smelling graduate lounge. The Ph.D. students had gotten together to celebrate turning in prospectuses. Exhausted sipping of craft beer on stained couches had gradually transformed into a liquor-soaked bacchanal as relief loosened them up.

Christ, how embarrassing. She'd definitely made out with Kabuki Kevin and maybe even Jameson the esoteric Buddhism guy. The last time any of them had paused to have fun was in undergrad . . . so naturally, her entire cohort had rapidly regressed.

Still, the overwhelming lightness of a completed prospectus outweighed the regret, the throbbing in her skull, and the time she'd lost by sleeping late. Swinging her legs out of bed, she walked ten steps to the cluttered kitchenette and measured loose-leaf *hōjicha* into a tea bag. She'd finished the work and let off steam. Now it was time to tend to the lower priorities, like regular meals and bathing.

Marina straddled her desk chair, sipping tea, and gazed out the grimy apartment window with an overwhelming feeling of peace. Inhaling the earthy scent of roasted green tea, she turned to the laptop to catch up on email.

The message whose ding had woken her was from her thesis advisor, Professor Johanssen.

> *Marina,*
>
> *I read your prospectus right away, due to my great interest in the research you've been engaged in the past couple of years. However, I am sorry to say it fell far short of expectations. I was taken aback to find you had been focusing on travel writing of the early Song Dynasty. Furthermore, I feel your approach doesn't promise to contribute any revelations to the existing scholarly body of work—material with which I'd expected you were already intimately familiar. In addition, given the dearth of* unplumbed *primary resources available within your—somewhat eccentric—chosen focus, the Chair and I worry you won't be able to shoehorn your research to-date into a more productive proposal. As such, we urge you to explore alternate lines of inquiry before submitting a new proposal to the Committee, next Spring.*
>
> *I apologize for bringing bad news, but I am here, as always, to advise you.*
>
> *K.J.*

Her heart stumbled, tripped on a rock, and fell into a gaping hole it would never emerge from. The room was very still; even her body's most basic organic processes seemed to have ceased.

No! I was done *with all that. I knew* what *to write. I thought it* was *good.*

Fuck, she'd practically felt the heavy, expensive paper of the thesis acceptance certificate in her hand, even though the actual writing of the dissertation would take years yet.

Wait. Was this a bad dream? She'd had plenty of nightmares that unfolded more or less the same way.

She went to the sink and drank a glass of water, also downing three ibuprofen. Then pressed her forehead to the dusty-cool refrigerator door for a few moments. But when she sat back down, the email still said what it said.

She leaned back in her creaking desk chair and thought about Buddhist hells. The blood pool hell, where women drowned in a lake of blood for the sin of having menstruated. The hell of boiling excrement . . . not sure how one ended up there. The forest of sword-blade trees where, blinded by lust, adulterers climbed through razor-sharp branches to reach the objects of their desire. Yeah, maybe that was where she'd landed. Trying to prove she had anything worthwhile to say to a bunch of academics felt a lot like climbing a tree made of knives.

Was the degree worth the cuts and slashes? Or would it prove as unsatisfying as a sexy phantasm conjured to balance one's karma? She'd happily clamber over knives to talk with seventeenth-century travel writer Xu Xiake, or tantric master Tsarchen Losal Gyatso. She'd gladly wade through a lake of blood if promised a glimpse of the landscapes they'd described: waterfalls suddenly emerging out of dense forest, a mountain whose majesty would ruin the beauty of all other mountains, white tents pitched on emerald fields like a garland of clouds. She'd fallen in love with wild, magical beauty described by long-dead wanderers. But those natural, historical scenes were as dead as their authors. Few now wanted to hear academics ramble about descriptions of descriptions of an impression—and those who did had just told her to forget it.

She hadn't cried, screamed, or broken anything. Presumably she was still in shock. She picked up the phone to call—who? Dad, who'd cheerfully supported her despite not having a clue what she studied? Mom, who'd only urge her to give up and move back to Ohio? Her childhood bestie, Ikue, who styled hair and thought terminal degrees were idiotic? Or Raquel in Art History, whose proposal had been accepted by *her* advisor, who claimed it was the most promising he'd ever seen?

No. Everyone in her life either believed she couldn't fail, or else was expecting her to. Both were equally unbearable.

As she stared at the blank screen, it lit up with a series of texts.

Marina!

-Not to pester if you're working, but I just acquired something really neat

-Think you'll find it fascinating, given your background

-I mean, area of study! You know what I mean. Aahhh

-You're not chinese, you're japanese right?

-Japanese AMERICAN

-Anyway if you're free, come over. I have the good bubblyyyy!

The last text was six champagne-glass emojis.

Marina was in no way equipped to deal with Caitlin's shit right now. But the only alternative was to crawl back under the sheets and pretend nothing was real. At least her sugar momma had better snacks and alcohol than her friends . . . not to mention far better sheets.

Caitlin's boxy brick house had gleaming glass sidelights and a copper roof. The severely pruned shrubs expressed a perfect Puritan disdain for nature. Forty-three-year-old Cait was the stereotypical New England heiress. Marina had become her Asian arm candy mostly by being bad at saying no to gifts and favors.

"Marina!" Cait gushed, throwing open crystal-clean French doors. "I can't wait to show off the new thing. Toss your shoes over there, please. Floors were polished yesterday."

Cait wasn't really her type, but once Marina had swiped right on Tinder, things snowballed. She'd come to Cait's house firstly to ogle the antiques, secondly to be treated to a nice dinners, and only thirdly . . . well, she hadn't minded the sex. On the app, Cait had shone like a bisexual beacon in a sea of men with premature hair loss confidently offering to eat Marina's pussy "like chicken chow mein." Cait's bland, rich-aunt demeanor was a refreshing change.

Still, if anyone had told Marina a year ago she'd be dating someone whose favorite book was *Eat, Pray, Love*, she'd have spewed out her three-buck Chuck. But, well . . . she'd gotten used to better wine. Also, she'd recognized Caitlin's Tinder pic from the donor page of the Asia Society newsletter. Not an academic; an enthusiast who'd funded Marina's advisor's endowed chair. So, why not get connected *and* spoiled at the same time?

Marina dropped her boots on the foyer's shining blue and white Mexican tile. Coming here had seemed ideal. To be . . . not alone, exactly, but with someone who didn't know her too well. Now she turned away, grimacing, pretending to straighten her boots as bubbles of hysteria gathered in the back of her throat. She would *not* fall on Cait and cry a river into that powdered clavicle.

Before they'd even gotten to the kitchen, Cait was nuzzling Marina's neck.

She playfully pushed her away. "Hey, is this a 'come see my etchings' situation? Your generation's version of 'Netflix and Chill,' I believe?"

Cait shrieked a laugh. "I'm not *that* old. You're just too attractive to keep my hands off of. Ugh, and I'd *kill* for that satiny skin!" She stroked Marina's bare right arm, frowning at the large tattoo there. A *kirin*, or *qilin* in Chinese: a mythical antlered beast symbolizing wisdom and luck. Marina'd had it done when she entered the Ph.D. program. Despite Cait's love of East Asian art, she'd never seemed to approve of the ink.

"I'll leave it to you in my will, stretched on canvas," Marina teased. "In case stress and sleep deprivation kill me. Now come on, show us the new treasure!"

The hallway was lined with charcoal rubbings from Thai temples. Princes, arhats, and dancing girls smiled faintly, seeming amused at their displaced existence here.

Cait opened a heavy, carved door pillaged from a ruined Vietnamese temple.

Glass cases lined a series of dim, interconnected rooms. This wing looked like the curated hoard of an avaricious but clueless dragon. To the left, a pair of Tang tomb guardians, snarling faces glazed yellow and green. To the right, a cheerful Korean folk painting of flowers and ducks. Once, Marina had asked about the collection's layout. Cait had replied, "Yeah, don't you just love the way these greens go together?"

Thus, all her fears had been confirmed.

But on that first visit she'd also been promised dessert, and Baked Alaska had melted her resolve. With men, you had to worry they'd kill you for laughing at them. By comparison, humoring an older woman's lack of curatorial knowledge was a cakewalk.

Now, Marina dredged up a smile for Cait. Remembering, vaguely, what excitement felt like. "I see a new case over there!"

The glass was unreflective; the overhead light seemed to die inside folds of black velvet. A burnished yellow gourd nestled there. Despite the harsh white track lighting, a warm glow flickered across the characters carved into its skin.

"Might look like some dried-up old squash," Cait said, "but this beauty dates from the Yuan Dynasty, early 1300s. It's thought to be a rare example of some sort of talisman. Let's see. What was it called—"

"*Fulu?*" Marina supplied. Her lady friend was always 'fuzzy on the details' of purchases.

"Right! But they're usually little coins, right?"

Marina smiled indulgently, gaze still on the gourd. There was definitely something captivating about it. "Yes. Or paper. Never heard of a gourd *fulu*. Not exactly convenient for toting around. Maybe to hold liquid?"

"Nope. The appraiser says the gourd's intact and totally empty. Not even one little dry seed rattling around in there."

"Weird." Marina frowned. "Symbolically, though, it makes sense. A gourd could represent heaven and earth, and the portal between."

Cait's laugh sounded embarrassed. "I should know better than to try and teach *you* something new!"

"Well, my area's more literature than art history," Marina backpedaled. The older woman's pride sometimes required dumbing herself down a little. But it was a welcome break from the constant snarky academic one-upmanship in her department. In contrast, Cait always absorbed Marina's words with interest and admiration.

Knowing that was probably what encouraged her to take advantage.

"Hey," she muttered as Cait leaned in to inhale the sandalwood-and-vanilla scent of Marina's shampoo. "If I was really careful, could I borrow it for a few days?"

Part of Marina was still drowning in anxiety; she should be trying to salvage something from those lost years of research. But another part had already latched firmly onto the hope that the *fulu* might be a mystery for her alone to solve. Maybe this enigmatic object would turn out to be her ticket to a totally untapped topic.

The following day, hunched inside a carrel in the theological library, she inhaled the musty tang of slowly-disintegrating paper. Every collection had its signature smell. This humid basement floor was especially funky, but at least it was quiet.

Usually, home base was the Jiankang East Asian Languages and Cultures Library and its acrid scent of radiator dust. But lately, it exuded a fug of PhD panic. So she'd dumped the contents of her carrel into a tote bag and decamped to the theological stacks.

The gourd clacked as she set it on the desk. The overhead fluorescents revealed a wavy texture in the lacquered yellow skin. Characters circled its rounded belly, their balance and grace taking her breath away. Still, though she'd learned Chinese cursive and seal scripts—in addition to reading her parents' native Japanese—this writing made no sense.

She scanned the stacks for a fellow student who might know about religious paraphernalia. Jaz, Masters in East Asian religions, was chatting with friends in a circle of armchairs. Perfect. She'd let Jaz turn in essays late when she was their TA. So they owed her.

She caught their eye and tilted her head. As they approached, Marina pushed the gourd under the carrel's wooden hutch.

"'S'up, Marina?" Jaz picked cat hairs self-consciously from a loose purple sweater.

"Weird-slash-vague question. Ever seen a Chinese script that didn't make sense? Maybe a Buddhist ritual thing?"

Jaz frowned. "Uh, no . . . maybe you're thinking of, like, Daoist magic script? That'd only have meaning between a teacher and their disciple, so you couldn't read it."

"God, all you religion people do is invent exclusive magic clubs." She smiled nervously, the tips of her fingers keeping the gourd from rolling back into sight.

Jaz snorted. "Where'd you see it? Want me to take a look?"

"Nah." Marina shrugged. "Not important."

After Jaz walked away, Marina grabbed a couple hefty books to pin the unwieldy gourd safely in place, out of sight. Then she headed to the Daoism aisle.

Just as she pulled a third book off the shelf, a loud, dry crack sounded. She dropped everything and sprinted back.

The gourd lay in halves on the red plush carpet.

The blood drained from her head, and she swayed in place. *I am so dead. How much did Cait say she paid? Oh wait, she didn't. So it was really expensive.*

Sinking to her knees, she scooped up the pieces like endangered bird's eggs.

Still, how weird. The carpet was so thick. Even this brittle thing should've just bounced. And how'd it fall, anyhow? She glanced up. The two books she'd stacked were now splayed open on the desk, to *Basilica of Venice* and *Sacred Mountains: Wonders of Taoist Architecture.* Had someone decided to browse, broken the gourd, and run?

The spines of both books had been savagely cracked. Carefully, she flipped over *Basilica.* The open pages showed a watercolor of "San Giacomo di Rialto," an eleventh-century church in Venice's San Polo district. And in *Sacred Mountains,* a color photo spread featured the eighth-century White Cloud Temple in Beijing, shrouded in mist.

Which all meant exactly nothing. She wrapped one half of the gourd in a spare cardigan, thinking to buy some magical museum glue online. But getting away with this was probably hopeless. Could a day *get* more depressing?

The inside of the other half caught her eye then. Stringy and rough, except for one smooth patch where Chinese characters, roman letters, and Arabic numbers had been messily scratched.

"Jian . . . kang," she whispered. "CLP two seven five dot E five. . . ."

She frowned. Arabic numerals weren't used in China in the 1300s. And the format looked like a catalogue number. The work of an appraiser?

No. Caitlin had said the gourd was intact. And the scratchings looked *exactly* like a Jiankang call number, right down to the section prefix.

The number was indeed assigned to a book in Jiankang. *Half-Eaten Peaches: China's Tradition of Homosexual Love Poetry.*

Marina slumped. Nothing to do with charms or magical writing systems. The faded paperback, from a defunct gay press, sported a cringey late-Eighties cover. Bare-chested, loinclothed Asian hunk biting into a glistening peach. Way outside Marina's area. But she flipped to pages 278-279, as the squash commanded.

To a far land I travel to be with my love, / our secret contained in the vessel of my heart. / How I long to spill the water of history / at his feet in a new land. / Will we also share the fruits of this new place / or will the faint taste of peaches be forever in my mouth?

So melodramatic. Marina wished she had the original Chinese to compare with. Or maybe love poetry just wasn't her thing.

The next read:

Did the savage horse-folk turn him cruel / Or did his own dead God create him thus? / I never saw his eyes so cold / In all the nights we spent together. / To leave me broken was not enough, / With his hateful parting gift, he has ended my life.

Hmm. Quite the change of tune.

I am weary. As darkness closes, / Recalling the story of Li Tieguai / I leave this body to reach for peace. / Shall I wander abroad as a hungry ghost / or follow in the footsteps of the great Immortals? / My love has cut our red thread, but a witch holds all the strings.

Huh? What kind of effing love poem was *that?*

At the bottom of the page, a short blurb provided context:

This book of verses was discovered in a Venice junk shop, with no collector's seal. However, the enfolding papers bore the name and rank of a Taoist monastic: Lie Jiao. His verses deviate from standard six-line poetic compositions. Though the first two express themes typical of homosexual love poetry—including allusions to the 'half-eaten peach' shared by legendary

Duke Ling and Mizi Xia—the last devolves into chaos and despair. The second alludes to "savage horse-folk," suggesting the lover turned against our scholarly Chinese narrator as a result of racial prejudice under Mongol rule. The evocation of Li Tieguai adds a rebellious flavor of Taoist magic. It refers to the Immortal Master who concocted the elixir of immortality in a drinking gourd, and whose body was burned by a disciple as his master was astrally projecting. This tale would have been important to a Taoist monastic as a symbol of escape from human frailty.

But why *is our narrator dying? Some theorize the poet is being treated by a female shaman for an STD. Today, in the midst of the AIDS crisis, the idea of a gay man dying alone from a misunderstood illness cuts deep.*

Marina barely registered the final paragraph. The editor had her at "elixir of immortality in a drinking gourd." What had she and Cait talked about? Oh, yeah: a portal between heaven and earth. Not a vessel. No apparent opening. But what if it *had* held something?

Perhaps she had fucked up even worse than she'd thought.

A warm June breeze whipped hair into Marina's eyes as she pushed Jiankang Library's heavy front doors open. Stepping out, she caught a movement to the left, and did a double take. She could've sworn one of the stone Fu lions flanking the entrance had tilted its head. Maybe a bird, landing on the statue?

But no bird or squirrel there. Though a pair of crows in a nearby tree were making a godawful racket.

Marina walked on, wondering how to explain the ruined gourd, as the peeling soles of her Oxfords slapped the sidewalk. Forget merely getting dumped. If Caitlin was enraged enough, she could convince the University to revoke Marina's grant. Though if she didn't come up with a better topic fast, she wouldn't need their money anyway, only Greyhound fare to Ohio.

Halfway home, she felt sure she was being followed. Either that, or she needed to see an eye doctor, because the peripheral flickers were getting worse. Palpable dread kept spinning her around, only to find an empty sidewalk. *This is how psychotic breaks happen,* she thought grimly, speeding up to pass a woman pushing a stroller. *You're a twenty-something high achiever, everything's peachy. Then one day the stress breaks you and you're telling people you don't need to bathe or eat because you're actually just an animated corpse.*

She'd never been superstitious, but her father was a slut for the supernatural. He purchased a new *ofuda*, a protection charm, for her apartment every twelve months on visits to her grandparents in Japan, because he firmly believed in the amulet's one-year expiration date. Three different *omamori* for traffic safety hung in his car ("drivers in America are way crazier, so I need more help."). Her mother complained about the charms cluttering up the house, too. "Rina, can you believe? Last night I made Papa watch Marie Kondo's show about clutter. But he say to me, 'talking to old clothes and appliances? She is just making comedy show!'"

For the first time, Marina was grateful for Papa's eccentricity. She stomped up the creaking steps to her third-floor apartment, jonesing for the protective bubble of the *ofuda*. Even if none of it was real.

Slamming home the chain, she glared at the calligraphed rectangle of wood and paper taped to the inside of the door. *What did you cost, thirty bucks? Better be good for* some*thing*. Kicking free of her boots, she headed for the kitchen nook for some calming lavender tea.

An incoming email made her phone ding. *Community Advisory: Theft of Stone Lions from Jiankang Library*, read the subject line.

"What the hell?" Marina muttered. "I just *saw* them."

Campus Police advise members of the community to report suspicious activity surrounding the Jiankang East Asian Languages and Cultures Library. Two lion statues from the library's entrance have been reported missing. The statues are five feet tall and weigh close to four tons apiece. A gift to the University from Beijing Language and Culture University in 1978—

An incoming call cut her reading short. Her father was in Japan this week; normally he never wasted international minutes.

"Hey, Papa. *Doushita no? Baachan to Jiichan, daijoubu?*"

"Grandma and Grandpa are fine. Today we ate shabu, *umakatta ze*. Anyway, sad news. I just learn they had to tear down the local shrine. I think this means our *ofuda* won't work anymore. You probably don't mind to wait until I get new ones, *ne?*"

"Ah . . . *sou ka*. That *is* sad, but I'm okay. Sorry, Papa, I gotta go."

She hung up, throat constricting. Of all the shitty fucking crap luck. Why did magical protection come with so much fine print? She turned back to the email, hoping to find out exactly when the statues had vanished.

Ding. A push notification obscured the email again. The Google Translate app.

[Translated from Chinese (traditional)]: They follow me.

"What the hell?" Marina shivered. She didn't remember looking up that phrase. . . .

Ding.

[Translated from Chinese (traditional)]: Because I break the gourd, they can find me. Can you help?

Marina's voice shook. "Help? Who the fuck *are* you?"

Ding.

[Translated from Chinese (traditional)]: I am Taoist monk Lie Jiao. Pleased to meet you. Hiding in this object for now, so please help me fight the spirits.

"Fight—*spirits*? Jesus, am I getting targeted by Chinese hackers? This makes no *sense*." Her hands shook, fumbling for the power button. *Turn the damn thing off so they can't spy anymore, take it straight to T-Mobile—*

Ding. [Translated from Chinese (traditional)]: Please do not turn off. We are both in much danger. If you do not listen, you will die by my enemies.

She stopped dead. "Who . . . what do you mean by *enemies*?"

Silence buzzed for excruciating seconds, until the phone chimed again.

Enemies are here now. Outside.

From the back yard of her building came a grating roar, like a building under demolition. She ran to the window. Rotting planks from the cedar fence were strewn across the neatly-mown lawn. "Oh my god," she breathed. The landlord would *shit*. She pressed her face against the cool window pane to see what was happening at the base of the building.

Campus police, rejoice! Your Fu lions weren't stolen. Nope, they've just followed me home, and are currently trying to climb the fire escape. Aw, Dean Harrison, they're so cute. Can I keep them?

Ding.

Transform this object into protection charm. I will show you how.

"Are you fucking *nuts*?" she yelled, feeling pretty fucking nuts herself. "I gotta get out of here. Those things could crush my head with one paw!"

Evil spirits are inside. If you have a charm, they cannot touch you. If you run, they will inhabit a person and stab you. Or bus, and run you over. You are not safe without fulu.

The squeal of metal rose to painful levels. How could the fire escape hold up under so much weight? Four tons *each*, the advisory had said. . . .

"No, no, no." Marina shook her head, backing away from the window for fear of locking eyes with one of those monsters. Would they be pools of darkness, have burning red pupils, or remain gray stone as blank as the day they were carved? "You're crazy. I can't just sit here while they climb through my window like hungry stray cats!"

It is necessary to remain calm. Fighting bad spirits is frightening, yes. Why not drink some baiju *for the nerves and get on with it. Quickly.*

Marina flung the phone down on the desk. "You're saying get shitfaced. Right now." Actually, if she was about to be crushed to death under eight tons of impeccable Chinese stonemasonry, it wasn't the worst idea.

That'll teach me to wonder if my day could get any worse.

The walls shook as stone clanged ever upward against metal. Louder, so they must've reached the second-floor landing. Why wasn't the Fire Department *wee-oo*ing over? Then she remembered: the landlady's family, who occupied the lower floors, were on spring vacation in Bermuda.

And she'd forgotten to water the hydrangeas, like she'd promised.

"You know what? *Fine.*" She sank into her desk chair, reaching into a file drawer to grab the handle of vodka kept for grading undergrad essays.

I see you are familiar with this calming technique.

"Oh, shut up." She grabbed a tiny screwdriver from the pen cup. "So what do I have to do—disassemble the phone, draw a pentagram in blood on the inside, put it back together inside-out. . . .?"

No, much easier. Only carve characters into the back. Magic writing learned from my master.

"Is there time to do this before they murder us—well, me, given you're *already dead?*"

Only if you hurry very much.

So there she was, carving magical runes into the back of her new-ish iPhone 8 with an eensy screwdriver, while a deceased monk critiqued her handwriting in an unnaturally calm, robotic female voice. Jiao had helpfully turned on Translate's audio output function, since she couldn't carve and read at the same time.

"Carve light," the voice advised pleasantly. *"At first you may make some mistake."*

Outside, a horrible scraping and banging said the lions had slipped and fallen a ways down the fire-escape stairs.

"Jiao, I'm freaking out." She paused to gulp air. "I focus better when I multitask. So please talk to me. You're sure this'll protect us from these . . . things following you?"

"Yes." Silence for a few seconds. Then, just when Marina thought he wasn't going to continue, *"When my body dies, I don't get proper rituals, so evil spirits attack.*

When I sleep inside gourd, they cannot find me. This symbol will protect, same function."

Made sense enough, she supposed.

"Left radical must be curvy, like a dancing leg," Translate's AI voice insisted.

She dutifully scratched away. Thanks to the vodka, a warm tingle of determination danced through her fingers. The linework became steadier as she followed Jiao's instructions with increasing confidence. I'm doing *magic*, she thought. Learning more from this ghost in twenty minutes than from three *years* of graduate study.

"If you've been sealed in there for hundreds of years, what woke you up?"

"You do, with books. I know places in them. Books make me wake and remember."

"So . . . you lived in White Cloud Temple during Mongol rule? Wow. But how do you know a church in Venice? Did you travel the Silk Road? It's crazy, but this is exactly what I—"

A crashing thud rattled the window panes like ice cubes in a glass. On the other side, the bunched swirls of an elegant gray mane rose into sight. Followed by two large eyes, white and smooth as bleached bone.

Marina had felt like pissing herself only once before, while staring into the predatory eyes of several cheetahs in a zoo enclosure. But *this* dread was worse, more primal still than a fear of being simply torn apart and eaten. This creature would consume her whole—body *and* spirit.

"Hurry, complete the magic writing! We are very close now." Somehow his urgency leaked into the app's robotic voice.

As she applied the screwdriver's tip to etch the final line, the window exploded inward. Marina screamed as glass spewed across the floor, shards incising tiny cuts in her bare feet.

She grabbed phone, screwdriver, and vodka, and scrambled into the bathroom. Ducked behind the shower curtain, hands shaking as she tried to dig the screwdriver's tip into the back of the phone. One unfinished line stood between her and a crushed skull.

Out in the main room, the floor groaned under enormous granite paws. Would the joists even hold under multiple tons?

Shit, she couldn't worry about that right now.

I must become formless like Li Tieguai. I am like a beacon attracting them, Jiao wrote. Mercifully, he'd silenced the phone and switched back to text. *Finish the* fulu!

Before Marina could protest, the screen went black.

She gasped, fumbled the phone, then dived for it, knocking over her bag. The vodka bottle and broken gourd clattered loudly into the tub.

If only she could leave her vulnerable, squishy body like Jiao and his Daoist Immortals.

The bathroom's heavy oak door ripped from its hinges and slammed to the tiles. She screamed as the shockwave ran up from the floor and through her body.

"Li Tieguai!" She gasped out.

The second lion lumbered in, splintering the fallen door beneath its paws like matchsticks. Unlike the ones that'd peered through the window, this beast's eyes were a shiny beetle-black. From over its shoulder, those eerie white eyes tracked her quivering movements like a cat watching a humming can opener. Two sets of lichen-rimmed jaws opened, uttering low, grinding growls.

Marina covered her head and yelled louder, "Li Tieguai! In the name of Li Tieguai, *leave me alone!*"

This outburst had two surprising effects. Well, technically, three.

The fluid, magically-animated granite stiffened with a crunching sound, and the lions shifted back into their original seated poses. The cap of the vodka bottle in the tub popped like a champagne cork. Glowing golden liquid spewed out into the broken gourd, spattering her feet and the dead cell phone.

As the floorboards groaned and screeched under the suddenly very-real weight of the statues, the screen of her damp iPhone flickered back to life. A horrible distorted voice, the combined shout of every possible electronic pronunciation aid and automated answering system, commanded:

"DRINK IT."

Marina grabbed up the gourd and tossed back the mystery liquid the way she would top-shelf tequila. The next thing she knew she was lying down under what felt like a weighted blanket. Sort of comforting, relaxing even. Except someone kept shouting at her.

"*Hunh*, stop yelling. I'm getting up." She gave the blanket a push; a heap of plaster and splintered floorboards cascaded off her. She looked up. Two jagged, perfectly aligned holes in the ceiling said she'd fallen two stories, into her landlady's tastefully-furnished midcentury-modern living room.

Well, it *had* been tasteful. The rubble and shattered hunks of lion were a little off-theme.

That finally got her pulse pounding. *Okay, the four-ton statues are in itty bitty pieces. Am I also missing some limbs, and just too shocked to feel it?* Dragging smarting legs from the rubble, she saw only shallow cuts from the shattered window. And then, speaking of intact, what else came rolling roundly out from the pile of debris to bump against her thigh?

The motherfucking gourd.

Well done, calling on Li Tieguai Laoshi, said a calm voice in her head. *I would have suggested this, but never imagined it would work for you. Much less that an Immortal would gift an uneducated barbarian an elixir of protection.*

"Wow, thanks. And you sound a lot less dumb when you're not filtered through a crappy app," she fired back, brushing plaster dust from her arms. His speech was indeed flawless now. She couldn't detect any accent—or even, in fact, tell what language he was speaking. It felt like the words were simply forming in her brain. "Where are you, anyway?"

You are touching me right now. Kindly stop, it tickles and is most unseemly.

She froze, then lifted her hand. The kirin tattoo on her forearm twisted to slowly blink its large yellow eyes at her, like a cat conveying trust.

Goosebumps broke out at the sight of her own pigmented skin suddenly shifting around. "Ugh, that's horrible! And it *tingles* when you move!"

I knew possession would be uncomfortable, which is why I chose to animate this qilin on your skin instead of . . . anywhere else. Clever to have this auspicious symbol with you always. Perhaps that is why the Laoshi chose to help you.

Marina laughed shakily. "Please hold that thought while I call my mom. She needs to hear that tattoos aren't just a 'gangster thing' from someone *else* who's old." She pressed the Home button on her phone. Nothing happened. "So is my new iPhone broken junk now?"

If you finish that last line, it will become a functioning talisman. Good to have, in case more demons are around.

"So, because somebody forgot to chant the proper mantra, you'll be pursued by vicious demons forever. Seems harsh. Hey, what if you just jumped back into the gourd? The Immortal Laoshi was kind enough to fix it for you, see?"

Out of the question. No one will coax me back in there—not you, not my lover, not her.

"Who— "

Please. Not right now.

In front of her lay a shattered stone paw. Lacey yellow-green lichen accented its curved claws. She wasn't to blame, but felt terrible nonetheless about the destruction of something so beautiful and old.

Just draw the last line. I will explain more after we are safe.

"You'd better. And please, save the bullshit about helping your spirit move on until we've gone through *everything*. How you got to Venice, how your ghost ended up in a magical squash, why exactly I had to get involved—et cetera." Marina threw herself onto a gritty red 1950s sofa, carefully wedging the miraculous *fulu* beside her. Digging through the coffee table drawer, she found a letter opener. "So, curved like a dancing leg, correct?"

No! He'd been short-tempered since she'd suggested he return to the gourd. *Since you are still imbued with power from the elixir, for the moment . . . let us try something bigger. It has never worked for me before, but now, perhaps . . . everything can be mended.*

Marina groaned. Her hand was cramping around the letter opener. "I have to start over?"

It is mostly the last line which is different. An easy fix.

She scored the final line, expecting a burst of energy, or maybe to become enveloped in a shiny bubble of pure magic. Instead, she inhaled a hot, ozone-scented wind.

Marina looked up from the phone.

She was no longer on her landlady's ruined vintage sofa, but kneeling on damp, uneven stones. The iPhone lay beside her, cracked and dead as before. The gourd, too, had come along. She was in the middle of a long, flat bridge. Hundreds of small carved lions stared down from its stone railings. Beyond them, acres of grass lined the dry riverbed.

"Shit!" She jumped up to run, but snarling lions lined the railings behind as well. She froze, heart hammering, until she realized none of them were moving. At least, not yet.

"*Jiao,*" she hissed. "Three important queries: what'd you just do, where are we, and should I expect to be mauled?"

The kirin's two-dimensional eyes stared ahead. He, too, seemed surprised to be under this muggy gray-blue sky, washed-out treetops just visible through a haze of yellowish smog.

Lugou Bridge, said his voice in her head.

"Lu—you mean, Marco Polo Bridge? Near *Beijing*?"

Marco Polo Bridge. Even telepathically, his voice was spiked with bitterness.

"That sigil wasn't for protection, was it? You tricked me!"

I am sorry. The secret writing says 'home,' which is very close to 'safety.' I assumed we would be taken to White Cloud Temple. They've the skills to perform final rites. But I suppose he is still the home of my heart. Even after everything."

"Wait." Her mind raced to connect the dots. The spirit awakening when the *fulu* touched the books about White Cloud Temple and the Venetian basilica. Desperate love poems, betrayal, death. "The 'he' in your poems. Who *is* it?"

The kirin circled her bicep, tufted tail tickling her armpit. His antlered head rose to just below the collarbone, close to her downturned face. "Only one other person knows my story, besides *him*. And confiding in *her* proved a terrible mistake."

"So tell *me*. Jiao, I really do want to help if I can. Why're we on this bridge instead of in your monastery?"

If I ever get out of China without a damn passport, she thought, *I'm going to write the most ridiculous dissertation*. This was all she had to cling to at the moment, in order not to run screaming to the nearest American consulate.

Simple. Marco said when he described China, he would praise this bridge. I suppose they ended up calling it after him. But to me, the place where we parted ways forever is ugly. Horrible. Years of secret passion ended when his family returned to Venice.

Marina hadn't realized she was gaping until a drop of drool fell on Jiao's draconic head.

"Ugh, sorry!" She wiped her mouth. "But . . . you're saying *Marco Polo*, the great explorer, was your *lover*?"

There is a long and noble tradition in China of love between—

"I'm not judging! I've had relationships with women."

A frosty pause. *Well, not between two* women. *That* is *abnormal*.

She swatted at the tattoo. Jiao ducked away, so she only smacked herself.

"Ouch. Okay, fine." She rubbed her smarting collarbone. "*Please* just reveal all your fucking secrets, already."

So Jiao began. His eloquence made her doubt he was telling the story for the first, or even second, time. He must've written a journal, as travelers did on those long, perilous journeys. Perhaps the poems in *Half-Eaten Peaches* weren't all he'd left behind. If she could get hold of his travel writings, along with this firsthand insight, what an incredible primary source. . . .

Then she shook her head. Just focus on the story!

My life would never have ended in Venice if not for Marco. He came one winter on business for the Khan, seeking translation of a text—I believe it was the Analects—*into the kingdom's official script. I was skilled at the new-fangled 'Phags-pa writing system, but from the moment I saw this serious, handsome foreigner, I couldn't keep my mind on the task. We talked over tea, ignoring the text on the table between us. He spoke many languages, traveled many places. I was ashamed to have never left the city. But he was interested in my studies. When he departed that day, he kissed my cheek in the way of Europeans. I overstepped, pulling him back to kiss his mouth.*

I expected rejection. He was a trusted advisor of the Khan, with much higher status than an ethnic Chinese. He only paused a moment before returning my kiss with even more passion. He called me beautiful in his native language. We made reckless love by the tea table where lay the forgotten volume of Confucian morality.

Marina swallowed. She hadn't expected the narrative to get steamy so quickly. Jiao had decided to trust her, clearly. But she wasn't used to swapping such intimate details, even with friends.

His position had him forever coming and going, but we corresponded. I wrote openly of my love, in the classical style. He was more reserved. Europeans have little precedent for expressing the beauty of this type of relationship. If we voiced such feelings in my country, he wrote, they would hang us in the public square. Our bodies would be burned along with our sinful missives. It shocked me, the cruelty of his countrymen, but that would not stop me when the time came to journey there.

Each time Marco returned to the capital, we met in secret. You know, I almost did not recognize this old bridge at first. We usually met in winter, when it was dusted with snow.

The last time, he laid a hand on my cheek. "So cold and white and sadly lovely—like the stone and snow."

I wept until my tears formed icicles. He tried to console me. "When I return to Venice, I can never tell the tale which matters most. But when I describe the Capital—even to my friends in the City of Bridges—I will call Luguo Bridge the finest in the world."

This was no solace.

In year seventy-seven of Yuan, he traveled so far even the Mongols' expansive post system could not deliver my letters. Still, I returned to this bridge alone, year after year. Knowing he would think of me standing here in the snow.

"That's . . . so sad. Being cut off like that." Marina had forgotten to breathe. She couldn't imagine waiting for someone that way. Couldn't even recall the name of her high school boyfriend, sometimes.

For twenty years, I did not know what had become of him, said Jiao. *But I heard he'd made it back to Venice, after Persia. He'd told such tales of his childhood in Venice. The marble churches, golden statues, bustling markets. The roads made of water.*

Meanwhile, a terrible sickness was spreading into our Capital. The blood-vomiting plague. Finally I had a reason to leave China and go to him. So I lied, telling my master I'd heard the Catholics in Venice knew of a holy elixir that could cure any illness. I requested he send me on behalf of the temple to learn their alchemy. I joined a caravan of Mongol traders for the better part of a year on the Silk Road. Many of my Mongol companions died. I cannot believe I survived. I lay awake listening to the wet choking as the plague took their lives. I survived because they shunned the company of the lowly Chinese. And of course, by making the strengthening elixir taught by my master; his last transmission to me.

"And you didn't . . . share that medicine with your traveling companions?" Marina asked.

The kirin's flat yellow eyes met her gaze. His was distracted, as if still lost on the long trail of silk, spices, and death.

I was a scholar, weak of body and unsuited to the road. In the same way, their minds were too weak for our mysteries. They were unschooled in the Dao, and not even Han. It would not have saved them. It was not for them.

"But you know," Marina said hesitantly, not wanting to offend him, "I'm not Chinese. I have no training in the Way. Yet Li Laoshi's elixir still saved me."

Jiao's tufted tail swept across her forearm like an angry cat's. *That, I don't understand. But it is certainly not the only thing about you I find odd.*

"Please," she said, "go on."

Only seven traders survived the road to Venice. We divided the goods of the dead. I took some bolts of silk, and tins of cinnabar pigment, because these could be carried in my pack.

Sweat was now coursing down Marina's back. Her ass ached from sitting on the uneven paving stones. She settled onto one side, head resting on shoulder. Looked steadily into the kirin's golden eyes as his words flowed through her brain like music, or dreams.

In Venice, no one spoke my language. I'd thought, Marco is so famous, all I'll need do is say his name. But no: the first week, people only stared, or laughed at my robes. Some bought silk, but acted like they couldn't understand me. Some asked if I could curse their rivals or ex-lovers. I sheltered in doorways, holding my goods in a death-grip, even while asleep. Sometimes I found a street market at which to spread my cloak and play the exotic silk merchant.

One day I at last recognized something. A church Marco had described. Its marble facade, the golden horses: San Giacomo di Rialto. "As a child I visited there often with my mother. We were close before she died," he'd sighed. "I barely knew my father or uncle, before they swept me away to see the world."

Finally, I felt close. My heart raced as I climbed the steps, with the same anticipation as I once walked to our bridge. The church was small, draped with rich silk hangings similar to the blood-red bolts I carried. Past rows of empty wooden benches I walked, gaze fixed upon the marble statue at the center of everything. I believe it was the Immortal named Jesus. His lean, graceful body draped in loose cloth, he held aloft a staff. Rays circled his head like a bodhisat-tva's fiery mandorla. His skin, so white and cold. I imagined Marco touching it to revisit his last memory of me. But, from what he'd said of Venetians' laws, he would no more be allowed to touch the marble face of Christ in public than to caress mine.

I was not alone amid the white marble and red silk. A man, over whose shoulders gray curls spilled, knelt on velvet cushions before the statue. So still and quiet, I'd mistaken him for part of the chapel. It was Marco, sunk in devotion, or despair.

I stood lost, unable to speak. In my many imaginings, I meet him on his own doorstep. He seizes me with a cry of joy and pulls me inside, somewhere we cannot be seen or overheard. But I had dreamed it all wrong, even his clothing. Instead of Mongol robes, he wore a fur-trimmed green cape over a high-collared tunic. A shapeless silk cap lay next to him like a small dead animal.

I approached and knelt upon the cushion too. So close, his cap was crushed beneath my knee. I clasped my trembling hands in supplication. The only prayer in my head was, Look at me, look at me. *Our elbows on the railing nearly touched. Under the incense haze, I detected his musk of sweat, cinnamon, and cloves. The first welcome scent in this noisome city.*

My nearby heat seemed to slowly thaw him. He turned his head to regard the stranger who knelt so close.

"Madonna santa," he whispered, as if praying still. Then, in Pekingese, "Are you really here? Or have my prayers again turned to sinful daydreams?"

Just then Marina and Jiao both flinched, as footsteps sounded on stone. She started up from her fetal curl, suddenly self-conscious. She'd been too absorbed to notice two middle-aged Chinese tourists, one with a chunky camera slung around his neck. As they passed, the tiny woman kept up her Mandarin patter to the perspiring husband, shooting Marina a dirty glance.

"Well fuck you too," Marina muttered, lowering herself back into the shade of the railing.

The kirin blinked and slowly relaxed his ink-lined muscles. Still, his hesitation to resume the story, and downcast yellow eyes, betrayed anxiety and pain. After a few moments he spoke again, the words more rushed now.

I tried to take Marco's hand, but he snatched it away. "Monsignore," he called over my shoulder to someone. "Per favore, aspetta un momento."

I tore my gaze from him to glance behind. A priest stood in the side doorway, his narrow dark gaze on us. Candlelight bounced from his embroidered red-and-gold cassock, dazzling the eye. I would never have noticed this stealthy man's presence among the richness of our surroundings.

The priest nodded at Marco, but remained. The tension in my beloved's body was plain. Still whispering, as if afraid the Priest might understand Pekingese, he said, "Wait in the square. I'll send a messenger. A friend who does not judge. She will provide us with somewhere private to meet."

He stood, nodding to the priest. The two disappeared into an ornate wooden box, the purpose of which I had no notion.

I was relieved I had found him, disappointed in the finding, and angry with his lack of affection. Could he not at least have greeted me as a dear old friend before this holy man? Were all forms of love forbidden in this wretched Western city?

Nevertheless, I still trusted. Stepping out into the sunlit square, I made my way to the fountain and sat upon its marble rim. Took off the unwieldy cloth pack of silk and cinnabar pigment, and propped it there as well.

There I stayed, reimagining the disappointing scene. Perhaps Marco had exited the building merely to escape me . . . had age diminished his attraction? His had only endeared him to me further. I was absorbed in heartbreak, eyes cast down on the dull gray paving stones.

After some hours passed, an olive-skinned, beringed palm entered my field of vision.

"Do not indulge unpleasant thoughts a moment longer. Come with me and all will be well."

My head snapped up. I was shocked to hear a woman's deep, melodious voice speaking perfect Pekingese. She was neither Han nor Mongol; nor did she quite look like the Italians bustling around us. Long, elegant face. Exceedingly long, thick dark braid draped over a gown of deep-blue brocade. And clever almond eyes which shifted from green to black, like the wings of a beetle, as she inclined her head.

I shrank away, thinking, Such an aura of beauty and power could only belong to a nine-tailed fox spirit. Has it come to help, or to trick me?

Marina frowned. "Hang on. In the poem, you wrote something like 'a witch holds our strings.' Is this the witch?"

Yes. The one called Vera. I wish by the Eight Immortals she had never found me in that square. I could not have known then, but Marco had instructed her to poison me so his sins would never come to light and disgrace his family.

He had a wife and children as well. I learned this in her villa just off the Canal Grande that evening. I also couldn't have known this seemingly compassionate noblewoman would . . . on the cusp between life and death . . . siphon off my spirit into a drinking gourd, to be kept always in the dark.

"Damn," Marina whispered, shocked and appalled. "Jiao . . . I'm so sorry. I didn't realize you were trapped against your will. I never would've suggested going back into the gourd if—"

"Yes, it was torment, alone in that well of pure darkness. Even though I was eventually drugged by boredom and loneliness into a kind of sleep. But Marina, I apologize for my harshness, and for the earlier deception. I did not mistrust you. You have been brave, and listened to me attentively. Even before my captivity, I have not had such a worthy companion in a long time."

Marina frowned. Something was shifting in the atmosphere. The humidity grew even thicker. Heavy drops fell out of the smoggy sky, splashing on stone. A distant rumble came from below, and the bridge shuddered. In the parched riverbed below, water trickled up from the earth, quickly cresting the tops of the dry grass.

Further down the bridge, a resonant voice issued from within the miniature rainstorm.

"You're a difficult disembodied spirit to find, Venerable Lie Jiao. Glad you finally called me to you."

The brief rainfall ceased abruptly. Several dozen yards down the bridge, a tall, thin woman emerged from the mist now rising off the river. She was dressed like a fashionable young Beijinger: black leather jacket and flowing skirt, a lacy parasol and gloves to keep the sun from her skin, eyes hidden behind round dark shades.

But Marina felt a thrill of dread when she noticed the thick dark braid draped over one leather-clad shoulder. "You!" she yelled, surprised at how steady her voice sounded. "Leave this poor man alone. Haven't you tormented him enough already?"

Vera nodded affably, shaking sparkling droplets from the dainty black parasol. "Restless spirits get like this, you know. Confused, angry; dangerous to themselves and others. Let me put him back into that gourd, just for a bit, and set him right again."

As she walked past, each miniature stone lion blinked and swiveled its head to watch.

Marina yelped and backed away.

"Oh, don't misunderstand." Vera waved a hand at the lions. "Those aren't mine, and they won't hurt you." She withdrew a brocade amulet pouch from her pocket. "Mustn't travel without one of these. The angrier and more regretful a homeless spirit like Jiao becomes, the stronger his scent to predators. In this case, our demonic guests."

The lions stayed put, though a few snarled as if wishing they could spring on her.

"Our friend Jiao has been putting you in great danger. It would be best if I took him away. Then these demons will have no reason to bother you."

"But I'm protected. They can't hurt me." Marina hoped she projected more confidence than she felt.

"Ah," Vera smiled. "Yes, for the moment. But the effects of that elixir will not last. I had to call in many favors to ensure that if Jiao got loose on his own, no bystanders would get hurt."

Don't listen! Jiao cried. *She wants to keep me imprisoned forever. This she-demon destroyed my body and entrapped my spirit. Don't let her consign me to that nothingness, that terrible darkness again!*

Marina held up a hand. "Stop walking. Stay there!"

Vera halted.

Marina hoped Jiao couldn't hear her thoughts racing as she weighed the options. Keeping him *was* no doubt dangerous. And in the end, it wouldn't get her anywhere if he remained merely a voice in her head. She needed something concrete to prove everything Jiao had told her was true, if she wanted to use it for her prospectus. And Vera could likely take him away by force, anyway—leaving Marina with nothing. On the other hand, if Vera had been the last to see him alive, she likely knew where his personal effects had ended up.

"I want something in exchange. His journals."

Jiao exclaimed, *You will give me up to this devil for a stack of paper?*

She was flooded with shame, until a sharp pain in the forearm made her cry out. Somehow, the kirin's long talons had pierced her skin from the *inside.* Rivulets of blood ran down her wrist. Those pale eyes turned a blazing orange, the pupils insanely dilated. Yellow tongues of flame licked out between its bared teeth.

"I'm *sorry,*" she gritted out through clenched teeth. "But I'm really not sure who the devil *is* anymore."

"Of course. I can arrange that," Vera said pleasantly, as if they were agreeing to trade houseplant cuttings.

The kirin tattoo flitted up, down, and around Marina's arm in agitation. *Please, no!* Jiao pleaded. Her skin grew hot wherever the illustrated flames licked.

Vera stepped forward, picking up the gourd. Cool fingers closed around Marina's wrist, holding that arm steady as the other woman pressed the vessel to it.

The kirin thrashed. A strange writhing sensation erupted just beneath Marin's skin, as if the cells were being squeezed, forced to regurgitate subsumed pigment. And then, the tattoo . . . vanished.

"Now, let's get you home," said Vera briskly.

As Marina stared blankly at her pristine, unmarked forearm, Vera pressed the cracked iPhone into her hand and closed her dirty fingers around it.

Marina face-planted hard onto a musty, faded red carpet. The 'home' talisman had whisked her directly back to Jiankang Library's quiet study floor. To her world, apparently safe and sound . . . and miserable. Sure, he'd tricked and even threatened her, but she'd just condemned Jiao's soul to eternal torture. And for what? A better dissertation topic.

Was that all she fucking cared about: proving herself to a panel of stuffy, middle-aged professors?

She stumbled down the white marble steps, past two empty, darker patches where the library's guardians used to sit. If she went to her apartment now, would the building be surrounded with cop cars, the broken stone lions lying inside like mangled corpses?

Good! she thought wildly. Maybe I'll just say I stole them. Turn myself in. That way I can pay for my crimes and secure my legacy at this stupid school *without* earning a degree.

But when she arrived a half-hour later, the driveway and street in front of her building were empty. Tension fizzed her blood as she turned the borrowed key in the lock. Outside, it all looked so normal Marina half-expected to find the living room tidy, the jade plants only a little dry from neglect. Instead she had to force the door open, shoving until a pile of lathe and plaster scraped across the floor, exhaling a cloud of white dust into her face.

The lions still lay where they'd fallen.

Picking her way across knee-high debris, she sustained a myriad of scratches on her calves. So the invincibility had worn away, just as Vera said it would.

Marina knelt next to one decapitated leonine head and laid a hand on the cool, dusty curls of its mane.

"Li Tieguai?" she whispered experimentally. Her breath disturbed the plaster dust, but nothing else stirred.

She leaned closer to the ruined statue's ear, tasting grit in the air. "I'm sorry. So sorry. I really messed up. If you can hear me, just . . . help Jiao. I'll deal with the rest by myself."

A week later, Marina was called to the Department Chair's office. Well, no wonder. She'd skipped out on TA duties, ignored her advisor's emails and Cait's texts. Not to mention abandoning her ruined home to camp out on a friend's couch, where she'd been living on granola bars and lukewarm Lipton's, while staring at Netflix on a borrowed laptop all day. Her broken phone lay abandoned under the couch with the dust bunnies and crumby wrappers. And her landlady would be home the next day.

She'd only left the house once, to visit a tattoo parlor. She could cut most everything else out of her daily life, but her arm felt unbearably empty without that kirin. And the pain and soreness from the needles made her feel a little less numb inside.

Now, in the Chair's office, she pressed a thumb against the still-healing skin, tracing imaginary scripts on his mahogany desk with the other. The pain blurred her thoughts as finger-smudges dulled the shining wood. What was taking the man so long?

Just get in here and tell me I'm on probation. Then I can tell you I'm done with studying, till I learn how to be a fucking human again.

The door behind her swung open. She took a deep breath, ready to start the tirade. But it wasn't the tweedy Chair who walked around the desk and sat down.

Vera was no longer dressed like a rich young Beijinger. Today she looked like a rich middle-aged New Englander. The ensemble could've come from Cait's closet: white linen slacks and heels, a fitted teal silk shirt, a heavy silver bracelet set with turquoise and diamonds, all topped with a blindingly white cotton sun hat. But the thick, dark braid was all Vera. The lack of sunglasses meant Marina could finally see her eyes. That eerie iridescence, shifting from green to black as she tilted her head, just as Jiao had described.

Vera gave Marina a small, noncommittal smile and set the gourd, balanced atop a brown paper package, on the desk between them.

Was Jiao trapped inside? Marina suffered a fresh gut-punch of guilt. She was lost for words.

Vera, of course, was not. "The journals, as we agreed. And, seeing as we're finished with this old squash, you can return it to the nice lady who paid far too much money for it."

"Is he . . . in there?" Marina touched the gourd. It rocked gently back and forth.

"Oh!" Vera laughed. "No, I let him out as soon as he calmed down. I'm sorry you got caught up in this tortuous fight between old friends. He's fine. You see?"

She pulled up one silky sleeve to reveal a crisp new tattoo: black line art of a snake circling her wrist. Its red tongue flicked lazily. "We'll head to Venice shortly. I've arranged for three resident monks from White Cloud Temple to meet us there. They'll perform the final rites for Jiao at Marco's resting place."

Marina blinked. "You're not keeping him bottled up?" The ball of guilt in her stomach unclenched and shrank a little.

"No, no. Contrary to what Jiao told you, that was never my intention. Our old-yet-short history is fraught with many misunderstandings. He was always rather impetuous and hard to reason with, even before."

"He said you and Marco conspired to kill him, to keep their affair secret."

"No. That's incorrect. But . . . when one dies as Jiao did . . . in a manner of speaking, they are traumatized by it. Their memories . . . quite unreliable. Left on their own, they grow ever angrier. And finally, one day, become demons. Those 'evil spirits' inhabiting the Jiankang lions, and the ones on the bridge, were once like him, too. The only reason Jiao was still lucid at all when you met him was the sleeplike state in which the vessel had kept him. Toward the end, when you agreed to relinquish him, he was teetering on the edge of that particular abyss."

"How *did* he die?"

Vera tapped her lips with one manicured finger. "Hmm. Simply put? Impatience and despair. All so *Romeo and Juliet*, it should've happened in Verona rather than Venice! I had him wait in my sitting room for our friend Marco. Whose confessions, by the way, do tend to get rather long-winded. Jiao and I got acquainted as he sat there for hours, growing increasingly distraught. Certain he'd been abandoned. I bid him wait calmly while I went to seek the tardy lover—who, it turned out, had been delayed by a jealous mistress. Marco could never be called faithful, yet he did love Jiao very much."

"Huh." Marina raised an eyebrow. "And so. . . ?"

"Are you aware that cinnabar is a toxic ore of mercury? In my absence, Jiao finally decided he'd suffered enough. He poured an entire tin of vermillion pigment into his tea." Vera made a face as if she could taste the metallic tang. "No matter how bad the suffering, it's very rude to commit suicide in someone else's sitting room. Anyway, I was gone for hours. When I finally returned with Marco, Jiao was on the verge of death. His lips stained a deep vermillion, like Chinese lacquerware. He was in agony, barely conscious, too insane with mercury poisoning to understand us. With his last bit of strength, he cried out to the Immortal Li Tieguai."

Marina's eyes stung. *Jiao, you poor fucking idiot. You could've been happy. Or at least, as happy as one could be in a strange country, with a cheating boyfriend.*

"The floor shook." Vera continued. "The air split open. Golden rain fell into the drinking gourd Jiao carried at his belt. Desperate to help somehow, Marco held it to his lover's crimson lips . . . but Jiao did not revive. Instead, the life flowed out of him instantly. When the sigils appeared on the gourd, and its mouth closed over, I knew he'd been sealed inside."

"So, then what . . . you just held onto him for a few hundred years? Like some old ripped pants you meant to stitch but never got around to?" Marina was having trouble sympathizing with someone who'd gripe about a suicide because it happened in her living room.

Vera's eyes shifted to black. "I'd intended to obtain the proper rites immediately. But time got away from me, as it tends to do when one has . . . so much of it. Marco died not long after Jiao took his life, so he wasn't there to push me. I travel where and when a certain Bazaar takes me. However, several decades later I returned to Venice, and rediscovered his vessel among my things left stored there. I had intended to deal with him as soon as I tied up business in that city.

"But I must admit . . . I do not know precisely what happened. Either the gourd was stolen, or perhaps . . . perhaps I mistakenly bartered it away. I'm neither infallible nor blameless in this messy affair."

"And it took hundreds of years to find him again." Marina shook her head. "But you only knew Jiao for a few hours. Why go to all this trouble?"

Vera smiled. "He gave me a tin of cinnabar in exchange for a Tarot reading. Wanted me to make his future with—or without—Marco clear. I was unable to render that service before he died."

Marina stared, unable to keep the obvious question bottled up anymore. "So, um . . . what *are* you, exactly?" Unsettling images from fantasy novels and old fairy tales were floating through her mind. Mysterious fae bargains, inscrutable otherworldly transactions, magical deals whose vague wording always doomed their makers.

Vera laughed, a slender finger tugging at her expensive collar as though she was embarrassed. Very obviously an act. "Me? Just a woman with certain principles. And very good connections. I have Jiao to thank for providing an introduction to a Daoist Immortal that night. I rather think that merits me footing the funeral expenses."

The snake on her wrist nodded its flat head.

"And so I came here in person to ask: what can I do for *you*, Marina? Besides the journals, I mean. Jiao wants you to have them anyway. If you hadn't risked your own life, we would not finally be concluding this centuries-old transaction."

Marina looked down, picking silently at dry cuticles under the desk. She'd answered quickly enough when she'd betrayed Jiao for the journals. But now her mind was blank. She wished she knew what Jiao was saying, inside Vera's head.

"Honestly? I don't know. I'm kind of a mess. Guess I always felt special because I was smart. Ambitious. But the further I get in life, the smarter and more ambitious everyone around me gets, too. There's nothing left for my pride to hold onto."

Vera nodded, perhaps even in sympathy.

"Then I thought, *surely* I must be special when a goddamn Daoist Immortal answers my prayers. But it turns out that wasn't anything to do with me, specifically, either. Forget special. I'm actually a shittier person than I ever realized. One who'd rather bend over backward proving myself to assholes I don't like, than help the people I do."

"Well, whatever *you* think, you clearly proved yourself to Li Laoshi. Why else would he have put that wreck of an apartment so nicely back in order? Seems he was touched by your appeal on behalf of Jiao."

Marina blinked. "The house? That's great. I haven't even been back. But . . . the lions are still missing from the library."

"Ah, well. The Laoshi can be a bit of an old softy when it comes to cats. As I understand it, when he put your house back to rights, he gave the lions leave to stretch their legs and roam around for a while."

"But . . . the evil spirits, they left the statues. How can they roam?"

Vera clucked her tongue. "Those pieces are at least three hundred years old, my dear. Naturally, they've developed their own version of a soul, by now."

"So," said Marina a little hollowly. "Everybody's been taken care of." She felt like a splinter forced from a wound. The problems she'd caused were healing around her, squeezing her out in the process.

"Mm. Except for you, Marina. Which brings me to a follow-up question: if you're not too busy at the moment, would you like to come along to Venice, and help reunite these two?"

Marina bolted up so abruptly, before the last word had even left Vera's lips, her chair fell backward onto the floor. "Ditch school and help perform a ceremony to reunite tragic gay historical lovers? Count me the fuck *in*."

Vera laughed. She rose and came around the desk to right the chair, but Marina beat her to it. "I don't know you terribly well," Vera murmured, "but I wouldn't say you're that shitty a person."

"Oh." Marina froze, hands tightening on the wooden backrest. The chair's rigid Shaker design had just reminded her of someone. "I better take care of another thing first. Do you, uh, have a cell phone? Is that a stupid thing to ask someone who's, like, a thousand years old?"

"Not at all." Vera produced a thin silver smartphone. No case, yet not a smudge on the glass. Clearly it'd never been used.

Marina dialed Cait. "Hi. Yeah, it's me. Sorry for not answering your calls earlier. I'm leaving the *fulu* with Dean Harrison. You can pick it up from his office. Afraid I couldn't find out a damn thing about it. But you definitely have a rare treasure there."

She grinned at Vera, who dipped her head to suppress a laugh.

"Oh, and Cait? Please don't take this badly. But I feel like we've just been using each other, and I'm pretty over it. I hope you find somebody who makes you happy, though, really soon."

The angry buzz of Cait's voice, near-incoherent thanks to the marble building's poor reception, permeated the room.

Marina picked up. "Cait, I . . . sorry, you're breaking up. No pun intended! Did you just say . . . some *lions* broke into your house and stole a bunch of art? Oh . . . just the pieces that looked like animals. Wait. No? Oh, the animal artworks left on their *own*. Uh huh, uh huh . . . um, not to be judgy, but have you been taking your Prozac dose with too much wine, or something?"

More staticky screeches were cut off as she pressed END, giggling uncontrollably.

Vera's green eyes sparkled with amusement. She picked up the journals and held them out to Marina. "Reading material for the flight. No need to take notes. Just read them for the pleasure of knowing."

That had always been what drove her, before. Before she got lost in the posturing, the sucking up, the backstabbing, the frantic networking. Marina took hold of the package gingerly, feeling the weight and irregularity of the ancient pages through brown paper. OK, no notes, but she would *definitely* wear gloves. She wasn't a barbarian.

"Actually," she said, "I think I'd rather talk with Jiao on the flight. If it's all the same to you, can he ride with me instead?"

She held out her arm. The tattoo was healing, but still shiny and taut. The new design was a Fu lion, its eyes and curved claws touched with vivid cinnabar red. Vera laid her cool wrist against the still-sensitive flesh. Marina felt a tingle as the lion shook itself and stretched like a housecat, extending vermillion claws. She closed her eyes and smiled widely as Jiao's voice filled her head.

Hello, friend. Shall we take one last journey together?

This long, carefully-rolled up scroll came to us recently, after its second owner's unfortunate death by plague. See how large it is, all the pages curled in upon themselves repeatedly, until it forms a sort of thick staff or rod? The parchment pages within—some clean, fair copies, others with crossed-out lines and musing scribbles—make up a lengthy play based on a famous Greek myth. One meant to be performed before a popular audience, no doubt. But in the 14th century such secular themes, in all types of art, were still frowned upon, their display or performance forbidden. Thus were the creative voices of artists often stifled, even in Venice, by the heavy hand of Rome. However, at the Night Bazaar we've always prided ourselves on offering a haven for the talented and the misunderstood. As well as a venue in which to put diverse works before an appreciative crowd. But sadly, even here, after the admission coins have been collected, the lines all spoken, and the final curtain rung down, there's sometimes still a price left to be paid.

ISMENE IN VENICE
by Gregory Fletcher

I

I followed Antonolo out of the cathedral and into the gray, damp morning, toward the rectory next door. Stepping softly, trying to refrain from making a sound, I left the gravel path and veered off toward the side window of the cabinet room, where Father Marco always held audiences. Crouched below the sill, I'd be able to overhear every word without being seen.

I couldn't help spying. Like a proud father, I was excited for Antonolo. Now the six plays he'd been writing over the last few years would be pronounced ready for production. His future reputation as a great writer would be traced back to its beginning, here, at this very moment. His fame would soar to match that of the great poets of ancient Greece, whom he so revered.

I peeked over the sill. No one in there yet. The heavy, carved wooden table held fresh, unlit tapers in two brass candelabra. But no scrolls.

If my wife still lived, God rest her soul, we would celebrate the rest of this day with such a feast! We'd both always thought of my friend as the son Our Heavenly Father had never blessed us with, though in truth I was only ten years Antonolo's senior.

Just then footsteps approached the interior room. I heard Father Marco already paying compliments. "You've shown such constant focus, my son."

My hands covered my mouth so squeals of delight would not emerge and reveal my hidden presence.

"Your perseverance has astonished us all," he added, rather drily.

I couldn't have agreed more. Endless nights, working by candlelight, Antonolo wrote on into the dawn, making every revision suggested by the Fathers. That passion was indeed God-given, and His bountiful glory was finally about to be bestowed on the worthy Antonolo.

"Alas," Father Marco added, heaving a sigh.

I waited, but an unfathomable silence hung in the air, like the foul stench of death that afflicted our beleaguered city.

"You hand the scrolls back to me as if this were the end," Antonolo said at last.

Father Marco cleared his throat. "Secular plays have been banned for hundreds of years, my son. It's God's will. Let us not debate it further."

"But Father, my work was inspired by the Holy words preached from the pulpit: pride, lust, gluttony, hatred, avarice, and anger."

"Where God's words shall properly remain. Let this secular obsession go. Unless, of course, you're unhappy here?"

I was stunned at the threat implied. Antonolo must've been, as well, for he remained silent.

"If it makes you feel any better, my son," said Father Marco, "know that your penmanship has been praised as some of the finest in all of Venice."

A crunching of gravel approached, then stopped behind me.

I glanced over one shoulder and saw a young boy staring with suspicion. One of the orphans, no doubt. I grimaced and flicked a hand toward the back of the rectory, where, in another building the Carmelitani order of nuns ran the foundling home. There I'd first met Antonolo. I'd been senior altar boy, and he the youngest; about the size of the *ragazza* now jeering and running away from me.

More crunching drew my attention then. Antonolo, stomping back to the cathedral.

I rose and rushed after him.

Inside the nave, dozens of volunteers were still reviewing their parts in next Sunday's Passion Play. Gurian stepped into Antonolo's path before I could reach him. "The Holy Twelve is short by one," he said. "And I don't have to tell you,

I've more than earned the right to replace him." Thanks to his narrow, rounded shoulders, and soft chubby curves, Gurian had been playing Mary Magdalene for the last decade.

Antonolo didn't answer, but only looked distracted. I tried to intercede. "Who's missing?"

"Paladin." Then Gurian turned back to Antonolo. "I thought you would've known."

My stomach quivered. Hadn't I just seen Paladin in Mass this morning? I thought back.

No, I had not.

Others around us stepped closer to hear the sad news.

"His wife and child too," Gurian added. "All gone within the week."

"Dear Heavenly Father." Antonolo shook his head.

I blinked and lowered my gaze to the geometric inlay of the tiled floor. The stone had cracks running through its connected burgundy octagons, as if illustrating how the Black Death had torn apart the families of our congregation.

Antonolo was always our source of news on births, marriages, and deaths of parishioners, because he lived, worked, and dined within the Church. But the plague that had hovered like a carrion crow over Venice for months had deterred the priests from making house calls to give Last Rites. Thus, information had all but dried up.

"The Passion Play *must* have twelve Apostles," Gurian insisted.

Clearly the bad news had drained away the last of Antonolo's strength, so I brought things to a close in the only way I knew how. "Since we could perform it in our sleep by now, I bid you all a safe journey home. Godspeed."

Everyone nodded and dispersed. All, that is, except Gurian.

At last I said, "Very well. Be on the lookout for a new Mary Magdalene."

Clapping his fingertips together, Gurian ran after the others to announce his promotion to one of the Holy twelve.

Antonolo hung his head. "I've outlived my purpose here. I am no longer needed."

I tugged on the end of my graying beard. "Certainly not! The Passion Play needs you. The living Nativity needs you. And who else could manage church volunteers so deftly?"

He shook his head. "I fear this performance may be my last." He walked away, past the shadowy row of columns stretching the length of the nave.

"Though where else is there for me?"

I scurried after him. "Having shelter in God's house during such dark times is a blessing."

"True." He nodded. "Only pestilence and death await me outside those doors."

Muffled footsteps stumped towards us. Clearly Bini's. His limbs were too short for his barrel-chested body. From a burlap bag hung over one shoulder, he strewed herbs and rushes across the floor—lavender, thyme, meadowsweet, and marjoram. A chore he undertook whenever the stink of death in our streets crept inside. He'd also come here from the orphanage. But he and Antonolo were the only ones who had room and board within the church, thanks to their duties. Bini scrubbed floors, ran errands, rang the church bells, emptied chamber pots, and cleaned the *necessarium*, where the local princes of the church emptied their bowels.

He offered Antonolo the covered plate clutched in his free hand. "I was bringing it up to your room."

Antonolo looked wounded. "I'm no longer welcome at their table?"

I struggled to find consoling words. "Perhaps the Fathers realized how upset you'd be and chose not to be burdened with your disappointment."

It didn't sound as comforting as I'd intended.

Bini climbed the steps of the curving, walled staircase up to their rooms. We followed, more slowly. At the stone archway that was Antonolo's, Bini pushed aside the faded blue velvet curtain—a discarded drape from an old confessional. The dim, windowless room had a small ventilation hole that let in a square beam of light. Bini pulled some altar candle stubs from one voluminous sleeve and left them on the table.

Antonolo dropped the six scrolls into a basket, scowling at the candles. After Bini left, he snapped them in half and dropped to his knees beside his bed, pounding the straw mattress into shape. Then stretched out with an exasperated sigh. Breathing deeply, drifting off.

"Yes, sleep will do you good," I said.

Once outside the church, I realized home was the last place I wanted to be. Two rooms of emptiness. No wife, no child, no rest. Only long walks until exhaustion made sleep possible. So I began my usual trek, walking from street to street, over a canal bridge, to the next street or alley, and so on. Shutters were closed tight; people boarded up inside with their fear and dread. The only sounds were my own muffled footsteps on cobblestones, the occasional squeak of a rat, and splashes against the walls of the canals.

Long after nightfall, still too wakeful to return home, I stepped into an alley and was greeted by a foul, gagging waft of Death. I shivered. Was The Grim Reaper now at my side?

Wooden heels clacked nearby. I jerked my head around, checking either side. No one there. Behind me, then?

Not a soul. Only that rotting putrescence. I lurched away, fanning the air before me, as if that would help. Through watering eyes I noticed a woman walking toward me some distance ahead, wrapped head to toe in a hooded cloak. The same height as my departed wife, Fea.

As we drew closer, she stared in my direction and opened her mouth to speak. Instead of a voice, though, a cold breeze brushed my ear. *"Pietro."*

I halted, frozen with fear and longing. "Fea?"

Midnight bells tolled just then from the cathedrals. When I looked back, no one was there, before or behind me. How had she vanished so quickly?

But at my feet, close to where she'd been standing, lay a length of red ribbon embroidered with two tiny words. I had to bend and squint to make them out:

Night Bazaar

A young man leaning against a nearby building whistled, and held out a bucket. I walked over to look inside, wherein lay jumbled many such ribbons.

He jerked his head toward the open door. "Like nothing else in town. No wishes forbidden, no desires banned here."

Did I dare ask? I thought of Antonolo and couldn't help myself. I whispered, "What about . . . by chance, are there any secular performances to be viewed?"

The boy gave a crooked smile and inclined his head again. "Step inside and see."

Antonolo needed to meet other writers of plays. To know he wasn't alone in this world. I held up the ribbon. "Is this good for two?"

The boy pointed at my feet. I looked down, saw a second ribbon lying on the cobblestones, and snatched it up. "Tomorrow night, too?"

"We'll be gone by sun-up. Never in the same place twice."

But it was still hours before dawn. So I knew exactly what I must do.

II

I rushed up the stairs of the church and burst into the dark room to shake Antonolo's shoulder. "Wake up, wake up." I set his shoes on his chest, then felt around for the cloak he always flung over the one chair.

"Don't need cheering up, Pietro." He rubbed his face. "I need sleep."

"You've slept away twelve hours already. Please, trust me. You'll want to see what I have to show you."

He sighed, but sat up. There came a rustle as he tied the leather laces of his shoes. He rose and went over to the table, turning back to shove a plate of food at my chest. "Eat. You've been losing too much weight since. . . ." He trailed off.

No matter. I knew exactly what he meant. Since Fea had passed away.

I gladly accepted the cold potatoes and boiled egg. In the dimness sat a second dish, still covered, as if he hadn't eaten at all. "You have money?" I asked. "You may need it."

We left the plates on the table. Antonolo flung his cloak about his shoulders and went to the curtained arch. I felt my way behind him, and followed up the stairs to Bini's room, directly above. With no curtain screening his room, he lay snoring away, sound asleep.

Antonolo made his way to a large, misshapen storage basket. He rooted to the very bottom. There came the muffled jingle of coins as he whispered, "Bini has a knack for finding fallen *monete*."

We left the room. Antonolo paused on the landing. "The stairs are steep and narrow. Put your hand on my shoulder." I did so, and he slowly led the way down the two dark flights.

We left through a side door, emerging into an alley. The moon lit the thick, dank mist from the canals so it looked like drifting milkweed floss. Now I led the way. Keeping to the shadows, pressed close to buildings so as not to risk a fall into a strange canal, I retraced the way toward that strange, so-called Night Bazaar.

After a few blocks, I broke the silence. "When the Basilica finally presents a secular play or two, Santa Maria Assunta won't be far behind." I wasn't sure I believed this, though. "Our times will surely become more enlightened before you know it."

Antonolo snorted. "I'll be long dead before any such enlightenment arrives." He threw up his arms. "Oh, ravaged city of thousands dead, plucked and discarded. Where's our Oedipus when we need him most?"

He'd always had a flair for drama.

"No thanks," I teased. "Venice has enough problems without adding a king who murders his father and marries his mother."

He scowled as if I had blasphemed. "Oedipus didn't *know* the king and queen of Thebes were his parents. And *twice* he saved that city from the Black Death. We should be so lucky. But, no, all *you* remember—"

"Is that he was the father of Antigone, Eteocles, and Polynices."

"And? You're forgetting the second daughter."

I frowned. "Who?"

"Antigone's sister."

"Oh. Um . . . what's her name?"

"*Ismene.*" A long, bitter silence, before he muttered, "Being strong-willed and ambitious—it's exhausting."

Was he still speaking of Ismene?

Finally, I spotted the same young good-for-nothing leaning against the building with his bucket. I dropped in our ribbons, and he flapped a hand for us to enter.

The deserted building was large, scarred from a recent fire. Its outer stone shell looked solid enough, but many of the interior walls seemed to be missing. We walked through a maze of parti-colored tents of all sizes. Oil lanterns hung at the entrance to each. Dozens, perhaps hundreds of people were milling about, examining merchandise. I'd expected African masks, Byzantine relics from Constantinople, Chinese long-stemmed wooden pipes. But the exotic goods on display were items I'd never seen before. Miniature beasts with fangs, oblong smooth wooden handles—but for what? Baskets that jiggled; something alive inside. I wanted to stop to look more closely, but instead led Antonolo past it all. Searching for anything that might resemble a dramatic performance.

At the entrance to the last tent stood another young man with a leather bucket. When he thrust it our way, I saw many coins, even half-ducats inside. Much laughter from within the tent said some sort of performance was in progress.

We deposited one penny apiece, and the boy pulled back the canvas flap.

Inside, we picked our way slowly through a dim space. Stepping around dozens of mesmerized men sitting on the floor, facing three male performers lit by a row of candles. Dressed as a Zoroastrian priest, the one in the center wore a purple cloak and had the dark skin of a Moor. Two paler fellows sat on either side of him. One guzzling from a goatskin bag; the other picking his teeth as if they'd just finished a meal.

We found an empty spot and sat. The tent was warm and stuffy, thick with hot candle fat, smoke, and male sweat. How much of the play had we missed?

Antonolo's eyes sparkled now, lit by the flames of more candles suspended in metal dishes by ropes of different lengths. Higher and off to the far left hung a large oil lantern with the brightest flame of all.

I pointed to it and whispered, "It's the north star."

Antonolo nodded, pressing a finger to his lips to shush me.

The player in the middle yawned. "Shall we continue while the stars shine bright?"

One companion pulled his foot from a boot as if nursing a blister; the other opened a tied-up cloth and counted what looked to be gold pieces.

"Melchior, put that away," scolded the King of Arabia. "Let's not attract trouble."

As Melchior retied the pouch around his waist, he passed gas. A crude but surprisingly effective jest. The audience guffawed. The young man attending to his blistered foot grimaced and pressed his nose to a small, ornate bottle. The faint, rich scent of frankincense drifted to us.

The middle character took out a small glass vial and poured a single drop of glistening oil onto one palm. With his fingertips he massaged temples and earlobes.

"Balthazar, enough myrrh," the man on his right complained.

"Enough of your nagging," he snapped back.

The beardless, younger traveler with the frankincense scowled. "Walk your royal black ass back to Egypt, for all I care."

I whispered to Antonolo, "You see? They're headed to worship the baby Jesus."

He shushed me again, more sharply, but no longer looked sad. He was as entranced as the rest.

Balthazar, Melchior, and Caspar grudgingly picked up their belongings and left through a back flap in the tent. By then some of the suspended candles were guttering. Audience members stomped their feet and cried out approval, then rose to leave the tent.

A boy came in through the same back flap to replace the dying candles with fresh ones. I stood, intending to peruse other exhibits. But Antonolo remained seated. Hoping for another performance, clearly.

Outside the tent, I followed the chiming of finger cymbals. Belly dancers from far-off lands gyrated and writhed, all but naked, showing sinful stretches of smooth, bare flesh. When one kohl-eyed houri beckoned, I was drawn toward her as if ensorceled. I stopped mere inches away, inhaling her sweet scent. She lifted the veil at her bosom and exposed one brown nipple.

I knew I should feel incensed, and loudly denounce her as a harlot. Before I could, with a twirling movement of one hand, she spread her fingers. My mouth opened silently, instead. She crooked her little finger and my tongue sprang forth. I knelt, forced relentlessly down as if someone leaned on my shoulders. The harlot pressed her most secret place against my tongue, writhing in pleasure. Only when my knees buckled and I collapsed did onlookers drag me away and help me to my feet.

Someone shoved a small leather bucket laden with coins at my chest. Not daring to look up and meet those ensorceling eyes again, I flung in a penny and hurried off.

On the next aisle a bare-chested man carried a pale-yellow snake thicker than his arm and longer than he was tall.

The sight of its pale, throbbing length wrapped around his shoulders and waist made me feel somehow even more wicked than the houri had. Yet my hand rose to touch the snake. I grabbed an onlooker's arm, and cried, "I beg you, drag me away!" And he obliged.

Finally, I discovered a Godlier booth, one which sold products to shield one from the Black Death. It offered such nostrums as bodypainting, herbal wrappings, or the painful-looking application of Oriental needles. I examined a cloth meant to be worn around the neck or over the face like a mask. It smelled delightful, whatever its supposed curative powers. At the very least, it would block the stench of death. I purchased it for three coppers. If only Fea had owned such an item to protect her from the disease that stole her from me!

Back at the tent, the young man with the bucket stopped me. "Last performance. Over."

"But I have a friend inside."

"No more," he grunted. "See for yourself."

The interior of the tent was empty, but faint voices drifted from the back. I made my way to the flap where the performers had gone in and out.

"Cinnamon? Eucalyptus?" asked a familiar voice.

I started. Was that Antonolo?

"Correct. Now, one more," a stranger replied. The basso of the dark-skinned performer who'd played Balthazar.

"Rosemary?" Yes. Antonolo, to be sure. I stuck my head past the flap.

He was standing inside, turned away from me, his backside stark naked! His cloak, blouse, stockings, smallclothes, breeches, and shoes lay nearby in a heap. In front of him knelt a shirtless man, running a cloth over my friend's naked flesh.

Dear God, had he too been ensorceled?

Someone tapped hard on my shoulder. Two men forcibly turned me around and led me out to the front entrance of the bazaar. I recognized them as the other performers. They marched me back to the front door. ¯

Outside was the faint glow of sunrise. Clearly, the bazaar was closing for the night.

One of the players flapped both hands at me: *Go, leave.* That simple gesture left me with an awful feeling—as if I were being discarded. Undoubtedly how Antonolo had felt when Father Marco returned the six scrolls.

I left, crossing myself, praying he would be safe. My eyelids were drooping; exhaustion had arrived. Finally, I could go home to sleep, and hope not to dream of poor ravaged Fea. To know nothing more, until I woke again.

III

Around noon I rushed to Santa Maria Assunta, hoping to find Antonolo asleep, as before. But his bed was untouched. I sat at his table and waited, after a while nibbling at the plate of food delivered by Bini. Boiled cabbage and sardines today.

When another plate came in the early evening, I felt as surprised as Bini looked to find me still waiting. Where had the time gone? More alarming—where was Antonolo?

I waited out the evening in a sweat of apprehension, then retraced my steps back to the Night Bazaar. But the boy who'd collected the ribbons had told the truth. They were gone, moved to some other location.

I walked street after street, crossing each bridge of every canal in Venice. Listening for the faintest sound of exotic flutes and drums, or cries of debauched revelry.

Hours later, a boy carrying a wooden crate crossed my path. He'd tied a cloth over nose and mouth; the very same as I had purchased at the Bazaar. Haunting the shadows, hugging walls, I followed.

A few blocks later he tripped over a lifeless body left in the street and fell to all fours on the cobblestones. "God's teeth," he cursed, gathering up scattered merchandise from the crate. Then he glared down at the poor, rotting corpse, and drew back one foot.

"Please, no-no-no," I said, stepping out beneath the light of a torch racked at the corner. I pointed to the cloth around his face, which had slipped below his chin. "Take care."

He shrugged, retied it, and went on his way.

I followed, for the hour was late. Perhaps the urchin worked at the Bazaar.

After traveling up and down several alleys, he did indeed lead me to its new location, in an old warehouse. While he complained of his misadventures to the same boy holding the same bucket of ribbons at the entrance, showing off scraped and bloody hands and elbows, I sneaked inside without paying.

I found the performance tent again, and dropped a penny in the leather bucket thrust my way. The boy mumbled, "Hurry up, last performance."

Only a few open spots remained on the floor. The crowd intently watched as a long-bearded player paced within a space shaped like a large cross, outlined by candles on the floor. This night the audience sat on three sides of the makeshift stage. The cross' top arm was up against the back flap of the tent.

The bearded one wore a turban held in place with a hemp circlet. Like some ancient Hebrew prophet worked in stained glass, he wore a rough tunic that hung to his calves, crudely belted.

A female character entered, wearing a loose robe. The man portraying her had shaved his beard. His head was draped with a long cloth like the wimple Holy Sisters wore. "She" slipped off her sandals, but froze like a startled deer when she saw the bearded man across from her.

"Oh, Husband," she said softly. "You must be famished." And she turned toward the back of the tent, where some clay pots and stacks of wooden platters stood.

The bearded man snapped his fingers. "You are surprised to find me at home so early?"

She nodded uncertainly.

"Then tell me, obedient wife, where have you been?" His eyes narrowed in accusation.

"I . . . fetched water from the well in the square. Tidied up the house, and baked bread. Did you have to walk all the way to Sepphoris to find work today?

And carrying your tools, too?"

"What good is a carpenter without tools?" He circled her, then suddenly picked some small thing off the back of her robe. "What's this . . . a withered grape leaf?"

She lowered her gaze. "I...also found work in the vineyard today." She pulled a few coins from a cloth pouch. "And was paid a good wage."

He counted the money. "No one makes so much from a *bit of work* in a vineyard."

"Please, Joseph, you're hungry. It makes you cross. Let me—"

He snarled and shoved her to the floor. "This isn't the first time, is it?" He stood menacingly over her. "God help you, Mary, you'll be stoned to death in the streets one day."

"Joseph, please, lower your voice."

The pudgy man sitting next to me stared, eyes wide. He crossed himself and muttered, "No! Not Mary."

Another said, louder, "What blasphemy is this!"

I was revolted too. Tempted to leave. And yet . . . I had to see what would happen next.

She reached out and embraced his knees. "I am yours, and yours only."

Lip curled with disgust, he pointed down. "Fornicator, God will judge thee!" Then he slapped her face, the smack of hand on cheek ringing out through the tent. "Is it my fault there's no work in Nazareth? That I must walk miles to Sepphoris?" He groaned and covered his face. "Exhaustion has been my downfall as a man—not my desire." Real tears ran from his eyes.

My stomach quivered. I had to bite my lip not to join him in weeping.

He drew back to strike her again. This time her arms shielded her belly.

He gasped. "You're...Mary, no. Tell me you're not with child."

I shook my head, unable to fathom such a wicked turn of events.

"I can make it right," she pleaded. "Hear me out, husband."

"You can only spend eternity in the fires of Hell! There's no hope now. We must move where no one knows us. All the way to Bethlehem."

"With you at my side, we can live in a stable for all I care."

"You have destroyed us!"

"No. We will create such a story as no one will dare to doubt. A great tale that will follow this babe for all its years, and beyond." She kissed his hands and rose to stand beside him. "Only believe in us, my husband, and watch others come to believe in this child."

"I haven't the strength to do such a thing," Joseph said.

"I'll help you. Together, we possess the strength to create a new world." She turned away, and stepped over to the clay pots at the tent's back wall.

Joseph sank onto the floor cradling his head.

Mary returned with a wooden platter of flat bread and oily green olives. He sat up and composed himself. She pushed the food toward him. As he took a few bites, my mouth watered. Then he looked up at her, and pointed to the food. "Eat, Wife."

She shook her head. "I am not worthy to break bread with you."

"But you must. For . . . the child."

With each bite, he sat taller. Straighter. His eyes narrowed again, but in curiosity rather than suspicion this time. "What is this story we will tell?"

She half-smiled, seeing she'd not only won back her husband, but that he would do as she'd bidden.

If only I'd had something to throw, a rotten potato or a bad egg, I would've done so. The audacity of these heretic players!

Yet the audience around me leapt up, stamping their feet in approval. All the while Joseph continued to eat, gazing intently at his wife, as if no one else was inside the tent. He inclined his head toward the back flap. They rose and stepped closer. And then, Holy Father forbid, met in a passionate, lustful embrace.

I looked away in disgust.

By the time my eyes were drawn back again he was leading her away, apparently to their bed. The audience roared with delight.

Merciful Mary, Mother of Jesus, I was surrounded by heretic heathens.

As everyone filed out, chattering about what they'd seen, I looked for Antonolo. No sign of him, but I heard voices behind the back flap, and stepped closer to listen. One was his, so I lifted a corner and peeked inside.

The one who'd dressed as Our Lady was helping Joseph remove a false beard.

"You used too much pine resin." The clean-shaven player shook his head. "A couple drops generally does the trick."

"I didn't want it to fall off. Ow! Now it's pulling out the few beard-hairs I possess."

It was Antonolo!

"You just feared being recognized," the one who'd played Mary said. The Moorish King of Arabia, from last night's performance. The one I'd spied kneeling before Antonolo as in blasphemous worship. "On the count of three," he said. "One—" And with that, he ripped off the false beard.

Antonolo shrieked bloody murder.

Two more men tromped noisily into the main tent. I scooted off to hide in the shadows. One player carried a fistful of coins he jingled with satisfaction; the other clutched a full wineskin. They pushed on through the back flap.

"To Antonolo!" one cried. "Vera wanted you to have this. The Lady Fortunato recognizes talent when she sees it. Now, where's your money pouch?"

"I . . . I've never needed one before," Antonolo said.

"Get yourself a pouch to hold coins. You'll need to carry it from now on."

"Luca has always dreamt of a rebirth of the Arts," the other man said. "As if we live in ancient times!"

"A Renaissance," Luca corrected him.

"If such a thing is even possible," the other said doubtfully. "But with Antonolo and Luca on stage, maybe it's not merely a dream."

I scurried out then, into the maze of booths and tents, dodging jongleurs and mountebanks and prognosticators, beside myself with disgust and worry. All around me the purveyors of filth were dismantling their stalls, packing away goods. Men carried packed crates out the entrance. I picked up a small chest and followed one. Surely at some point Antonolo must exit here as well. Then I would follow and confront him openly about the ungodly spell he'd fallen under.

The workmen circled the building and headed down to a canal, where they were loading everything onto a barge tied up to a pier. I climbed aboard too, then veered off to the stern where crates were already stacked head high. I found a gap between two rows and slipped in to hide.

Before long Antonolo and Luca boarded. They found their own place between the piles of crates, sacks, and rolled-up tents. Hidden from the street, but if I craned my neck, still in my line of vision.

The barge jerked as the line-handler pushed us off from the pier. Two sweating men began oaring it. Where were we headed? Surely not toward open sea, or more likely, a new pier. Not one of the nearby islands, I hoped, for then how would I get back?

Luca handed a small wooden bowl to Antonolo. He poured in a few drops from several tiny glass bottles, then swirled the mixture with a cloth. He rubbed this over the back of Antonolo's neck, then around his ears. Pulling off my friend's tunic, he ran the cloth along his ribs, chest, and under his arms. Just as I'd suspected—a potion created with dark magic.

Did Antonolo object? No! He only said, "I've missed oranges this season."

Luca handed the cloth over and slipped off his own tunic. To my surprise, Antonolo wiped down his companion with equal care. Luca leaned forward to sniff at his neck. From ear to ear, and down each arm, and back again, like a hound in rut. From nipple to nipple, then down the center of his belly. And yes, lower still.

I wanted to shout damnation, but dared not make a sound. No telling who else was on this damnable barge. Soon their shining torsos melded, like a conjoined statue of sin. Had any abomination ever looked quite so artful?

No, I could watch no more.

Covering my eyes, I crouched and rocked. How to return Antonolo's life to the place it had been only days before I'd found this cursed Bazaar?

"Shall we go for your belongings?" Luca said at last.

Antonolo shook his head. "Not yet. After Sunday's Passion Play."

Had any woman ever bewitched a man as quickly as Luca had seduced my dearest friend?

"No, it's impossible," Luca responded. "By then we'll be out at sea."

"To what city, what country?"

Luca shrugged. "That's Vera's decision, not mine. She decides such matters."

"But . . . as yet I have no Mary Magdalene," Antonolo said. "And then who would play Jesus? No, I cannot possibly depart so soon."

For a brief moment I was hopeful. But their faces moved closer, their mouths sought each other again. Once more the sweet aroma of that devil's potion stunned them into a sinful silence louder than any words.

I covered my eyes, trying not to groan aloud.

When the barge finally docked at a pier on the Grand Canal, Luca and Antonolo were the first off. They hurried to a nearby gondola. When men came to lift the crates and unload them, I simply picked up one too, and followed. The sun was just rising as I set down my burden and slipped away, back home. Such exhaustion would ensure a few hours of rest.

Around noon I rushed to Santa Maria Assunta, but Antonolo was nowhere to be found. I prayed for his soul, tempted to line up with the other congregants at the confessionals. But my admission would doom him to a heretic's pyre.

He arrived a little after Nones, the public mid-afternoon prayers.

I rushed up to rebuke him.

"Forgive me, Pietro," he said, before I could even speak. So earnestly I fell back, seeing anguish in his eyes.

"No, it was I who took you to the Night Bazaar. I blame myself."

He shook his head, then stared at a young man standing with his back to us, replacing a row of burnt-out votives with new candles. The boy's shoulders were narrow and rounded as a girl's, his hips slightly curved.

Antonolo stepped closer and tapped him lightly on the back.

When the fellow turned toward us, it was Gurian. Who said with enthusiasm, "So, have you found a replacement? Mary holds a dear place in my heart, so I will happily share my many nuances of the role."

Antonolo sighed and shook his head. "From the back, I thought *you* the perfect replacement. Please, Gurian, would you honor me by portraying Our Lady one last time?"

"But I'm one of the Holy Twelve now! It's not possible to play both."

"I promise, you can be any Apostle you choose next year."

Gurian went pale. "I've already told everyone—I'll look a great fool. No, I'll find someone else for the part yet."

"And dress him in the proper clothing?"

"Yes, yes, of course." He set the basket of candles on the floor, and rushed out.

Antonolo headed up the side stairs, but climbed on past his own room to Bini's. I followed quietly behind. He knelt at the basket of soiled clothes in Bini's chamber and dug to the bottom for the coin pouch. He added several; ill-gotten gains from his unholy work at the Bazaar. Then he buried the pouch deep again.

He walked past me without a word, seeming to have forgotten my presence. So I followed, to his room. He pulled back the curtain, then flinched and gave a muffled cry, startling me as well.

He thrust out both hands before him, whispering, "No, you must leave now. You should not be here, in my chamber." He stepped inside and closed the drape. "Why did you follow me?"

Someone else was inside the room with him.

"Is this *Antigone in Venice*?" The deep voice was Luca's.

"No, one of the six plays Father Marco rejected. *Anger*, to be exact."

"Where's *Antigone*?"

I'd thought I knew all of Antonolo's works, finished or in progress. How strange I'd never heard of this title before.

"Never mind," Antonolo said. "I'm not even certain it's worthy of notice."

"You're sounding more and more like her. Antigone's hopeless sister."

"What if I am Ismene?"

"If you can write of Antigone's strength, then you possess it within yourself. I saw it emerge in last night's performance."

"Ha. A fleeting moment."

"Antonolo, moments eventually turn into days. And days to months. Now, where is the play? I'm desperate to read it."

"No. It's hidden for good reason. In my version, Antigone condemns both the Doge's Palace and the Church. In the end, when she's left in a cave to die, she screams, 'A plague on your city. A plague will be the death of you all!' And now look at the state of fair Venice."

"Impressive, Antonolo. Maybe you're the soothsayer Tiresias, too."

"No, you were right. I'm merely poor hopeless Ismene."

The sharp report of a slap pierced the air. I winced, then lifted one side of the drape and peered inside.

Antonolo sat on one side of the mattress looking stunned, gingerly cradling one cheek. Luca knelt on the other side, running his hands beneath it. "Nothing," he said, then leapt up and overturned both chair and table to examine them, as if something valuable was hidden underneath.

"Stop," Antonolo commanded. "I won't ask again."

Luca smiled. "Ah! There it is. Antigone in the flesh." He went over and embraced Antonolo. "Your strength is intoxicating. Don't ever doubt it again." Luca frowned suddenly. He slowly turned and met my gaze. "Ah. Whose audience is this?"

I dropped the curtain and stepped back, flushing hotly.

Antonolo lunged through it, pulling Luca along by one arm. I backed away, tripping over my own feet, to fall ignominiously on my *culo*. "Antonolo, wait!" I called. "I must speak with you."

Without slowing, he shouted over one shoulder, "Meet me later, Pietro. I'll return anon."

And then they were gone.

After hours of waiting, I finally realized a great truth: If I was going to save Antonolo from Luca, it would require more drastic measures.

IV

I decided to return to the barge the heathens had tied up on the far side of town; my aim to catch Antonolo before he was kidnapped. Still, even knowing Venice as well as I did, wrong turns delayed my progress. By the time I arrived at the pier, the barge was gone. Not a soul in sight on the neighboring gondola. Waiting till sunrise for the other one to return . . . that might be too late. But finding the Bazaar's new location also seemed impossible.

At a loss, I walked the streets looking for any sign of the abominable den of heretics.

"Pietro," a woman called. She stood across the canal, wrapped in a blanket, arms open in supplication. As I gaped at this apparition, she collapsed.

I ran to the closest bridge and bolted across to the other side. When I reached her, though, I hesitated. She wasn't moving. And the cloth was pulled up now, covering her face.

"Fea?" I reached out and flipped back one corner.

It was no living woman but a decomposing corpse. I recoiled so violently, one scrambling boot kicked the body, sending it tumbling into the canal.

Dear God! I crossed myself, gagging at the foul stench on my hand. Somehow, the little food in my stomach remained.

Her body drifted farther out.

Now a gondola was approaching, carrying two men, the bigger of the two with an arm around the other. "You'll be fine. You're only exhausted," the large one said. "Not used to working through the night."

It was Luca and Antonolo, being ferried back the way I'd just come. I crouched behind a bollard until the gondola oared past my hiding place.

"But what about Antigone and Ismene?" Antonolo's voice drifted faintly back.

"We have plenty of others to perform the role. It needn't be you."

I ran crouched along the seawall, behind them, following.

"Your Ismene was weak," Antonolo added. "A weeping ninny. Whining and frail."

"Isn't she all of those things?" Luca demanded. "She brings nothing to her world. She might as well be dead."

The gondola tied up at a pier, and Luca helped Antonolo board a barge with a small cabin on deck. They both stepped inside it, but after a few minutes, Luca hurried off to re-board the gondola—presumably, returning to the bazaar for tonight's performance. But his words still rang in my head: *She brings nothing to her world. She might as well be dead.*

Surely, a king's daughter such as Ismene would have grown up stronger, more ambitious. As Antonolo had once been, before Father Marco's constant *no-no-no.*

I waited an hour before slipping quietly onboard. What I did from this point on would have to be improvised, but I felt certain modifications to my original plan would ensure success.

A lighted lantern hung on the door to the crude cabin. The floor of the small wood-paneled room behind it held two pallets, side by side. Antonolo lay asleep on one.

Now was the time. I must act quickly to save him. "Wake up, wake up!"

He rolled away, mumbling, "Just a bit longer."

"Wake up, Antonolo. It's Pietro."

He bolted upright, panic in his eyes. "How'd you find me?"

I crossed myself, hating the lie that must be told. But I had no choice. "One of the boys from the Bazaar approached me after the performance tonight. Several men there have fallen deathly ill. One is Luca, who calls for you. We must leave right now."

Antonolo made no objection. We left the barge and headed north. The faster we moved through the streets and over bridges, the less time he'd have to question my story.

In an older part of town lay a modest plot of land I'd inherited. It held only a small stable which had belonged to childless older cousins—the closest thing to parents, though they'd been too poor to raise me themselves. For years, I'd rented out the four stalls and hayloft above. My dream of acquiring my own horses never materialized. Both home and stable remained barren.

"In here," I said breathlessly.

Once Antonolo stepped through, I slammed both wooden half-doors shut, and slid the heavy oak bars in place. Thank the Holy Father, saved at last!

"Forgive me, dearest friend," I called. "I knew no other way to rescue you."

Still, I needed to see him there, safe inside. I'd removed the ladder that normally led to the hayloft, and set it under the lone window, against an outside wall, out of Antonolo's reach. I climbed it now and, below the rotting shingled roof, threw open the wooden shutters to look inside.

Antonolo gazed up. "I must get back. Luca and I—"

"No!"

"But I've found where I belong."

"On Satan's path? To be stoned to death? Or burned at the stake. Antonolo, you know not what is best. You're too weak to resist their spells. Too naïve. Look at yourself, at what's become of you already."

"So you're going to leave me here to die? As you did with Fea?"

A shiver shot up my spine.

"A goose is walking over my grave," Antonolo added.

It was what my wife used to say, when she felt the sort of chill that turns one's skin to pimpled gooseflesh. During her last days, neighbors had whispered of pestilence even though Fea had grown ill before this outbreak. Or had she perhaps been its first victim? She'd had her own suspicions, though. One night, fevered and sleepless, she'd whispered, "God has no use for barren women."

The next morning, she had vanished from our house. Antonolo and I searched everywhere; it was here we finally found her. By then with the delirium and black boils. I'd even swear that once she levitated above the hay. We wrapped stones in the blanket to keep her earthbound. After she breathed her last, by then blind, her blackened body had shriveled and warped into deformities we'd never seen before. Bumps, bulges, twisted limbs. As if her soul had been squeezed violently out to join Our Lord in Heaven.

Or so I continue to pray.

"I am sick," Antonolo said, still gazing up.

"No, the trance is broken. Now, you are safe." I started to climb down.

His next words stopped me. "You saw me? In the Bazaar play."

I looked in again and nodded reluctantly.

"Pure blasphemy, no?"

"Their punishment will be eternal, even if the inquisition doesn't get to them first."

He sat abruptly in the straw and covered his face. "If only you really knew them, Pietro."

"Why do you think they must move to a new place each night? They'll be publicly flogged. Chained, imprisoned. Burned in flames that sear forever."

He heaved a great sigh, then lay back on the straw-covered dirt floor and scooped mounds of hay over himself.

"There are blankets stacked in the corner." I climbed down and found a piece of white limestone in the dirt. On one stable door, I scrawled a large letter:

Q, for Quarantine. Not the first time I'd warned strangers off in this way. Then I pressed an ear against the wood.

Inside, Antonolo was muttering, "I bring nothing to my world. I might as well be dead."

Every day I brought food tied up in a cloth, and dropped the bundle from the hay-loft window, along with a full skin of water.

Antonolo fingered the material, a moth-eaten altar cloth. "From Bini?"

"Why should it go to waste? Food is scarce."

He fetched the bundle and beckoned. "Come, eat." He untied the cloth to reveal boiled potatoes and onions. "There's plenty."

My stomach rumbled. But, for the first time in my life, I couldn't trust him. "Later. When you're free."

"Isn't that up to you, Pietro?"

"Don't fool yourself, Antonolo. I know alchemy when I see it. Like those wicked potions rubbed onto your skin."

"Not potions," he mumbled through a mouthful of potato. "Herbs and oils. Luca learned medicine from a Chinaman, and he hasn't been ill a day since. Including during the time spent in Messina, when they had plague."

"He survived Messina? Few others did."

"I need rosewood, frankincense, yellowed flowered Mediterranean plant, and spruce."

"To keep you healthy?"

"No. Strong and confident."

I shook my head, and did climb down then.

He shouted after me, "Pietro, come back. I'll forget all about Luca and the Night Bazaar. I've a new idea for the Passion Play. It's brilliant. Are you listening?"

"Go on." I stepped closer to the door.

"From the small circular opening at the top of the dome," he continued. "An angel is lowered on a rope, after Jesus is taken from the cross and entombed. The angel carries Jesus, both of them pulled up to the top as if it were Heaven."

It was the most outrageous mechanical idea he'd ever proposed. "Despite the combined weight of two men?"

"Well, yes . . . the rope would have to be stout enough to hold us both."

"As if Father Marco would ever allow such a dangerous stunt!"

"If I must die, why not go the way of gods?"

That did it. I slammed both fists against the door, and his blasphemy. Then walked away, without another word.

Three days later, when I pushed back the two beams for the last time, it wasn't me Antonolo acted happy to see. Bini stepped inside with a covered plate, and Antonolo embraced him like a long-lost relative.

"My good friend. I feared you were no more," Bini said, patting his back.

Antonolo bolted the food as if famished. After finishing the salted pork, though, he tore off a hunk of bread, and handed the rest to me.

"I prayed you'd survive," Bini continued. "And just in time."

Antonolo furrowed his brow. "What do you mean?"

"Tomorrow's annual Play, of course."

"It's Saturday already?"

Bini nodded. "The effects of the fever Pietro mentioned. He said you might speak like a lunatic."

When Antonolo looked my way accusingly, I shrugged. Feeling proud I'd thought of all sides of this story. And relieved, for I could not lose Antonolo. He was all I had left.

Bini repeated, louder, "Yes, tomorrow is Sunday. Come now." He beckoned with both hands, as if to a child.

For the first time since early Wednesday morning, Antonolo stepped outdoors. When I passed, he took hold of my arm and whispered, "Are they imprisoned, or have they set sail? Oh, please, not burned at the stake?"

"From what I've heard, simply run out of town. You're safe."

"Safe?" He lifted his nose to sniff the air. "Smells like Black Death to me."

"Let's return you to Santa Maria Assunta," Bini said. "Where you belong."

I couldn't have agreed more. And I wasn't alone. Whenever we crossed paths with a member of the church, they gazed at Antonolo with relief and crossed themselves.

"Back from his death bed," Bini announced. "Thanks to the mercy of Our Lord."

The priests and sisters welcomed Antonolo back warmly. Even Father Marco looked happy to see him again. "You must join us for your meals again," he said.

Antonolo nodded, smiled, but said little.

Inside his room, though, he clapped in delight. Bini had scrubbed the flagstone floor and re-stuffed the mattress with an abundance of herbs and fresh, sweet-smelling hay. "Oh, my dear friends," he said, "I can promise you this: I will never be a burden again." Then to me, "And I promise, no grand new ideas. I'm perfectly happy keeping things just as they are." Then his eyes widened, and he gasped, "Oh! Gurian. Did he find a suitable replacement for Mary Magdalene?"

Antonolo was back to business as usual. I couldn't have been more pleased. Our ordeal had come to an end.

V

As soon as the two-hour Sunday mass ended, Father Marco took his place at the pulpit, untying the ribbon on the scroll of narration for the annual Passion Play. The players moved amongst the congregants, dressed in homemade Biblical costumes. As Antonolo reached the center of the nave, costumed as Jesus, the crippled and blind approached to be healed by His holy touch.

He circled the outer sanctuary, and one by one the disciples joined him. When all twelve were following, they stopped in the center of the nave. Jesus broke a loaf of bread and passed pieces to each apostle. Sweet Gurian was smiling so broadly by then, his unseemly exhilaration was a bit unnerving.

As Antonolo passed the goblet of wine, two Roman soldiers appeared.

I frowned. This was well before their cue, which came after Judas's betrayal. In one year's time, the two players had matured from timid to confident. They looked strong, with military bearing. Also, their costumes seemed more convincing than the simple tunics I remembered from the previous year.

Each took hold of one of Antonolo's arms and dragged him toward the west doors. I could see him inclining his head, trying to redirect them to where the next scene with Pontius Pilate was supposed to take place, at the front altar.

A woman stepped out to block the way. A veil concealed her face. My respect for Gurian's casting talents rose. He'd exceeded all expectations in finding a feminine Mary Magdalene. Even Antonolo appeared surprised.

"You don't recognize your faithful disciple?" she asked. "It is I, Mary of Magdala."

Oh dear. Gurian had not made it clear to the new player that speaking the parts was forbidden. All narration was to be done solely by Father Marco.

Antonolo jerked free of the soldiers and lunged forward, to unveil her.

It was Luca! I pushed closer. He pulled out a bottle and dabbed oil onto his fingertips. As he reached for Antonolo, I tried to pull my friend to safety, but the two soldiers shoved me away. Now I recognized them, too: other performers from the Bazaar.

"Grapefruit." Antonolo glanced at me. "And lemon. And . . . lavender." As if he was telling me he was safe amid the sharpness of citrus and the perfume of French blossoms.

Luca massaged Antonolo's temples. "Yes, for confidence, strength, and self-love."

I tried to reach him again, but a large, scowling soldier held out a spear to block my path.

"It's not safe for you here," Luca said to Antonolo. "We must go now."

Those standing nearby seemed mesmerized by this new experience: an actual conversation between Mary Magdalene and Jesus. Though one cynic behind me muttered, "Mary the Whore!"

Luca stroked Antonolo's face with the ends of his long, perfumed hair.

A blacksmith gasped, "You dare touch our Lord and Savior?"

The Doge's barber tapped his shoulder. "It's Mary the Prostitute. What did you expect?"

The narration suddenly paused. Up at the altar, Father Marco was squinting our way.

"Come with me now," Luca said, hooking an arm through Antonolo's.

With all my strength, I tried to push past the soldiers, but they slammed me against a nearby column, banging my head against the marble. A heavenly constellation flashed before my eyes. I groped behind me to steady myself, but no use. I slid down it to the cold stone floor.

The shorter soldier unfurled a whip and sneered at Antonolo, "Do you know what we've risked, coming here?" He cracked the snaking leather on the tiles.

Congregants scattered out of the way. Luca rushed to Antonolo's side and caressed his face. "Think only of the love we'll have."

"Please, just go now," he whispered.

The whip cut a strip from Antonolo's robe, mere inches from Luca, who yelped and jumped back. "No, stop. I don't want this!"

Antonolo stared hard at him. "I do not possess your courage."

Again, the whip snapped. Antonolo's legs buckled. The sharp crack came again, then a fourth and fifth time. The cloth on his back was shredding. Streaks of blood stained it as if he truly was Jesus being flogged through the streets.

Father Marco pounded a fist on the scroll, frowning nearsightedly at the wretched excess of this new drama. The other priests in attendance rose and walked out through the Chancel, shaking their heads disapprovingly.

Luca lifted Antonolo's face to his. "Our lives together will be glorious."

"I lack your confidence," Antonolo whispered, grimacing in pain.

Father Marco turned back to the script, as if in a hurry to get it over with. Proclaiming at the top of his lungs, "Crucify Him!"

The two boys in charge of the wooden cross had been awaiting their cue on the far side of the sanctuary. They dragged the ten-foot pine cross over, staggering under its weight.

"The Passion of the Christ is complete," Father Marco exclaimed speedily. "Father, into Your hands I entrust his Spirit. Faithfully, this man was the Son of God. It is done. And thus ends our play. Get you gone, one and all. In peace. God speed you on your sinful way." And with that, the old priest left the altar, hobbling after his *fratelli*. The congregants and volunteers followed close behind, some throwing back frightened or disapproving looks at the players. Soon only about a dozen still stood in the nave and transept.

Gurian came over and squatted next to me. "When were these strange additions made? Why wasn't I informed?"

"They are not. . . ." But there was no time to explain. I grabbed his shoulders and cried, "Get the Doge's guards here immediately. Run, you fool!"

He pulled away, gaping. "Pietro, that's quite a bump on your head."

"Gurian, for the love of God, do as I say!"

The two young men laid the cross next to Antonolo, then lowered him onto it. They were to position his arms so that he could slide middle and pointer finger past the nails already safely hammered in, as usual, then tie him securely to the crosspiece before lifting it.

Luca pleaded, "You are strong. Confident! Everything can be ours. Only say the words!"

"I was so, once," Antonolo agreed, "for a short time. Dry your eyes. I forgive you." Then he lifted his head from the cross and kissed Luca on the lips.

Gurian clapped a hand over his mouth. "Mary, Mother of God, what sacrilege is this!"

Antonolo drew back to say one final word to Luca. "Go." Then turned his face away.

Luca's expression hardened. "Ismene, you bring nothing to this world. You might as well be dead." He took a wineskin from his belt, lifted Antonolo's head, and forced it to his lips.

Antonolo choked and sputtered; wine dribbling from the corners of his mouth. The two soldiers knelt on either side of the cross, wrapping the leather straps around the crosspiece. But too loosely. And then they did another odd thing: yanked the big nails free of the wood, and centered each in the middle of Antonolo's palms.

"No!" I screamed, finally realizing what they meant to do.

Yet they went on, hammering both in, as blood spurted and Antonolo screamed.

A woman great with child fainted dead away. Gurian dropped to his knees and vomited.

The Roman soldiers positioned Antonolo's feet atop one another, and drove a large spike through both. Then they raised the cross and set it inside the heavy, specially-forged iron base. Supported only by a wooden wedge beneath his bare feet, Antonolo hung helpless, dragged down by the weight of his own body, unable to breathe.

Gurian bolted out, along with the last remaining onlookers. And where were Luca and his two evil colleagues? They'd snuck out like dogs, along with everyone else.

My head still reeled from the blow. "Bini!" I shouted.

Running footsteps echoed: Bini, rushing from the sacristy at the front end.

Antonolo's arms were stretched to the limit, his torso sagging. Gasping for air, face taking on the pale blue tinge of the Virgin's robe. Blood oozed from his hands and feet, dripping onto the floor.

"Lord have mercy. Christ have mercy." Bini reached up and touched the crucified one's bloody feet, then examined his red, sticky fingers in disbelief. As he gazed up at Antonolo, the dying man groaned and exhaled a final breath.

Bini screamed then. So piercing a cry, I feared I'd faint from the ferocity of his heartbreak.

Antonolo's eyes were still open, glazing over like those of a plague victim fallen dead in the street.

More footsteps approached. Father Marco had returned. He peered up at Antonolo in disbelief. "Well, this one won't be rising from the dead." He turned my way. "And what happened to you?"

Appalled at his lack of compassion for one he'd known all his life, I wept, refusing to answer, or even look at him. Finally, as if abashed, he began reciting the Last Rites. I was too overcome with grief by then to make the proper responses.

Fea. I'd failed her first. *Antonolo.* Gone, too. My whole family, dead.

I remained in the church, too dizzy and lightheaded to rise. The cross was removed by the Doge's guards when they arrived. Bini washed Antonolo's blood from the marble tiles with clean rags and a basin of water.

"Fetch Antonolo's possessions and leave them at the side entrance when you finish," Father Marco ordered, and then he left.

Bini went off to do his bidding, emerging a few minutes later carrying the six scrolls. I took the lot, cradling them the way one might hold a cherished *Neonato.*

"Anything else here you want?" Bini inclined his head at a meager little pile. "All that is left behind will be burned. Father Marco's orders."

When I tried to stand, the terrible dizziness returned.

Bini steadied me, casting a concerned glance at the bump which still made my head throb. "No trouble getting a *Medico* to come here. Easier than to your home."

I shook my head. Then, an arm around my shoulders, he helped me to the side staircase and slowly up the steps to Antonolo's room. Once we pushed past the faded blue curtain, he lowered me onto the mattress. "Ah," I sighed. It felt good to lie down. My gaze took in the room, stripped so bare it now held not a single thing of Antonolo's.

Bini moved the lone chair to the archway and pointed at the hanging blue drape. "Father Marco said I might have it for my room." He stepped up and pulled down the curtain. "Strange," he said, inspecting the rod. "Not made of wood or iron." He slid the material off. "Why, it's a very long, rolled-up parchment scroll."

He carried it over. I sat up and unrolled the top leaf, recognizing Antonolo's neat yet sweeping hand. I'd read all his dramas, but none had been such an obviously large work. *Antigone in Venice*, it said in loose, flowing script. The play Luca had searched for in vain.

"You keep?" Bini asked. "I never learned my letters."

If Antonolo had wanted me to read it, then surely he would have —

"No," I said. It'd been hidden all this time, thus not intended for my eyes. I retied the scroll and handed it back. "You keep it. I'm sure this meant a great deal to Antonolo. All his heart, labor, and passion live within it."

Bini nodded and slid it back through the top pocket of the drapery. Then scooped up the material and headed upstairs. After a moment, he bellowed down, "It fits!"

He returned and pointed to the six small scrolls I was still cradling against my chest, for comfort. "His life is with you, too, Pietro."

My eyes were full of tears; they trickled from the corners when I nodded.

"I'll fetch the doctor," he said, and left through the now-open archway.

Though the plague is gone now, these many months later, I still ponder how everything could have gone so awry. After all, I did my best to save dear Antonolo, Jesu knows. It was the least one Christian must do for another. And that much of it I would not change, though I miss my old friend every day.

Bini was not wrong, either. For I never feel alone now, as long as Antonolo's writings are close at hand. His words, recorded in those scrolls, bring *everything* to this world: all that has been, and is, and will yet be. They are the sole light and joy of this, my solitary life.

That necklace you eye so longingly here at the Baubles, Bangles, and Beasts stall has a long and fascinating history. I knew its former owner, who had a most interesting second profession, as well. Sorry? Oh no, a much older vocation even than that one . . . do you recall that we noted, earlier, around the world there's an infinite variety of the sea nymph you probably know best as 'mermaid'? Well, in far-flung places, these mythical beings have many different names: Graeae, Mari-Morgen, Nix, Rusalki, Ningyo, Merrow . . . and of course here, in Venice, Sirena. Whatever name they go by, sea nymphs still have much in common: They swim more gracefully and faster than all other denizens of the Deep; they have no need of clothing to warm them, nor even of air to breathe. Not in their true form. And yet, a mermaid appreciates a nice piece of jewelry as much as any Venetian noblewoman. The difference is, the jewels of a sea nymph tend to be imbued with magical, often hypnotic properties. Which certainly must come in handy when plying your trade requires capturing the complete attention of your . . . er, customer. Ah, but you are putting the necklace back. So you have changed your mind about the purchase. Well, no doubt it's for the best. One should never try to own or control that which one does not really understand or truly care for. As this coming tale will make quite plain . . .

PLENTY OF FISH IN THE SEA

by Lenore Hart

(for Natalia Molchanova)

I rise from the floor of the Deep, swimming toward the quivering lamp-glow of a full moon. Below lie the reefs, their phosphorescence pulsing.

A school of needlefish fin up madly in my wake, then flick past. The small fry may fear I'll attract a larger predator, but barracuda and sharks always take care to avoid me. I swim with arms extended, a wedge to part the water. Undulating eel-like to foil the drag of this salt-infused sea, through even the strongest currents. Layers of cold that hit other creatures like a heart-stopping ice bath, snatching away breath and warmth and life, are a balm to me.

For I can be just as sudden. Just as cold.

Ashore, I draw in a slow, deep breath. Letting my lungs slowly inflate, wincing at the acidic burn of oxygen. On the stretch of smooth white sand, footprints large and small crisscross like trails in a forest without trees. Some are darker, still damp with seawater. I'm already dry, save for my dripping dress. The hem will stay wet no matter how long I'm ashore.

Smoothing creases from sea-green silk, I stroll toward the tiki bar at the Blue Lagoon Condos. A thatched patio overlooks beach and the onyx waves beyond, dark as an old bruise. A breeze bellies my skirt like a sail, carrying me over the golden sand. Fiddler crabs flee in my wake to the fragile safety of dune grass.

Once on the patio, I brush sand from my soles and slip on silver sandals. Then enter the bar, trailing a finger across the glass of a massive saltwater aquarium that runs its length.

Clownfish, gobies, batfish, and wrasses freeze behind its glass, then abruptly flee, abandoning a single startled seahorse whose tail is clamped around a branch of coral. The fish all huddle in a mass at the tank's far end, mouths agape, finning madly to stay in place.

At a small round table I sit and drape my skirt in attractive folds around pale, slender legs, tossing long black hair over one shoulder. Turning sideways, I face the curved bar crafted of sawn driftwood, my hands on the glass tabletop.

A young woman in a short black skirt and sleeveless white shirt hurries up. "Hope you weren't waiting long. Welcome to the Cove Bar," she says breathlessly. "What can I get you?"

"Hmm. Let's see." I draw the moment out, anticipating the various tastes to savor. Finally going with the usual. "A beach-plum margarita, please."

She nods. "Sea salt or sugar on the rim?"

"Salt. Extra, in fact. Please."

As she weaves away gracefully between tables, I lean back to survey the room. Rough-hewn pillars support the ubiquitous palm-thatch roof. A giant version of the lopsided huts people build behind houses, to create the illusion they're vacationing on a Polynesian island instead of working themselves to death to own that sixty-by-fifty patch of green. This floor is spacious, though, paved with colorful patterned Mexican tiles. It holds twenty rattan tables and more wicker chairs like the one I'm sitting in. It's already late. The crowd has dwindled to the truly desperate and the truly intoxicated.

The waitress returns and sets my drink on a coaster printed with palm trees and flamingos.

"Thanks." I take a sip, licking salt off my lips. "Mm. Delicious."

A plastic card materializes in my palm and I hand it over.

She runs it through a little machine pulled from her apron pocket. Glancing at the embossed name before giving it back with two curling slips of paper. "There you go, Miss. . . Morgan. Would you like a receipt?"

"No." I scrawl in a generous tip, and tuck the card into a sharkskin shoulder bag.

She nods. "You're welcome." The arm holding the round tray hangs relaxed at her side; its wrist is encircled by a bracelet of purple bruises. "So, are you . . . waiting for someone?"

"Yes. I am." I glance at her nametag. "Shayna."

I stare into her eyes, green gaze holding her still while I read what's below the surface: a small room, bright with sunlight. A shelf of books. A table holding a bowl of apples, one slightly withered. A worn couch draped with an orange bedspread. Fist-sized holes in the plaster walls. A coffee table with one badly-mended broken leg.

I blink and lean back in my chair, letting go.

She shakes herself, blushes, and looks away. "Oh. Um, well . . ." She steps back, clearly misunderstanding my sudden interest. No doubt she's often hit on by all genders, all persuasions.

To put her at ease, I glance around. "But I don't think he's here yet."

True enough, for *she* is certainly not who I've come for.

"Oh! Right." She looks down and frowns. "Hey, your skirt's dripping. Want a towel?"

I shake my head. "No thanks. Who knows? Might go wading again later."

"Call if you need anything else." She walks back to the bar, hips swaying, tall heels clicking over gleaming tiles. The black shoes look hard-worn, one sole thinner than its mate's. Throwing her stride off, creating an imperceptible limp only a predator would notice.

Whatever money Shayna makes, she's not spending it on herself. A student working her way through college? A high-school dropout who decided only she could love her baby well enough, and kept it? Or maybe she lives at home and gives all her money to a sick mother.

One thing I know from the bruises, and that quick gaze inside: she's in thrall to a bad man.

I sip my drink, enjoying the fresh lime juice, the tequila of excellent quality. No cheap bottled mix with a chemical aftertaste. I savor every tart, citric, salty sip. There's just an inch of cloudy, golden liquid left in the ridiculously-large goblet when an angry male voice rises over at the bar.

A thirtyish man with blond hair, dark stubble, and a faded golf shirt has been nursing a glass of draft IPA like a stingy baby. Now he shoves his stool back, and stomps over to the waitress' station, to speak urgently to Shayna.

When she turns away he grabs one arm. She pulls free, but the red imprints of hard fingers are already rising on the soft, smooth skin like stigmata.

"Stop," she hisses. "Come on, Derek. I'm working."

No one else seems to hear, or at least they don't react. The bartender is tall and broad-shouldered, with close-cropped curls and smooth dark skin. Close to forty, amber eyes framed by laugh lines. He probably didn't see the argument, since he's turned away, laughing tolerantly at a rambling story told by a customer midway down the bar. Two seats farther a young couple are twined like fouled anchor lines, leaning in from separate stools, paying attention only to each other.

I smile at their oblivious bliss, for I too have enjoyed the sweet press of a lover's swollen lips, having performed this same ritual in all my various forms.

But the angry man isn't done. He follows Shayna as she wipes down tables, keeping his distance whenever she halts at one that's occupied. His cowardice, that hint of belly from beers past, remind me of the red grouper: afraid of bigger fish, darting out to catch a fingerling, then hiding in his hole again to eat.

Shayna stops before me to ask, "Like a refill?"

I nod and hand over my empty glass.

As Derek passes my table, scents rise off him in waves: stale barley, musky male sweat. And something metallic: the sharp stink of meanness. He's muttering imprecations in Shayna's wake, yet she doesn't tell him to go away, or ask for someone to help eject him. So then I know what's to come will hurt her more, as they say. But what's good for us often feels more painful than the things we desire instead.

"Let me work. We'll talk later," she throws over one shoulder, like a bone to distract a growling dog.

He grabs her arm again, holding it down next to him out of sight, giving the wrist a vicious twist.

She yelps and drops the bar rag.

"Hey, Shayna?" The bartender opens a gate and steps out, crossing muscular arms. "Everything good?"

She waves him off. "Fine, Jeff. I just . . . tripped."

He frowns, narrowing his eyes at Derek, but steps back behind the bar to resume polishing glasses. Glancing their way occasionally.

This Jeff is nothing like the other. When I cradled the bowl-like glass he'd held to pour in my drink, and pressed it to my forehead, there shimmered before me like sea mist an image of a young woman. His wife . . . who's some kind of . . . wise woman? No. A teacher, at home with a baby. Their daughter. A girl they have hopes and dreams for.

So, a good man. I'm glad I'll never have to visit him.

But my feelings aren't the point. This is a job, a family trade I was born into long ago. It's what we Morgans do.

I rise and walk through the tables behind Shayna and Derek. Sidling past on my way to the bar, letting my breasts brush his arm. To ensure he's hooked, I gaze back and flash a smile.

At the bar I fish a lime wedge from a metal garnish tray and suck on it. Then turn and lean my back on the polished countertop, spine arched, elbows propped, displaying my charms to best advantage.

Derek swaggers up. "Hi." He turns to lean beside me, gaze snagging like a fishhook on my low neckline. "Stayin' here?"

"Mmm. But only tonight."

He raises an eyebrow. "Yeah? Got plans?"

I peer up through a curve of dark hair. "Not yet."

He scoots closer, glancing toward the tables as if to make sure Shayna's watching. "Why not get outta here, then? Just you and me."

I shrug. "I have another drink coming." Hard not to sigh at how pathetically easy this is. "And what about your, um, girlfriend?"

He snorts. "*She* doesn't give a shit."

Shayna returns to the bar, head high, spots of color heating each cheek. She impales a green olive on a bamboo pick as if it's my heart, then plunks it into a martini glass on the black rubber mat. Anger rolls off her in yellow and red bands that undulate like Sargasso weed in a rip current.

I like the anger. It means she's still whole, still wants things for herself. Still *has* a self. Hasn't yet disappeared into the demands of someone louder and meaner. In a different life, we might've been friends. I'd like to walk over right now and whisper, *Someday you'll thank me. I know this because I'm older, so very much older, and have seen endless schools of his sorry kind swim past.* I'd add, just before turning away, *There will be more. Next time, maybe one who deserves you.*

But to do that now would run counter to my task. For I come not in friendship, but with a sword. So I look away from her, back to him. "What's your name?"

"Derek." He grins, but doesn't ask for mine. "So, we're on?"

I smile and raise a hand to caress the large, luminous gray pearl hanging from a silver chain around my neck.

"Hey, that's nice." He peers at it. "A present?"

I nod. "A long time ago."

He frowns. "Like, from a husband or boyfriend?"

"No. A pirate."

He laughs cautiously, as if he suspects I'm making fun. Strange how, when one tells the truth, people tend not to believe it.

Years ago I once sat in a Savannah bar, waiting while a good-looking man in an Armani suit paid our tab. On the wall opposite, a screen showed four people sitting around talking. A woman in black-framed glasses was saying, "Men are afraid women will laugh at them. Women are afraid men will kill them."

Which is, of course, true. I was just surprised people were still discussing the fact as if it were news. For any woman who loves too well, but not wisely, the most dangerous person in the world is probably her partner. The poorly-chosen person, male, female, or gender neutral, sleeping next to her. Though in my long experience it is the male who does the most damage, still. So I'd stared at the screen back then, reflecting on how little the world had changed over the centuries. Until my companion turned from the cashier, tucking a shiny black card inside his wallet.

Then I'd picked up his empty highball glass and pressed it to one cheek. The cool crystalline surface spoke to me back then, like a neighborhood gossip, of his many sins. How he liked to pinch his young wife's upper arms, twisting the soft pale flesh until it purpled and she begged him to stop.

Of course he would never stop. Which was why I'd been there in the bar in the first place.

"I'm not laughing at you," I say now, as sweetly as possible, to Shayna's man. Stroking one hairy forearm, gazing up without blinking.

"Uh, sure." He slugs back the dregs of his beer. "Put it on our tab," he calls across the bar.

Jeff the bartender, pouring my second drink into a silver blender, just grunts. His mouth tightens at the corners.

I lay a twenty and a ten on the bar-top, and sigh. Regretting the excellent drink I won't be having now. Feeling regret, also, for Shayna.

As I step away, Derek hesitates. Perhaps he's reconsidering and won't come after all? He lifts his empty glass again and stares down, as if he's decided to have another.

All I really want is to return to the water, submerge myself, and wash away the petty stink of their mediocre kind. "Hey," I say, lifting the gray pearl again. "Tick tock, mister." I swing the pearl like a tiny pendulum, then slide it between my lips.

He blinks and swallows, gaze riveted on my mouth. "Right. Let's get the fuck out of here."

I steer Derek to a pool on the other side of the condos.

"How 'bout we go to your room?" he suggests.

"I like getting acquainted outside, in the fresh air. Being near water makes me feel, you know . . . freer."

He smiles at that. I can see myself in his mind. How he imagines this night will go: me naked at poolside, him gripping my long dark hair, forcing my head back . . .

So predictable. I sit on the tiled edge, dangling my legs in the cool water. "This is nice," I say, though it reeks of chlorine, of bleach and mildew and body oils and stale sweat from the soles of all the bare dirty feet that've trod the concrete shore of this false sea. At the deep end, a half-deflated raft bumps morosely against the ladder like a drowned sailor.

Derek drops beside me and slips an arm around my waist. "Nice isn't what I was thinking about." He nuzzles my neck.

This is always the tricky part. To not just stiffly tolerate but seem to actually enjoy the press of human hands, that hot breath on my skin. For theirs, up close, is not wet and smooth as silk, nor scaled and beautifully iridescent. It's dry and flaky, with oily blotches, red patches, pimples, and scabs. I recall, ages ago, how shocked I felt the first time I laid eyes on a human being. They always feel dry, hot, and sick to us. Weak, fearful, and puny. Something to be avoided. Yet since this is the task I was assigned in the great scheme of things, I must tolerate such intimacy for a time.

It's not like the old days back in Germany. I was born on a high, flat-topped mountain whose flattened crest cradled a deep, turquoise lake. Its waters were pale brown, yet pure and sweet. Tinted and preserved by the tannin in fallen leaves which drifted down from the nearby beech and spruce forest, ancient home to the lynx, the brown cave bear, and the gray forest wolf. A boulder-studded cliff rose abruptly on one side out of the water; a great wall. No one could scale it, not even us. Snowy edelweiss, violet gentian, and their poisonous sisters, arnica and wolfsbane, grew tucked into the cracks and crevices along its stony face.

On the other side of the lake wound a narrow trail lined with tall waterweeds. It was used by those who worshipped us; the path they walked up, carrying offerings. But in more recent times our mountain was assailed by sudden, violent storms, great winds, and drowning rains, making it uninhabitable for my sisters and me. This was none of our doing, but that of the people who lived below and had fouled the earth. The ones who'd stopped coming to make offerings or ask for favors.

In the old days, our father was also prone to terrible fits of rage. When displeased he simply flooded the land and drowned houses, even whole villages. That had always seemed crude to me, and cruel. It punished the innocent as well as the guilty.

Well, the Old Ones never worried much about justice. Still, gradually my sisters and I defied him, and each in her turn was banished. Sent away from his displeasure, to ply our watery trades elsewhere.

That lost quiet at the heart of our lake I can only experience now while submerged in the Deep. Times have changed. We had to change, too. I have merely altered the old rules to suit myself, you see.

Though now, as Derek slides a hand into the low neck of my dress, I think, *Some things never change at all.*

"I hope Shayna doesn't see us out here," I murmur.

He grunts noncommittally and buries his face in my breasts, wet-lipped, rooting like a baby seal.

Suddenly, unable to stand another second of his touch, I push him off and stand abruptly. "Let's go down to the beach."

"What?" He raises his head. "Why? Here is fine."

I lift the pendent again, letting it sway.

He catches the movement and stares, following its trajectory as if entranced by the orbit of a tiny full moon. I slide the cool gray orb into my mouth, then pull it out and roll the wet pearl slowly over his lips.

"Wait." He shakes his head, blinking. "What was I just—"

"Never mind. Come." I take his hand and pull him to his feet. He follows down the broad wooden steps and out onto the beach, without a word of protest.

We sit on the damp golden sand, and I pull a silver comb from my sharkskin bag. "Comb my hair," I order.

He pulls the gleaming teeth through the long dark strands. Clumsily at first, snagging the teeth on small knots. Whenever he jerks too hard I hiss.

"Sorry," he mumbles, and begins again, more gently. Soon the strokes are regular, the lift and descent of the comb smooth and fluent. When I glance over one shoulder his eyes are blank, mouth slack.

As he labors, gray clouds gather in the dark night sky. Their pulsing golden veins are lit by some far-off squall. A rising wind tugs at our clothes like an impatient child.

Storms make me melancholy. Homesick, I suppose. So I sing the old tune my sisters and I once sang for our father.

> *The wild-fowl are calling, come back to the lake!*
> *O, nixies come back or your proud hearts will break . . .*
> *The gray mists are rising! Beware, O beware!*
> *For though you are slender, and though you are fair,*
> *Your treacherous waters, O nixy king's daughters,*
> *Can slay the unwary. Beware!*

After the final chorus I say, "Put down the comb, and get up."

I lead him toward the water until the ocean swirls around our ankles, then our knees, cool as silk, its lace edges spun of white foam.

When the cold sea reaches my waist, I grip his arm. "Stop here."

He halts obediently.

"Look out, and then down into the water." I point to a spot a dozen feet beyond us. "What do you see?"

He narrows his eyes, body tense, gaze fixed. "Oh my God," he breathes. "I see it! The towers. The buildings. And . . . the women!"

I don't need to ask what he thinks is out there. Mortal imaginings are more or less always pitifully the same: silver and gold objects. Crystal buildings that glow and sparkle beneath the waves, studded with diamonds, furnished with gold-washed chairs and tables. Streets paved with gold bricks, or coins, or both. Rooms populated with busty, beautiful women who have only one name on their plump, luscious lips. *Derek*, they all whisper, cupping absurdly large breasts, running their hands over waspish waists, down long curved thighs. *Derek, we wait for you and you only. Please, come and fuck us. Let us take you into our bodies, into our mouths. Oh, how we all lust for you!*

I have to suppress a yawn. It's become boring now, so many centuries of the same thing, over and over. Or has just one cocktail made me sleepy? Jeff, the nice bartender, did pour with a generous hand. His soul is expansive, kind, interesting. If he were not already attached to a woman and child, I might go back later and work a little magic between him and Shayna. She deserves a kind, thoughtful partner.

But my rules are clear: No meddling when the pre-existing bonds are favorable. So . . . back to work.

"Would you like to go there, Derek?" I whisper in his salt-damp ear. "Or would you rather stay here, be a kinder person, and treat Shayna with love and respect?"

Because it's possible even a bad one can change. Though this doesn't happen as often as you probably want to believe. Also, if it seems at this point that the deck is stacked against poor Derek, I assure you he'll have another chance. In fact, more than one.

He's looking conflicted now. His mouth works. "I . . . I want . . . want to. . . ."

I straighten, suddenly interested. I'd felt sure this would be a quick job. Predictable, over and done with very fast. "Yes, you want—?"

He grimaces as if he's lost the knack of making language, of stringing words together in a straight line. One arm rises stiffly to point ahead at a roiling patch of water from which a faint phosphorescent glow emanates. "I want *that*. Them. All of it. All of them!"

Of course he does.

Derek wants the selfishly impossible: a fantasy world full of willing women, all turned toward and worshiping him, his obedient slaves. Any woman in sight his to grab, to have, by virtue of . . . well, of being Derek. Plus he'd also like great wealth without making any effort. Oh yes, and the right to do whatever he likes, without responsibility or punishment or remorse, afterward.

I shrug. "Sure. Fine. Let's go, then." I tow him out deeper, then deeper still, until our toes no longer touch the sandy bottom. Without another word, for words are useless now, I dive, pulling him along. Straight toward the Deep.

We descend head down, face to face, sinking rapidly. At first he maintains that rapt look of eager anticipation, as we draw nearer to what he perceives to be Paradise.

Are you sorry? I ask him, in my mind. *Even a little bit?*

No, he responds without moving his lips. *Take us deeper.*

But it's not going to be that easy for him. Rising off to the left are some new, watery images. The faces of all the women he's ever hurt.

Oh, Derek! So many. You've been a busy boy, I chide. *Won't you decide instead to change, and return to the world, now?*

Even so many accusing faces seem not to faze him. He shakes his head, stubbornly looking down again, toward the very depths, where everything he has ever wanted but not bothered to earn still beckons.

So I grip his head and turn it to face them again. All the women he's wronged in his life.

The greedy, rapt look slowly fades. This time he's actually paying attention. Flashing before his eyes now he sees not nubile sylphs walking streets paved with gold, opening slender arms to draw him in. Instead, it's a parade of all the sad, hurt, angry faces he's ever deceived, abused, lied to, and betrayed. The girlfriends. The battered ex-wife. The date rapes in college. The paid escorts on business trips. So many slaps, punches, curses, and kicks. Soft flesh bruised like a dropped peach.

Well, at least he *sees* all his sins now.

I recall that he never asked my name. That he never bothers to ask for things at all, but simply takes. I press my face closer and whisper it now. *My name, Derek? It's Mari,* I say. *Mari Morgan.*

At this revelation his eyes widen in horror. He convulses in my arms, thrashing and kicking.

Too late. I anticipate every feint and punch and kick to break free. One flailing hand snags on my necklace. The soft links of purest Spanish silver part. It breaks free and floats away, out of reach. Drifting down, down, to land somewhere far below. No matter. There are plenty of pearls left in the sea.

Gradually Derek's arms and legs slow their frantic jerking. The deeper he sinks, though, the more we see. All the way back to his original sin. Above all the old transgressions, an even older image forms.

A little girl standing on a playground. A thin child with blond hair and two missing front teeth. *Ellie.* She gave him a cookie once, at recess. He accepted and ate it, thinking that such a willing gift made her stupid. An easy mark. So then, wondering what else might be had, he pulled her behind the equipment shed, pushed her to the ground, and clamped a hand over her mouth. There he yanked up her dress, ignoring her struggle, the crying.

That night the girl's mother, a divorceé who cleaned houses for a living, had called his parents. Derek's father picked up. "I'll take you to court and bankrupt you," he said smoothly. "You'll lose your miserable little job. Is that what you want? Because no one threatens my son."

After his father hung up, Derek had tensed, expecting a lecture, or at least a time-out in his room. Instead his dad had clapped him on the shoulder and winked. "Just be more careful next time, son."

Behind his back, Derek's mother had frowned. Her mouth tightened. But she'd said nothing to either of them.

So then he had understood: *This is how the world works.* That he should simply take whatever he wanted, whenever he saw it.

So, there's blame to go around. But that's not my problem. Flawed elderly parents are someone else's responsibility. Like any growing thing, sins have roots. The truly unforgivable act is knowing your misdeed, yet never trying to do something to redeem it.

At this point we are suspended in the dark murk of The Deep, a place neither sun's rays nor moon's beams can illuminate. Our only light is the green phosphorescence of plankton, the blinking of the odd, passing angler fish.

Derek no longer tries to break free now. Air contracts as you descend, so there's still enough oxygen in his bloodstream to get him to the surface. He averts his face from the image of his little classmate, her bruised back and scraped legs. Avoiding her look of dawning horror as again, in the image, he tears her dress. Instead he gazes longingly down at the golden towers and beckoning women. Choosing, finally, the intoxication of the Deep.

Only once has a man truly repented as I pulled him down. Only once has one declined the golden city. Only once have I been compelled to let go. To allow the accused to rise and swim unmolested back to shore. So he might crawl out of the waves and collapse gasping onto the sand, beneath the bloodshot eye of dawn. Unharmed, but changed.

Derek's clearly not going to be the second one. So, as we fall faster toward the pale-green glow of the deepest reefs, I clamp my hands on either side of his ribs, take hold, and press.

As we sink, he grows thinner. Then smaller and shorter, changing shape.

This is, I admit, my favorite part. The deciding. What sort should he be? A clownfish, perhaps?

No. There's nothing funny about Derek.

But he *was* weak. Cowardly. A small man in a way that has nothing to do with his former height or bulk. Hiding the transgressions, living off others, intent on destroying them. Especially the women. Always looking for someone prettier, something easier, a situation that required less work. A connection that required even less from his unmovable, anchor-stone heart.

As I slowly open both hands again, I feel the tickle of his frantic squirming. My fingers loosen, then part and let go.

Derek shoots out from between my palms and swims off, his flat disks of eyes rolling back fearfully, in case I'm in pursuit. His stubby fins churn the water in terror. He wriggles frantically, swimming hard for the shelter of the deepest reef, which no longer glows quite as brightly. Which is, of course, not really paved with gold. Nor is the branching coral truly made of crystal, or the silver spires studded with jewels. This world is not really inhabited by curvaceous, scantily-clad young women, but rather by far less accommodating creatures.

Beneath an undulating cluster of sea fans, a dark cavity slowly opens. In his haste Derek must not notice this calculated movement, because he swims on. Directly into what he has probably assumed is the safety of a coral cave.

In fact, it's the gaping maw of a red grouper. Those jaws snap shut. The big fish withdraws, again hidden by the shadows of the lower reef.

Oh, well. Sometimes there is justice, and sometimes justice is imperfect, or unattainable. I am only one, after all. A single Mari-Morgen cannot find and correct all the outrages of this world.

But by the gods, she can try.

Above, a full moon lights the dark skin of the sea. The long night stretches ahead, and there is still time remaining. Yes, I think, already rising again. Why not? Perhaps one more.

This green and white-striped silk tent draped with ancient tapestries marks the end of your tour. Within it, I tell the fortunes of only a select few. This Christmas Eve night I had the honor of spreading my cards for the family of the French Templar, Jacques de Molay. The knight has been imprisoned by King Philippe, who owed him a great deal of money—and kings never like to pay their debts if they can help it. The Templar's woman and child came seeking a reading, for they were fleeing for their lives and desired knowledge of how they might arrive safely at their next destination. And where was that? Of course I cannot say; you understand. What I can tell you is that the women carried something so vital, so important to the world, they will be hunted for centuries by evil men, and so must always take great care. The cards also showed me that mother and daughter would eventually be parted, though the knight's line would endure. But how all of that will come to pass is the very subject of this final story. . . .

THE BOOK OF AMAL

by Kaylie Jones

Venice
New Year's Day, 1348

Esperanza my beloved daughter,

The Veritas will be yours now by the drop of blood that Habiba my mother spilled upon this coffer, so that none other but you, or your own daughter, or her daughter after her, will be able to open it.

Forgive me for withholding the truth all these years. I should have told you long ago but I was afraid, worried for your safety. Now it is time for you to have the Veritas, though I urge you not to do as I did. You are still young, but one day soon you will have a daughter, this I know. You must tell her this story, but tell it slowly. Then, when her time comes, she will not find herself alone, as you will be now.

My mother was called Habiba—the Loved One—though she could neither remember the date of her birth nor the name she bore before she was made a slave. She was freed from bondage by the enemy, a Frank, the Infidel Templar

Knight Jacques de Molay, during a battle against the Mamluks of Egypt, near the city of Homs, in the Levant. This was in the last month of the year 1299, by the Christian calendar.

It happened in this way. The Christian Knights came charging into the harem and began slaughtering the women and children. But Habiba sat quietly, with the posture of a queen, reading her cards as the Grand Master of the Knights Templar approached, his bloody sword raised. She looked up at him without fear and without judgment, and he slowly lowered the sword. Habiba was a tall, thin girl in the early bloom of womanhood, with golden-brown skin that glowed in the sunlight streaming through the barred windows. She had the blackest hair and eyes the Knight had ever seen. Just below her right collarbone was a dark birthmark in the shape of a crescent moon.

The Knight asked her in Arabic what this mark meant.

She gazed at him calmly and said, "I believe it is the birthmark of my family." When the Knight asked for her name, she told him she was the property of the Eighth Mamluk Sultan of Egypt, Al-AsIhraf Salāh ad-Dīn Khalil ibn Qalawūn, and did not know her true name, but that the Sultan called her Habiba.

"Well," said the Knight, "Habiba, you are now free."

"I will never be free," she replied, "for I have no home, no land, no family, no name, and no memory of my life before, only knowledge of what will come after."

Then she bargained with the Knight. "If you will offer me shelter and not molest me in any way, I will open your eyes to a greater truth."

The Knight laughed, but he was charmed, and so he agreed. He told her he would take her as far as Jerusalem, and then she would be free to make her own way in the world. As the army set forth the next day, the Knight allowed Habiba to ride upon a horse, unlike the other slaves, who were made to walk behind the soldiers.

By the waxing crescent moon, which for Habiba was when the dark veil between the known world and the unknown world was thinnest, she spread her cards for the Knight upon a little table in the tent he had provided. She laid his hands upon the spread, and with her own hands pressing down upon his, she imparted to him a vision.

The landscape was the same vast desert plain on which the Crusaders' army had just done battle against the Mamluks. But upon the terrain was a black road, straight and narrow as a ribbon of black satin, the likes of which the Knight had never seen, and upon the road a caravan of horseless carriages rolled at incredible speed. A terrible sound filled the air, like the wind of a catapult projectile but a thousand times louder. From the sky fell cylinders that contained some sort of naphtha, which smashed into the caravan with extreme force and precision. The horseless carriages burst into flames and flew off the road in every direction.

Jacques de Molay stood up suddenly, throwing Habiba, the table, and the cards across the tent. "What is this you are showing me? This is witchcraft!" he shouted.

Habiba pulled herself to her knees and began to calmly gather the cards scattered about the rug. "This is a bad thing," she said without emotion, "for if I lose one card, the spread will not be true."

The Knight stormed out of her tent without another word.

But the next night, after their long and exhausting progress toward Jerusalem, he returned to Habiba's tent. He apologized for his fury of the night before and asked her to show him more.

She told him she would show him more, but if he ever raised a hand to her again she would slit her own throat and he would never know the truth.

On that second night, Habiba and the Knight saw, beyond the veil, images of his own long-forgotten childhood. Of himself as a very young boy sitting on his mother's lap, and practicing swordplay with a wooden stick, and running through an apple orchard in bloom. He was reminded of the love he'd once held in his heart for his people and his land. All that was gone now, for he was a shell of a man whose heart was filled only with the lust for blood and treasure.

The Knight was utterly bewildered by these images. When Habiba lifted her hands from his, he murmured, "*Haec est veritas.*"

This is the truth.

But Habiba only heard the word Veritas, for she did not speak that language.

The Knight stood, thanked her, and bowed before he left.

The invaders continued their grueling march toward Jerusalem, believing their god favored their victory and that they would secure Jerusalem for the Christians for centuries to come. But on the third night, when the Knight came to see her, Habiba the former slave shared a vision of the Knight's enemies, at home with their wives and children, drinking tea and playing with their infants.

He saw that without their terrifying armor and curved gleaming swords and pointed helmets, the Mamluks were only men. They loved their families and their god as much as any Christian.

Jacques de Molay threw up his hands. "I do not like this vision at all," he told Habiba.

She countered that she had no control over the visions, and to complain of them was like complaining to God of the desert heat and the lack of water.

The Knight was still in an exalted state over the Templars' victory over the Mamluks at Homs, and that was good, for otherwise he might have slit her throat himself.

The following night, she brought forth a vision of the Sultan's armies, thousands upon thousands of Mamluks approaching Jerusalem. The Knight refrained from throwing Habiba and her cards across the tent, but he was clearly angered. He once again accused her of witchcraft, but moments later a messenger rode into the camp and told the Grand Master of the Knights Templar that his Mongol allies had retreated, and the Sultan's Mamluk army was fast approaching the walls of Jerusalem.

The Knight was overcome with emotion, because now he believed Habiba. Under normal circumstances he might have stayed in the Levant and confronted the Sultan's superior forces, and died an honorable death in battle, which was the destiny for which he had always been groomed. But he was so captivated by Habiba's cards he ordered his men to retreat to the coast, where their ships awaited them.

He asked Habiba to come with him to Cyprus, for now he felt compelled to know more.

Habiba my mother never told me why she agreed to sail away with the Knight. Perhaps she truly had nowhere else to go; or, perhaps, she already knew that her destiny was entwined with his.

Several months later, in the gardens of Kolossi Castle near the town of Limassol on the island of Cyprus, the Knight admitted to Habiba that he no longer believed in the righteousness of his cause. He was already an old man, long past fifty, with graying locks and deep-set, troubled eyes, but Habiba did not see his age, and she no longer feared him. What she saw was a man struggling to understand a larger truth he could no longer deny. She felt a deep compassion for him, perhaps even love, for he was entirely alone.

The Knight had understood that God is impartial, and the kingdoms of Europe were deluded in their blind arrogance, in their belief that they could hold the Levant against the Mohammedan heretics, who also believed that God was on their side. The Knight also understood the Christians had set in motion a war that would continue for a thousand years, for he had seen the future.

It was there, in Kolossi Castle, a beautiful fortress of golden stone, that he at last broke his sacred vow of celibacy. A little over a year later, in the second year of the new Christian century, I, their only child, was born. The Knight was disappointed that I was a girl, for he had wanted a son.

Habiba laughed and told him that a daughter was much more important. She held me up to him and displayed the birthmark on my right thigh, the same as hers, a dark crescent moon that appeared silvery in the light. She named me Espérance, though she would not convert to Christianity and my father did not force her, for by then he no longer believed in his god, nor any god so limited in scope. And yet, he baptized me himself, perhaps as a rite of passage, perhaps as a safeguard against the fires of Hell, if such a Hell exists.

The Knight continued to wage war on the Mohammedans in the name of Christianity, attacking by sea their ports along the coast. He knew the war was lost but he also knew no other way to live. But his heart no longer thirsted for blood and he no longer slaughtered innocents. His men thought he was bewitched, but they were no fools, those Knights. Habiba's foresight had already saved their lives countless times.

While Habiba my mother and I lived in Kolossi Castle, the only fortress the Templars still held in that part of the world, Habiba developed a friendship with a young blue-eyed Knight called François Boissevain de Vièrnes, who had been a child of ten when he first became Jacques de Molay's squire.

François Boissevain was related to Philippe IV of France through the King's wife, Queen Jeanne of Navarre. The Knight François was Queen Jeanne's first cousin. Yet, as the third son, he'd been sent off to be a celibate soldier of God. This, or the regular priesthood, was his only option. Now, at sixteen, he was tall and already strong, a great swordsman, and deeply devoted to Jacques de Molay his master.

When the Knights were not away waging war, my father and the Knight François liked to sit with my mother and me by the large fireplace. Once, and I remember this so clearly though I was but a small child, my father reached over and took up Habiba's embroidery, to try it for himself. It was a funny sight, the Grand Master of the Knights Templar attempting to embroider the hem of a linen shirt with large callused hands. At last Habiba grew irritated at his messy sewing and gently slapped him away, for she had to undo the stitches he'd made and start again. Young François seemed startled by her familiarity with his stolid, formidable hero, and he too began to soften toward us. He even allowed me to sit upon his back and play at being a knight upon a charging horse.

In 1306 by the Christian calendar, King Philippe IV sent a messenger to Kolossi Castle with a sealed letter demanding that the Knights Templar return to France. The king wanted to discuss in person the Templars' loss of the Holy Land.

Habiba reminded Jacques de Molay of her visions of him broken-limbed and in unimaginable pain.

But the Knight my father only shrugged. He said, "You opened my eyes to the Veritas, and I now know God is God, and God does not care about fortune, or land, or custom. Man is driven by greed and will always be so driven, and his greed will forever be hidden behind falsehoods spread by zealots."

He would bring this message, this truth, back to the King of France, who was his friend.

The Knight once again offered Habiba her freedom and a great deal of gold to make her own way in the world, but she would not leave him. She asked him to take us along to the kingdom of France, for she thought she could protect him with her cards. She would dress as a nun, a convert, while I, still only a small child, would be presented as the orphaned daughter of a brave knight felled in battle. We would not stand out, for the knights had many servants.

Because my father so deeply honored Habiba's counsel, and no longer felt complete without her, he agreed. Habiba had not once steered him wrong or told him of a thing that would come to pass that did not come to pass.

After a long and difficult voyage, in the beginning of the Christian year 1307, we arrived in Paris, in the company of a cohort of sixty Knights Templar. François Boissevain, now almost twenty years of age, was among them. I was but five, and do not remember much, only what Habiba my mother later told me.

The Grand Master of the Knights Templar was the richest man in the entire kingdom of France by then. He had loaned a great deal of gold to the King, known as Philippe le Bel, though there was nothing beautiful about him. The Knight my father and the King had been close friends in their youth, and Jacques de Molay had stood godfather to the King's only daughter, Princess Isabelle of France. In fact, Jacques de Molay had loaned King Philippe so much pilfered treasure that the Knight now practically owned all the lands of France. Philippe le Bel had no intention of repaying his debts, and he could not fathom that the Knight was no longer driven by greed.

Habiba warned him of the dangers of facing a jealous king whose coffers were empty, and a frightened pope who wanted the Church to retain control over the kingdoms of Europe.

The Knight my father only nodded sadly and said, "If I cannot convince King Philippe of this Veritas, there will be no hope. No hope of ending this calamity that will continue for a thousand years and bring about the end of days."

In Paris, the Knight prostrated himself and deposited at the King's feet a vast treasure from the Holy Land. This was only a small portion of the Knight's treasure, but he misled Philippe into believing it was all. We traveled then to Poitiers, a miserable city that I remember stank of death and sewage, where the Knight my father was to meet with Pope Clement V.

The Knight never thought of himself as free of sin. His own hands were drenched in the blood of innocents, for in the beginning he had believed that the only way to win the war was to kill every Mohammedan in the Levant. But now he said to Habiba my mother, "My only path to redemption is to convince them to accept the Veritas."

On the day he was to meet Pope Clement he gave my mother eighteen chests filled with gold, jewels, and priceless heirlooms that had belonged to the Sultans of Egypt and even to the Pharaohs before them. He told her that if he did not return, she must use the treasure only for good, to atone for his sins. He also ordered François Boissevain, whom he trusted above all others, to hide the chests in the crypts of the ancient Abbaye Saint-Hilaire in the Vaucluse.

"In case I do not return," he added. My father then laid his hand on the Knight François' right shoulder and told him that once the treasure was secured in the Abbaye Saint-Hilaire, the young man would be released from his oath, free to return to Navarre and to marry.

But François fell to his knees before his master and swore, "I will never abandon you, your woman, or your child until the end of my days."

At this, my father smiled and lifted the fair young man to his feet. "I leave feeling a great peace in my heart," he said.

And finally, before he rode off on his white Arabian horse, the Knight told Habiba, "The only persons you may trust completely are those who cannot be bought. I count the Knight François among these. Luckily for you, there are still a few like him left in the world."

My father was arrested that very day.

My mother and I fled, in the company of the Knight François and the ten most loyal knights of my father's cohort, to the Abbaye Saint-Hilaire.

Within days of our flight, Habiba saw in the cards a new calamity. King Philippe had not only had Jacques de Molay arrested, he had swiftly ordered the arrest of all the Knights Templar in the kingdom. François Boissevain de Vièrnes, as a Prince of the Blood of Navarre, was not beholden to the King of France. He could have left us at the abbaye and returned safely home to Navarre, but he chose to remain with us.

Habiba sent messengers, and a few Templars were able to flee the country.

King Philippe agreed to allow Pope Clement to interrogate seventy-five Knights Templar in Poitiers. During their progress toward the city, Philippe diverted the four most powerful knights, including my father and Guy, the Grand Preceptor, and had them escorted in chains to the Royal Fortress of Chinon, near Poitiers, where they were imprisoned, and beyond the Pope's reach. The four were tortured without mercy.

Habiba understood that there was no possibility of planning an escape from this well-guarded fortress, and she began to despair.

Alone in her monk's cell in the Abbaye Saint-Hilaire, she spread the cards, and spread the cards, and spread them again. But she could not understand the intricacies of the politics, nor the backstabbing and papal bulls and writs and accusations that were thrown against her Knight. They made no sense to her at all. The Templars were accused, among other sins, of spitting three times on the Cross of Jesus and of raping children, both male and female.

This made her laugh, but it was an ugly and vengeful laugh.

One night, when we had been at the Abbaye Saint-Hilaire for six months, as the waxing crescent moon rose over the distant hills, Habiba my mother took me into her cell. She sat me down at the small round table upon which she read her cards. I was not yet six years old.

"You must read for me," she said, "for I am blinded by love and by rage."

She laid out the cards and ordered me to press my hands upon them. She placed her own hands over my small ones, her grip heavy as iron, so that I could not move at all. The dark veil lifted from my eyes, and I saw a terrible room filled with unimaginable instruments of pain. I smelled blood and burned skin and urine and excrement.

I swayed and felt myself losing consciousness, but my mother lifted one hand and slapped me across the face. The sting brought me back to that horrific room, where I saw the Knight my father lying naked, chained to a wooden board, his shackled feet slathered in pig's grease. His torturers were roasting his heels over an open brazier and he was screaming. He no longer had any fingernails or toenails, and his fingers were broken. Now they were burning his feet, urging him to confess. He had held out until now, six whole months, refusing to confess to crimes of which he was not guilty.

In his torment he shouted at the inquisitors, "You are all fools! You know nothing! *Vidi Veritatem!* I have seen the Truth! You are neither godly nor pious men and you are not doing God's work. Jesus gave his life for peace! For *peace*, not war! I brought back the greatest treasure of all. I brought back the Veritas! I brought back the map to the future and I have seen it. We have brought down upon ourselves a war that will last a thousand years and we will all go down in history as murdering barbarians!"

They pulled the board away from the brazier and raised it so that my father was now vertical and eye-level with the Papal Legate, who approached him with mincing steps, suddenly quite pale. He brandished his jewel-encrusted crucifix at my father and crossed himself. "Verily, you are a heretic," he whispered, awed by the words that had escaped from the chained man before him. "And where is this map?" he asked in a coaxing voice.

My father the Knight laughed. "It is well hidden and you will never find it. Never!"

My mother removed her hands from mine. I slipped off the wooden stool and onto the floor in a dead faint.

We left the Abbaye Saint-Hilaire at dawn.

All night the Templars and Carmelite monks and Habiba had worked to pack the eighteen chests of treasure into barrels filled with Franche-Comté, prized above all other wines in the western world. Journeying south by river to the sea, we traveled under the escort of the Knight François, and several monks from the abbey, and the ten remaining Templars, who no longer wore their white surcoats emblazoned with the red cross of their Order. On the barge that carried us south was a false relic from the Holy Land, a piece of wood purported to be from the cross of Jesus, which was really only a sliver of wood from an old beam in the abbey, which the monks had set in a golden chalice for all to see "on its way to Rome." The monks and the Knights warned the common folk who stood on the riverbanks witnessing our passage that to come anywhere near the barge with thoughts of pilferage would cause instant death and an eternity in Hell.

People are greedy, but they are also stupid and superstitious. The subterfuge was effective.

Upon reaching Venice, Habiba my mother procured this very palazzo. We have lived here ever since, protected by the Knight François, the ten former Knights Templar, and the monks of Saint-Hilaire.

For the next seven years, Habiba spent the Knight's gold on good deeds: she built an orphanage and a women's hospital. She helped the Jews, who were being persecuted. On the Island of Cyprus she had watched the Knights' commercial enterprises at work, how they sent ships filled with sugar and silk to Europe. She had learned as well their system of accounting, for she was very intelligent. In Venice she also became a lender of gold to honest people. She did not charge interest on the money, for she believed in a barter system of favors, and that every act of kindness brought back six kind acts.

And during those seven years, Habiba saw flashes of the horror of her Knight's imprisonment. Everyone believed she was a saintly woman, but then they never witnessed her rage. Once, when I was ten, she pressed my hands again upon the cards. I saw my father's future execution. He was tied to a stake with another man, and a miserably small coal fire bit at their feet and legs and I smelled their burning flesh. I pulled back my hands and shut my mind, and told her, "I saw nothing." She gripped me by the wrist and held my palm over a candle's flame, shouting, "This is nothing—*nothing* — compared to what they will do to your father the Knight if you do not open your mind to the cards!"

Habiba also believed she could speak to him across time and space. Once a month, she sat in her apartments in the palazzo, spread her cards by the light of the waxing crescent moon, and spoke to her Knight in his fever dreams of the curse she had set upon his tormentors.

"King Philippe's sons will never procreate," she whispered to him, "and the Capet line of French kings will die out." She told him of the imminent death of Pope Clement, and of the war of men that would never end until humankind understood the Veritas. And that the cards, which were the map, were safe. "They will be passed down through the generations." Which meant through me, her daughter.

She tried to comfort him in his distress, so he would understand that time meant nothing and everything at once.

On March 18, 1314, by the Christian calendar, Habiba saw the Knight stumble in chains on shattered limbs to the public scaffold that had been erected in front of the great Cathedral of Notre-Dame of Paris. There the four most senior Knights Templar were expected to publicly confess to heresy. Habiba spoke into the Knight's fevered mind, urging him to confess, and be set free. Why not confess? "The words given to such men are meaningless, in any case," she whispered. All Habiba wanted was for him to return to her and live in peace in the sanctuary of the free republic of Venice.

But he refused, for he had fought valiantly against the Mamluks, and would not allow shame and humiliation to blacken his name.

The four chained Knights were pushed to their knees upon the scaffold, where the Papal Legate read their forced confessions aloud before the crowd. Two of the Knights had been completely broken by torture, and they wordlessly nodded their assent. But Jacques de Molay my father pulled himself up on his shattered feet, raised his shackled arms to the sky and shouted for all to hear, "I do confess my guilt, which consists in having, to my shame and dishonor, suffered myself, through the pain of torture and the fear of death, to give utterance to falsehoods, imputing scandalous sins and iniquities to an illustrious order, which hath nobly served the cause of Christianity. I disdain to seek a wretched and disgraceful existence by engrafting another lie upon the original falsehood."

He was interrupted by the Papal Legate and violently pulled off the scaffold, along with his compatriot Guy, the Grand Preceptor, who, emboldened by my father's words, also refused to confess.

At nightfall the two Knights were brought out once again from their dungeon and carried to the Ile aux Juifs, where they were tied to stakes. The King's men jeered as they lit with torches the slow-burning coal fires, insuring the Knights' suffering would be long and horrendous. Habiba spoke through her cards, telling my father to curse King, Pope, and Church with his last words, for all assembled on the Ile aux Juifs to hear. By then the flames licked at his bare, broken feet. My father raised his head to glare at the dais, where the Papal Legate and King Philippe sat watching impassively in their embroidered robes. He shouted, "Neither Pope Clement, nor you, King Philippe, will survive the year. King Philippe, your Capet line will perish with your three barren sons. And you will all face your reckoning before the only King who matters, the King of Heaven, who does not abide cruelty, nor lies, nor greed. Let Evil swiftly fall to those who wrongly condemned us!"

A loud gasp rose from the gathered crowd.

It took my father four hours to die.

After that day, Habiba my mother grew more silent and morose. She often sequestered herself in her wing of the palazzo, unwilling to speak or accept any kind of comfort, for she could not shake from her mind the ordeal of her Knight, my father.

Three years after his immolation, a courier arrived with a sealed letter from Queen Jeanne of Navarre. François Boissevain de Vièrnes' two older brothers and their wives and children had all died of a fever, and François had now inherited the title of Marquis de Vièrnes, and all the domains of his family.

Habiba smiled with bitter satisfaction at this news. She said to the newly anointed Marquis François, "Now you may wed my daughter."

I was seventeen when we married in the Basilica of Saint Mark, with all the pomp and grandeur to which the Marquis de Vièrnes was entitled. Documents with official seals from the Doge and the Patriarch of Venice reassured Habiba that I, her only daughter, would no longer be in danger.

"And so you must stop being so fearful," she told me. "You are safe now."

But I never felt safe. I was still terrified to lay my hands upon her cards. In her despondency, my mother rarely forced me, which was a relief. But still, I feared every day that she would ask.

For eight years I despaired of having a child. But Habiba had seen you, my daughter, in a vision, and was convinced only my own calamitous fear kept me from this most sacred covenant.

I went to see the Patriarch of Venice, who told me to read the Bible and pray. I lit candles to the Virgin and prayed on my knees that she might give me a child. For eight years I prayed, until one morning Habiba came out of her apartments to tell me that I had succeeded in my duty. I was twenty-five years old by then, but I felt no fear of dying in childbirth, for I knew that child was you, my Esperanza.

During the months of my confinement my mother did not try to force me to read her cards. But as soon as you were born, my Esperanza, she started once again to spread her cards and press my hands upon them and demand that I tell her what I saw. I shut my mind and refused to pass beyond the veil. She whipped me on several occasions, which was not unusual, for whipping is considered quite beneficial to stubborn and recalcitrant children. But I have never whipped you, my Esperanza, and I forbade every person in our employ from whipping you, even your strange Nguni Master of the African combat staff, who had refused to teach you, a girl, until I paid him his own weight in gold.

I could not always close my mind to Habiba's cards. Yet the visions were so horrifying I sometimes fell to the floor, unconscious. This angered my mother so deeply she would throw me bodily out of her apartments and lock the door, believing she had failed. Or, more precisely, that I, her only daughter, had failed her.

On the evening of March 18, 1330, by the Christian calendar, Habiba's personal servant came to my apartments and said, "Your mother is asking to see you." I crossed the long, cavernous main hall of the palazzo and approached her door with dread in my heart. She was sitting propped up in bed and beckoned me to approach. I wanted to run from her but I did not, for knew I would regret it the rest of my life.

I sat on a chair by her bed and listened as she told me that this night would be her last of this existence. "I do not know what awaits me beyond, for no vision of the afterlife has ever come to me." She told me the story of her life and, with tears streaming from her eyes, said, "I have spent my entire life trying to understand the cards' designs."

The glimpses she'd been given of the future and the past and the present depended not on her. She had always felt like a charioteer who had dropped the horses' reins in a careening race along a dark and twisted road that led she knew not where. The more she'd fought to control the visions, the less she'd understood. She believed this was because she had been enslaved as a small child, and so had not been taught by her people how to truly employ the gift she had been given.

Then she handed me this small coffer and told me not to fight the visions, only to immerse myself in their dark waters and let the current take me where it willed. She also gave me her brooch, which had been my father the Knight's and which he'd always worn into battle. It is a representation of the Knight's original family crest, with his own additions of the moon and stars.

Habiba died at one minute before midnight, exactly sixteen years after her Knight. You were only a small child, my Esperanza, and so you do not remember her passing.

For years now I have kept the truth from you, for I did not want you to live in terror as I had done. The vision that always comes to me when the dark veil is lifted between the worlds is of a black fog arriving from the East, and within the fog are countless merchant ships. For years this dark miasma has haunted my sleeping and waking hours, growing in intensity. And then, two years ago, I dreamed the roiling fog turned into rats spilling from the ships. I awakened in my bed to the Marquis François your father leaning over me, his kind face contorted with worry. I begged him to cease going to the port himself to examine our shipments from the East.

He only laughed and patted me as if I were a frightened child. He did not trust anyone but himself to properly oversee our enterprises. He never believed I could see beyond the veil.

And you remember this horror. A few days later the Marquis your father returned from the port feeling unwell. By nightfall he had a terrible fever. The next day his body was covered in black pustules. He was dead by the following morning. I would not let you see his body, for I did not want that sight to forever haunt your dreams.

I was never as strong as Habiba my mother, though you, Esperanza, are stronger than us both. You have been educated by the best minds in Venice, you have four languages, and you read *The Epic of Gilgamesh*, *The Histories* of Herodotus, Homer, the Greek philosophers, and the Q'uran. And you are the only girl in Venice who had a Nguni Master of the combat staff. You know the Bible, too, and that is good, for you will need that knowledge in this Christian world.

When we went to the Night Bazaar in Saint Mark's Square on Christmas Eve that gypsy seer confirmed my worst fears. The pestilence that killed the Marquis François your father has returned and this time it will spread across the world entire. My beloved, my Esperanza, you must leave Venice at once. I am old now, forty-six, and already weak. Habiba my mother did not believe our line could die from illness, as long as we remained strong and brave. But I have never been able to keep my fear at bay. I have never lived a day without fear but made sure that you, my daughter, would grow up strong and capable, educated by the best masters our fortune could buy.

Our path splits here. You must never despair, nor succumb to fear as I have.

The pestilence will bring devastation the likes of which humanity has never seen. In my visions I saw bodies piled to the sky all over the known world, millions of dead. People will believe it is the Apocalypse, but life will continue, only worse than before, because those same people are driven by greed and they do not learn.

You must go now to Navarre, to Vièrnes, where you will be recognized as your father's rightful heir. In Vièrnes there is a fortress, built long ago by the invading Roman army, and later generations of Navarrese built upon those ruins, to protect the land from invasion. It is abandoned now, but stands high in the foothills of Vièrnes. Fill the moat with fire and kill every rat you see. Do not ever harm cats or dogs but take them in and treat them well, for they will be your best defense. You must take all the knights you can gather, and their families, and the monks of Saint-Hilaire, and all the gold you can carry, and stay there, in the fortress surrounded by fire. Wait for the pestilence to pass. Afterward, you must always help the poor and downtrodden, and others in dire need of shelter, for they will remember, and one day they will help you in return.

Your title and your lands will never be wrested from you by greedy men, for in Navarre, as in the free republic of Venice, women may inherit their husbands' and fathers' property. In Navarre, they honor the matrilineal line and do not abide by the new French Salic law, which was put into place to stop King Philippe IV's daughters from inheriting the throne. You also have the documents and the seal of your father the Marquis and his ancestral line to protect you.

My very own Esperanza, you are now only twenty-one. But in the future you will bear a daughter. This I promise upon my soul, for I have seen her. Tell no one about Habiba's cards, nor that you are the natural and only grandchild of Jacques de Molay. Stay away from Spanish Navarre, for in their religious zealotry the Spaniards will burn you without a second thought, for your birthmark alone.

Go quickly. But do not travel by water, nor stop to rest in cities. Watch for friends along the way, for they will know you by that same mark. You must guard the cards with your life. Look for the sign, the right-sided crescent moon, and pay close attention to numbers. Three is our most powerful number. And nine, for nine is three times three. Also the number one, for it is the beginning of all things. Ten is also the number one, for zero has no value. Beware of the numbers five and seven, for they are incomplete.

Most importantly, my beloved, do not let fear blind you to what the cards have to say.

A terrible war that will last one hundred years has already begun. The kingdoms of France and England both claim the throne of France because Philippe le Bel's sons died without progeny, thanks to Habiba's curse. Unlike my mother, I have no talent for curses and therefore cannot guide you. The French and the English will continue to fight in the name of God, and freedom, and peace, backed by powers beyond our comprehension. Some will turn a blind eye. Some will prefer total annihilation to change. They are the most dangerous, for they couch their greed in zealotry and arrogance. They will use fear to pave the way, but do not fear, ever, and do not love blindly. For if you fear, or if you love without clarity, you will not see the map clearly either. Nor be able to use the cards that will guide your way.

I have seen one more thing beyond the veil. In Navarre, one day a great king will rise and bring peace to the land, and your descendant will be there to show him the way of the Veritas.

In France you must call yourself Espérance, but our one true name is Amal, which means hope in the tongue of Habiba my mother. This coffer, which she gave to me, I now give to you, as well as Jacques de Molay's brooch, which will be recognized by our allies.

We will be with you always, as long as you hold the map.

Your loving Mother,

Espérance de Molay Boissevain de Vièrnes

AFTER THE BAZAAR . . .

The plague had come, leaving behind too many bodies to count and mourn, much less bury. Soon the city was sick unto death. At the same time, we denizens of the Night Bazaar were slowly being forced out of Venice. No longer welcome, impugned by the ignorant or the ostentatiously pious. By holy hypocrites and insolent bureaucrats. And by those simply fearful of what they did not understand—what matter, in the end!

There was no choice but to leave, and look ahead.

I lived a rather conventional life for most of my time in *La Serenissima*. Even before then I'd led previous existences, in other times and places . . . having been, among other things, a seer, a priestess, a circus performer, and a horsewoman, long before Marco Polo returned from the East. Centuries before plague rats scurried down a mooring line at the Rialto, to let fester their contagion along the canals and alleys that carry Venice's life-blood.

But to finish our story there, we departed Venice, taking along those vendors, performers, and other associates who'd also found life in Italy somewhat . . . constricting. Our rootless banishment was not wholly involuntary, though. In the end we found it far more pleasant to roam the world, rather than sit and molder in one beautiful but damp place. To go elsewhere, and even *elsewhen*, as the mood so took us. Since now we possessed the *means* to do so.

And, having tarried with us for a time, don't you agree?

The city's loss was our gain, as we set our sails and our sights on new places: Athens, Constantinople, Tangiers, Bruges, Beijing, New York, Paris, Nuremburg, and so on.

But where to *next*, precisely, for our nocturnal marketplace of the strange, the forbidden, and the occult? We've heard rumors that London is/was/will be interesting. (For one who traverses Time, tenses can prove a terrible tangle.) Once it was naught but savage, untamed woods filled with wild woad-painted Celts who worshipped the Raven Goddess of Nightmares, and of War. Their Druids were renowned for both wisdom and secret dark ceremonies; they erected stone temples to chart the heavens. These so-called pagans faced down wild boars and cave bears, and finally even the well-drilled legions of Rome.

But by the nineteenth century the country's great rivers were lined with castles and bridges, and even hushed temples to great learning. Their grassy yards stalked by nothing more frightening than a black-gowned Cambridge don with a pudding-pot on his head. The stone halls that once hosted drunken revels and councils of orthodoxy and heresy had become repositories of literature and history and science. The standing stones, merely quaint sights for badly-dressed tourists to gawk at. A net of iron and steam and wires was growing apace, bringing both new light, and deeper darkness, to the intricacies of human life. No need any more for the vague inconvenience of *Wonder*.

And yet, is there not possibly still *some* magic and wildness to be found in Albion? Perhaps we shall travel there next, in our never-ending journey through space and time.

Perhaps *you* will also be one of the Invited then, as well. . . .

I look forward to it!

Yours in the Mystery,

Madame Vera.

CONTRIBUTORS

 **APHRODITE ANAGNOST** is the author of the novels *Memoir of a Death Angel* (an Amazon Best New Author semi-finalist) and *Passover* (A Chanticleer Paranormal Book Award winner co-authored with Robert Arthur). Find Anagnost, a country doctor, horse trainer, and equestrian book editor, on Twitter @AphroditeAuthor, on Facebook, and at XenophonPress.com.

* * *

 The first volume of *The Night Bazaar* included **GREGORY FLETCHER'S** "Friends of Vera." His Young Adult novel *Other People's Crazy* came out in 2019 to rave reviews from sites like Litpick. His nonfiction craft book, *Shorts and Briefs*, features short plays and brief principles of playwriting. Fletcher's own plays have had twelve Off-Off-Broadway productions, and four essays appear in various journals. A Dallas, Texas native, he earned theater degrees from Cal State Northridge, Columbia, and Boston University. For more visit gregoryfletcher.com.

* * *

 **ROY GRAHAM** is a writer from New York whose work has appeared in *Rolling Stone*, *Playboy*, *Motherboard* and, once, on the back of several million Chipotle bags. He received his BA from NYU and is currently in the MFA program at Rutgers Camden.

LENORE HART is the author of eight novels, and series editor of *The Night Bazaar*. She also writes as Elisabeth Graves. Her poetry, nonfiction, and short stories have appeared in a variety of magazines and literary journals. She's a Fellow of the Virginia Center for the Creative Arts, and an Irish Writers Union and Irish Writers Centre member. Lenore teaches in the MFA program at Wilkes University, and at the Ossabaw Island Writers Retreat. She lives in coastal Virginia. Find more at lenorehart.com, lenore_hart_author on Instagram, and Facebook @LenoreHartAuthor.

* * *

KAYLIE JONES' latest novel is *The Anger Meridian*. She's the author of the acclaimed memoir, *Lies My Mother Never Told Me*. Her novels include *A Soldier's Daughter Never Cries*, released as a Merchant Ivory Film in 1998; *Celeste Ascending*; and *Speak Now*. She's written book reviews and articles for *The Los Angeles Times*, *The New York Times*, *The Paris Review*, *The Washington Post*, *The Rumpus*, *Salon*, *Huffington Post*, *The Guardian UK*, *Confrontation Magazine*, and edits the anthology *Long Island Noir*. Kaylie teaches at SUNY Stony Brook's MFA Program in Writing, and in the MFA Program at Wilkes University. She co-chairs the James Jones First Novel Fellowship, which awards $10,000 yearly to an unpublished novel. Her imprint with Akashic Books, Kaylie Jones Books, is a writer's collective in which the authors play a fundamental part in the publishing process.

* * *

REBECCA LANE was telling stories before she could write. She went on to tell them in grad school, earning an MFA in Creative Writing from NYU. She's been published internationally, and has been active with S.L.A.T.E Charity for several years, supporting their work for writers and students. She lives in northeastern Pennsylvania with her husband and their two daughters.

CAROL MACALLISTER is published across the genres, and is also an exhibiting fine artist. She holds MFAs in both disciplines and has won numerous awards and competitions. Author of *Blackmoor Tales* (Northampton House Press) she's also edited and published collections of poetry and fiction, and serves as a judge for the Bram Stoker Awards, National Federation of State Poetry Societies, and AWR Journal. Find more about her at carolmacallister.com.

* * *

EDISON MCDANIELS is a brain surgeon, audiobook narrator, fiction author, and baseball fan; not necessarily in that order. He lives in Wisconsin, not far from his beloved Minnesota Twins. He does not own a dog. Learn more about his writing at www.SurgicalFiction.com.

* * *

DANA MILLER graduated from Wilkes University with an MFA in fiction and screenwriting. Her debut novel, *Twisted Fate* (Northampton House Press) received a starred review from *Publishers Weekly*, and was an Award-Winning Finalist in the Fiction: Romance category of American Book Fest's 2019 Best Book Awards. She lives in Pennsylvania with her husband and two Sphynx cats, and is at work on her second novel. See more at danammiller.com.

* * *

CORINNE ALICE NULTON, an academic adviser at Penn State, shares her love for language with reluctant freshman, jotting down her own words in the breaths between. Her short story "Ember and Ash" appeared in volume one of *The Night Bazaar*. Her play *14 Symptoms* was featured in the Brick Theater's Game Play Festival in 2014. Her ten-minute play *Flesh* was a finalist at the Kennedy Center in 2012. She's the drama and poetry editor for *Door is a Jar* Literary Magazine.

Nearly fifty of **DAVID POYER's** novels and books of creative nonfiction are in print. He's been translated into Japanese, Dutch, Italian, Hungarian, and Serbo-Croatian; film rights have been sold for several of his novels. He teaches at Wilkes University and the Ossabaw Island Writers' Retreat. His latest novel is *Overthrow*, published by St. Martin's/Macmillan in December 2019. Peruse more of his work at poyer.com.

* * *

Originally from Virginia's Eastern Shore, **NAIA POYER** holds a BA in art from Swarthmore College and an MTS in East Asian Religions from Harvard University. As a queer agender writer and artist working in higher education, they hope to contribute to LGBTQIA representation in media and in everyday life. Poyer works in Harvard's Department of East Asian Languages and Civilizations. Also a professional graphic and book designer, they created the cover for the 2017 and 2020 *Night Bazaar* anthologies. More on Facebook @NaidBookDesign and website www.naiadartdesign.com.

* * *

FAE TYLER, assistant editor for the 2017 and 2020 *Night Bazaar* anthologies, graduated from Swarthmore College with degrees in Art and Fantasy Writing. She is a fashion designer and photographer of the beautiful, strange, and fierce. Her work can be seen at FaeTyler.com.

* * *

Born in The Netherlands, **MAU VANDUREN** grew up in a family of doctors, accountants, artists, and musicians; pillars of society and freebooters. He spent many years in international consulting as an information specialist, where he endeavored to serve the human element in his projects. He writes nonfiction history, and detective and fantasy fiction. Mau and his wife Jackie find friends and enjoy nature in Parksley, Virginia.

ALSO FROM NORTHAMPTON HOUSE PRESS

If you enjoyed your visit to *The Night Bazaar: Venice*, don't miss the first volume in
the series, when the Bazaar appeared in present-day New York City!

The Night Bazaar
Eleven Haunting Tales of Forbidden Wishes and Dangerous Desires
edited by Lenore Hart

Available in ebook   ISBN 978-1-937997-79-3
And in trade paperback   ISBN 978-1-937997-78-6

*"Appealing to those who like their fantasy served with a side of psychological horror,
this anthology is sure to please!"* – PUBLISHERS WEEKLY

NORTHAMPTON HOUSE PRESS

Established in 2011, Northampton House Press publishes selected fiction, nonfiction, memoir, and poetry. Check out our list at www.northampton-house. com, and Like us on Facebook—"Northampton House Press"—as we show-case more innovative works from brilliant new talents. We can also be found on Twitter @nhousepress and on Instagram at nhousepress.